.

Titles include:

Stephan Karschay
DEGENERATION, NORMATIVITY AND THE GOTHIC AT THE FIN-DE-SIÈCLE

Colin Jones, Josephine McDonagh and Jon Mee (editors)
CHARLES DICKENS, A TALE OF TWO CITIES AND THE FRENCH REVOLUTION

Jock Macleod
LITERATURE, JOURNALISM, AND THE VOCABULARIES OF LIBERALISM
Politics and Letters 1886–1916

Kirsten MacLeod
FICTIONS OF BRITISH DECADENCE
High Art, Popular Writing and the *Fin de Siècle*

Charlotte Mathieson
MOBILITY IN THE VICTORIAN NOVEL
Placing the Nation

Natasha Moore
VICTORIAN POETRY AND MODERN LIFE
The Unpoetical Age

Kristine Moruzi and Michelle J. Smith (editors)
COLONIAL GIRLHOOD IN LITERATURE, CULTURE AND HISTORY, 1840–1950

Sean O'Toole
HABIT IN THE ENGLISH NOVEL, 1850–1900
Lived Environments, Practices of the Self

Tina O'Toole
THE IRISH NEW WOMAN

Richard Pearson
VICTORIAN WRITERS AND THE STAGE
The Plays of Dickens, Browning, Collins and Tennyson

Laura Rotunno
POSTAL PLOTS IN BRITISH FICTION, 1840–1898
Readdressing Correspondence in Victorian Culture

Laurence Talairach-Vielmas
FAIRY TALES, NATURAL HISTORY AND VICTORIAN CULTURE

Marianne Van Remoortel
WOMEN, WORK AND THE VICTORIAN PERIODICAL
Living by the Press

Palgrave Studies in Nineteenth-Century Writing and Culture
Series Standing Order ISBN 978–0–333–97700–2 (hardback)
(*outside North America only*)

You can receive future titles in this series as they are published by placing a standing order. Please contact your bookseller or, in case of difficulty, write to us at the address below with your name and address, the title of the series and the ISBN quoted above.

Customer Services Department, Macmillan Distribution Ltd, Houndmills, Basingstoke, Hampshire RG21 6XS, England

---

Oscar Wilde, Wilfred Owen, and Male Desire

Begotten, Not Made

James Campbell
Associate Professor, University of Central Florida, USA

First published 2015 by
PALGRAVE MACMILLAN

Palgrave Macmillan in the UK is an imprint of Macmillan Publishers Limited, registered in England, company number 785998, of Houndmills, Basingstoke, Hampshire RG21 6XS.

Palgrave Macmillan in the US is a division of St Martin's Press LLC, 175 Fifth Avenue, New York, NY 10010.

Palgrave Macmillan is the global academic imprint of the above companies and has companies and representatives throughout the world.

Palgrave® and Macmillan® are registered trademarks in the United States, the United Kingdom, Europe and other countries.

ISBN 978–1–137–55063–7

This book is printed on paper suitable for recycling and made from fully managed and sustained forest sources. Logging, pulping and manufacturing processes are expected to conform to the environmental regulations of the country of origin.

A catalogue record for this book is available from the British Library.

Library of Congress Cataloging-in-Publication Data
Campbell, James, 1964–
Oscar Wilde, Wilfred Owen, and male desire : begotten, not made / James Campbell, Associate Professor, University of Central Florida, USA.
pages cm. — (Palgrave studies in nineteenth-century writing and culture)
Includes bibliographical references and index.
ISBN 978–1–137–55063–7 (hardback)
1. Wilde, Oscar, 1854–1900—Criticism and interpretation.   2. Wilde, Oscar, 1854–1900—Relations with men.   3. Owen, Wilfred, 1893–1918—Criticism and interpretation.   4. Owen, Wilfred, 1893–1918—Relations with men.   5. Male Homosexuality in literature.   6. Male homosexuality—Great Britain—History—19th century.   I. Title.
PR5827.H63C37 2015
828'.809—dc23   2015018354

Typeset by MPS Limited, Chennai, India.

To Maura, Brendan, and Owen

Contents

Acknowledgements

This book began to take form in a 2007 National Endowment for the Humanities Summer Seminar held at the William Andrews Clark Memorial Library, and I can think of no better place or group of people to help get it started. Bruce Whiteman, Carol Sommer, and Scott Jacobs were instrumental in making the considerable resources of the Library and of UCLA easily available, and Patrick Keilty, Noah Comet, and Adam Seth Lowenstein were incredibly helpful making it all work smoothly. I owe each of the participants immense thanks: Rachel Ablow, Gregory Castle, Loretta Clayton, William A. Cohen, Ellen Crowell, Lois Cucullu, Chris Foss, Neil Hultgren, Elizabeth Carolyn Miller, John Paul Riquelme, Felicia J. Ruff, and Molly Youngkin. Joe Bristow, who organized the endeavor and created an inspirational environment, has the gratitude of myself and, I am confident in claiming, all of the other participants as well.

I am also grateful to the College of Arts and Humanities at the University of Central Florida and its Dean, José Fernandez, for the award of a research sabbatical that greatly aided the completion of the project. Thanks are also due to my UCF colleagues Anna Maria Jones and Kate Oliver, co-laborers in the field, as well as Kevin Meehan for the longest book loan in the history of the codex, and to François-Xavier Gleyzon for help with André Raffalovich's French. The Interlibrary Loan office of the UCF library proved equal to almost any request, no matter how obscure. They are brave people.

I owe thanks as well to the staff of the Rosenbach Museum and Library in Center City Philadelphia, especially Elizabeth Fuller, who quite literally let me in from the cold to access the manuscript of the long version of 'Mr W. H.'

Benjamin Doyle and Tomas René at Palgrave Macmillan have been expert editors; their professionalism and patience are greatly appreciated.

My interest in Wilde is recent, relatively speaking, but my interest in Owen goes back to my doctoral work; I thus need to thank Gerald Bruns, Joe Buttegieg, Seamus Deane, Barbara Green, Krzysztof Ziarek, and especially John Matthias, who first got me really thinking about Owen.

Some debts are intellectual, some are personal; the most profound are those that are both at once. In this category I must thank Paul Puccio, whose company and conversation sustained me through my early years at UCF and whose trace is here still, and Kathy Hohenleitner, my first and best reader; like Dorian to Basil, she is never more present in my writing than when no image of her is there. And to the MOB for keeping me sane by occasionally driving me crazy.

An earlier version of Chapter 1 appeared in *Wilde Discoveries: Traditions, Histories, Archives*, edited by Joseph Bristow, and I am grateful to the University of Toronto Press for permission to reprint the work here. I also want to thank the anonymous reviewers who provided valuable feedback on the chapter. An early version of Chapter 6 was presented at the 2014 MLA convention in Chicago, and I am grateful to Jesse E. Matz for organizing the panel on '1914 in 2014: Our Great War', as well as all of those who participated in the ensuing discussion.

A Guide to Abbreviations

The standard but incomplete edition of Oscar Wilde's works is: Wilde, Oscar, *The Complete Works of Oscar Wilde*, gen. ed. Ian Small, 7 vols to date (Oxford: Oxford University Press, 2000–).

Individual texts are cited using the abbreviation *CWOW* followed by a volume number. The following volumes are used:

CWOW1:   *Poems and Poems in Prose*, eds Bobby Fong and Karl Beckson (Oxford: Oxford University Press, 2000).

CWOW2:   De Profundis, *'Epistola: In Carcere et Vinculis'*, ed. Ian Small (Oxford: Oxford University Press, 2005).

CWOW3:   The Picture of Dorian Gray: *The 1890 and 1891 Texts*, ed. Joseph Bristow (Oxford: Oxford University Press, 2005).

CWOW4:   *Criticism*: Historical Criticism, Intentions, The Soul of Man, ed. Josephine M. Guy (Oxford: Oxford University Press, 2007).

CWOW5:   *Plays 1:* The Duchess of Padua, Salomé: Drame en un Acte, Salome: Tragedy in One Act, ed. Joseph Donohue (Oxford: Oxford University Press, 2013).

Other texts are abbreviated:

CP&F: Owen, Wilfred, *Complete Poems and Fragments,* ed. Jon Stallworthy (London: Chatto and Windus, Hogarth Press, and Oxford University Press, 1983).

OCL: Owen, Wilfred, *Collected Letters,* eds Harold Owen and John Bell (London: Oxford University Press, 1967).

WCL: Wilde, Oscar, *The Complete Letters of Oscar Wilde*, eds Merlin Holland and Rupert Hart-Davis (New York: Henry Holt, 2000).

Introduction

'Perverse we all are somehow'
(Wilfred Owen, 'Perversity', 1917, *CP&F*, p. 108)

This book traces the development of Oscar Wilde's thoughts and theories about the artistic importance of male same-sex relations and contends that these theories were passed on to Wilfred Owen, who in turn used them to articulate his ideas about the physical and cultural damage caused by the First World War. My interest lies in Wilde's articulation of male same-sex desire in his literary texts and in how Owen received, employed, and subtly changed these ideas under circumstances vastly different from those under which Wilde had formed them. While I remain attentive to the differences between literature and other forms of writing and insist that Wilde's fiction demands to be read as fiction, I am nonetheless making an argument that Wilde needs to be taken seriously as a queer theorist.

Considering Wilde as a theorist of same-sex love means breaking away from the waning but still popular vision of him as a gay icon. As I explain in greater detail in Chapter 3, Wilde scholarship in the 1990s, especially Ed Cohen's *Talk on the Wilde Side* and Alan Sinfield's *The Wilde Century*, argued that Wilde became the template for subsequent gay male identity. As true as this may be, my interest here lies less in what subsequent culture has made of Wilde than in how Wilde himself understood male same-sex relations and of how he expressed his understandings in his literary texts. I am also interested in how Wilde's understandings differ both from those of his contemporaries, including the burgeoning discourse of late nineteenth-century sexology, and from later forms of sexual identity politics. I also stress the importance of classically based ideas about same-sex desire at the end of the

1

nineteenth century, including the possibility that stereotypes of sexual deviancy were operative during the time of Wilde's career, though these stereotypes were certainly not those of the twentieth-century gay man. But primarily I am concerned to attempt to locate and analyze Wilde's thoughts about same-sex love within his literary texts, and I endeavor not to assume that Wilde's ideas prepare for or predict later normative patterns of gay and straight, or of camp and square.

Although my approach differs from that of Cohen and Sinfield, I am nonetheless operating from a similar post-Foucauldian assumption, one well articulated by Jeffrey Weeks to the effect that 'sexuality is not a given that has to be controlled. It is an historical construct that has historical conditions of existence.'[1] As a result of acknowledging these historical conditions, it is necessary to admit first that the common cultural understanding of what we now call homosexuality simply did not exist during Wilde's lifetime and, though Wilde's very public trials for acts of gross indecency certainly did play a role in creating the identity of the gay man, I hope to show that the creation of such a new sexual identity did not take place instantaneously at the time of these trials in 1895. Certainly Wilde belongs in the epoch that 'initiated sexual heterogeneities', as Foucault puts it, but the heterogeneities of late nineteenth-century England are not identical with our own.[2] Secondly, the construction of Wilde as a foundational figure of the gay man has tended to take place through reading and interpreting Wilde's public image and at the expense of reading and interpreting his texts.[3] Thirdly, de-emphasizing Wilde's role as ur-gay icon allows room to address other, potentially more interesting questions, two of which will recur several times in what follows: If Wilde was not gay, what was he? What did he think he was? The short answer is that though Wilde was not gay, he was queer, and that his particular theorization of queerness both informs several of his literary texts and became a legacy he was able to pass on to a later generation of writers, including Owen. That Wilde's theory itself concerns the passing on of legacies through generations in acts of queer filiation is, in these circumstances, less an irony than the operation of a cultural logic.

I have named Wilde's primary conception of the cultural role of male same-sex attraction 'male procreation'. In its simplest form, it describes and idealizes an uneven but harmonized relationship between two men in which one man begets ideas that are gestated by the other. The male couple thus becomes the means by which culture not merely replicates itself, but generates new ideas through a fecund mental interaction between men of sufficient education and talent. Rather than a symbolic mimicking of biological procreation, moreover, Wilde's investment in platonism allows him to value this non-material form of creativity above that of physical reproduction. Male procreation will be subject in the chapters that follow to critique, increased complexity, inversion, and accusations of abject failure; some of these pressures are applied by me, while some are applied by Wilde in an extended process of ironically distressing and distrusting his own idealized invention. Similarly, Owen brings to male procreation the pressure of a cultural situation that Wilde could not have foreseen, yet one that he would have had to confront had he lived long enough to see his own eldest son destroyed by it: the violent mass death of young men in the Great War. But however it is inflected, the logic of male procreation lies at the heart of this book.

The upshot of this logic is that the study cannot end with Wilde himself; if Wilde's theory of male procreation has any validity outside his own imagination, the theory will work by being passed on. Thus the trajectory of my project places Wilfred Owen as the recipient of Wilde's filiation theory, which is to say it makes Owen the symbolic son of Oscar Wilde. My argument is that Owen was the heir of several of Wilde's ideas about sexuality, creativity, and filiation, and that Owen, who never met Wilde, received these ideas from Wilde's surviving contemporaries as well as younger men who became influenced by his memory and example.

In this context a word about the title is probably useful. 'Begotten, not made' is the standard translation of the Greek of the Nicene Creed (γεννηθέντα οὐ ποιηθέντα in the original). The language reflects an attempt to establish as heterodox the Arian beliefs that Jesus became the son of God (rather than always having had that status), always remained subordinate to God the father, and was not necessarily a pre-existent being. For the architects of the Nicene formulation, it was necessary to contend that Christ was not created as other beings were created; he was not made as an act of *poesis*, but begotten as an act of *genesis*. As the second person of the Trinity, he was created in a way distinct from the origins of the rest of creation. God the Father is his father in a distinct and different way from his paternal relationship to all other created beings.

Whether the distinction between 'begotten' and 'made' actually solves the theological problems it was invented to elucidate remains an open question for some and is well outside the scope of this project. In repurposing it for Wilde's male procreation, I mainly want to call attention to Wilde's borrowing of religious as well as reproductive language (though in early Christian formulations, these languages are often identical). As is usually the case with his appropriating the language of orthodoxy, Wilde's usage forms his own trinity that is part reverent, part gently ironic, and part blatantly perverse. His distinction between making and begetting is a real one, and it moves artistic and cultural creation into a realm of imaginative reproduction quite distinct from a paradigm of manufacturing. But it does so, as one expects with Wilde, from a queer angle that undercuts most of the assumptions of orthodoxy, both religious and sexual.

Biographies and historical categories

Oscar Wilde was born in Dublin in 1854 to a distinguished Anglo-Irish family. His father was a physician who was knighted in 1864 and was deeply interested in Irish folklore, an interest he shared with his wife, Jane, who also published Irish nationalist poetry under the name of Speranza. Wilde was brought up in a literary house, and he excelled at school from an early age. He moved from Portora Royal School, an Anglo-Irish version of the English public school, to Trinity College where he won a demyship to Magdalen College, Oxford. After coming down from Oxford he announced himself a professor of aesthetics and spent a year in North America professing the English renaissance of art. His initial writings, notably *Poems* in 1881, and his first plays, *Vera* and *The Duchess of Padua*, were not successful, and Wilde turned to journalism to pay the bills of his household; he married Constance Lloyd in 1884, and they had two sons, Cyril in 1885 and Vyvyan in 1886.

Wilde spent much of the late 1880s as a reviewer, a job in which he was able to put his prodigious reading talents to work. Since many of his reviews were unsigned, collecting them has proven a difficult task. He became editor of *The Lady's World* in 1887; he renamed the venture *The Woman's World* and made it a more serious and politically engaged magazine. Nonetheless, the daily grind of editing was not something that Wilde felt to be rewarding, and he ended his involvement in late 1889.

Wilde's sustained career as a literary writer begins at this point as he started to publish the texts by which he still is known: fairy tales; short stories; the two versions of *The Picture of Dorian Gray* (1890 and 1891); the nonfiction collected in *Intentions* (1891), including the dialogs 'The Decay of Lying' and 'The Critic as Artist'; 'The Soul of Man under Socialism' (1891); *Salome*, first in French (1893) and then in English (1894); and the four social comedies, *Lady Windermere's Fan*

(1892), *A Woman of No Importance* (1894), *An Ideal Husband* (1895), and *The Importance of Being Earnest* (1895). This career was interrupted and all but ended when in 1895 he initiated legal proceedings for libel against the Marquess of Queensberry, who had left a card for Wilde at the Albemarle Club accusing him of 'posing' as a 'somdomite' (Queensberry's penmanship and spelling were equally unstable). Wilde's case against Queensberry fell apart when the latter's defense moved from an analysis of the supposedly sodomitical content of Wilde's literary writing, especially the 1890 version of *The Picture of Dorian Gray*, to the production of witnesses prepared (and paid) to testify to Wilde's sexual assignations with men. Wilde was quickly arrested and tried twice under Section 11 of the 1885 Criminal Law Amendment Act for 'gross indecency with other male persons': the first trial ended with a hung jury, while the second convicted Wilde, following which the presiding judge sentenced Wilde to two years penal servitude with hard labor, the harshest possible result. In the second year of his term Wilde wrote an extended letter to Lord Alfred Douglas, his former lover, the son of the Marquess of Queensberry, and, as far as Wilde was concerned at the time, the reason why he was imprisoned. After release, Wilde found literary production almost impossible. He was able to write 'The Ballad of Reading Gaol' and publish it anonymously in 1897, but this was to be his final work. He lived as an impecunious and alcoholic exile in France and Italy until the end of November of 1900, when he succumbed to cerebral meningitis in Paris.

Such is the outline of Wilde's life as an author, but to understand his legacy more fully, we need to return to 1886 when Wilde was in only the third year of his marriage yet already had two young children. It was at this point that Wilde was introduced to Robert Baldwin Ross, a young Canadian who was preparing for entrance to King's College, Cambridge the following year. Richard Ellmann claims, based on recorded confessions of both Wilde and Ross, that Ross was Wilde's first male sexual partner and furthermore, that the teenaged Ross seduced Wilde.[4] Wilde would go on to have a number of relationships with other younger men, most notably John Gray by 1889 and then, most destructively, Lord Alfred Douglas by 1892. But Robert Ross, known almost exclusively as 'Robbie' or 'Bobbie' among his friends, remained an important presence throughout Wilde's life as well as a guardian of his memory after his death. Wilde was able to confide in Ross about both his initial infatuation with Douglas and his growing dissatisfaction with that relationship. Conversation with Ross was the inspiration for both 'The Portrait of Mr W. H.' and 'The Decay of Lying'. Ross was with Wilde at his arrest, visited him in prison, helped to attempt to manage his funds after his release, was with him at his death, and served as his literary executor after his demise. He befriended Wilde's orphaned children, worked to establish the copyright to Wilde's works in order to discharge his bankruptcy, and defended Wilde's name and reputation when Alfred Douglas had turned on Wilde's memory and sought every opportunity to repudiate their former relationship. Ross furthermore raised funds for the relocation of Wilde's remains from a modest grave in Bagneux cemetery to Père Lachaise, and he commissioned Jacob Epstein to carve a sphinxlike sculpture for the new tomb; in 1950 Ross's ashes were placed in a compartment built into this tomb. Ross, in other words, most fully embodied the ideal of male procreation in Wilde's life and after it.

As mentioned previously, Oscar Wilde and Wilfred Owen never met. Owen was only seven years old when Wilde died, and Owen did not come from the kind of family that allowed him easily to join the artistic milieu that Wilde inhabited. Owen's family, for instance, could not afford to send him to any university to develop his poetic ambitions, yet alone the kind of institutions Wilde had been privileged to attend. Had it not been for the war and the appalling casualty rate among junior officers, it is doubtful whether Owen would have been able to obtain a commission in the British Army. But by the autumn of 1915, when Owen enlisted in the Artists' Rifles, officer cadets were no longer expected to hail exclusively from the social elite. Owen underwent extensive training throughout late 1915 and all of 1916 and was sent to France as a platoon commander on New Year's Day of 1917. Here he was exposed to intense fighting, including rare moments of large-scale movement as the Germans consolidated their positions on the Hindenburg Line, voluntarily withdrawing from a front that had remained more or less static since the end of 1914. Owen was removed from combat with neurasthenia by May of 1917 and was sent to Craiglockhart Hospital in Edinburgh where he was treated for shell shock and, perhaps more importantly for his psychological well being, he met and befriended the established and older war poet Siegfried Sassoon. Sassoon helped Owen to develop and refine his style, after which he wrote the poems that have become more or less synonymous with British disillusion about the mythical glories of twentieth-century warfare. Owen spent late 1917 and early 1918 training troops and working on his poetry. He returned to France and combat in the summer of 1918 and was killed in action a week prior to the Armistice.

The popular understanding of Owen tends to assume that his desire to articulate his feelings about the war drove his poetic ambitions. In fact, Owen thought of himself as a poet in the making from an early age and only with Sassoon's help was he able to move toward his mature voice of formal innovation in the service of unromanticized visions of the war and its effects on young men. Until Craiglockhart and Sassoon, in other words, Owen tended to keep poetry and war in mentally distinct categories, and poetry was far more a release from the pressure of combat experience than a means of expression for it. Sassoon gave him a way to bring war and poetry together but, even more than that, he also introduced Owen to a potentially appreciative audience for the kind of poetry he was beginning to be capable of writing. He introduced him to Robert Ross.

By 1917 Ross was an established figure in the London art world, having managed the Carfax Gallery and worked as the art critic for *The Morning Post*. He was politically well connected, counting the Asquiths among his friends, and knew most of the British literati of the first two decades of the twentieth century. His rooms at 40 Half Moon Street in Mayfair were by all accounts a shrine to the 1890s, and many of the rooms were maintained and rented to young literary men, Siegfried Sassoon and Wilfred Owen among them. Ross and his partner, More Adey, another former initiate of Wilde's inner circle, presided over a world in which skepticism toward the conduct of the war and an acceptance of same-sex attraction were established social norms. As such an audience had at least in part made Sassoon's war poetry possible, it would soon provide the same service for Owen.

Part of this audience was Charles Kenneth Scott Moncrieff, an officer some four years older than Owen who had been wounded in April of 1917 and was then working in the War Office. Though not nearly as distrustful about the management of the war by the politicians and general staff as was Sassoon, Scott Moncrieff was at least as dedicated to literature and same-sex love, and much less inhibited about his expression of the latter than the chaste Sassoon. Scott Moncrieff had at minimum a close friendship with Owen; Scott Moncrieff's biographer, Jean Findlay, characterizes it as Scott Moncrieff falling in love with Owen, though Owen did not fully reciprocate the emotion. In any case, Scott Moncrieff wrote three sonnets to Owen, two of which he published in G. K. Chesterton's *The New Witness*; these sonnets are addressed to Owen as 'Mr W. O.' and in an accompanying letter Scott Moncrieff places them in direct descent from Shakespeare's sonnets to the beloved youth through Wilde's theory of male procreation as outlined in 'The Portrait of Mr W. H.'

This material trace of influence is not the only evidence for Owen's understanding and use of male procreation as either an idea or a trope.

In my final chapter I read three of Owen's most well known war poems as examples of the workings of male procreation, and I contend that these interpretations would be equally valid or invalid irrespective of Scott Moncrieff's direct placement of Owen into the explicit tradition of a specifically Wildean male procreation. Owen was clearly familiar with Wilde as a writer without Scott Moncrieff's intervention, and Owen's familiarity with the idea of male procreation would be little more than a bit of biographical trivia if it did not affect the way in which he articulated the war and, consequently, also affect the way in which subsequent culture has come to understand the Great War at least partially through Owen. Wilde's influence on Owen is itself a case study in male procreation; it may be the best available recent instance of it. And, as I will make a case for at the end of my final chapter, seeing Owen's poetry as a product of male procreation, as begotten by Wilde and gestated by Owen, makes Owen's widely accepted influence not just on First World War poetry but on the very meaning of the war itself as a cultural text into the product of same-sex desire. The commonly held understanding of the Great War, against which recent military historians have come to rail, is Oscar Wilde's parting gift.

Placing Owen in the context of Wilde is admittedly an unusual way to read him. Part of the originality of the connection lies in the relative obscurity of Robbie Ross, who was certainly a public figure in the early twentieth century, but not someone who left a substantial trail of literary texts by which he would remain well known after his own day. Moreover, his early death from a sudden heart attack in 1918, just a month prior to Owen's death and the end of the war, insured that Ross would remain a pre-war figure. To the extent that the war is often constructed as a break that severed wartime from pre-war culture, Ross looks now like a holdover from the 1890s without relation to the post-war culture of modernism.

This matter of the division between eras, whether expressed in terms of nineteenth vs. twentieth centuries, pre- vs. post-war, or Victorian/Edwardian/Georgian vs. modernist, has not always been a helpful organization for considering the culture of 'transitional' periods. In a very real sense, the difference between 1888 and 1918 is no more or less transitional than that of any other thirty-year period; the mutual reinforcement of a change of centuries and monarchs, as well as the intervention of the Great War, has made connections between figures on either side of traditional categories of historical organization, if not more difficult to make, then at least less often made. Despite all of the profound changes that have affected our understanding of cultural knowledge and its production, traditional categories of historical organization have been remarkably intransigent. Much has changed in the last few decades in our understandings of literature, text, sexuality, and so on, yet the categories of Victorian and modern often seem to hover free of revision. In its own small way, I hope that this project does something to relax these categories.

Finally, a word about what constitutes the texts grouped under the signifiers of 'Wilde' and 'Owen' is necessary. Though I will have occasion to address some of Owen's most obscure poetry because the Wildean influence is most obvious in it, I also connect Owen's best known war poems to the queer sensibility he developed as a recipient of the theory of male procreation. On the other hand, the texts by Wilde himself that are subject to my closest attention are often not the ones by which he is now best known. I have largely avoided the social comedies, including *The Importance of Being Earnest*, in favor of his longer fiction and *Salome*.[5] As I point out in the first chapter, following an important distinction made by Regenia Gagnier, Wilde had two styles, the satiric and the seductive. The former dominates the society comedies while the latter is given freest rein in the prose and in *Salome*. The seductive prose not only best represents Wilde's thoughts on queerness, it also more than occasionally incarnates it.

Wilde and Owen as discourse

Richard Ellmann made the question of Wilde's sexuality into the cornerstone of his 1987 biography, stating that 'homosexuality fired [Wilde's] mind. It was the major stage in his discovery of himself.'[6] Whether the term 'homosexuality' is truly apposite for Wilde's situation—it was never a word he used himself—is a question that can and will be addressed later. For now, we can use Ellmann's immensely influential biography to mark a starting point for the inclusion of sexuality in Wilde studies, which might be tantamount to saying that Ellmann marks the beginning of Wilde studies as a discourse. Wilde was certainly not ignored by literary critics prior to 1987, but the matter of his queer sexuality was much more likely to be seen as embarrassing or distracting than central to a critical investigation. Having already established himself as a frank and insightful biographer with his 1959 *James Joyce*, Ellmann both solidified Wilde's status as worthy of extended critical attention of the kind Ellmann had previously lavished on Joyce, Yeats, Pound, and Eliot, while also marking a bold step toward allowing sexuality to play more than an auxiliary role in both biography and literary interpretation. Ellmann's Wilde biography was completed under very difficult circumstances and, as I will have occasion to indicate more than once, it makes several problematic assumptions about the matter that so fired Wilde's mind, but it certainly marks the beginning of an era for Wilde studies.

It would be inaccurate, however, to represent Ellmann as the single voice that heralded the arrival of Wilde studies. In 1986, a year prior to the publication of Ellmann's biography, Regenia Gagnier's *Idylls of the Marketplace* appeared and read Wilde in the contexts of his audiences, both in terms of how Wilde manipulated his audiences and of how Wilde's audiences marked his placement in economic and historical patterns far too vast and powerful for any single artist to manipulate. While Gagnier's work is unabashedly scholarly, Neil Bartlett's *Who Was that Man?*, published the year after Ellmann's biography, took a distinctly different approach to Wilde by making him the recipient of an extended and subjective consideration of gay male culture in London. Barlett constructs several different and self-consciously contradictory Wildes as reflectors and precursors of modern homosexuality; his work displays an intimate knowledge both of Wilde's texts and of Victorian queer culture, but its purpose lies in negotiating gay lived experience in the moment of its writing rather than literary criticism in any traditional sense. Yet it takes its place alongside the work of Ellmann and Gagnier in the inauguration of Wilde studies. Bartlett demonstrates that dealing with Wilde is never only about reading his texts. His early career as a public and self-promotional figure led up to a moment of equally public notoriety in 1895 as his life and career were crushed as efficiently as the British justice system could manage it. And the punitive legal action applied not only to Wilde, though he had to bear the burden of it, but also to the sexual actions of which Wilde was convicted and which made Wilde the signifier of same-sex behavior that remained illegal in the UK until 1967 and that remained socially stigmatized well after that. Bartlett makes clear that studying Wilde entails addressing his legacy as the public face of same-sex desire; my angle in this book lies in stressing the ways in which Wilde's ideas about same-sex desire do not necessarily reflect those of Wilde's later readers. Yet Wilde nonetheless remains an inescapable figure in attempting to articulate ideas about queer thought and behavior on either chronological side of his public downfall.

Scholarly interest in Wilde has remained strong since the late 1980s with a noticeable increase in attention in the mid-1990s, corresponding roughly with the centenary of his trials. In an overview of Wilde studies

Ian Small describes the three main strands that had developed by the turn of the millennium: the gay Wilde, the Irish Wilde, and the consumerist Wilde.[7] My project seeks to extend the first of these strands, but with the caveat that was already becoming necessary at the time of Small's writing that the continuity between Wilde's conceptions of sexuality, those that were thrust upon him in 1895, and those through which we see him now, is anything but straightforward. Put succinctly, my purpose is to demonstrate in what ways Wilde's persona and texts differ from subsequent versions of homosexuality while retaining their queerness, which is to say their insistence on disturbing commonly accepted notions of appropriate sexual identity and behavior.

Wilde studies may well have attained the status of a discourse; Owen studies has not. A good share of the most important work about Owen has occurred in the context of assessing the literature of the Great War more generally, whether defined as written by combatants or as any writer's response to the war's effects on lives and culture. Slowly over the course of the twentieth century, Owen's poetry has gone from being all but completely unknown at the end of the war to becoming practically synonymous with war poetry. Owen was championed by the leftist pylon poets of the 1930s; his first complete edition was edited by C. Day Lewis. Benjamin Britten's use of Owen's poetry in his popular 1962 *War Requiem* exposed Owen's work to a wider audience, and he has since become a fixture of British school curricula. By the early twenty-first century, this obscure war poet who had been promoted by ardent socialists had one of his poems identified as the favorite of incoming Conservative Prime Minister David Cameron ('Dulce et Decorum Est' is the specific title Cameron picked).

Scholarly work on Owen began with D. S. R. Welland's *Wilfred Owen: A Critical Study*, which was published in 1960 but had its roots in Welland's doctoral thesis of 1951. Wilfred Owen's younger brother Harold published a biography not only of Wilfred but of the entire family in 1963. The three-volume *Journey from Obscurity* tends to portray Owen's poetry as drawing on images that attain their full meaning only when placed in the context of Owen's pre-war biography, especially his childhood. Jon Stallworthy published the first critical biography of Owen in 1974, and he relies quite a bit on Harold Owen's *Journey from Obscurity*, as well as Owen's *Collected Letters*, co-edited by Harold Owen in 1967, and interviews with Harold Owen. After completing the biography, Stallworthy went on to edit and publish Owen's *Complete Poems and Fragments* in 1983, bringing together and attempting to date all of Owen's verse, including juvenilia, incomplete texts, and variants.

Stallworthy's reliance on Harold Owen as a source became an issue with the publication in 1986 of Dominic Hibberd's *Owen the Poet*. Hibberd believed that Harold Owen had effectively censored his brother's letters and his biography; he furthermore thought that Harold had done so in order to protect Wilfred from accusations of cowardice and homosexuality. Wilfred Owen was invalided out of combat in 1917 with neurasthenia and, although no formal accusation of cowardice survives, such categories as post-traumatic stress did not exist at the time, and neurasthenia was often read as code for moral or psychological weakness. Wilfred's sexuality seemed a subject that Harold wanted actively to avoid, while Stallworthy would only allude to it very obliquely: he writes, for instance, that Owen 'wrote more eloquently than other poets of the tragedy of boys killed in battle, because he felt that tragedy more acutely',[8] but Stallworthy does not make explicit why he thinks Owen's feelings were so sensitive. Similarly, Stallworthy addresses the role that Robert Ross played in Owen's literary development, but he does not mention Ross's connection to Wilde and the London queer demimonde.

It would be an exaggeration to claim that Hibberd, either in *Owen the Poet* or in his 2002 biography of Owen, made sexuality as central to Owen's literary voice as Ellmann had done for Wilde. Nonetheless, Hibberd did claim Owen as a gay poet. Though I think the term anachronistic, Hibberd's refusal to see such claims as the accusations that Harold Owen had perceived them to be indicates not only a change in how Owen could be read, but also an increasing admission in the academy and in Anglo-American culture more generally that same-sex desire was an admissible topic for serious discussion and not merely a cause for either scandal or embarrassed silence. As I explore in more detail in the chapters on Owen, Paul Fussell's 1975 *The Great War and Modern Memory* characterized the war as, among other things, an outbreak of temporarily socially sanctioned homoeroticism; his placement of Owen's verse specifically in this context offers one possible way to address the different approaches of Stallworthy's and Hibberd's biographies.

A bit further afield from work particularly on Owen but nonetheless wholly relevant is the more recent concentration on the relationship of the First World War to masculinity. This can largely be seen as occasioned by Fussell's connection between the war and homoeroticism, and it has generally taken the form of an exploration of the limitations of the male bonding that the war occasioned, if not enforced. Joanna Bourke's 1996 *Dismembering the Male*, for instance, admits that 'wartime experiences may have given greater potential for experimentation in intimacy between men', but she insists that 'these same experiences ultimately crushed such sentiments'.[9] Similarly, Sarah Cole's *Modernism, Male Friendship and the First World War* (2003) stresses the damage the war inflicted on male homosocial bonds, though Cole also points out that the war was by no means the only reason why nineteenth-century homosocial institutions largely waned in the age of modernism. Santanu Das in *Touch and Intimacy in First World War Literature* (2005) also emphasizes the damage done to male bodies and to male bonding during the war, while additionally finding a profoundly novel emphasis on tactile senses and the breakdown of corporeal boundaries that the material conditions of the war produced. All three of these books also testify to an increasing ability to talk about gendered bodies and bonding without necessarily having to insist that desires and relationships be categorized as hetero- or homosexual (or Fussell's problematic alternative of homoerotic). Although my emphasis remains on Wilde's and Owen's interactions with the queer cultures of their times, this recent work that takes up masculinity largely without regard to differences of self-identified sexual orientation has important implications for the second part of this book.

The continuing importance of queer

Perhaps the initial question to be posed about taking up Oscar Wilde as a queer theorist is, is it not a bit obvious? Wilde practically invented the twentieth-century queer, after all. His spectacular career, followed by an equally spectacular downfall, made his name synonymous with same-sex desire in the English-speaking world well before such words as 'homosexual' or 'gay' became common parlance. To cite only one example, in E. M. Forster's *Maurice*, posthumously published in 1971 but written just prior to the outbreak of the Great War, the only words Maurice can find to express his condition are 'an unspeakable of the Oscar Wilde sort'.[10] Wilde's own name became a kind of transitional term between the 'Uranian' and 'invert' of nineteenth-century sexology to the 'homosexual', 'gay', and 'queer' nomenclature of a twentieth century dominated by Freudian object-choice as the primarily constitutive element of sexual identity. Does not doing queer theory with Wilde pretty much add up to a case of demonstrating the self-evident?

Yet I think the case is more complex than it initially appears. If 'Wilde' first became a byword for sexual perversion, then a code word for a sexual identity, and by the 1960s and 70s a name to conjure with in the burgeoning homosexual rights movement, it does not follow that the various significations attached to Wilde's name reflect very much on the queer content of his writing. As I demonstrate in the first two chapters, Wilde did become associated with criminal sexuality through the publication of 'The Portrait of Mr W. H.' and the 1890 *Picture of Dorian Gray*, but it was not until his trials, conviction, and imprisonment in 1895 that he became the public face of a connection between art, infamy, and heterodox sexual practice. The name of Wilde that became a publicly traded commodity in the twentieth century had much more to do with his role as a sexual convict, whether considered as justly punished or insensitively martyred, than the content of his literary texts. Moreover, the Wilde who was convicted of gross indecency had gone to prison denying his guilt; if he became a martyr, it was against his best efforts. Wilde the public figure was made into a symbol of sexual deviance, but one who necessarily had to deny the implications of the texts of Wilde the writer.

All this goes to say that the queerness of Wilde as a public figure and the queerness expressed in such texts as 'The Portrait of Mr W. H.' and *The Picture of Dorian Gray* does not amount to the same thing. It is the latter queerness on which I want to focus in this book. I want to concentrate on the idea of male procreation and its relation to emerging understandings of the genealogy of modern sexuality. I take as a given here that homosexuality and heterosexuality are not trans-historical constants, but relatively new cultural understandings of how attraction between human beings can work. Moreover, Wilde's writings come at a crucial time in the development of what we now call sexuality, which means that it is all too easy to fall into anachronism by seeing them as examples of a postdated ideology of homo- and heterosexuality. I want to investigate their role in the formation of modern homosexuality, but this means that we cannot assume that these texts are, as it were, already homosexual. I will thus tend to emphasize the differences between Wilde's implicit understandings of sexuality and our received and hegemonic early twenty-first century understandings, however incoherent and contradictory they may well be.

One other general concern about Wilde needs consideration. In the earlier stages of the development of gay and lesbian studies in the academy, one of the most significant techniques involved was the recovery of lost voices. In a move parallel to that of second-wave feminism's rediscovery of many forgotten texts written by women, an alternate canon of gay and lesbian texts was soon assembled. But in many cases the construction of a homosexual canon involved less the recovery of long neglected texts than the reconsideration of canonical material in a new light. It might even be possible to construe Wilde's own 'Mr W. H.', with its interpretation of Shakespeare's sonnets as poems expressive of a uniquely same-sex love, as one of the first instances of this movement. But Wilde's writing itself hardly needs recovery in this sense. Wilde has been read (or actively not read) as symptomatic of same-sex love since his trials—as I will show, such readings in fact began with the 1890 publication of *Dorian Gray* and featured prominently in the first trial. If Wilde is in no need of recovery, however, he may well be in need of rereading. Unless we wish to assume that human sexuality is a transhistorical constant, an assumption I do not wish to make, one of the first things to do in such a rereading is to historicize Wilde's ideas about sexuality.

Attempting to do so has given me occasion to return to some of the foundational texts of queer theory from the 1980s and 1990s, and I find it impossible not to be struck by how radically and how quickly some things have changed. Confronting a culture that either ignored queer sexuality and hoped it would go away (perhaps with the assistance of HIV) or actively and often violently opposed it, early queer theorists fought back with an admirable brio and a sense that the stakes could not be higher. Now, in early 2015, we in the US find ourselves in a situation in which the Supreme Court has agreed to rule on the constitutionality of gay marriage later in the year. Meanwhile, lower court rulings against state bans on gay marriage are allowed to stand. Already over seventy percent of the US population has access to legal same-sex marriage, and it seems increasingly unlikely that the Supreme Court will reverse the momentum it has allowed to build. Meanwhile, all of the constituent parliaments of the United Kingdom except the Northern Ireland Executive have likewise legalized same-sex marriage. In a political scene in which it often seems that expecting a glacial pace of change is asking a bit too much, the cultural shift on the acceptance of same-sex relations has been dizzyingly quick. Politics and the law in many ways are just starting to catch up to cultural shifts that were unforeseeable only thirty years ago when the US Supreme Court upheld a state anti-sodomy law that outlawed consensual homosexual sex in private (Bowers v. Hardwick, 1986).[11]

And yet, it may be an appropriate time also to ask why the massive cultural shifts of the past few decades have found legal manifestation, in the US and UK at least, almost exclusively in the issues of same-sex marriage and the right of homosexuals to serve openly in the military. Why, in other words, have the most salient and noticeable changes found expression in the trajectory of making it easier for 'them' to live more like 'us'? Certainly the discourse of civil rights has been instrumental in making the possibility of increased individual dignity possible for many people and should not be blithely dismissed, especially when compared to the rollback of civil rights for gay people in Russia and much of Africa, but it also seems that merely extending the discourse of non-discrimination into the realm of sexuality inevitably serves to solidify current dominant understandings of sexuality. In other words, recent cultural changes have increased the possibility of more honest and livable lives for many, but they have done so mainly through demanding adherence to the unspoken rules of sexual orientation: that each person is either gay or straight, that their erotic desire will flow through either a same-sex or a cross-sex channel in perpetuity, and their object choice reflects a deep-rooted identity that precedes even the earliest individual sexual acts and experiences.

Wilde's idea of male procreation requires none of these assumptions. As my first chapter illustrates, in 'The Portrait of Mr W. H.' (1889) Wilde constructs Shakespeare's sonnets into the *locus classicus* of male procreation, and a fluidity of desire and object choice abounds in the erotic triangle that plays out when one decides to construct these lyric poems into a narrative. As Eve Kosofsky Sedgwick is careful to point out in an essay that contains no direct reference to Wilde's interpretation of the sonnets 'within the world sketched in these sonnets, there is not an equal opposition or a choice posited between two such institutions as homosexuality (under whatever name) and heterosexuality'.[12] Moreover, the same-sex relationship of the sonnets is not imagined as an alternative to cross-sex relations and their accompanying forms of marriage and procreation; rather, the relationship with the beautiful youth is often articulated precisely within these systems. Neither Shakespeare's nor Wilde's conception of male procreation, in other words, assumes that a person is either gay or straight or that her object choice either determines or is determined by some deep-seated personal identity. Moreover, it does not reject the gay/straight dichotomy so much as it precedes it: like Shakespeare, Wilde lacked access to the twentieth-century, post-Freudian articulation of desire. Much hinges, I think, on whether one assumes that this is the case because Wilde had yet to discover the truth about desire, or because his own articulation was no more or less inevitable than what replaced it. I make the second assumption.

I thus read male procreation as an alternative to post-Freudian theories of same-sex desire but not as necessarily preferable to them. Male procreation has the advantage of long pedigree; as one would expect from Wilde, who was before all else a student of classics, it has sturdy roots in ancient Greek thought. Socrates' ideas in the *Symposium*, for instance, are much easier to harmonize with a conceptualization of same-sex desire as a form of mental procreation that is not at all exclusive of cross-sex physical procreation than as an expression of an underlying putative reality in which all human beings are erotically focused on either members of their own sex or members of the opposite one—though Aristophanes' creation myth in the same dialog works better with the latter theory, which may well demonstrate that deep disagreements about same-sex love go back at least as far as ancient Athens.[13] As intriguing an idea as it may be, however, male procreation in both its Shakespearian and its Wildean manifestations remains exclusively male. Though Socrates in the *Symposium* credits the priestess Diotima for the genesis of his ideas, by the Renaissance at least platonic love has become decidedly and singularly masculine.

Such a state of affairs leaves Wildean male procreation open to accusations of misogyny, and it is not my intention to avoid such charges or to explain them away. In fact, it is better to admit them up front: no matter what conclusions scholars may wish to draw about Wilde's relation to the various strands of feminism in circulation in his time, his version of the generation of cultural innovation through the mental and verbal intercourse of male persons excludes women. Almost the only mention of women in his posthumously published 'The Portrait of Mr W. H.', the text in which he most directly outlines the idea of male procreation, is that Shakespeare's female characters inspired new styles of behavior in women; even feminism itself, in this version of cultural reproduction, is a product of male procreation. Moreover, when Wilfred Owen was exposed to these ideas, it was at a time when combat experience during the Great War drove a wedge between soldiers and civilians, and women joined older men as the primary symbols of willful noncombatant ignorance in Owen's mature poetry. Nonetheless, there is little in the theory itself to prevent its appropriation by advocates of female same-sex desire. Though male procreation is what interests and motivates Wilde and Owen, female procreation may well have inspired writers less ensconced in the male homosociality of the late nineteenth and early twentieth centuries.

Wilde's scheme of male procreation leaves plenty of room for queer disruption, and this is primarily where I see Wilde's pre-Freudian idea as having relevance for our own time. Seeing Wilde's writing as an attempt to intervene into ongoing discourses about effeminacy, same-sex desire, and cultural progress, and seeing his intervention as something that does not easily line up with subsequent developments with which later culture has become far more comfortable, can help us to avoid a complacency, if not an outright smugness, about being on 'the right side of history'. Overconfidence about trajectories of progress is far more tempting in an area wherein drastic change has been observable in the space of a single generation, but its cost may well lie in a rigidity about what constitutes progress. We are no more reaching the end of historical change in sexuality and queerness now than we reached the end of history with the cessation of the Cold War. Looking at Wilde's version of queerness not as a stepping stone on the path toward our inevitable terminus, but as an ideal that had meaning for Wilde and for Owen while not, with a few exceptions, surviving Owen's war, gives us a gentle reminder that the patterns of history are not always easily predicted. This is not to say that Wilde's procreation ideal is merely a cultural dead end; as I hope to show in my final chapter, it lingers now in the popular understanding of the First World War. But seeing Wildean queerness as something that does not fit easily into the genealogy of subsequent concepts about same-sex desire reminds us that our own models of sexuality are not the only ones that have ever been and thus are not the only ones that ever can be. Changes in models of sexuality will continue, irrespective of which side of history our current trajectory may end up on, and it is impossible to tell what part a Wildean queerness may eventually play in it.

   If extension of the discourse of civil rights into sexual orientation has become the new normal, and queerness is that which refuses to conform itself to the sexually normal, then it would seem inescapable that our new normal will produce a new queer. I can make no prediction about the forms it may take, but increased attention to sexual dissidence prior to the cultural dominance of orientation and object choice can make us more attuned to discontent within the new normality that equates the extension of tolerance to homosexuals with the attainment of a culture without a need for sexual dissidence.

Wilde's theory of male procreation is the central concept to the book, and the first chapter is dedicated to it and the text that most fully embodies it, 'The Portrait of Mr W. H.' Most centrally, I see the text as offering a theory of cultural reproduction through erotic connections between two men; in doing so, it also intervenes in late Victorian discourse on male same-sex desire by attempting to recuperate effeminacy in a positive light. Nonetheless, Wilde also qualifies his faith in this idea of platonic male procreation by offering it in a story that continually undercuts any attempt at sincere belief on the part of character, reader, or writer. The theory itself and the fictive qualification of it become insolubly linked in the legacy that the story passes on.

The second chapter takes up the 1890 version of *The Picture of Dorian Gray* as both an extension and a reconsideration of the male procreative theory. I submit that the novel can, in fact, be read as an illustration of the ideal of male procreation gone awry. I look carefully at two particular words: 'worship' and 'personality'. 'Worship' characterizes Basil Hallward's relation to Dorian: he accurately appraises the young man's worth, the words 'worth' and 'worship' being etymologically related. Basil's worship is a textbook application of the principles of male procreation, but it is undercut both by Basil's naiveté and Lord Henry's failure to value Dorian properly. Both Basil and Lord Henry are fascinated by Dorian's personality, which I read in light of John Addington Symonds' use of the word. Symonds claims that personality for the Greeks was a matter of appreciating the interaction of body and soul within a single human being; it is thus neither a matter of pure fleshly desire nor can it be divorced from the flesh and placed completely in a rarefied platonic realm. The portrait, however, betrays the union of flesh and spirit on which the ideal of personality rests: the portrait, rather than Dorian's actual body, displays the state of Dorian's soul. Wilde thus creates a fictive scenario that at once illustrates and destabilizes the theories presented in 'The Portrait of Mr W. H.'

Throughout this chapter, I employ the symbol of the green carnation as a helpful metaphor. Wilde used the green carnation among his coterie during public occasions: when asked what it meant, he would deny that it had any meaning at all. I contend that *The Picture of Dorian Gray* attempts to work in a similar fashion. Wilde wants his novel to promote male same-sex love among those readers who will be sympathetic to such a message while he wants to be able to deny any such hidden messages to readers who would reject them if they could discover them. As illustrated both by the reviews of the 1890 version of *Dorian Gray* and by its use against Wilde in the first trial, unsympathetic readers were fully capable of looking beneath the surface.

The third chapter considers Wilde as a queer theorist and uses several recent texts in queer theory to situate him both in the late nineteenth century and in his subsequent reception. The first step is to differentiate Wilde as a queer icon from Wilde the writer of literary texts that engaged with sexuality. Wilde went to prison denying the sexual actions of which he was convicted, and his legal case at his first trial centered on the aesthetic defense of denying any ethical or political meaning to his writings. The Wilde who has functioned as a gay martyr for the past century is not the same Wilde who wrote 'Mr W. H.' and *Dorian Gray*. I situate the latter figure in terms offered by David Halperin in *How to Do the History of Homosexuality* by carefully considering Wilde in each of the four pre-orientation possibilities that Halperin articulates (effeminacy, paederasty, friendship, and inversion). Seeing a pre-orientation era history of sexual deviance helps to explain why Queensberry was able to accuse Wilde of posing as a sodomite despite the fact that the stereotype of the gay man did not exist at the time of the trials.

I then turn to Wilde's theory of male procreation and consider its relations to more recent scholarship in the field of queer theory, focusing on the work of Lee Edelman, José Estaban Muñoz, Heather Love, and Judith Halberstam. Wilde's use of symbolic children is easily subject to critique as a symptom of Edelman's cult of the child; Wilde's ideas look much more productive when seen in terms of Muñoz's queer future as a utopian vision or when considering children as proto-queers, as Halberstam does, rather than enforcers of straight values, as in Edelman. Finally, using Love's idea of queer failure, I consider how Wilde's ideal of male procreation never actually works in any of his texts. His literary children are ill-behaved and fail to do what their parent instructs them, and I conclude that for Wilde, such failure is the point. Male procreation remains a beautiful idea, but an impractical one.

The fourth chapter begins with consideration of Wilde's prison letter, which provides insight into the idea of male procreation by blaming Lord Alfred Douglas for failing to be either a proper lover or friend; Wilde both characterizes Douglas as a child and negatively compares him to Wilde's biological son, Cyril. Doing so demonstrates the relation between male procreation and filiation, or the proximity of the relationship of son to that of lover. Of course, such admissions bring up the specter of incest as well.

In order to address incest, I take up *Salome*; moreover, I do so in the context of its performance in 1918 and the legal controversy that erupted when the producer and star of the play sued the radical right-wing MP Noel Pemberton Billing for libel when he accused the production and the play itself of being both rife with sexual perversion and detrimental to the British war effort. My reading of the play concedes that it does in fact represent aberrant sexuality, but it does so by questioning any communal sense of normality that would allow an accusation of perversion. I interpret the play as a confrontation between a

Hellenistic culture that expresses itself through visuality and simile and a Judeo-Christian culture that employs aurality and metaphor. Salome becomes uncomfortably caught between these two worlds, asking for a compromise and receiving instead condemnation from both sides for her articulation of desire.

The fifth chapter sets up Wilfred Owen's poetry as a product of male procreation as well as its cultural endpoint. I begin with Yeats' objections to Owen, which are couched in aesthetic terms but contain a sexual questioning as well: Owen's 'overwriting' cannot be divorced, I contend, from his status as a Wildean writer. Moreover, both Owen and Wilde inherit their tendency of seductive reveling in diction from Keats, a figure with whom both were almost religiously obsessed and a figure that generated sexual objection throughout the latter half of the nineteenth century.

I trace Owen's knowledge of and relationship to Wilde's ideas through Owen's poetry. The earliest clues lie in the self-consciously decadent turn his poetry took at the outbreak of the war, which is due largely to the influence of Laurent Tailhade. Owen wrote an untitled poem at this time that looks very much like a shortened version of Wilde's 'The Sphinx'. I look carefully at a number of non-war poems that reveal a gradually developing ability to use a specifically masculine beauty as their focus. Most importantly, however, Siegfried Sassoon provided Owen not only with the poetic encouragement that enabled him to begin to write about his combat experience, but also with an introduction to the London literary world presided over by Robbie Ross. This world, under whose influence and for whom as audience Owen would either write or revise practically all of the war poetry for which he is now famous, took male procreation as its model and functioned with the spirit of Wilde as its absent center.

In the sixth and final chapter, I continue to consider the influence on Owen of the Ross circle, among the members of which was C. K. Scott Moncrieff. Scott Moncrieff wrote a number of sonnets to Owen, whom he addressed as 'Mr W. O.' Scott Moncrieff thus consciously brought Owen into the tradition of male procreation articulated by Wilde's 'Mr W. H.' I read three of Owen's most well-known war poems, 'Disabled', 'Dulce et Decorum Est', and 'Strange Meeting', as poems about male procreation. In each case, the persona confronts the war through his encounter with a single soldier: in 'Disabled' the subject is overtly eroticized while in 'Dulce' eroticism is resolutely denied. 'Strange Meeting' is unique in that it demonstrates the male procreative principle in collapse: the meeting of persona and other should have been culturally productive, but the war has destroyed both the men and the idea of cultural progress itself.

The book ends, however, with the idea that male procreation continues to affect how we understand the First World War. Recent military historians have critiqued the popular understanding of the war as wasteful and pointless, and they have pinned the responsibility for this misreading on the war poets, Owen chief among them. Although I am skeptical of this revisionist claim of historical objectivity, I am willing to grant that contemporary understandings of the war remain largely inflected by Owen. Rather than a tragedy, however, I read this situation as a victory for male procreation: a small minority position has altered the way in which a major historical event is experienced for several generations after the events themselves. Wilde would be proud.

Lastly, I should point out that this project has been written and organized as a book rather than as a collection of more or less discrete if thematically connected essays. Although the constituent chapters can, I trust, be read independently without too much loss of meaning, the later chapters do assume familiarity with the concepts introduced and defined in the earlier ones.

1

Sexual Gnosticism: Male Procreation and 'The Portrait of Mr W. H.'

'You must believe in Willy Hughes. I almost do myself.'
(Wilde in conversation with Helena Sickert)[1]

In *Sodom on the Thames*, an exploration of late-Victorian male same-sex love through its legal manifestations leading up to the Wilde trials, Morris B. Kaplan dedicates considerable space to the homoerotic coterie surrounding William Johnson Cory, author of the foundational Uranian poetry text, *Ionica* (1858, revised 1891). As William Johnson, he had been one of the leading masters at Eton from 1845 to 1872, when he resigned under a cloud of scandal and adopted a new surname. Among his pupils was Reginald Brett, an aristocrat who was to attain immense political influence in the first two decades of the twentieth century. Brett allows Kaplan to trace Johnson's influence because Brett preserved a lifelong correspondence with a group of friends centering largely on the twin themes of remembrances of Johnson and amorous adventures with boys. In 1892 Brett wrote to a fellow old boy about 'Teddie', a fifteen-year-old Etonian for whom Brett had developed considerable affection. I will use Kaplan's description of the relationship:

> [Brett] entertains the youth at home with his wife and family; Teddie visits with the approval of his parents and of the Eton authorities. [Brett's] love for Teddie has important paternal and pedagogical aspects, but it is also intensely erotic. The sentiments and practices of love between them are not easily translated into contemporary terms.[2]

This is something of an understatement. Early twenty-first-century culture's passion for the child as victim and the pedophile as ravening

23

predator would suspect Brett's motives from the beginning. What surprises us about this relationship is how above-board it is: in correspondence Brett is nervous, not that he will be caught in a sexually compromising position with Teddie, but that his letters to the boy might be read by unintended readers and the depth of his emotional attachment exposed. While our culture is apprehensive that pedagogy will spill over into pedophilia, late-Victorian culture seems to operate more from the assumption that pedagogy without *philia* is hollow. That this love-as-*philia* could also participate in love-as-*eros* is testified to by Johnson Cory's loss of position and change of name.[3]

Critics since Michel Foucault have, of course, come to be careful about assuming that pre-twentieth-century sexualities can easily be fitted into the standard gay/straight dichotomy of later culture. Whether one agrees with Alan Sinfield's argument that Oscar Wilde is the template on which twentieth-century gay identity and sensibility are built,[4] constructing Wilde unproblematically as a gay man is a trap into which we have become less likely to fall. But this creates another problem: if Wilde was not gay, what was he? What did he think he was? Without the gay/straight dichotomy, how do we negotiate his sexuality and his construction of his and others' sexuality? In a culture in which Regy Brett can at eleven o'clock at night go upstairs in his own house and gently caress fifteen-year-old Teddie's head, knowing and recording it as a profound emotional experience, and do so with the apparent knowledge both of Teddie's parents and Brett's own wife, what does and does not constitute homoeroticism?

I propose to address this question through the Wildean text that I find most directly confronts sexual identity: 'The Portrait of Mr W. H.' (1889, revised ca. 1891). I will explore the internal logic of its theory of male procreation and demonstrate how it is based on an analogy with sexual reproduction. Beyond this, I also want to investigate how both the story and the theory are inflected through gnosis, or the idea of a secret, nonobvious meaning that lurks beneath the more readily apparent. The story operates simultaneously as theory, fiction, and quasi-religious text in which belief is frustratingly at once desirable and impossible.

Initiation rites: texts and codes

The story is also one of Wilde's most narratologically complex pieces and has, with the possible exception of the prison letter/*De Profundis*, the most convoluted textual history. It was written in the first four months of 1889 and was rejected by the *Fortnightly Review*. It first appeared in print in Wilde's second choice of venue, *Blackwood's*, in July. Apparently, it made something of an impact, though not enough to warrant much of a mention during Wilde's first trial, at which Edward Carson used *The Picture of Dorian Gray* (1890, revised 1891) and 'Phrases and Philosophies for the Use of the Young' (1894) as evidence for Wilde's putatively unnatural beliefs and behaviors.[5] Like the more famous and legally more damning *Dorian*, 'Mr W. H.' exists in two versions. But the publication history of the story presents a kind of reverse image of that of the novel, in that where *Dorian*'s second and lengthier version is in many ways quite a bit tamer than its initial appearance in *Lippincott's*, the expanded version of 'Mr W. H.' pushes to their cultural extremes ideas that are left merely implicit in the initial version.[6] Significantly, the longer 'Mr W. H.' was a posthumous publication, only seeing print in 1921 following an extended and inadequately explained loss of the manuscript.

Wilde worked on the text for some time. He began writing on the central idea, a theory of the homoerotic meaning of Shakespeare's sonnets, as early as 1887, though it seems that he conceived of the piece as an essay rather than a story at this early stage. Its publication two years later was only a midpoint in its development, as Wilde continued to expand the story even as it appeared in *Blackwood's*. Within weeks of its appearance, Wilde attempted to convince William Blackwood to publish a small volume containing a version of the story expanded by some 3,000 words, specifying only that 'I have many more points to make' (*WCL*, p. 407). Wilde even went so far as to have Charles Ricketts paint a portrait of Willie Hughes for a frontispiece for the expanded book; it was sold for a guinea at Wilde's post-trial bankruptcy auction and subsequently disappeared (*WCL*, p. 412). Horst Schroeder, who has written extensively on the textual history of several of Wilde's texts, sums up the story's post-publication life thus:

> I assume therefore, first, that in the autumn of 1889, i.e., before *The Picture of Dorian Gray* was written (1890–91) and before Wilde met 'Mr. W. H. redivivus,' as Shaw once characterized Alfred Douglas (1891), an enlarged version of *Mr. W. H.* already existed, and second, that this version already showed the distinctive features of the enlarged story as we know it today, viz. the exposition of the Platonism of the Renaissance, the chapter on the Dark Lady, and the discussion of the boy actors of the Elizabethan and Jacobean stage.[7]

The version to which Schroeder refers is not the final, posthumous version we have, which must date from 1891 or later, but it is close to it.[8]

At the time of the breakup of the Bodley Head, the publishing partnership of John Lane and Elkin Mathews, in late 1894, Wilde expressed a desire that Mathews publish the story (*WCL*, p. 604), which he declined to do 'at any price' (*WCL*, p. 607). Lane was tentative about taking on the book, while Wilde understood him to be under the obligation of honoring a previous agreement. Unsuccessful negotiations continued until the legal debacle of early 1895 nullified the matter (though not before Wilde had his revenge by naming the butler in *The Importance of Being Earnest* 'Lane'). The manuscript eventually turned up in the hands of Lane's former office manager, Frederic Chapman.[9]

The story of 'Mr W. H.' is tightly constructed. The unnamed first-person narrator relates his discussions of literary forgeries with an old friend named Erskine. Late at night, Erskine tells the narrator about his college friend Cyril Graham, a beautiful effeminate figure who specialized in playing women's roles in Cambridge productions of Shakespeare. Cyril, relates Erskine, had committed a forgery in order to provide material proof for a theory of Shakespeare's sonnets in which he claimed to believe. The Cyril Graham Theory of the Sonnets postulates that they were written to a young actor in Shakespeare's company named Willie Hughes. Hughes was a young man who, like Cyril, brought life to feminine roles: 'the boy-actor for whom he [Shakespeare] created Viola and Imogen, Juliet and Rosalind, Portia and Desdemona, and Cleopatra herself'.[10] Hughes functioned as both inspiration and instrument to Shakespeare, inspiring him to his greatest creations and embodying them onstage. The sonnets chronicle Shakespeare's love for the boy, his theory of artistic creation, and the interruption of his love by the Dark Lady, who temporarily inserts herself into the masculine relationship. The only problem with the theory is its complete lack of extratextual support: there is simply no record of a Willie Hughes in Shakespeare's company. So Cyril Graham hires a painter to fake an Elizabethan portrait of Mr W. H., which convinces Erskine of the theory's validity until he stumbles across the painter himself. He extracts a confession from Cyril, who claims he still believes in the theory without proof but had the painting forged to convince Erskine. That night, Erskine relates, Cyril killed himself as an act of faith in the theory. Wilde's narrator is 'converted at once' (p. 42) by Cyril's tale of art and pathos, and he devotes himself to poring over the sonnets and expanding the theory's applications and subtleties. Having perfected the theory, he finally overcomes Erskine's doubts, only to lose confidence in his own explanations. The newly devoted Erskine apparently replays the fate of his young friend, sending the narrator a suicide note from the Continent, where he has gone to do further research. When the narrator arrives, however, he learns that Erskine had known he was dying of consumption and attempted to forge his own death into martyrdom for the cause.

This plot sketch applies equally to the *Blackwood's* and the posthumous version; Wilde's additions to the text do little to expand its storyline. Almost all of them concern the narrator's ruminations and expansions on Cyril Graham's basic ideas. Most of these, in turn, focus on the intellectual justification of male homoeroticism in terms of neoplatonism. It is thus quite easy to conflate Wilde and his narrator: just as his character in the story, Wilde himself pored over the sonnets and made them the catalyst for his expanding ideas on male same-sex love. The text of 'The Portrait of Mr W. H.' became the receptacle for Wilde's thoughts about the matter that would land him in prison. Unlike such late-Victorian contemporaries as John Addington Symonds and Edward Carpenter (and even, in his own way, Lord Alfred Douglas), Wilde left no sustained text theorizing his view of homoerotic love. Symonds, for instance, wrote two privately printed tracts on male–male love that Wilde may or may not have read;[11] Carpenter's output on homoerotic love largely postdates Wilde's criminal conviction, though Carpenter's pamphlet *Homogenic Love and Its Place in a Free Society* (1894) was withdrawn by its publisher at the time of the Wilde trials.

Rather than explicate his theories of male same-sex love in a nonfiction text that would need to be published discretely and would appeal only to a very select audience, Wilde chose to hide in plain sight. *Blackwood's* was a solidly conservative literary forum, albeit one with a background in literary controversy dating back to its publication of Shelley. And 'Mr W. H.' engages with homoeroticism on a blatant, though platonically disembodied, level. It is ironically much less oblique on this matter than the passages from the *Lippincott's* version of *Dorian Gray* on which Edward Carson seized during the first trial while pleading justification for the Marquess of Queensberry's accusation that Wilde was posing as a sodomite. The passages from *Dorian* were subject to a hermeneutics of suspicion not only by Carson but also, for instance, by the author of a negative review in the *Scots Observer* that implicitly pegged the novel as homoerotic by linking it to the 1889 Cleveland Street male prostitution scandal through a mention of 'outlawed noblemen and perverted telegraph boys'.[12] But the same type of hermeneutics was perhaps operative in the novel's role in initiating the relationship between Wilde and Bosie Douglas: when Lionel Johnson lent his copy of *Dorian* to Bosie, the latter became entranced with it and soon arranged to be introduced to Wilde at his home.[13] As Douglas Murray's biography makes clear, Douglas experienced both emotional and physical erotic relationships with other young men at Winchester and Oxford prior to meeting Wilde and was thus open to understanding *Dorian* as a coded text.[14] It was possible, in other words, to read between the lines of *Dorian* for a novel about homoeroticism, whether the reader was sympathetic to or appalled by the results. But 'Mr W. H.' does not require this kind of code breaking.

This is not to say that the text presents no hermeneutical problems. We do not have to decode a love that dare not speak its name lurking in the interstices of the unsaid. Nonetheless, we are offered the possibility that the text means more than it at first says. As I will develop momentarily, its construction of male homoeroticism is resolutely neoplatonic, which is to say, ultimately disembodied. Yet the concern of the text is love, a love that participates in both *philia* and *eros*. One of the primary cruxes of the text is how it plays with the body, both as symbol and as material reality. This is, after all, a narrative about same-sex love that develops from a physical analogy.

The physical analogy in question is reproduction: sexual intercourse, fertilization (or 'begetting'), pregnancy, and delivery. The discovery (or invention) of this interpretation is perhaps the narrator's primary contribution to the Willie Hughes theory and represents his breakthrough in expanding what Cyril Graham has left him. Graham's interpretation does not clarify why Shakespeare wants the young man of the sonnets to marry and father children; the narrator's solution is to interpret the children as nonphysical entities, 'immortal children of undying fame' (p. 53). Instead of the production of bodies through physical intercourse, Wilde's theory promotes a 'marriage of true minds' that will produce ideas through mental intercourse. Although this initially sounds like a parodic version of physical procreation, once the reader understands the importance that Wilde and his narrator make the analogy bear, the reverse seems truer: the physical production of additional human beings is a pale imitation of the actual creative process, which is thoroughly intellectual, deeply erotic, and exclusively male.

Most immediately, the theory is illustrated by Willie Hughes fathering, or begetting, Shakespeare's art, which gives birth to not so much the sonnets that express this idea as the characters within the plays that immortalize Shakespeare and are constitutive of his ideas. But the enthusiasm of Wilde's narrator transforms this procreative code into more than an explanation for the birth of the sonnets and/or the homoerotic inspiration of Shakespeare's drama; the relationship between

Willie Hughes and Shakespeare becomes the *locus classicus* for the secret engine that drives cultural progress. The Renaissance is sired by Greek platonism on the minds of sixteenth- and seventeenth-century artists in the same way that Willie Hughes sires Shakespeare's plays. Masculine homoerotic relationships produce cultural change: the 1484 translation of Plato's *Symposium* by Marsilio Ficino begat the Renaissance and thus continued the lineage of what Wilde calls 'the Romantic Movement in English Literature' (p. 69), of which he considered himself a part. Lurking beneath the recorded text of Western culture there hides a homoerotic genealogy, an occult version of the patrilineal lists sprinkled throughout the Pentateuch. Only in this case, rather than the sons of Noah begetting the races of the world (Genesis 10), the sons of Plato (or perhaps Socrates, who sired Plato's dialogues) beget new generations of ideas.

Of course, the entire story is constructed to illustrate this procreative concept. While Willie Hughes sires the sonnets on Shakespeare, Shakespeare in turn (and in a reversal of implied gender roles) begets the Willie Hughes theory on Cyril Graham. Thereafter, Cyril, obviously playing the role of Willie Hughes himself, inspires Erskine to preserve the theory despite his avowed lack of belief in it; Erskine inspires the narrator to take up and expand the theory, thus inspiring the story as the reader receives it. The narrator's primary amorous relationship, however, is more with Cyril Graham and/or Willie Hughes than with Erskine, which demonstrates how convoluted and overdetermined these genealogies can be. Moreover, there is a missing link in the cultural history portrayed: Wilde tacitly endorses a belief going back to the beginning of his literary career as a 'Professor of Aesthetics' who toured North America lecturing on, among other topics, 'The English Renaissance in Art'. Wilde's own era, he hoped, was to play the role of the Quattrocento by offering yet another rebirth of platonism and male friendship, this time inspired by the translations of Oxford professor Benjamin Jowett rather than Ficino's.[15]

To summarize, then, Wilde presents in 'The Portrait of Mr W. H.' a theory of masculine relationship that so closely parallels cross-sex procreation that it becomes impossible to determine with any precision which is the original and which is the analog. He makes homoerotic fecundity a matter of art and of ideas: new philosophies and new ways of making and critiquing art are produced by masculine inspiration. Not surprisingly, a strong vein of classicism runs through this theory, which ultimately traces its genealogy back to ancient Greek culture generally and Plato's dialogues specifically. Also unsurprisingly, this platonic background encourages a distancing from the body. These fertile mascu-line relationships may rely on physical beauty as a means of inspiration, but they do not require sexual contact. The body is a shadow of the soul, and physical expression is unnecessary and, theoretically at least, potentially deleterious to the ideal relationship. A version of this atti-tude would shortly become the basis for the relationship between Basil Hallward and Dorian Gray (though not, importantly, for that between Dorian and Lord Henry). It is, perhaps, also behind the view expressed in 'The Critic as Artist' (1890, revised 1891) that 'the mere creative instinct does not innovate, but reproduces' (*CWOW4*, p. 145). In this case, criticism is the homoerotic procreation of ideas while 'mere' creativity is instinctual and comparatively bodily, the equivalent of the vulgar realm of action that is denigrated in favor of pure contemplation. 'Reproduction' is the opposite of the creation of new ideas, or, as Wilde's Gilbert has it, 'There is no mode of action, no form of emotion, that we do not share with the lower animals' (*CWOW4*, p. 146). Like procrea-tion, doing is a symptom of animal existence; we free ourselves from slavery to action only by embracing pure thought. From this angle, at least, physical enactment of homoerotic inspiration would seem to represent a betrayal, not just of a beautiful ideal but also of the sphere of human culture itself.

These ideas of homoerotic spiritual procreation form the bulk of the material into which Wilde poured his energies following the story's appearance in *Blackwood's*. In one of these added sections the narrator reflects on the utterly Wildean question of the meaning and purpose of art. He decides that art can never really show us the exterior world but only illuminate the interior of our own souls. This Paterian epistemol-ogy is applied to aesthetic situations in which we are surprised by art and suddenly 'we become aware that we have passions of which we have never dreamed' (p. 91). This revelation leads Wilde into the lan-guage of gnosticism:

> I felt as if I had been initiated into the secret of that passionate friendship, that love of beauty and beauty of love, of which Marsilio Ficino tells us, and of which the Sonnets in their noblest and purest significance, may be held to be the perfect expression. (pp. 91–2)

This is the heart of the matter of the expanded text. The Willie Hughes theory provides the narrator with a hermeneutic experience that changes him entirely. Having been initiated into the mystery of homo-erotic reading, the reader can no longer read innocently, and thus the text is changed. And if the text of 'The Portrait of Mr W. H.' has its desired effect, its reader will also emerge changed from the encounter with hidden knowledge. Not only will he or she be unable to read the sonnets in the same way, all of Shakespeare will likewise be changed, and the entire interpretive experience will now involve searching for the hidden and dissatisfaction with the obvious. The reader has been introduced to a level of meaning that is not accessible to the uninitiated and now reads with a difference.

Conversion and the roles of sex

It is not very difficult, of course, to move from this gnostic herme-neutics back to sexuality—perhaps we never left it. The reader comes to understand that the sonnets concern same-sex love and that this same-sex love is a secret driver of cultural progress. Once the code has been broken, once we realize that 'children' are not literal children but the 'children of the mind' produced through the artistic union of the two Williamses, Hughes and Shakespeare, it becomes all but inevitable that we consider the next hermeneutical leap: is the enlightened reader to understand that the avowedly disembodied and platonic sexual-ity that produces ideas rather than bodies is itself a code for physical same-sex intercourse? Does the marriage of true bodies underlie that of true minds? The surface of Wilde's text denies the possibility; in fact, it would not be particularly difficult to see 'Mr W. H.' from a doctrinaire Freudian perspective in which it illustrates a conscious form of subli-mation: unacceptable sexual desire leads to the production of art. But rather than accept a discourse, whether sexology or Freudianism, that is overtly hostile to Wilde's purposes, most recent criticism has celebrated the text's sexual indeterminacy. Lawrence Danson puts it well:

> On the question the forensic reader finds most urgent—is the sort of love designated by these discourses criminally culpable? is it in fact fully sexualized?—Wilde makes the mutual elucidations perfectly self-cancelling. . . . Is this 'transference of expressions' only a linguis-tic dodge that directs us to go on understanding *body* where mysti-cally it seems to put *soul*? Or would such a coded reading merely reproduce the error of those 'who find ugly meanings in beautiful things?'[16]

Danson ultimately declares that, '[i]n a century that could not name Wilde's love without making it "unnatural," the deferral of naming could be an act of resistance'.[17] Linda Dowling disagrees with Danson but not really, I think, that much:

> Yet not to see that Wilde's very lack of specificity may itself constitute an aesthetic choice wholly independent of the mechanics of repression and resistance is to make the mistake of reductionism—as if Basil Hallward, to take one salient instance, employs such a phrase as 'the visible incarnation of that unseen ideal that haunts us artists like an exquisite dream' simply because he somehow lacks a language of properly 'homosexual' denotation.[18]

But it is not reductive to claim that Wilde's refusal to name may have effects that are at once both aesthetic and cultural/sexual. While the temptation to identify Wilde's desires with our constructions, as if Wilde were an early-twenty-first-century gay man waiting impatiently for the term to be invented, is a real temptation and a basis for many popular (mis)conceptions of Wilde as cultural icon, to refuse this identification does not, of course, mean that we must accept the surface platonism of Wilde's text at disembodied face value.[19] Once Wilde has invited us to make one act of decoding, how do we decide not to make another?

William A. Cohen contributes to the discussion:

> The relationship between literariness and sexuality is not simply unidirectional, as if a prior, secret sexual meaning takes refuge behind the guise of literature. . . . Neither the literary nor the sexual can be considered primary. As a result, the imperative to interpret—and to sustain interpretability—becomes paramount in both endeavors, which perpetually require each other.[20]

This approach is reflected in Richard Halpern's *Shakespeare's Perfume*:

> Wilde's commitment to the sublime in his prose fiction overrides any attempt to make same-sex passion acceptable to a broad public, just as, in his personal style, Wilde chose brilliant and devastating wit over ingratiating tactics. . . . The void of silence he creates is so absolute, the walls of secrecy and dread surrounding it so steep, that trying to fill it with any merely finite content, including sodomy, will ultimately disappoint. Wilde does not render sodomy sublime so much as he creates a sublimity that sodomy cannot possibly answer to.[21]

For both Cohen and Halpern, then, there is no secret meaning lying beneath the surface, or at least not a single one. Interpretation cannot hope to discover the one true meaning of the text; taking the step of reading the sonnets as homoerotic love letters that mask a theory of cultural production does not allow us legitimately to proceed to a de-sublimation of Wilde's neoplatonic fiction into its physical reality. Or to put this in the terms I have been using, Wilde's gnosis wants to stay gnostic. Though it is willing to expose polyvalence, it is not willing to have this polyvalence pinned down to specific, limited content. Whether for reasons aesthetic or cultural, it defers the question of physicality.

Though I accept to a certain extent these insistences on deferral, I am hesitant to believe that the body will so easily be banished to indeterminacy. In one of the critical works that inaugurates the contemporary era of Wilde criticism, Regenia Gagnier claims that Wilde had two basic styles. On the one hand, the first style, which she identifies with sadism, is a parodic subversion of Victorian journalistic language and dominates Wilde's social comedies. It chides the audience for not being worthy of the text Wilde offers to them and might be identified stylistically with Halpern's 'brilliant and devastating wit'. On the other hand, the second style is more evident in works such as 'The Portrait of Mr W. H.', which is dominated by purple prose rather than wit and attempts to appeal to an idealized audience. Rather than punish, such writings seduce—and thus come close to the 'ingratiating tactics' that Halpern claims Wilde rejected.[22] It is precisely this seductive quality that makes sexuality a constant undertone in the story, that makes 'Do you believe in Willie Hughes?' as much a come-on as an interrogation of interpretive convictions.[23] But rather than attempt to insist that, despite all the valid objections just cited, we must reinscribe sexuality as the sole hidden signified of the text, I want to introduce a third term: religion.

Of course, by insisting on calling 'Mr W. H.' a gnostic text, I have been using religion all along. Gnosticism is a term usually used of debates within early Christianity in which certain sects, later declared heterodox, claimed that a special knowledge was necessary to understand correctly the message of Christ. Only those initiated into the secrets could understand the nonobvious meanings. 'Mr W. H.' is gnostic, then, in the sense that it initiates the reader into a nonobvious interpretation of the sonnets and implies that such meanings are not meant for the majority of potential readers, who would greet the interpretation with misunderstanding and hostility (Erskine demands that Cyril 'in his own interest . . . not publish his discovery till he had put the whole matter beyond the reach of doubt' [p. 43]). But there is another sense in which the work participates in a discourse of religion without leaving that of sexuality, and that is in its trope of conversion.

If I have failed to distinguish thus far between Wilde and his narrator in the story, I will need to make the distinction now. The question of religious belief is especially relevant to the story as a piece of fiction, as opposed to a theory (whether of Shakespeare's sonnets or of male procreation). A cycle of skepticism and fanatical belief recurs throughout the fiction, as Cyril converts a doubting Erskine; Erskine converts a doubting narrator, only to lose his own faith; and the narrator finally reconverts Erskine, who becomes a pseudo-martyr to the cause, while the narrator becomes an apostate. Belief in Willie Hughes seems a kind of zero-sum game: when the missionary makes a convert, the missionary's faith passes out of him into the new believer, leaving the missionary bereft of conviction. The narrator is fully cognizant of this phenomenon, remarking that '[p]erhaps the mere effort to convert any one to a theory involves some form of renunciation of the power of credence' (p. 94). But the narrator does not speculate on why this should be the case.[24]

Gnosticism is a matter of experience rather than faith. Gnosis is something to which one is granted direct access, or at least something to which one believes one has been granted direct access. Wilde's youthful experience of Freemasonry at Oxford would have made him intimately familiar with the concept.[25] Yet this sexual gnosis is constructed not as an alternative to belief but as antithetical to it. And here I want not so much to queer Wilde as 'straighten' him by claiming that the theory of male procreation, which 'Mr W. H.' both embodies and ironizes when it appropriates cross-sex procreation for queer relations, borrows more than it bargains for. Although Wilde clearly wants to appeal to the code of Greek associations so well exemplified by Pater and Symonds, his appropriation of neoplatonism can easily slip into a rarefied form of bourgeois sexual purity. From this angle, the refusal of sexual embodiment ties homosexual procreation to distrust of physical sexual pleasure. Rather than entertain ideas of physiological and mental changes brought about by sexual contact between men—ideas supported by Symonds, for instance—Wilde chooses to make the flesh a mere adjunct to the soul, a 'veil' that must be 'pierced' to free 'the divine idea it imprisoned' (p. 67). Wilde both reinforces and distances himself from the overwhelmingly sexual imagery here by stressing that neither he nor his narrator is its author: the 'fine phrase' comes from Symonds's analysis of Michelangelo's sonnets.[26] The flesh is not the point, but the flesh is not so much transcended, as in Plato, as pierced, as in penetrative sex.

There is a danger, however, in relying too much on Symonds's formulations for the theoretical basis of Wilde's construction of same-sex desire. Though Wilde clearly is reading Symonds as though both have been initiated into the mysteries and thus understand the code, at a fundamental level, Symonds's construction of Greek love is opposed to that implied by Wilde in 'Mr W. H.' and other texts. For Symonds, effeminacy is a betrayal of true Greek homoeroticism. What he identifies as 'Dorian' sexuality is martial in sprit and only later became infected with 'the Scythian disease of effeminacy'.[27] Symonds sets up a struggle within classical Greek sexuality in which the essence of Dorian manliness constantly wars against 'Oriental' pleasure seeking and effeminacy. For Wilde, of course, effeminacy is indispensable, and I think it is not too anachronistic to claim that, despite his working outside the medical discourse of sexology, Wilde's theory of homoerotic procreation implies a version of what the sexologically informed Carpenter presented as inversion. And there is always, as Eve Kosofsky Sedgwick points out, buried within this understanding a hidden heterosexuality,[28] but in Wilde's case it is quite a complex one.

Effeminacy and procreation may imply symbolic heterosexuality, but the assignment of gender roles is anything but rigid. As the narrator of 'Mr W. H.' claims, 'of all the motives of dramatic curiosity used by our great playwrights, there is none more subtle or more fascinating than the ambiguity of the sexes' (p. 72). And who precisely plays the heavily gendered roles of mother and father to homoerotically generated children is a very fluid affair. In the sonnets, Willie Hughes is the father and Shakespeare the mother, but the Hughesian ephebe Cyril Graham gives birth to the theory by the fatherhood of the sonnets themselves. Or perhaps Erskine inspires Cyril to produce the theory, but this does not prevent Erskine from playing the role of inspiring the narrator to revitalize the theory. Individual male characters can both father and mother, creating a free-for-all of sexual role playing with but one rule: a participant cannot play more than one role at the same time. Gender may be fluid, but it is never transcended. One may inspire/beget the theory, or one may believe in/gestate it, but never both at once. Hence the story's mechanics of belief: Erskine convinces the narrator of a theory in which he can no longer believe; as soon as the narrator convinces Erskine of its validity, the narrator ceases himself to be a believer.

Ascribing male procreation to the platonic sphere means that physical same-sex relations become simultaneously an actualization and a betrayal of the secret engine that drives Western culture. In the fictive world of 'The Portrait of Mr W. H.', this allows Wilde to accomplish two important feats. First, he can say that if Shakespeare and Willie Hughes were physically intimate, such a relationship is symbolic, but also constitutive of real (though nonmaterial) creation. It is thus, in terms of a justice higher than that allowed by the 1885 Criminal Law Amendment Act, neither a crime nor a sin. Just as importantly, it allows Wilde to say that the physicality of the relationship is not the issue. As Wilde would say on the witness stand during his second trial: 'It is beautiful, it is fine, it is the noblest form of affection. There is nothing unnatural about it. It is intellectual, and it repeatedly exists between an elder and a younger man, when the elder man has intellect and the younger man has all the hope, joy, and glamour of life before him.'[29] 'It' is 'the Love that dare not speak its name', and it is here again unabashedly platonic, though perhaps not in the popular sense of the word.

For if we continue in this biographical vein, I think we discover the bad conscience of this platonism. Wilde claimed 'The Portrait of Mr W. H.' was itself a product of what it describes: it was begotten by Robert Ross, with whom Wilde had a relationship that was at once physical and intellectual (*WCL*, pp. 407–8). But the insistence on an impermeable division between the flesh and the intellect, between homoerotic sex and what it was supposed to be a symbol of, led to the pattern of Wilde's later relationships, in which rent boys played the role of the embodied literal and Douglas the role of the rarefied intellectual inspiration. Wilde's prison letter to Douglas is largely concerned with the outcome of this arrangement: the panthers with whom Wilde feasted would eventually pounce, and the ephebic English aristocrat would frustrate rather than facilitate Wilde's artistic creation. The prison letter begins with an indictment of Bosie as a poor inspiration and a destructive force in Wilde's creative life: 'my life, as long as you were by my side, was entirely sterile and uncreative' (*WCL*, p. 685). Much later, Wilde returns to the theme of failed *paiderastia* in relation to Douglas: 'the "influence of an elder over a younger man" is an excellent theory till it comes to my ears. Then it becomes grotesque' (*WCL*, p. 767). Throughout the letter Wilde blames both Douglas and himself for continuing a relationship that not only was spectacularly unsuccessful in living up to the creative homoeroticism modelled in 'Mr W. H.' but also so directly undercut its paradigm that it would seem to invalidate the theory entirely.

But Douglas's failure adequately to play the role of Willie Hughes, Cyril Graham, and/or the narrator of 'Mr W. H.' may not have caused

Wilde to abandon his ideals.[30] Within four months of leaving prison, Wilde wrote to Douglas: 'I feel that my only hope of again doing beautiful work in art is being with you' (*WCL*, pp. 932–3). Perhaps the ensuing reunion did not work out as Wilde had hoped, but his need to reconnect with a male muse points out Wilde's continued belief in the necessity of male procreation even in the face of overwhelming disapproval from family and friends and a heartfelt belief during his imprisonment that the relationship with Douglas was little more than a destructive parody of what it should have been.

Inverting inversion

In concluding my argument, I want to return to my earlier questions: If Wilde was not gay, what was he? What did he think he was? These are difficult questions, since there is no accepted nomenclature. 'Homosexual' comes from the medicalizing sexological discourse of the late nineteenth century, and Wilde seems to me to avoid the term studiously in his letters.[31] 'Invert' likewise comes from sexology and is used by Carpenter and Havelock Ellis as well as, for strategic reasons, Symonds when publishing with Ellis.[32] Perhaps the best term would be *Uranian*, introduced into English from the German of Karl Heinrich Ulrichs. Wilde did use this term, for instance in a letter to Robert Ross dated February 1898, precisely in the context of his return to Douglas: 'It is very unfair of people being horrid to me about Bosie and Naples. A patriot put in prison for loving his country loves his country, and a poet in prison for loving boys loves boys. To have altered my life would have been to have admitted that Uranian love is ignoble. I hold it to be noble—more noble than other forms' (*WCL*, p. 1019). Ulrichs invented the term as an allusion to Plato's *Symposium*, a connection of which Wilde no doubt approved. But he may not have approved of Ulrichs' grounding of the term in the inversion trope (*anima muliebris virili corpore inclusa*), an aspect of sexology that Wilde was anxious to avoid. As Joseph Bristow puts it, 'to fix, to name, and to classify "homosexuality," as the sexologists were attempting to do in the 1890s, was for Wilde to sign its death warrant'.[33] In using Ulrichs' word, we need not assume that Wilde has become a wholesale subscriber to his definitions.

So what does Uranianism mean to Wilde? The idea of effeminacy is central to 'The Portrait of Mr W. H.' It is also, as pointed out above, one of the main differences between Wilde's and Symonds' conceptions of homoeroticism, as effeminacy is anathema to Symonds. It is, apparently, necessary to Wilde: Cyril Graham is identified as effeminate, though Erskine is quick to point out that he was also 'a capital rider and a capital fencer' as well as 'wonderfully handsome' (p. 36). Similarly, Willie Hughes's forged portrait displays a lad 'of quite extraordinary personal beauty, though evidently somewhat effeminate' (p. 34). Where effeminacy means weakness to Symonds, it seems to mean creativity to Wilde.[34] The effeminate man is less tied to rigid gender roles and thus more able to negotiate the dance of paternity and maternity that the generation of mental children requires. He can ride and he can fence, but he has no time for team sports (Cyril 'had a strong objection to football' [p. 36]); above all, he can act. Effeminacy gives the ephebe flexibility in roles ideally suited for the stage and for life conceived as a theatrical event. Since he is neither isolated nor swallowed in the crowd, the effeminate youth can explore beauty that is not tied to the flesh.[35]

Despite all the emphasis on the beauty of Cyril Graham and Willie Hughes, we get little in the way of direct physical description of them. We know that Cyril was beautiful, but most depiction of him concerns his family and his activities at Cambridge. For Wilde, spiritual procreation requires bodily beauty, but it also requires a beauty that moves us beyond the flesh. The combination of masculine physicality with feminine delicacy of form, which is embodied by both Cyril and Willie, in Wilde's view moves the ephebe away from the body and towards the platonic ideal. This model is based, I believe, on Wilde's association of the body as pure flesh, as opposed to symbol of the platonic ideal, with the female body.

We see this most directly through the story's engagement with the Dark Lady, who is subject to much more direct, and much more pejorative, physical description than any of the male characters. She is 'black-browed, olive-skinned' (p. 78) and ultimately of a sinister nature as she drags Willie Hughes away from Shakespeare's spiritual love and embroils him in a nonproductive cross-sex affair. To rescue his beloved, Shakespeare seduces the Dark Lady himself and likewise becomes temporarily lost to the flesh, though not before expressing his distaste for the relationship in several misogynistic sonnets. But perhaps an even better illustration of Wilde's gender dynamics can be located in a brief moment in the frame story: when Erskine stumbles across the artist who has forged the portrait of Mr W. H. around which the story revolves, it is the artist's wife who gives him away. Erskine describes him as 'a pale, interesting young man, with a rather common-looking wife—his model as I subsequently learned' (p. 45). During the exposure of Cyril's dishonesty, the artist tries vainly to cover it up and thus protect both his reputation and that of his client, but his wife's material interests give him away because she thinks that Erskine might want to buy the preliminary drawings of Mr W. H. Rather stereotypically, the woman's greed trumps the male artist's honor; her devotion to pecuniary interests far outweighs her respect for her husband's professional status, let alone his artistic relation to the platonic ideal. She gets her reward in the form of a five-pound tip from Erskine. But most significantly, this gross materialist is the artist's model and thus the physical model for Mr W. H. himself.

The image offers an illustration of the workings of Wilde's gender ambiguity. The body of the artist's 'rather common-looking wife' provides the femininity to the artistic composite that is the forged portrait of Willie Hughes. This clearly, however, is not where the beauty comes from, and the beauty testifies to the ephebe's relation to the platonic ideal. Beauty is thus a product of the masculine, which can imbue even a common-looking woman's body with a trace of the ideal. The wife as a woman does not even rate a name; the wife as Willie Hughes is an immortal. Like the Dark Lady, the wife is tied to the flesh. Once animated with the spark of masculinity, he testifies to the immaterial ideal. In a sense, this is an inversion of *anima muliebris virili corpore inclusa*. Rather than a man's body entrapping a woman's soul, a man's soul warms the flesh of a feminine body—so much so, in fact, that the body becomes a sensitive, delicate, and beautiful expression of masculinity. It is, in other words, an inversion of inversion.[36]

And so it would remain, in a neat little Wildean paradox of gender relations, if Bosie had had his way and the theory had remained a theory rather than an exercise in fiction. But this theory cannot be played out in life any more than the story of 'The Portrait of Mr W. H.' can be treated as nonfiction. The fictive, or literary, will intervene, interrupt. The story's awareness of itself as an act of fiction—and, above all, its constant offering and withdrawal of the theory as a thing in which the reader might seriously entertain belief—ensure that there will be no one great Truth about queerness, no sexological taxonomy, no perfect platonic mind sex. The theory is unsustainable; even a willingness to die for it is not guarantee of its validity—rather the opposite: 'No man dies for what he knows to be true. Men die for what they want to be true, for what some terror in their hearts tells them is not true' (p. 100). Wilde would apparently both embrace and betray this Uranian idealism on both sides of his prison sentence. The Uranian gnosis of 'The Portrait of Mr W. H.' is a lie, but a lie by all means to be believed.

2
Shades of Green and Gray: Dual Meanings in Wilde's Novel

'I take it as a symbol. I cannot help it.'
(*The Green Carnation*, p. 138)[1]

'For when the work is finished it has, as it were, an independent life of its own, and may deliver a message far other than that which was put into its lips to say.'
('The Critic as Artist', *CWOW4*, p. 158)

The cult of the green carnation

In February of 1892 Wilde asked a number of his friends, including one of the actors, to wear a green carnation to the opening night of *Lady Windermere's Fan*. When one of the chosen coterie, Graham Robertson, asked about the meaning of the gesture, Wilde replied that it meant 'nothing whatever, but that is just what nobody will guess'.[2] The green carnation would become a recurring symbol in both Wilde's writing and his dress: he would wear one again at the opening night of *The Importance of Being Earnest* two years later[3] and would have Salome promise to reward the Young Syrian for allowing her to speak to Jokanaan by dropping 'une petite fleur verte' (*CWOW5*, p. 519).

Calling it a symbol, of course, would appear to be misleading. Symbols refer to something other than themselves, and Wilde seems to have designed the green carnation to function in a precisely opposite manner: it was to be a symbol that meant nothing. This negative symbology is also a theme in Wilde's writing, most obviously in the 1887 short story 'The Sphinx without a Secret', in which a woman cultivates an air of mystery around her doings, only to have revealed that she maintained a secret address merely to give herself the appearance of having something to hide. Her life was, in fact, in all ways irreproachable; she loved the romance of the appearance of having a secret life much more than the content that any secret life could bring. Her mystery symbolized nothing, and the reader is left to consider that it is not coincidental that her secret is discovered only after her death, for her mystery was so dear to her that it is doubtful that she would have enjoyed life without it.

So on the surface, the green carnation is precisely all surface. Its purpose is to nurture mystery in order to obscure the fact that there is nothing behind the symbol. And it toys with an interpreter's desire to know what is behind the symbol; that there is nothing there 'is just what nobody will guess'. It is a teasing, even flirtatious, gesture. The interpreter wants to know what this symbol means, so the interpreter asks. 'It means nothing', replies the bearer of the symbol. The interpreter is hooked: it must mean something. What is it hiding? What does it mean, really? The more meaning is denied, the more the interpreter is convinced, not only that some meaning is there, but that it must be important if it has to be so carefully obscured and disavowed. And Wilde laughs quietly to himself, having illustrated the paranoia of hermeneutics. The green carnation, it turns out, is like one of Henry Wotton's cigarettes: 'it is exquisite, and it leaves one unsatisfied. . . . The perfect type of a perfect pleasure' (*CWOW3*, p. 55).

'Those who read the symbol do so at their peril' Wilde was to warn his audience in the Preface to the second edition of *The Picture of Dorian Gray* (*CWOW3*, p. 168). Again, there is a kind of mocking tone to the admonition: Wilde knows it would be fruitless to warn a reader against interpretation. In fact, as we will have occasion to dwell on in some detail, the Preface represents a reaction to the kinds of interpretations several critics had assigned to the content of the first edition of *Dorian Gray*. People will ask just what the green carnation means; nothing can dissuade them from that. But Wilde warns us that there is nothing to see, and that our investigations into deeper meaning, like those of Erskine and the narrator of 'The Portrait of Mr W. H.', are apt to end in disappointment and heartbreak. And perhaps not for the reader only: as Wilde was to discover, the peril is not limited to the reader of the symbol but extends to its bearer as well.

So, forewarned, we will attempt to look beyond the surface of the green carnation. Perhaps the first quality of the carnation on to which we might fixate is its physical structure. Ironically, an attempt to look beyond the surface of a carnation is immediately frustrated by its appearance of being all surface. It lacks the obvious center of the flower so prominent in sunflowers and lilies (to choose only flowers with heavy aesthetic associations). It appears to have no sexual organs. Of course, carnations do have stamens and ovaries, but they are unusually discreet about hiding them. But initially, the flower seems uniquely suited to representing a lack of secrecy. At second consideration, however, it is a perfect symbol for secrecy precisely because it seems to have nothing to hide, so it hides its secret very well.

Wilde's carnations, however, were not merely carnations, but also green. At the end of the nineteenth century green carnations could only be created through dyeing white flowers. The green carnation is thus conspicuously artificial or unnatural.

Lastly, though the etymology of the word 'carnation' is disputed, most sources cite at least the possibility that the word derives from the Latin *caro*, or 'flesh'. If this derivation is accurate, it probably stems from the flower's original pinkish-white color reflecting the common skin tones of Europe. The association may also be inflected by popular Roman Catholic traditions that claimed the first carnations sprung up from the Virgin's tears at the Crucifixion, in which case the step from carnation to incarnation is a small one. In either instance, the flower is a symbol of the flesh, sacred or secular, wounded or whole.

The green carnation thus seems to symbolize secret, unnatural flesh. And though it is not the case that all of the young men invited to wear the (non)symbol at the opening of *Lady Windermere's Fan* were practitioners of same-sex love, at least some, including Robert Ross and Edward Shelley, were sexual intimates of Wilde. It is thus possible to read the symbol as simultaneous disavowal and confession. To those on the outside it is a symbol for nothing, a playful prank at the expense of people's need to ascribe meaning to everything; to the initiated, it is a hiding in plain sight, an appropriation of the codes of masculine dress that mocks mainstream constructions of masculinity and does so right under the noses of those who would be most offended if they knew.

It may also bring some additional light to the question if we consider the immediate context of the opening of *Lady Windermere's Fan*. Although not Wilde's first dramatic production (*The Duchess of Padua* had opened in New York over a year earlier under the title of *Guido Ferranti* but had not been a success), *Lady Windermere's Fan* was Wilde's first play to open in London. Its venue, the St. James's Theatre, was one of the most solidly established of the Victorian West End, having staged many of the most popular plays of Boucicault and Pinero. Already recognized as a fiction writer and essayist, Wilde now wanted to announce himself a playwright on a grand scale. He did so by writing a play that mimicked the salient features of melodrama, including a pure hero-ine, a child of unknown parentage, a woman with a history, a villain with sexual designs on the heroine, and a convoluted plot involving characters desperately working to keep their secrets hidden. In Wilde's play, however, the heroine, who is the child of unknown parentage, is sufficiently impure to plan to run away with the villain. This secret, as well as the fact that the heroine is the child of the woman with a history, remains a secret at the end of the play, thus denying the usual melodramatic culmination in which all is revealed. The play at which the green carnation was introduced, then, treats its audience as part of the initiated. The characters never learn one another's secrets, but the audience is privy to all. As far as the play is concerned, it is given the audience to know what the symbol really means, and it is left to them to contemplate whether people are not happier when they are allowed their illusions.

When called to the stage by sustained applause, Wilde gave a contro-versial curtain speech in which, among other things, he congratulated the audience on the success of their performance,[4] thus turning the convention of the author's opening night speech into an occasion for metatheater. The role of the audience in *Lady Windermere's Fan* is to know the secrets (Lady Windermere's parentage and her willingness to leave her husband and child) that remain undisclosed to the charac-ters themselves. They are to know the secrets, know that they remain secrets, and applaud loudly for the play that celebrates the wonders of continued ignorance—and the man in the green carnation who brings it all to them.

One person influenced by the *petite fleur verte* was the journalist Robert Smythe Hichens who in September of 1894 published anony-mously *The Green Carnation*, a short novel in which two of the main characters, Lord Reggie Hastings and Esmé Amarinth, are transpar-ent stand-ins for Lord Alfred Douglas and Oscar Wilde. Hichens had befriended Douglas in Cairo in early 1894, and he briefly became part of the Wilde circle in London later in the year. The novel constitutes an attack on aestheticism; in it, Hastings/Bosie emerges as potentially redeemable while Amarinth/Wilde does not. The plot centers on a week in the country hosted by a Mrs. Windsor; in attendance are Amarinth, Hastings, and Lady Locke, a young widow with a nine-year-old son, Tommy. During the week, Lady Locke becomes fascinated by Reggie but appalled by Amarinth; when Reggie finally proposes, she refuses him on the grounds that he is merely an echo of his mentor. Overall, the novel reads as a kind of prose parody of one of Wilde's social comedies with Lady Locke playing the role of the pretty Philistine with an inflexible and traditional sense of morals (i.e., Lady Windermere from *Lady Windermere's Fan*, Hester Worsley from *A Woman of No Importance*, and Lady Chiltern from *An Ideal Husband*). Unlike Wilde's plays, however, the narrative sympathy is strongly with the inflexible character, who is allowed to reinscribe bourgeois morality in the face of decadent fatuousness.[5]

The green carnation itself is an icon throughout the text. When Lady Locke first sees Reggie wearing the flower, she asks Mrs. Windsor 'Is it a badge?' (p. 17). When asked for clarification, Lady Locke expands with:

> I only saw about a dozen in the Opera House to-night, and all the men who wore them looked the same. They had the same walk, or rather waggle, the same coyly conscious expression, the same wavy motion of the head. When they spoke to each other, they called each other by Christian names. Is it a badge of some club or some society, and is Mr. Amarinth their high priest? They all spoke to him, and seemed to revolve round him like satellites round the sun. (p. 17)

Whether Hichens had attended the opening night of *Lady Windermere's Fan* or not, he clearly had heard about the sartorial events surrounding the evening. Lady Locke displays the hermeneutics of suspicion on which Wilde depended, and there is a distinctly sexualized tenor to this suspicion. Further in the same conversation, Mrs. Windsor claims that a kind of mental cross-dressing is common in London society, and these young men are indulging in their freedom to explore it: 'Really, Emily, you *are* colonial! Men may have women's minds, just as women may have the minds of men' (p. 18). Lady Locke's conservative sensibility is suitably dismayed, but it is not until she overhears Reggie offering to procure a green carnation for her son Tommy that her distaste for Reggie's morals overcomes her attraction to his looks. The scene with Tommy plays as a seduction (pp. 150–2) and thus connects the green carnation, obviously if not overtly, with both effeminacy and pederasty. The narrative voice comments on the scene's role in Reggie's ultimate rejection: 'Although possibly she hardly knew it, the scrap of conversation that she had chanced to overhear between Lord Reggie and Tommy had really decided her to meet the former with a refusal if he asked her to be his wife. It had opened her eyes, and shown her in a flash the influence that a mere pose may have upon others who are not posing' (pp. 184–5). As the Marquess of Queensberry would also within the coming year, Hichens offers an accusation of posing.

The Green Carnation was quite popular and caused a considerable disturbance for Wilde, who even went so far as to accuse indirectly his friend Ada Leverson of having written it (*WCL*, p. 615). The conversations in the novel display an intimate familiarity with Oscar and Bosie's table talk, and may even reproduce actual discussions more or less verbatim. The idea that someone who had evidently been allowed into the inner circle had then turned around and published private discourse in a context so clearly designed to undercut the entire spirit of Oscar's views must have been disconcerting. The dichotomy implicit in creating the cult of the green carnation (a phrase the novel itself uses [p. 207]) begins to become less clear-cut. Initially, the reading of the symbol depends upon the existence of two audiences: those who will not understand that the symbol means nothing even when they are told, and those who will realize that it means something without being told. The latter group should consist entirely of those who are sympathetic to the meaning of the symbol. The existence of *The Green Carnation* demonstrates the breakdown of this system. Hichens knows what the symbol means, and judging by the satiric tone of the novel, he does not approve and even goes so far as implicitly to threaten to betray the meaning of the little green flower to those who would not sympathize. The mentality necessary to break the code, in other words, does not guarantee sanction of the content of what had been encoded. Did Hichens himself don the green carnation while he listened to Oscar's repartee and then rushed home to make his notes?[6]

My purpose in this chapter is to read Wilde's most famous piece of prose, *The Picture of Dorian Gray*. I want to do so under the aegis of the green carnation, for *Dorian Gray* operates as a novel rather like the green carnation operates as a symbol: it represents what it refuses to acknowledge and splits its audience into those who understand and those who remain ignorant. As with *The Green Carnation*, the two parts of this split audience fall out in unpredictable ways. Like the green carnation, *Dorian Gray* is playful and flirtatious, yet it also knows that it is playing with fire.

The two editions of *Dorian Gray*

Like 'The Portrait of Mr W. H.', *The Picture of Dorian Gray* exists in two distinct versions;[7] also like 'W. H.', *Dorian Gray*'s later version has become the text that is almost exclusively reprinted in collected editions of Wilde, as well as stand-alone editions of the novel. Again like 'W. H.', Wilde began considering a longer edition of *Dorian Gray* before the first edition had even been published. In May of 1890 he wrote to an unknown publisher that he wished to bring out the story 'with two new chapters as a novel' (*WCL*, p. 425); when the novel was eventually published by Ward, Lock and Company in 1891, it had been expanded by seven chapters. It is this longer, twenty-chapter version that has become popularly identified with *The Picture of Dorian Gray* since Wilde's death.

However, the 1891 edition differs in more than mere length from its 1890 predecessor. Originally published in a single volume of *Lippincott's* magazine, a US venture seeking to expand its market into Britain, the thirteen-chapter *Dorian Gray* is the text that generated considerable controversy and first linked Wilde's name to criminal sexual behavior in the press. W. H. Smith, then the largest bookseller in Britain, had withdrawn the issue of *Lippincott's* that contained *Dorian Gray* in reaction to the bad press the story had generated. The 1891 version, though longer, is in many ways a reaction to the *Lippincott's* version's stormy reception, and it reflects the sexual accusations by consistently toning down the physical and mental intimacy between the three male characters that dominate the narrative. The 1891 edition, moreover, was presented as an expensive art book, skillfully designed by Charles Ricketts, and available in two sizes and prices. Even though it was produced in limited print-runs, sales of the 1891 edition were disappointing: the impact seems to have been made in 1890, and the later edition failed to extend the text's hold on the public imagination, either through appreciation or prurience. As Joseph Bristow has it in the Introduction to the 2005 Oxford University Press edition that printed complete and separate texts of the two versions, 'the 1891 edition departs so much in size and scope from its predecessor that it does not so much constitute a revision of an earlier work as a wholesale rethinking of it' (*CWOW2*, p. xxx). It is thus both unfortunate and ironic that, though the 1890 *Dorian Gray* made the text's cultural impact, it has been the 1891 *Dorian Gray* that has subsequently taken credit for it.[8]

For these reasons, I have chosen to use the 1890 *Lippincott's* version in the following interpretation. I will occasionally refer to the 1891 version largely for purposes of contrast, but my focus remains the *Dorian* that created controversy and the *Dorian* that Edward Carson cited as evidence for justification of Queensberry's accusation during Wilde's first trial. Overall, I will focus on the use of two words in the text: 'worship' and 'personality'. I want to continue the investigation into Wilde's implicit and self-consciously literary understandings of same-sex sexuality, which will mean reading *Dorian Gray* as in some ways the sequel to 'The Portrait of Mr W. H.' This is not to claim that *Dorian Gray* simply reiterates the male procreative theory of 'Mr W. H.'; rather, *Dorian Gray* gives us both a glimpse of male procreation in action, and it demonstrates how the theory can be abused. Its creation of an all-male erotic triangle allows Wilde to explore the implications of male artistic procreation in both its ideal and ethically flawed forms.

Howbeit in vain do they worship me

It is rather commonplace to read Chapter 2 of *Dorian Gray*, in which Lord Henry Wotton is introduced to the title character, as a seduction.[9] It is that, of course, but it is also an impregnation. Lord Henry's famous monolog, in which he profoundly influences Dorian by, among other things, explaining to him the immorality of influence (*CWOW3*, p. 20), culminates in a moment of silence just prior to Basil Hallward's announcement of the finishing of the portrait. As Dorian considers all that Lord Henry has said, his gaze falls upon 'a furry bee' that has begun to pollinate the sprig of lilac that Dorian has just let fall from his hand (CWOW3, p. 26). The narrator initially portrays the bee as a kind of distraction from the rapid mental processing in which Dorian is engaged at the time:

> He watched it with that strange interest in trivial things that we try to develop when things of high import make us afraid, or when we are stirred by some new emotion, for which we cannot find an expression, or when some thought that terrifies us lays sudden siege to the brain and calls on us to yield. (*CWOW3*, p. 26)

Yet it would not take an overly sensitive reader to recognize a more than coincidental relationship between this triviality and what it intrudes upon. Dorian is at this moment being pollinated; he is undergoing a specifically sexual yet non-physical influence in which Lord Henry's words form the grains of pollen that produce new and frightening thoughts within Dorian's mind. He is, in other words, undergoing the type of artistic procreation delineated in 'Mr W. H.' Moreover, the floral image, like that of the green carnation, seems to ask to be interpreted to its limit: the sexual reproduction of flowering plants often relies upon the participation of a third party. The bee facilitates cross-fertilization by transferring pollen from one flower to another (in this case from Dorian's discarded lilac to 'the stained trumpet of a Tyrian convolvulus' [*CWOW3*, p. 26]). The bee itself, however, is gathering nectar from the flowers and is not concerned with its role in fertilization. Its reproductive role is played, as it were, unconsciously.

I am not claiming that the bee image is strictly allegorical. Neither Lord Henry nor Basil need correspond directly to the bee. In the homosocial erotic triangle the novel so carefully constructs, both Henry and Basil play the role of the fertilizer of Dorian. This may well be part of the metaphor as floral cross-pollination requires three parties: two flowers and a bee. It is cross-sex in a strict biological sense in that pollen (male gametes) is transferred to ovule (female gametes) on the body of an insect. But the insect is a medium rather than a full participant in this process. It is integral to the life cycle of the plant, yet it does not contribute any genetic material itself. Likewise, Henry and Basil are both fertilizing Dorian, Henry with his ideas and Basil with his worship of the young man outlined in the first chapter of the novel. Yet the sexual/reproductive relationships are even more complex: Dorian is initially fascinating to Henry because Dorian fascinates Basil. Henry's fascination leads to the conversation that so greatly stirs Dorian's mind, and it is the outward display of the effects of this inward process that causes Basil's picture to capture Dorian at his most intriguing: 'I don't know what Harry has been saying to you, but he has certainly made you have the most wonderful expression' (*CWOW3*, p. 23). Put in terms of 'Mr W. H.', it is obvious that Dorian's physical beauty begets the painting that represents Basil's best work (*CWOW3*, p. 88) and 'one of the greatest things in modern art' (*CWOW3*, p. 29). Yet it would be just as accurate to claim that Henry begets the expression that begets Basil's painting, and that Basil begets the obsession that causes Henry to generate the expression in Dorian. As in 'Mr W. H.', male procreation is anything but simple.

Yet within this imagery of cross-pollination another factor is introduced. At the very moment of gestation, after Dorian has called for silence following Lord Henry's verbal ejaculation and while Lord Henry watches for the results thereof, Dorian reels and considers what is going on inside himself: 'he was dimly conscious that entirely fresh impulses were at work within him, and they seemed to him to have come really from himself' (*CWOW3*, p. 22). Such thoughts open up the paradoxical tensions within Lord Henry's seduction, which, after all, is a philosophical rejection of influence that is designed to influence its subject. Likewise, Dorian is influenced by an outside source to consider whether the new ideas he currently experiences do not in fact emanate from within. Wilde, of course, is perfectly capable of reveling in such paradox entirely for its own sake, but it is worth considering whether the possibility of self-pollination might be introduced here. The influence of either Lord Henry or Basil on Dorian might be a cooperative affair with the influencer begetting a new Dorian only inasmuch as the influence (in the form of words or paint) allows the subject to listen to interior voices to which he had been hitherto deaf. Dorian might thus be seen as pregnant with a new version of himself, a version that comes at least as much from his own material as that of any putative father.

However we negotiate the complexities of male procreation in this seminal chapter, the most salient fact is that a male erotic triangle is productive of both an art object and a new version of a character. The former, in which Basil and Dorian give birth to the titular painting, I will characterize as a product of worship. The second case of paternity, in which Lord Henry and Dorian give birth to a new version of Dorian, I will characterize as a birth of personality. These are not mutually exclusive terms: the loves of Basil and Lord Henry have a certain amount of overlap, and the creation of personality may well result in the creation of an object of worship. But one of the tasks Wilde sets himself in *Dorian Gray* is the differentiation of two kinds of male same-sex love and thus two kinds of male artistic procreation. It would be an exaggeration to claim that Basil's worship is ethically perfect while Lord Henry's obsession with Dorian remains purely destructive, but I do think that Wilde offers these two extremes as a kind of illustration of the extent to which male–male love can vary from the quasi-religious, artistic, and platonic (Basil's worship) to the manipulative, sterile, and destructive (Lord Henry's influence).

The term 'worship', unlike most of Wilde's favorite words, is resolutely Anglo-Saxon. As a noun, the *OED* defines it as 'condition of being worthy, honor, renown', while as a verb in its earliest iterations (thirteenth century) it means to recognize as worthy, 'worthy' and 'worship' in fact having the same Anglo-Saxon root (*weorð*). This sense is preserved in the title 'worshipful' and the usage of the term 'your worship' for mayors and magistrates in most nations of the commonwealth. Its ties to sexuality as well as religion are illustrated in a phrase from *The Book of Common Prayer* that Wilde must have spoken at least once in his life: 'with my body I thee worship'. In the context of the Anglican rite of marriage the term implies that sexuality is a conference or recognition of worth. The religious sanctification of sexuality recognizes its worth, and the participation of the couple in sanctified sex represents a mutual recognition of the worth of each other in the sexual context of the relationship. To worship, then, is to recognize the (true) worth of that which is worshipped, and in the context of a world in which the trace of the Anglican marriage vows will subtly affect the connotation of the word, to place worship within the framework of sexuality will function to a certain extent to sanctify it.[10]

This sexualized usage of the term 'worship' is first outlined in Basil Hallward's explanation of his relationship to Dorian Gray in the opening chapter of the novel. The context for Basil's employment of the term is his rather coy semi-explanation/semi-refusal to explain his fascination with Dorian. The green carnation moment comes almost immediately in the novel when Basil is maneuvered by Lord Henry into admitting the name of his new aesthetic obsession. When Lord Henry queries why Basil should want to withhold such information, Basil replies:

> Oh, I can't explain. When I like people immensely I never tell their names to any one. It seems like surrendering a part of them. You know how I love secrecy. It is the only thing that can make modern life wonderful or mysterious to us. The commonest thing is delightful if only one hides it. (*CWOW3*, pp. 5–6)

The explanation reads as a reiteration of 'The Sphinx without a Secret' and thus introduces the question of audience, i.e., the differentiation between those who wear the carnation and those who ask about it. For the latter, Basil's secretiveness is a smokescreen that hides the fact that he has nothing to hide. For the initiated, Basil's confession that he has nothing to hide obscures the nature of his worship.

Basil introduces the word mid-way through the first chapter in a roundabout way. He claims that his happiness relies upon seeing Dorian every day if only for a few minutes: 'But a few minutes with somebody one worships mean a great deal' (*CWOW3*, p. 12). Lord Henry latches on to the word immediately, claiming incredulity that Basil could care for anything as much as his art. At the beginning of Chapter 2 Lord Henry comes to agree with Basil's summation and his diction: 'No wonder Basil Hallward worshipped him. He was made to be worshipped' (*CWOW3*, p. 19). Taking the word at its literal, etymological level for the moment, Basil is merely valuing Dorian at his true worth. This worth, moreover, is primarily aesthetic: 'He is all my art to me now' (*CWOW3*, p. 12) is Basil's justification of his worship. Dorian is not a distraction from art; he is art. Basil's worship of Dorian is thus an act of artistic appreciation, the fascinated gaze of an enraptured attendee at a surprisingly good gallery opening. His worship is the acknowledgment of this inspiration, both when Dorian is the direct subject of the artwork and when he is ostensibly absent from it: 'He is never more present in my work than when no image of him is there. . . . I see him in the curves of certain lines, in the loveliness and the subtleties of certain colors' (*CWOW3*, p. 13). The worthiness of Dorian lies in how he allows Basil to see more so than what (or whom) Basil sees. Dorian has thus impregnated Basil as much as Basil has impregnated him: there is a mutuality to this aesthetic/erotic relationship that allows it to achieve, potentially at least, true reciprocal creativity. As an ideal, it hews closely to the paradigm of male procreation that runs through 'Mr W. H.'

Two of these three instances of the word 'worship' in the first two chapters of the novel are cut in the 1891 version.[11] In Chapter 2 the sentence 'he was made to be worshipped' is cut entirely; only 'no wonder Basil Hallward worshipped him' (*CWOW3*, p. 181) remains. The effect of these changes is complex: in the 1890 edition, Lord Henry's observation in Chapter 2 is a direct quotation of Basil's confession in Chapter 1, as well as an enthusiastic agreement with it. Moreover, the agreement is couched in terms, not so much of Lord Henry's concurrence with Basil's taste, as an acknowledgement of worth, just as the Anglo-Saxon would have it. The passive voice of 'made to be worshipped' brooks no disagreement, as though Dorian's worth is not a matter of individual judgment but a topic of universal aesthetic accord. In the 1891 edition, however, Lord Henry is no longer citing Basil directly; his 'no wonder . . .' statement is still substantially an agreement with Basil's worship, but it implicates Lord Henry less directly in the adjudication of Dorian's worth. To exaggerate slightly, it is as if the 1891 edition has Lord Henry say, 'I can see why Basil rates him so highly', which is not the same statement as, to further paraphrase, 'he must be rated highly'. Moreover, since this is the first instance of the word 'worship' in the 1891 edition, Lord Henry seems to be exposing something about Basil in ascribing the attitude of worship on his part toward Dorian. Here, Basil never confesses; Lord Henry confesses for him.[12] Basil's worship of Dorian is thus less a universally accurate assessment of his worth than it is an idiosyncratic obsession. It is not unjustified, but it is also not necessary.

Basil's worship of Dorian is the central issue for Chapter 7 as well. Dorian's refusal to allow Basil to view the portrait becomes the occasion for Basil's confession to Dorian, a confession that is particularly revealing in the 1890 edition: 'It is quite true that I have worshipped you with far more romance of feeling than a man usually gives to a friend' (*CWOW3*, p. 90).[13] The diction of both 'worship' and 'romance' is tied to sexuality by the immediately following sentence: 'Somehow, I had never loved a woman.' This is as close as Basil, and perhaps Wilde, can come to an explicit invocation of same-sex desire. The addition of 'romance' to 'worship' moves the latter term from one of appreciation, however tinged by sexuality, to one of *eros*. At this point, Basil's secret becomes a positive desire rather than an empty core that he hides for the sake of loving secrecy itself. In terms of the green carnation, the confession turns the portrait from a symbol that means nothing to an icon that threatens to reveal the core of Basil's life: his 'idolatry' (*CWOW3*, p. 91) of Dorian. Moreover, Dorian is cast as the audience for this hermeneutic revolution; Dorian is the recipient of the coded message about which Basil hopes him to be at least sympathetic, though he fears that Dorian might like him less than he does or will 'laugh at' him (*CWOW3*, 89). Dorian plays his role by pretending that Basil's reasoning, which is a revelation, is in fact what Dorian himself saw when he looked at the painting: a kind of self-portrait of the artist's worship. Basil fears that he has revealed himself in the painting; he has not, but Dorian allows him to believe that he has. Dorian thus functions as perhaps the least ideal type of audience for Basil's aesthetic confession: he feigns understanding and sympathy, but he feasts on another's secret while hording his own. Dorian Gray thus fictively predicts Robert Hichens as much as Alfred Douglas.

Yet this question of audience in Chapter 7, tied as it is to a predictive metatextual possibility (that *Dorian Gray* could be read as unsympathetically as Dorian Gray reads Basil's confession), leads to another twist: Basil confesses what he had felt or had feared that his art revealed about his desire, but he claims no longer to fear such exposure. He wants to display the picture, and he announces a complete reversal of his aesthetic theory: 'I cannot help feeling that it is a mistake to think that the passion one feels in creation is ever really shown in the work one creates. Art is more abstract than we fancy. Form and color tell us of form and color,—that is all. It often seems to me that art conceals the artist far more completely than it ever reveals him' (*CWOW3*, p. 91). Basil does not disavow his worship, but he does distance himself from the possibility that his confession is reflected in his art. Wilde thus offers his readership another green carnation: by having Basil, the only productive artist of the triangle, mouth the standard aesthetic disconnection between artist and subject, Wilde gives the audience the kind of theory it has come to expect from him. This theory also, of course, functions as an insistence that there is no secret hidden meaning to art, that the green carnation means precisely nothing. The fact that this articulation directly contradicts Basil's earlier theory ('every portrait that is painted with feeling is a portrait of the artist, not of the sitter' [CWOW3, p. 7]), leads to another metatextual possibility. How much of Wilde does *Dorian Gray* reveal? Is the purpose of the story to reveal a hidden portrait of the artist, of his secret soul, or to provide a carefully crafted aesthetic object that tells us merely of the writer's ability to write?[14] Different answers to these questions would dominate the reception of the 1890 edition, and Wilde expressed considerable frustration at what he took to be misinterpretations of his work. Yet Basil's contradictory theories express Wilde's own dance in and out of his text: the artist confesses his secret soul to those who sympathize, while to the prurient and philistine, the green carnation reveals nothing. This is the ideal, anyway, yet as we have just seen, the novel itself predicts the inevitability of unsympathetic reading.

Basil's aesthetic vacillation also replicates the ebb and flow of passion in 'Mr W. H.' It is when the portrait leaves Basil's sight that he ceases to believe in his doctrine of self-revelation, just as the narrator of 'Mr W. H.' becomes an apostate of his own religion as soon as he (re)converts Erskine. In the previous chapter, I tied this flexibility of belief to Wilde's celebration of effeminacy, and I think that much of that idea continues to obtain here. Though never referred to as 'effeminate' in either edition of *Dorian Gray*, the 1890 edition says of Basil, 'Rugged and straightforward as he was, there was something in his nature that was purely feminine in its tenderness' (*CWOW3*, p. 87). This combination places Basil in the line of Cecil Graham's blending of athleticism and effeminacy, a mixture of gender traits that allows platonically idealized masculinity to become embodied. Basil articulates two contradictory theories. He cannot make up his mind as to whether art reveals or conceals the artist, just as Wilde wants to have it both ways: to one audience, art reveals the inner secret, while to another it reveals only itself and conceals its maker. Basil's effeminacy marks him as the proper character to express this ambiguity; as an example of Wilde's preferred ambiguity of the sexes that nonetheless privileges a platonic masculinity, he embodies the same-sex desire that may or may not constitute Wilde's true confession—depending on who hears it.

The word 'worship' is also used in a heterosexual context during Dorian's brief and tragic courtship of Sibyl Vane. In announcing his infatuation to Lord Henry, Dorian exclaims 'My God, Harry, how I worship her!' (*CWOW3*, p. 44). By the following chapter, he has expanded this estimation of her worth into something universal: 'I want to place her on a pedestal of gold, and to see the world worship the woman who is mine' (*CWOW3*, p. 55). When the fall comes, this universal estimation of worth is one of several ideals that the disappointed Dorian flings in the girl's face: 'The world would have worshipped you, and you would have belonged to me. What are you now? A third-rate actress with a pretty face' (*CWOW3*, p. 63). Dorian's disenchantment stems from having been mistaken in his worship or, in other words, of having misidentified the worth of the object evaluated. When Sibyl was an artistic ideal, she was worthy of the highest estimation; when she loses her talents as an actress, she no longer interests Dorian. The ethical implication, of course, is that Dorian has failed to see Sibyl as a person (and perhaps also as a woman) rather than as an *objet d'art*. By the morning, he has begun to realize his mistake and thus regret his actions. Lord Henry, however, convinces him once again to look at the event aesthetically and thus retain distance and control over his reactions and emotions ('you must think of that lonely death in the tawdry dressing-room simply as a strange lurid fragment from some Jacobean tragedy, as a wonderful scene from Webster, or Ford, or Cyril Tourneur' [*CWOW3*, p. 80]). Dorian is thus sufficiently calloused to withstand Basil's critique in Chapter 7.

Dorian's mistake is certainly related to the over-expansion of the aesthetic as a category, but it is also worth considering the gender dynamics of the situation. Sibyl interrupts the exclusively male homosocial triangle that constitutes the main dynamic of the novel. Her death both restores and permanently alters the relationships that constitute the triangle. Dorian and Lord Henry conspire to keep Sibyl as an object within the confines of the aesthetic, the realm in which male procreation occurs. Where the artist's wife in 'Mr W. H.' was ennobled into art and masculinity by posing as the model for Mr W. H. himself, Sibyl is murdered into art. Henry is perversely correct in his summation of Sibyl: 'The girl never really lived, and so she has never really died' (*CWOW3*, p. 80). Her attempt to operate as a conscious subject within art dooms her. When she is a good actress, one gifted with 'genius' in Dorian's estimation (*CWOW3*, p. 45), she is unaware of herself as an artist. When she becomes self-conscious, she becomes a bad actress. 'I knew nothing but shadows, and I thought them real' (*CWOW3*, p. 62) is her explanation. The ability to stand outside of art and manipulate it, to treat life as an aesthetic object, is an ability reserved to men. It may also be an illusion reserved for men. But for now, Sibyl's death preserves the masculine sanctity of art. Only men can procreate aesthetically, and Dorian's worship of Sibyl is misplaced in that he values her worth as an artist, which must be, according to the paradigm of male aesthetic procreation, illusory.

Basil makes a similar mistake in his estimation of Dorian. Basil initiates the entire discourse of worship, and he returns to it when he re-enters Dorian's life as a moral scourge. After Basil demands from Dorian a direct explanation of his behavior and its effects on others, Dorian offers the portrait. Basil is shocked to discover that the work both is and is not recognizable as his own, and he interprets it as evidence that his worship has been misplaced: 'God! What a thing I must have worshipped! . . . I worshipped you too much. I am punished for it. You worshipped yourself too much. We are both punished' (*CWOW3*, p. 135–6). Basil's worship had been, or had at least appeared to be, a purely aesthetic judgment, a more or less accurate estimation of Dorian's value. At this moment, Basil is forced to recognize the effect of having aestheticized Dorian. Dorian has become what Lord Henry wished him to be: a spectator of his own life and thus an escapee from the suffering to which the non-aesthetically enlightened are subject (*CWOW3*, p. 86). Though Dorian has fulfilled Lord Henry's wish, Basil must now face the idea that his own worship has been as responsible for Dorian's deleterious effect on himself and others as has Lord Henry's fascinated manipulation of the lad. Basil's worship has led to Dorian's vanity ('you met me, devoted yourself to me, flattered me, and taught me to be vain of my good looks' [*CWOW3*, p. 135]) and to his tendency to see himself entirely in aesthetic terms. Basil thus finds himself co-procreator with Lord Henry, an arrangement that questions the neat breakdown between Basil's worship and Lord Henry's manipulation or, to put it another way, between platonized idealization and bodily sexuality.

The quasi-allegory I am offering, then, amounts to a scheme in which Basil's worship represents the idealized platonic conceptualization of male same-sex love, the Hellenic model conceived in Benjamin Jowett's Oxford and fostered by Pater and Symonds. Lord Henry's fascination, on the other hand, represents, if not a more purely physical, then a more sexualized and manipulative type of relationship in which the pleasure of the older, aristocratic subject is privileged over the effects of the taking of that pleasure from the ephebic object of desire. Basil's love prompts an internal monologue for Dorian that presages Wilde's trial speech cited at the end of the previous chapter:

> The love that he bore him—for it was really love—had something noble and intellectual in it. It was not that mere physical admiration of beauty that is born of the senses, and that dies when the senses tire. It was such a love as Michael Angelo had known, and Montaigne, and Winckelmann, and Shakespeare himself. Yes, Basil could have saved him. (*CWOW3*, p. 96)

Dorian, apparently, has read Pater's *Renaissance*; moreover, he has found himself within the proper audience of that text and registers a sympathetic response to its coded celebration of Hellenic homo-eroticism as the hidden engine of the enlightenment of post-Medieval culture. Lord Henry's relationship to Dorian, however, is that of an artist commanding an instrument. Lord Henry configures Dorian as an extension of Lord Henry himself, and though the attraction is at least as intellectual as that of Basil, it lacks nobility. In the 1891 version, Wilde has Lord Henry investigate the circumstances of Dorian's early life, and insofar as they feature a beautiful young orphan raised by an unsympathetic uncle, they parallel those of Cyril Graham. In the 1890 edition, Lord Henry reflects that 'to a large extent, the lad was his own creation' (*CWOW3*, p. 47); in 1891 this is extended into a musical metaphor:

> Talking to him was like playing upon an exquisite violin. . . . There was something terribly enthralling in the exercise of influence. No other activity was like it. To project one's soul into some gracious form, and let it tarry there for a moment; to hear one's own intel-lectual views echoed back to one with all the added music of passion and youth; to convey one's temperament into another as though it were a subtle fluid or a strange perfume: there was a real joy in that—perhaps the most satisfying joy left to us in an age so limited and vulgar as our own, an age grossly carnal in its pleasures, and grossly common in its aims. (*CWOW3*, p. 199)

The physical implications of the diction here, the joy in 'projection' into a 'gracious form' and the conveying of 'temperament' in the form of a 'subtle fluid' are unmistakably copulative, yet they are deployed as an overt rejection of vulgarity and gross carnality. And though it would be possible to construct this passage as a clear outbreak of sublimated sexuality, there are other possibilities. Most interestingly, to my mind, is the idea of filiation: what Lord Henry is attempting to create in Dorian at this point is less a lover than a son.[15] His fantasy is that of a younger incarnation of his own self, mimicking his views with the added vigor of youth. He desires not so much Dorian himself but Dorian as a reitera-tion of Lord Henry.

On the surface, the passage itself echoes a metaphor in 'The Portrait of Mr W. H.', one that similarly uses a musical instrument as an illustra-tion of homoerotic procreation: 'I saw that the love that Shakespeare bore him [Willie Hughes] was as the love of a musician for some deli-cate instrument on which he delights to play.'[16] Yet the remainder of the paragraph from which this sentence is drawn, while admitting that actors form a kind of human medium through which the theatric art expresses itself, also stresses the give and take between artist and implement. Willie Hughes is the instrument through which Shakespeare expresses his art, but he also affects the art that is thus expressed. Without Willie Hughes, the narrator insists, there would have been no Juliet, no Imogen, no Cleopatra; Willie Hughes functions as much as an inspiration for the creator of his roles as he does as of a mere product of them. Lord Henry, on the other hand, seems to hold Dorian in no such high esteem. The lad is his fascinating creation, but Dorian does not reflect back on his creator in a divine feedback loop of eroticized creativity. Like Basil, Lord Henry appreciates Dorian; he may even love him. But, unlike Basil, Lord Henry does not worship Dorian.

Cult of personality

One of the most perplexing elements of the diction of *The Picture of Dorian Gray* is its deployment of the term 'personality'. In contemporary usage, personality most often refers to that which makes a human being unique, what sets him or her apart from the species at large. It may also be something that a person either possesses or lacks, lack of personality functioning basically as a synonym for dullness. It thus can (and probably should) strike a first-time reader of *Dorian Gray* as rather odd that Basil claims that 'I knew that I had come face to face with some one whose mere personality was so fascinating that, if I allowed it to do so, it would absorb my whole nature, my whole soul, my very art itself' (*CWOW3*, p. 8) when describing his initial encounter with Dorian. Basil has not even yet spoken to Dorian, so how can he know of what the young man's personality consists? Lord Henry is likewise capable of prolix mediations on Dorian's personality while at the same time treating the lad as a kind of *tabula rasa* (e.g. *CWOW3*, p. 47–8), mere clay in the sculptor's hands. Clearly, Wilde ascribes to the term 'personality' shades of meaning that no longer commonly obtain today.[17]

Moreover, popular usage has for years made 'personality' the precise opposite of physical attractiveness. The cliché of a 'great personality' operates as an open code for 'ugly' on both sides of the Atlantic though in all probability it is, like most iterations of 'lookism', more often applied to women than men. Since Basil is immediately stunned at the first sight of Dorian and fears being overwhelmed by the attraction, Dorian certainly does not have a great personality in this euphemistic sense. Yet, again because this panicked attraction occurs just as Basil first sees Dorian, personality must be something that is immediately apparent in the physical presence of its possessor. It need not be synonymous with staggering good looks, but it cannot be separate from them.

In 1883 John Addington Symonds privately published ten copies of a pamphlet he had written ten years earlier. 'A Problem in Greek Ethics' accesses questions of homoerotic attraction, as is usual for Symonds, through classical Greek ideals. 'Greek love', for Symonds, is 'a passionate and enthusiastic attachment subsisting between man and youth, recognized by society and protected by opinion, which, though it was not free from sensuality, did not degenerate into mere licentiousness'.[18] As mentioned in the previous chapter, Symonds also took great pains to distance Greek love from effeminacy: 'Greek love was, in its origins and essence, military. Fire and valour, rather than tenderness or tears, were the external outcome of this passion; nor had *Malachia*, effeminacy, a place in its vocabulary.'[19] In addition to these theorizations of ancient same-sex desire, Symonds also wrote about the place of personality in the Greek world. This place, in Symonds' formulation, lies at the absolute center:

> What the Greeks worshipped in their ritual, what they represented in their sculpture, was always personality—the spirit and the flesh in amity and mutual correspondence; the spirit burning through the flesh and moulding it to individual forms; the flesh providing a fit dwelling for the spirit which controlled and fashioned it.[20]

For a number of reasons, it is currently impossible to know with any certainty whether Wilde read this tract. Wilde's library was sold at auction following his bankruptcy; although the auctioneer's catalog from the sale has survived and does not list this text, it may not represent Wilde's entire book collection. Moreover, though Wilde probably did not own Symonds' pamphlet, he may have read it nonetheless, perhaps through George Ives' library.[21] On the other hand, we need not assume that Wilde's use of the term requires Symonds' definition as a legitimizing precedent: I cite the passage mainly to demonstrate what Wilde might have meant by 'personality' and that his usage was not entirely idiosyncratic.

Personality in this context is thus a negotiation with platonism. Rather than a version of the platonic ideal in which the body is unimportant because it merely houses the *psyche*/soul that is capable of maintaining a relationship with the ideal realm, personality testifies to the possibility of the body cooperating with its animating spirit and thus participating in the ideal. Beauty in this conception is anything but skin deep: it is evidence of an incarnation of the ideal. An appreciation of beauty in this formulation is an admiration of the way in which the spirit informs the flesh. Personality is thus the realization of the Renaissance ideal with which the narrator of 'The Portrait of Mr W. H.' becomes so intimately involved, the 'mystic transference of expressions of the physical sphere to a sphere that was spiritual',[22] the 'dream of the incarnation of the Idea in a beautiful and living form'.[23] It is a simultaneously physical and metaphysical beauty that Willie Hughes and Cyril Graham have and that their admirers worship; it is the quality that Dorian initially has, yet from which his portrait will alienate him.

With this definition in mind it becomes a bit easier to understand the importance of Dorian for Basil's artwork. In his attempts to explain to Lord Henry, Basil moves from claiming that 'his personality has suggested to me an entirely new manner of art' (*CWOW3*, p. 12) to 'the harmony of soul and body,—how much that is!' (*CWOW3*, p. 13), which hints that it is Dorian's integration of spirit and flesh that has inspired the artist. Yet at the same time, Basil fears the influence of Dorian's formidable personality. In addition to the terror of absorption he feels on first meeting Dorian, Basil also expresses his conviction that 'as long as I live, the personality of Dorian Gray will dominate me' (*CWOW3*, p. 15). Such fears lead us to the conclusion that personality needs even more refinement of meaning: potentially, if we assume that all human beings have both soul and body (which is not to assume that the soul is synonymous with an essence or can easily be made the subject of positive knowledge),[24] any person by definition 'has' personality insofar as their spirit and flesh intertwine. But clearly the precise combination of *psyche* and *soma* that is Dorian Gray is so rare as to be not merely remarkable but positively frightening. For Basil, Dorian's personality is potentially absorbing: it may overwhelm Basil's ability to use it toward artistic ends. He feels himself in danger of simply worshipping Dorian's personality without that worship resulting in productive gains for art. Such a result would be sterile and thus a betrayal of the ideal of male procreation. This fear also forms the reason for Basil's tendency to hide his feelings from both Dorian and Lord Henry: in addition to a palpable sexual jealousy, Basil also does not want to acknowledge, either to himself or to others, the extent of his dependence on Dorian. Rather he wants to achieve a balance between worship and artistic use, between domination and aesthetic distance. His constant negotiations between these poles help to explain his inconsistent aesthetic theories remarked upon above, as well as his needing to be prodded into speech by Lord Henry.

Lord Henry negotiates with Dorian's personality from a different angle, but he comes to a similar conclusion. While ruminating on Dorian's announcement of his love for Sibyl Vane, Lord Henry determines that 'now and then a complex personality took the place and assumed the office of art, was indeed, in its way, a real work of art' (p. 48). Again, if we stress the idea that personality is a result of a combination of both physical and psychological aspects, we can see that Henry is congratulating himself on his use of Dorian as a medium or, perhaps more properly, as artistic media that already combine body and soul in a remarkable way. Henry has created Dorian out of Dorian himself; one way to put this is that Henry believes himself to have made Dorian out of the elements of Dorian's own personality combined with other elements added through Henry's influence. Like Cyril Graham, Dorian Gray is already an aesthetic object insofar as the combination of soul and body in both cases qualifies as personality, which is to say that it allows the flesh to be spiritualized and the soul to be incarnated. Or perhaps it would be more accurate to say that, since such is ostensibly the case in all human beings, in the case of the personality the twin elements are combined in such a way as to illustrate what should be the case for each person but usually is not. Most mortals, it would seem, are either predominately fleshly or ethereal; only the elect manage to demonstrate both simultaneously. At this moment in the text Lord Henry has convinced himself that he has successfully accomplished male procreation: Dorian is his offspring, his lover, and his project (both in the sense of being the result of an extended task and in the sense of his being that into which Henry has projected himself). Henry has begotten Dorian, yet the relationship will ultimately prove sterile.

Out of these ponderings comes Lord Henry's internal monolog on the relations between flesh and spirit:

> Soul and body, body and soul,—how mysterious they were. There was animalism in the soul, and the body had its moments of spirituality. The senses could refine and the intellect could degrade. Who could say where the fleshly impulse ceased, or the psychical impulse began? (p. 48)

There is, of course, a platonic paradox in these thoughts. If classical Platonism privileges the ideal over the physical, Henry's Platonism wants to combine these two elements in such a way that they cannot be distinguished, even if they remain theoretically separable. In this version, the ideal can only be accessed through the physical, which one might expect, yet the reverse would also be true: the physical cannot be experienced without the ideal, the flesh without the spirit. Dorian's attractiveness lies in his personality, his unique combination of spirit and matter. To desire the one involves the other; desiring likewise involves the subject who desires on both a fleshly and a spiritual level.

Yet the centerpiece of the novel is Dorian's virtual divorce of flesh from spirit. The picture, which accurately represents his personality, i.e., his body as imbued with his spirit (for 'there is nothing that art cannot express' [p. 12]) becomes changed by Dorian's desire for youth into a portrait of his soul that excludes his body. Dorian expresses the idea in precisely these terms to Basil, claiming that the picture portrays his soul (p. 130). From the moment of Dorian's granted wish, then, he is no longer an actual personality. Though he appears to be the definitive illustration of the ideals of Wilde's modified platonism, the best possible illustration of spirit burning through flesh while body supports soul, he is in fact a mockery of this ideal. He betrays the principle of male procreation by begetting ruined lives rather than ideas and crime rather than art. Once the picture has been inspired and produced through the mechanism of male procreation, the erotic triangle of Dorian, Basil, and Henry becomes sterile.[25]

From this angle, *The Picture of Dorian Gray* is the negative side of 'The Portrait of Mr W. H.' Where 'W. H.' represents male procreation as the hidden driver of human cultural progress, *Dorian Gray* represents male procreation gone tragically awry. Once Dorian has become a parody of personality through separation of soul from body, it seems that nothing can recuperate the homoerotic ideal. Where 'W. H.' hoped for a new English Renaissance brought about through a rebirth of neoplatonism that would parallel Ficino's evocation of that philosophy in the fifteenth century, *Dorian Gray* seems to throw up its hands in despair at the thought that a quattrocento spirit could ever warm the flesh of a late Victorian era. Moreover, this tragic collapse from the heights of Greek love is brought about through art, the very institution male procreation is designed to support. It is, after all, the picture of Dorian Gray that initiates the breakdown of his personality, the divorce of his flesh from his spirit.

To investigate why the picture fails so miserably in its ostensible task of illustrating male procreation, we need to return to the figure of Basil Hallward. I want to contend that Basil is both the conscience and the bad conscience of the novel in that he is a kind of moral irritant to Dorian and in so functioning he belies the hard break between ethics and aesthetics that Wilde would plead immediately following the publication of the *Lippincott's* version and that he would most famously make a centerpiece of the Preface to the 1891 edition. By insisting on personality, which is to say on the inseparability of the body and soul, Basil insists as well on the inseparability of art and behavior that Wilde would publicly deny in the press, in the 1891 Preface, and in his trials. Basil thus undercuts Wilde's self-representation as an aesthete insofar as that position is synonymous with the pronouncements of (among other Wildean masks) Gilbert in 'The Critic as Artist', who insists that 'all art is immoral' (*CWOW4*, p. 174), and aligns the novel instead with such aesthetic-ethical interventions as 'The Happy Prince' and 'The Young King'.

In Basil's midnight inquiry into Dorian's behavior, the artist invokes an idea that Wilde had first explored in one of his earliest pieces of fiction, the short story 'Lord Arthur Savile's Crime'. In the story, a young aristocrat meets a palm-reader at a reception; the palm-reader reveals that Lord Arthur is destined to become a murderer. The story soon turns into a parody of Victorian respectability in that Lord Arthur decides that, if he is fated to kill, he should embrace his doom as a duty and eliminate a harmless relative as soon as possible. A series of botched assassination attempts ensues which quickly turn Lord Arthur's tragedy to farce. But the first two of the six parts of this story contain moments of stark terror when the protagonist believes that something deeply private and hidden, so hidden in fact that he himself did not suspect it, has become obvious to at least one other person. 'Could it be that written on his hand, in characters that he could not read himself, but that another could decipher, was some fearful secret of sin, some blood-red sign of crime?' (p. 18).[26] In this moment of terror, the worst possible fate is that in which others can read the soul written on the body: the body becomes a text through which others may read meanings that should remain secret. And, in a twist on the Green Carnation trope, these others are not assumed to be favorably disposed to the message of the revealed text they now can read. Even the bearer of the text, its subject more than its author (for Arthur Savile does not write himself as a criminal), is surprised and horrified by the meaning of the text he discovers on his own body. The terror of this moment is so pronounced that the remainder of 'Lord Arthur Savile's Crime' turns to dark comedy to extricate itself from continued confrontation with it.

In Basil's final altercation with Dorian, he expresses an idea that reflects the Arthur Saville moment and the meaning of personality as a simultaneous presence of *psyche* and *soma*:

> Sin is a thing that writes itself across a man's face. It cannot be concealed. People talk of secret vices. There are no such things as secret

vices. If a wretched man has a vice, it shows itself in the lines of his mouth, the droop of his eyelids, the moulding of his hands even. (*CWOW3*, p. 128)

There may well be traces here of positivist criminology, the type of thought promulgated by Cesare Lombroso and Max Nordau, for instance, the latter of whom would turn Wilde himself into evidence of inborn criminality in his 1892 volume *Degeneration*. But we need not go to the promoters of *fin-de-siècle* biopower for the only possible explanation of this insistence on the inseparability of body and soul. Rather, this belief in the physical manifestation of vice represents the negative side of the idea of personality. Dorian has personality to the extent that his body and soul are in such harmony that it makes an immediate impression on an aesthetically/erotically sensitive observer. To see him is to know him to a certain extent, since seeing his body allows a glimpse into his soul. The quotation above is spoken in the context of Basil's refusal to believe any of the rumors of evil behavior circulated about Dorian; if Dorian acted badly, for him of all people the results would be betrayed by immediate physical evidence. In the neoplatonic world of personality, beauty is a guarantee of spotless behavior. The portrait, by breaking this connection between body and soul, breaks the connection on which Dorian's personality rests. His body is now illegible; only the picture can be read.

This reading of the body as text is reflected in the second chapter of *Dorian Gray* when Dorian, while considering the information with which Lord Henry has impregnated him, or perhaps, as he insists, while trying not to consider it, begins to meditate upon language: 'Words! Mere words! How terrible they were! . . . They seemed to be able to give a plastic form to formless things. . . . Was there anything so real as words?' (*CWOW3*, p. 22). Language here is implicitly placed into the same paradigm as the neoplatonic mutual implication of soul and body. Words are the *soma* to thought's *psyche*, and the combination of thought and word produces the linguistic equivalent to personality. A kind of neoplatonic semiotics is implied in the construction, perhaps inflected through the prolog to the fourth gospel: the word becomes flesh, but the flesh also becomes warmed by the indwelling *logos*.

What happens when we gender this body read as semiotic text? In the previous chapter I characterized Wilde's take on effeminacy as a matter of a masculine soul incarnated in a feminine body which results, to put it in *Dorian Gray*'s terms, in an effeminate personality. To spell out the implications of Dorian's semiotics in Saussurian terms, the signifier (as sound image) plays the role of the body while the signified (as mental construct) assumes the part of the soul. The sign, being the combination of the two, constitutes the linguistic personality. In order for the semiotics of embodiment to become the semiotics of effeminacy, the meaning must be taken as the masculine part of the word that warms the flesh of the feminine signifier that, as in the titular portrait of Mr W. H., produces a body that is effeminate rather than feminine (or female). Meaning effeminizes the word, the most real thing in existence.

All of this is to say, then, that the language of *Dorian Gray*, the words out of which it is made, are themselves effeminate personalities. His characters may or may not be sodomitical (as Edward Carson described them in the first trial), but the language itself is effeminate according to the internal logic of its own engendering of the word. The text of *Dorian Gray* strives to become what it represents: aside from its characters, its very words embody effeminacy. Its purple prose, its obsessions with the obscure (especially in the ninth chapter), and its calling attention to the language out of which it is made all function within the gendered parameters Wilde sets out and produce a text that does not so much represent effeminate sexuality as embody it. At least it does so for those who are sufficiently sensitive to its personality, i.e., those who know *that* the green carnation means—ultimately a more important distinction than *what* it means.[27] But the novel had its share of readers who believed they had an answer for the latter question.

Dorian Gray: two times tried

The first Wilde trial, in which he sued the Marquess of Queensberry for criminal libel, was unusual in many ways, not least of which was the fact that Queensberry's lawyer, Edward Carson, used the 1890 version of *Dorian Gray* as evidence of Wilde's posing as a sodomite and thus as justification of his client's allegation. But this was, in fact, the second time that the novel had been the basis of an accusation of criminal behavior. The reviews of *Dorian Gray* were extremely mixed and often hostile. The most vociferous was that published in the *Scots Observer*, but it was not an isolated case. The review in *St. James's Gazette*, for instance, mentions the possibility of the prosecution of Wilde or his publishers,[28] while the *Daily Chronicle* indulges such adjectives as 'unclean' and 'effeminate'.[29] As mentioned above, the controversy eventually rose to such a level that W. H. Smith withdrew the *Lippincott's* issue from its stalls.

The *Scots Observer* review, however, was the most noticeable and in many ways the most damning. Consisting of only a single paragraph, it accuses Wilde of writing 'stuff that were better unwritten' and of taking as subject matter incidents 'only fitted for the Criminal Investigation Department'.[30] It ends on the note that Wilde, though a talented writer, is currently producing only for 'outlawed noblemen and perverted telegraph boys'. The review also manages to employ the word 'unnatural' twice and to state that the novel's main interest is 'medico-legal'.

This review, as well as Wilde's response to it, has become something of a set-piece in Wilde criticism, so I will need to plead indulgence while I briefly go over old ground in explicating its rather packed content. The 'outlawed noblemen and perverted telegraph boys' alludes to the Cleveland Street scandal. In the summer of 1889 London police had uncovered a male prostitution ring in which young telegraph messengers had supplemented their income in a brothel at 19 Cleveland Street in the West End. Their clients seem to have been largely drawn from the better classes: Lord Arthur Somerset, the Extra Equerry to the Prince of Wales, was one of a number of aristocrats named in deposition. Not named but subject to endless rumor was Prince Albert Victor, eldest son of the Prince of Wales and thus second in line to the throne. Somerset, tipped off by the government that prosecution was imminent, escaped to Europe and lived there for the rest of his life (an exile both much longer and more comfortable than Wilde's post-prison existence). The Cleveland Street affair was the subject of great public resentment, as it was widely felt that aristocratic or even royal criminals had been spared prosecution by a government that applied a different standard of justice to different social classes. Henry Labouchère, the author of the law under which Wilde would be prosecuted, was instrumental in bringing such accusations to the floor of the House of Commons.[31]

Through an allusion to current events the *Scots Observer*'s anonymous reviewer, then, explicitly links Wilde's novel to sexual criminality. Use of the word 'unnatural' likewise confirms the association, and 'medico-legal' conjures the emerging discourse of sexology, which constructed sexual differences primarily in terms of pathology (e.g., Richard Krafft-Ebing) and the legal implications of such medical definitions (e.g., Karl Heinrich Ulrichs). Moreover, the reviewer writes that 'Mr. Oscar Wilde has *again* been writing stuff that were better unwritten' (emphasis added), which implies a critic familiar with the recent contents of *Blackwood's Magazine*, in which 'Mr W. H.' had appeared in 1889, as well as with Continental sexology. The reviewer has, in other words, detected in the text the trace of male same-sex desire, the same quality that Bosie Douglas and his Oxford coterie would find so fascinating in their obsession with the book and its author. The green carnation has in this instance failed—or perhaps it has succeeded too well. The green carnation has a more or less specific meaning, the toleration if not celebration of male same-sex desire, that must co-exist with its avowed lack of any meaning at all. If the flower is to work as designed, the specific meaning should be available only to interpreters who will accept it. To those who would turn away in disgust, or worse yet call for the police, the flower must defer all meaning. No one will accept that the symbol is meaningless, but to those who would reject its bearer, the symbol must not be allowed to rest on a determinate meaning. Whether this determinate meaning is seen as synonymous with the truth is less important than the symbol's ability simultaneously to sustain play for one audience while subtly hinting at an open secret for another. Both audiences will suspect a code, but only one should be able to convince themselves that they have broken it.[32] Yet in this instance, the reviewer has solved the cipher and delightedly exposed the secret to unsympathetic eyes, his own included.

In replying to these barely disguised charges, Wilde dared not address them directly. In his 9 July 1890 letter to W. E. Henley, the editor of the *Scots Observer*, Wilde first insists on a clear demarcation between the artist and the work of art. Alluding to Keats's observation that Shakespeare had experienced as much delight in the creation of Iago as in the creation of Imogen, Wilde then claims that surrounding Dorian Gray with 'an atmosphere of moral corruption' had been an aesthetic necessity to the novel (*WCL*, p. 439). He then goes on to turn the tables on his accuser:

> To keep this atmosphere vague and indeterminate and wonderful was the aim of the artist who wrote the story. I claim, sir, that he has succeeded. Each man sees his own sin in Dorian Gray. What Dorian Gray's sins are no one knows. He who finds them has brought them. (*WCL*, 439)

This is a particularly brilliant, if not quite ingenuous, move. While it is certainly true that many of Dorian's specific behaviors are only hinted at, it is also true that, for the reasons I have outlined above, the novel's self-conscious status as an overwritten text gives a sexual specificity to its 'vague and indeterminate and wonderful' prose. Though it is no doubt true that the reader brings his or her own sins to Dorian Gray (and to *Dorian Gray*), the reader need not acknowledge these things of darkness as their own. Quite the opposite: a reader, or a critic, might project these criminal desires onto the fictional characters precisely in order to disavow the desires in himself. Wilde no doubt knows that this can happen, and he perhaps suggests that it has happened in the pages of the *Scots Observer*. In washing his hands of specificity, he sets up another possible escape: any particular sins that Wilde might have had in mind while writing *Dorian Gray*, and might thus have inadvertently suggested through density of prose, are just as much impositions upon a 'vague and indeterminate and wonderful' text as any vulgar accusations from a Puritan journalist masquerading as a critic of art.

Consciously or not, Wilde testifies to this division between the artist who creates and the critic who interprets, even if those roles coincide in the 'same' human being, in the pronouns of the quotation. He writes of 'the artist who wrote the story' in the third person, and judges 'his' work a triumphant success. That Wilde might see his own sin in Dorian Gray thus remains a possibility, but if this occurs, the story reflects a different Wilde from the one who wrote it. As with the green carnation, there is once again the simultaneous avowal and denial of meaning. The reader may catch a reflection of Oscar Wilde in Dorian Gray, but this is not the Oscar who wrote the text; rather he is the one who reads and judges it. Taking the quotation further, we might say that this is an Oscar that the reader brings to the text, as Charles Whibley, the author of the review, as well as Bosie and the book's innumerable other critics, did.[33] The Oscar the reader brings to the text is not the writer and is thus not liable for whatever crimes the reader may bring. In the summer of 1890, Wilde probably had little reason to believe that he would ever have occasion to attempt to make this defense the basis of an actual legal case.

In 1891, however, Wilde did make many of his defenses of the 1890 edition the basis of his new Preface to the expanded version of *Dorian Gray*. First published in the *Fortnightly Review* in March, the new Preface in many ways represents a distillation of the *Dorian Gray* controversy as played out in the pages of the *Scots Observer*, the *St. James's Gazette*, and the *Daily Chronicle*. Argumentation and context are eliminated in favor of pith, and the impossibility of locating the artist within the work becomes dogma: '*To reveal art and conceal the artist is art's aim*' (CWOW3, p. 167; italics in original). '*Those who find ugly meanings in beautiful things are corrupt without being charming*', which seems aimed squarely at Whibley and Henley. To read *Dorian Gray* in the context of the Cleveland Street scandal constitutes a moral failure on the part of the reader. '*There is no such thing as a moral or an immoral book*': even if the reader does detect criminal behavior in the novel's characters, this does not mean that the author shares his characters' proclivities. '*No artist has ethical sympathies*': the artistic writer does not write to persuade but to delight the reader. *'It is the spectator, and not life, that art really mirrors'* (*CWOW3*, p. 168): again, Dorian's sins are those the reader brings to the book.

During the controversy itself, Whibley had taunted Wilde with the assertion that it must have been painful to him to have his story praised in moral terms by such religious publications as the *Christian Leader* and the *Christian World*.[34] Wilde had flatly rejected the contention, claiming that it was too much to ask that any one critic appreciate the work in both its ethical and aesthetic qualities. 'For if a work of art is rich, and vital, and complete, those who have artistic instincts will see its beauty, and those to whom ethics appeal more strongly than aesthetics will see its moral lesson' (*WCL*, p. 441). Two lines on, Wilde writes 'it is the spectator, and not life, that art really mirrors', which would be repeated verbatim in the Preface. Yet Wilde had been sufficiently flexible in his public exchanges with Whibley to use the phrase 'ethical beauty' in reference to the moral content of the story, a phrase that in two words connects ethics and aesthetics unmistakably.[35]

Thus in 1890 a connection between aesthetics and ethics is possible, if tenuous. Wilde masks it behind a kind of smoke screen, perhaps the product of the cigarette he refused to put out while addressing the audience on the opening night of *Lady Windermere's Fan*. But despite a conscious effort to obscure it, there is an ethical claim in *Dorian Gray*, though not necessarily in the moralistic terms used in the *Christian Leader* and the *Christian World*. But the ethical claim must be publically disavowed once the code has been broken. Prying eyes want to see behind the mystery and, as in 'The Sphinx without a Secret', the discovery of the truth, or rather the complete lack of it, will kill the secret's guardian. So, for the uninitiated, Wilde builds a wall between aesthetics and ethics: he builds it during the controversy in the press, he separates it from the materials of its construction by making it into a Preface that is initially published apart from the text it ostensibly prefaces, and he finally builds a new version of the text to fit this Preface. This version, the 1891 novel, becomes the text known as *The Picture of Dorian Gray* since Wilde's death, and by this I mean not only 'the text itself', but the mainstream interpretations of it as a keystone of the 'Aesthetic Movement'. With its Preface to pre-interpret it and its conscious retreat from its boldest statements about same-sex worship and the fascination of personality, the 1891 *Dorian Gray* stands as a monument to the separation of aesthetics and ethics. The green carnation, it wants to say, means nothing. It is a pretty though an unnatural flower—that is all.[36]

The 1890 edition, though, offers something quite different. True, it can and doubtless was read as a piece of mere aestheticism at the time, but reading the text's queerness not only re-historicizes and thus re-politicizes it, but also allows a reopening of the text's ethical stakes. By this I mean that *Dorian Gray*, and the 1890 version especially, relies on an ethics as well as an aesthetics of reception. If a reader is receptive to the text's encoding, he or she understands its implicit ethical claim: taking male same-sex desire seriously to the point of seeing *Dorian Gray* not as a facile celebration of the phenomenon, but as a critique of it. Where 'Mr W. H.' might, in its own self-questioning and self-limiting way, qualify as a textual celebration, *Dorian Gray* demands that the receptive reader see male same-sex desire at the center of the text, and that he or she sees how the individual same-sex relationships represented in the novel fail to live up to the platonic ideals on which they are based. When this queer reading becomes transparent to a readership not open to the ethics of reception that the text requires, however, this ethical meaning must be disavowed. At this point, the purple prose becomes prolixity for its own sake.

In 1890, this disavowal of queer ethics played out in journals and newspapers and may not have done any lasting damage to the next four years of Wilde's literary career. But in 1895, the venue changed from newspapers to courtrooms, and the damage to all aspects of Wilde's life was profound. As pointed out above, the 1890 *Dorian Gray* became one of the primary pieces of evidence in the case for justification of Queensberry's accusation; significantly, there was confusion in the courtroom when Carson used the 1890 *Lippincott's* version in his attack on Wilde's writing and Wilde's counsel attempted to respond using the 1891 volume.[37] I will want to return to *Dorian Gray*'s role in the trial, but first I want to investigate a much smaller text that also became a piece of evidence in the same trial.

In January 1893 Wilde wrote to Douglas in response to a sonnet Douglas had sent him. The first paragraph of the two-paragraph letter runs thus:

> My Own Boy, Your sonnet is quite lovely, and it is a marvel that those red rose-leaf lips of yours should have been made no less for music of song than for madness of kisses. Your slim gilt soul walks between passion and poetry. I know Hyacinthus, whom Apollo loved so madly, was you in Greek days. (*WCL*, p. 544)

Bosie Douglas inadvertently left this letter along with three others in the pocket of a coat he gave to Alfred Wood, a rent boy with whom both he and Wilde had had sex. Wood attempted to use the letter to blackmail Wilde. According to Wilde's testimony at the first trial, Wood received fifteen pounds from Wilde in order to go to America and Wilde received the letters.[38] Then, soon after the opening of *A Woman of No Importance*, a different young man first sent a copy of the 'madness of kisses' letter to H. Beerbohm Tree, the play's producer, and then came to Wilde's home in order to discuss the document. This new young man, William Allen, tried to extort money from Wilde by stating that 'a very curious construction could be put upon that letter' and claiming that someone had offered him sixty pounds for it. Wilde called Allen's bluff, declaring that 'If you take my advice you will go to that man and sell my letter to him for sixty pounds. . . . I myself have never received so large a sum for any prose work of that very small length' (p. 53). Having sent Allen away with a single pound, a third young man returned the letter to Wilde after only a few minutes, saying, 'there is no use trying to rent you' (p. 55). Interestingly, the judge asked for clarification of the term 'rent', but Wilde said only that it was 'a slang term' (p. 55). Presumably, Wilde allowed the context to suggest that the term served as a synonym for blackmail but of course left unspoken the term's prominence in the subculture of male prostitution.

The aesthetic defense is already implicit in Wilde's response to the proposed transaction: where Allen wants to sell him a letter, Wilde wants to discuss the value of a piece of short prose. But after his apparently facetious response to Allen's blackmail attempt, Wilde raises the stakes by claiming that the letter really is a piece of artistic prose with the potential for aesthetic, if not commercial, circulation: 'This letter which is a prose poem will shortly be published in sonnet form in a delightful magazine and I will send you a copy' (pp. 53–4). As Wilde's attorney was quick to point out, the publication did in fact take place. *The Spirit Lamp*, an Oxford undergraduate literary journal edited by Lord Alfred Douglas, published a French verse translation by Wilde's friend Pierre Louÿs in May of 1893. Wilde and Bosie thus transformed the text from a love letter between two men into a literary text on the assumption that doing so moved it out of the realm of the personal and legally actionable.

Wilde and Douglas had every reason to do so. Confronted with a document that could, and in fact did, become a piece of material evidence for an accusation of criminal conduct, they availed themselves of the literary apparatus to which they had ready access. In a textual equivalent of money laundering, they removed the taint of criminality from the love letter by transforming it into art. The underlying logic of such a move seems to be that if a text is aesthetic, it is thus not personal. If the letter is a prose sonnet, in other words, it cannot also be a love letter expressing the emotions and desires of one man concerning another. If the green carnation is merely a beautiful, unnatural flower, it cannot also be a symbol of same-sex love. My point, of course, is that the letter and the flower may be both, depending on the audience, but a public admission to that effect at the time of Wilde's trials would have been literary and legal suicide. But the spirit of this letter, or at least its role as a legal ruse, serves as a paradigm for the fate of *Dorian Gray*. And it should be clear that the timing of the translation and publication of the 'madness of kisses' letter in Douglas' *The Spirit Lamp* reveals that its function as a legal ruse preceded both the trial and Queensberry's accusation. Wilde and Douglas had arranged for the letter's appearance as a literary publication by May 1893, while Queensberry's card was not delivered to the Albemarle Club until February of 1895. Though it eventually formed the backbone of the aesthetic defense against Queensberry, the publication of the letter was initially a move against blackmailers. The assumption that a literary use precluded personal investment was thus a defense against everyone, from Her Majesty's judges to rent boys.

While attempting to explain Queensberry's accusation that Wilde was 'posing as a sodomite', Edward Carson's opening for the defense included an insistence that Wilde's writings and behavior not be separated: 'Mr Wilde, by his acts and by his writings, was putting himself in that position that people might naturally and reasonably infer from the writings and the course of life he was adopting, that he, Mr Wilde, was either in sympathy with, or addicted to, immoral and sodomitic habits' (p. 255). And though Carson was certainly not going to acquiesce to Wilde's contention that literature and behavior constituted completely separate realms, Carson did claim that 'if we had rested this case alone on Mr Wilde's literature we would have been absolutely justified in the course we have taken' (p. 254). Carson thus reads *Dorian Gray* as a text 'in sympathy with' sodomy, and he extends this sympathy from Wilde's writing to his behavior.

Wilde's defense against these tactics was to insist upon the separation of author from text that he had used in response to the reviews of the 1890 *Dorian Gray*, as well as in his successful attempt to forestall blackmailing by renters. This aesthetic defense was first introduced by Wilde's counsel, Edward Clarke. In his opening statement for the prosecution, Clarke recapitulated Wilde's defense of *Dorian Gray* in the *Scots Observer*, specifically the idea that readers bring their own sins to those of Dorian Gray. Clarke stated that the book 'hints at and suggests [. . .] vices and weaknesses of which Dorian Gray is guilty, but to attack Mr Oscar Wilde as being a person showing himself to be addicted to this sort of offence, because in the book he states that the person is a vicious creature in all ways, is surely the most strange inference' (p. 42). Wilde himself expanded the defense while being cross-examined by Carson. Carson probed Wilde on the subject of 'The Priest and the Acolyte', a story that Wilde did not write but that appeared in the same (as it was the only) issue of *The Chameleon* as Wilde's 'Phrases and Philosophies for the Use of the Young'. The anonymously published story narrates the romantic relationship between a young Roman Catholic priest and a fourteen-year-old boy, his acolyte. When they are discovered in one another's arms (though no overtly sexual contact is ever represented or alluded to), the priest tells his superior about his eternal search for an ideal and his lack of attraction to women. Seeing no way either to maintain the relationship or to live without his beloved, the priest celebrates a midnight mass for just himself and the boy but puts poison in the chalice, and the two die together in a liturgical suicide pact.[39]

On the stand, Wilde claimed to hate the story on aesthetic grounds. Carson attempted to maneuver him into an ethical condemnation, but Wilde would not budge: 'It is impossible for a man of letters to judge of a piece of writing otherwise than from its fault in literature' (p. 68). Changing angles slightly, Carson went on to have Wilde confirm that, as stated in the Preface to *Dorian Gray*, no book was in and of itself immoral. Carson then asked, 'Then, I suppose I may take it that in your opinion the piece was not immoral?,' with Wilde quipping back, 'Worse, it is badly written' (p. 69). Carson continued to badger Wilde for several minutes, prompting two attempted objections from his counsel, both of which the judge overruled. Carson could not get Wilde to call the story 'blasphemous', nor could he persuade Wilde to accept the conclusion that 'anyone who would allow himself to be connected with that article [the story] or who publically approved of that article would be, at least, posing as a sodomite' (p. 72). Carson was, however, able to extract from Wilde the judgment that he thought the story 'disgusting twaddle' (p. 72). Throughout the exchange Wilde was adamant that his criticism of 'The Priest and the Acolyte' was purely literary and wholly negative: 'what I disapproved of was the tone, treatment, subject, everything, the whole thing from beginning to end' (p. 71). It is a bad story, in other words, as a piece of fiction, though a better writer could presumably have made a beautiful aesthetic object out of very similar materials. Where Carson wants a moral/religious condemnation of blasphemy, Wilde will offer only the artistic condemnation of twaddle.

Though never named at the trial, the author of 'The Priest and the Acolyte' was the editor of the *Chameleon*, John Francis Bloxam, a friend of Bosie since their Winchester days. In an undated letter to Ada Leverson that dates from early December, 1894, Wilde had summed up his reaction to Bloxam's story in somewhat different terms from those used at the trial: 'The story is, to my ears, too direct: there is no nuance: it profanes a little by revelation: God and other artists are always a little obscure. Still, is has interesting qualities, and is at moments poisonous: which is something' (*WCL*, p. 625). Since Leverson had not read the story, Wilde's characterization of it as 'poisonous' is a bit of a private joke, or perhaps one with a payoff only after the issue appeared. But 'poisonous' is the only positive adjective Wilde has for the story, and it is clear in this context that the word is meant as a compliment. Evidently he does regard it as aesthetically inept, but not the 'twaddle' that he would dismiss at the trial. Its poisonous moments are its redeeming features.

The *Chameleon* itself, however, was anything but a purely aesthetic literary project. Although edited by Bloxam while he was still an Oxford undergraduate, the magazine was organized, named, and launched with the assistance of Bosie Douglas and George Ives as a specifically Uranian endeavor. Its title, chosen by Ives, testified to its strategy of camouflage; it was as close to an openly homophile publication as it was possible to achieve in the England of 1894. It was the venue in which Douglas initially published his most famous poem, 'Two Loves', with its famous ending line of 'I am the love that dare not speak its name'. As a subtitle, Bloxam used 'A Bazaar of Dangerous and Smiling Chances', and the journal was sufficiently dangerous that it published only a single issue. Whether Wilde thought Bloxam's story was aesthetically twaddle or not, he did apparently believe in his magazine. Or perhaps the more important point is that, despite having deep reservations about the literary execution of 'The Priest and the Acolyte', Wilde readily agreed to place 'Phrases and Philosophies for the Use of the Young' in an obscure journal edited by an Oxford undergraduate because he approved and wished to support the extra-literary cause that the magazine, necessarily tacitly, also supported.[40] In the trial he would say of Bloxam that 'it would be beneath my dignity as a man of letters to write to disassociate myself from the work of an Oxford undergraduate' (p. 73). Perhaps, but it was evidently not beneath his dignity as a man invested in same-sex desire to write to associate himself with this work, as he in fact did with 'Phrases and Philosophies'. The *Chameleon* was a green carnation: like *Dorian Gray* and the 'madness of kisses' letter, it should read differently to different audiences. It should be art for art's sake, meaning nothing but itself and having no ethical influence, to those who would be disgusted by its sexual meaning. To those predisposed to accept the sexual meaning, its literariness should form part of the implicit argument that male same-sex love can be an ennobling form of worship, an appreciation of the platonic concept of personality, and a worthy topic of enlightened thought. These meanings should be available exclusively to either audience—but they are not.

Bloxam's poison was what Wilde valued in *The Chameleon*. Poison was a fascination for Wilde: his 1889 essay 'Pen, Pencil, and Poison' traces Thomas Griffiths Wainewright's career as a writer and murderer and implies a connection between the two endeavors; Lord Arthur Savile uses poison among other assassination techniques; the titular Duchess of Padua poisons herself, as does Sibyl Vane; Dorian is metaphorically poisoned by Lord Henry's yellow book; the mother in 'The Young King' is poisoned; the danger of poison suffuses the orientalized backgrounds of 'The Birthday of the Infanta' and *Salome*; even the apparently pacific 'The Critic as Artist' mentions poison six times. Where the aesthetic defense denies all possibility of influence and effects of literature on behavior, the trope of poison testifies to literature's ability to affect or influence readers with or without their conscious knowledge. Bloxam's story, however aesthetically inept, has the ability to poison, which is to say, to affect its readers. If they are open to the story's implicit message of tolerance for same-sex love, as the ideal readers of *The Chameleon* would be, they recognize this poison as a denial of the bourgeois sexual ideology that not only rejects same-sex love, but refuses to grant it any space in which, and from which, to speak. If the readers are not the ideal minority, they will understand the poison merely as something vaguely dangerous to their own presuppositions. 'Poison' here might well be read as a kind of reverse of Derrida's play with Plato's *pharmakon*: where the *pharmakon* is a drug that may also be a poison, Wilde's poison may also be writing that opens up a possibility for the representation of that which had formerly been unspeakable. In either case, what is poison for one type of audience may be a healthful supplement to another, and no one, however much they try, controls how the text will read for any reader.

'Any work of art, even if it be great or small, is good for people. I think so' (p. 94). So said Oscar Wilde during his first trial, in the midst of presenting what I have characterized as the aesthetic defense. After years of denying any ethical role for literature following the initial controversy over the 1890 *Dorian Gray*, Wilde let slip his hope that literature was capable of more than mere presentation of beauty that would have no designs on the world into which it was made public. This moment is neither as famous nor as obvious as the other great slip during this trial, his admission that he had not kissed Walter Grainger, not because he disliked kissing boys, but because Grainger was 'peculiarly plain' (p. 207). But they are related. Both the aesthetic defense and Wilde's plea that kissing Grainger would be akin to kissing a doorpost (p. 208) are legal necessities. They are statements made necessary by the assumption of a hostile audience, one for whom the green carnation must remain a symbol without reference. This is not necessarily to claim that Wilde's contrasting statements, that art is good for people or that he preferred good-looking to ugly boys, represent the true, unironic Wilde. Rather, my claim is that Wilde's aesthetic defense is too often seen as his unironic stance, and that decontextualizing his aestheticism from its place in the history of homophobia tends to marginalize the role of his writings, as opposed to the legal actions associated with his name, in opening up possibilities for homophile discourse. It has too often been accepted that the green carnation means nothing without the necessary complement that the green carnation means, not just same-sex love, but a public, if coded, testimony to it.

The price of this claim is admitting that Queensberry and Carson got it right. Carson's claim that Wilde's writings, *Dorian Gray* chief among them, put him 'in that position that people might naturally and reasonably infer' that he was 'in sympathy with [. . .] sodomitic habits' (p. 255), is, I hope to have shown, true. Wilde's sympathies lay with a belief in the importance of male same-sex desire to culture, whether or not that culture chose to acknowledge the male procreation that keeps it going. He attempted to encode his representation of desire in such a way that it would be invisible to those who lacked the 'sympathy' that Carson identified; that Carson, Hichens, Queensberry, and no doubt plenty of others could and did break the code without the accompanying sympathy was inevitable. Wilde foresaw this inevitability, but he failed to take it seriously enough.

Despite the weight that Wilde has been made to carry over the past century, modern homophilic discourse has always had a problem with him as a public figure, if not as a brilliant writer. Wilde became a martyr, after all, by hiding his love, not by announcing it. He sued Queensberry on the basis that the latter's allegation of 'posing as a sodomite' was libelous because untrue. When Queensberry produced a list of witnesses willing to testify to the contrary, Wilde's counsel withdrew the suit and Wilde was soon arrested. He continued to defend himself against accusations through a mistrial and a conviction. This is, again, not at all surprising: Wilde was fighting for his life, his career, and his family; he only occasionally had a chance to use the legal proceedings to fight for the legitimacy of male procreation, and even then it was the disembodied Greek ideal for which he fought, not the right to act sexually based on that ideal. To the extent that we date the emergence of modern homosexuality to the Wilde trials, we are left with a moment in which an identity is formed, not because it wants to become visible, but because it is forced to enter into public discourse against its own preferences and assumed self-interest.[41] If the Wilde trials moved same-sex love from the realm of the unspeakable into that of the legally and medically legible, they did so despite Wilde's best efforts.

All of this means that Wilde's aesthetic defense, his effort always to hide the physical and often even the metaphysical varieties of same-sex experience behind a smokescreen of the impossibility of influence and the inefficacy of literature, can no more be taken as definitive than its complementary stance, that the green carnation, *Dorian Gray*, and the madness of kisses letter are documents in the history of same-sex love and thus tacit arguments that texts have implications for the way people actually live. That Wilde lied *in propria persona* might be no guarantee that we can read his literary representations of male procreation as unproblematic truth; as I attempted to show in the previous chapter, even 'The Picture of Mr W. H.' ultimately withdraws male procreation behind screens of irony and disbelief. But as one of Wilde's masks, and one of the most full articulations of the aesthetic defense, famously quipped in 'The Critic as Artist', 'Man is least himself when he talks in his own person. Give him a mask, and he will tell you the truth' (*CWOW4*, p. 185).

3
Love of the Impossible: Wilde's Failed Queer Theory

Wilde's collection of poems, generally known now as *Poems* 1881, constituted his first significant publication and his first resounding failure. Having been a conspicuous academic success, first at Trinity College Dublin and then at Magdalen College at Oxford, where he had won the Newdigate Prize for poetry in 1878, Wilde's post-collegiate attempt to announce himself as a leading aesthetic poet did not have the effect for which he had aimed. Most reviews were unenthusiastic and, in the most notorious instance of negative reception, the Oxford Union voted to refuse a copy of the book after having requested it in the first place (Ellmann pp. 143–7).[1] Many objections, including those voiced by the Oxford Union, centered on the poems' borrowing too heavily and obviously from the canon of English poetry.[2] There were also concerns about insincerity: on religious and political matters, one poem would often contradict the claims of another. At one point Wilde's poetic voice is democratic ('To Milton'), at another royalist ('Libertatis Sacra Fames'). In one lyric he waxes eloquent on the charms of the papacy ('Urbs Sacra Aeterna'), while in another he celebrates the rise of the Italian nation-state ('Humanitad'). At one moment he is a Protestant flirting with Roman Catholicism ('Sonnet on Approaching Italy' or 'Italia'), while at another he is a Swinburnian pagan calling back the classical gods at the expense of any form of Christianity ('Santa Decca' or 'The Garden of Eros'). To Wilde, of course, such inconsistency might well have been the point, but not everyone was convinced.

In addition to plagiarism and disingenuousness, the poems also contained enough sex to guarantee a few raised eyebrows. Most obvious in this regard was 'Charmides', a narrative poem with a classical setting in which the title character hides in the Parthenon until darkness and then disrobes and rapes the statue of Athena. The chaste goddess of wisdom does not take kindly to this, and she appears as a storm to Charmides' ship. Charmides jumps into the sea to meet his supposed lover and is drowned. His beautiful young male body is washed up near Athens and discovered by a dryad who falls in love with him. Her divine mistress, however, is the other chaste goddess of classical myth, Artemis, who finds her servant mooning over the ephebic corpse and promptly sends an arrow through her heart. The entwined young lovers are then discovered by the decidedly unchaste Aphrodite, who intercedes with Persephone to 'let Desire pass across dread Charon's icy ford' (*CWOW1*, p. 88). The poem ends in orgasmic bliss as the lovers are given their moment of joy in the land of the dead, and Wilde's persona averts his gaze from their posthumous consummation.

Whether or not this poem is a failure in aesthetic or cultural terms, it is also a poem about erotic failure. I think it is also worthwhile in the context that I want to develop in this chapter to claim that it is a poem about queer failure. Granted, all the *eros* in this poem manifests itself in cross-sex desire, yet it also does so in deviant forms of 'heterosexuality': necrophilia and whatever it is one decides to call statue rape (perhaps an extreme form of iconolatry). It locates successful sex, even for a cross-sex couple, only in the afterlife, and even then it is possible only through the intervention of love herself. Repressive forces, represented in the form of Athena's storm and Artemis' bow, make successful *jouissance* impossible on the mortal plane. Those who would touch the god by touching the body of an other cannot hope to gain true fulfillment of their desire on earth. Sexual completion is purchased only at the cost of death.

And yet Wilde's persona insists that, for a minority at least, sexual fulfillment must be sought despite the odds. In two stanzas early in the poem, the narrator directly addresses the reader and installs a binary division between those who will understand the poem and those who will not:

> Those who have never known a lover's sin
>   Let them not read my ditty, it will be
> To their dull ears so musicless and thin
>   That they will have no joy of it, but ye
> To whose wan cheeks now creeps the lingering smile,
> Ye who have learned who Eros is,—O listen yet a-while.
>   (*CWOW1*, p. 73)

Likewise a few stanzas later the persona repeats the direct address and claims that if the reader has never 'wearied from some dear / And worshipped body risen' (*CWOW1*, p. 74), then they will never truly understand Charmides' feelings nor the poem itself. Some people understand that sex is practically impossible, yet they seek it nonetheless. It is, perhaps, the impossibility, among other things, that they love.[3] This is the audience Wilde seeks: those for whom sexual desire is at once ideal and corporal, a combination that makes it virtually guaranteed to fail.

Interestingly, these two stanzas of direct address were removed from the poem in its 1882 edition, one of the few changes Wilde made.[4] Perhaps they called too much attention to the sexual content of the poem or perhaps their attempt to indict the reader in the 'lover's sin' made it too difficult for Wilde to distance himself from the poem by claiming it as only a piece of descriptive exoticism about pagan excess. The stanzas' inclusion in the first version of the poem makes the connection between this tale of queer behavior and the reader's own innermost desires quite overt. In its 1881 form the poem invites us to participate in Charmides' queer failure.[5]

Male procreation as queer theory

This chapter aims to take the implicit ideas of queerness articulated in 'Mr W. H.' and *Dorian Gray*, as outlined in the previous chapters, and to make them explicit. I will also contextualize them in terms of their relationship to our own, post-Freudian ideas about sexuality, as opposed to the classical ideas through which Wilde primarily thought about the subject. I make a case that, despite scholarly claims made mostly in the 1990s, we can claim Wilde as queer, though not as homosexual. I end by looking at Wilde's queer theory as a form of filiation, and I use recent queer theory by Lee Edelman, José Esteban Muñoz, Heather Love, and Judith Halberstam to understand Wilde's expression of queer sexuality through the trope of children.

One of the initial problems that a historical investigation of same-sex desire prior to the mid-twentieth century must confront is that of what precisely is being investigated and what it should be called. The twentieth century has bequeathed us a treasure trove of concepts and nomenclature, so much so that it becomes difficult to describe practices from earlier paradigms without domesticating them to our own terms. Most acutely, the formation of the contemporary idea of 'sexual orientation', with its combination of post-Freudian object-choice and personal individuation, has become so hegemonic that it can easily blind us to historical difference. At its most reductive, this means assuming that human beings have always been organized into two mutually exclusive categories of homosexual and heterosexual (though they have only recently come to be called by those names), and Wilde, for example, can best be understood as a homosexual who got caught in times less enlightened than our own. That Wilde and those around him might have understood themselves in other ways never becomes a question under this regime. As I alluded in the first chapter, however, to the extent that Foucault's account in the first volume of *The History of Sexuality* has become the basis of subsequent work in the field, we are now less likely to make such naïve assumptions. The contemporary model is so strong, however, that guarding against its tendency to think itself a transhistorical reality remains a concern.

The problem of what to call same-sex desire on the other side of a putative historical divide also afflicts this project. Foucault's first volume describes the formation over centuries of what we now call 'sexuality', which is to say an organization of knowledge about sexual desires and practices that functions to make its subject confess itself into the establishment of biopower. It is thus tempting simply to refer to the contemporary, hetero/homo organization as 'sexuality' and have done with it. To do so, however, would necessarily involve calling Wilde's implicit understandings of same-sex desire 'pre-sexuality'. There are lots of problems with doing so, not least of which is the suggestion that such earlier understandings are somehow less 'sexual' than later ones. Additionally, such terminology suggests a more discrete historical break than I am comfortable with; the change in understanding was ongoing during Wilde's lifetime and rather more gradual than 'on or about December 1910'. But if 'sexuality' will not do, what will?

I have settled on the term 'orientation' for several reasons. First, it is commonly accepted and has a popular if imprecise meaning. In most non-specialist usage, it tends to mean the hetero/homo dichotomy more or less exactly. It is also the term given the official imprimatur of the American Psychological Association, which distinguishes it from sexual behavior and again makes it coterminous with the hetero/homo continuum (while stressing that it is a continuum rather than a simple binary). I will thus use the term 'orientation' to refer to the dominant cultural belief that sexual identity plays out in terms of object-choice, and that object-choice can be mapped along a continuum with heterosexual at one end, homosexual at the other, and bisexual in the middle. My use of this term is not endorsement: the orientation system is unavoidable, but it is not historically inevitable. Moreover, as Eve Kosofsky Sedgwick has more than adequately demonstrated in her masterful introductory chapter to *Epistemology of the Closet*, the orientation system is a mess. It is self-contradictory both in terms of essentialism vs. constructivism and in terms of minoritizing vs. majoritizing assumptions. These self-contractions do little, however, to prevent people from using the system as if it were lucid, coherent, and without need of a history. And if our own system is messy, we should not expect perfect order and coherence from pre-orientation understandings. Sex is messy, and it is not the job of queer theory to pretend otherwise.

David Halperin's 2002 *How to Do the History of Homosexuality* offers an intriguing schematic for the possible understandings of same-sex desire prior to the early-twentieth-century ascension of orientation and the homo/hetero split that characterizes contemporary understandings of the subject. Such a schematic can be extremely helpful in at least three ways. First, Halperin provides us with four different and potentially overlapping models for mapping pre-orientation desire. Secondly, by giving multiple examples, Halperin prevents a futile search for a single understanding of pre-orientation sexual beliefs and practices. The four models he offers, in other words, can co-exist, overlap, and/or exclude each other in different times and places. Lastly, he consistently stresses that these earlier models do not cease to become operative once we have reached the necessarily arbitrary date at which we decide that the orientation model becomes dominant. Rather, these earlier models continue to inform, often in very subtle ways, how culture defines homo- and heterosexuality.

So I now reconfront the questions I posed at the beginning of the first chapter: if Wilde was not gay, what was he? What did he think he was? Having established interpretations of sexuality in his literary texts, especially 'Mr W. H.' and *Dorian Gray*, I want now to attempt to fit these interpretations, including the ideal of male procreation, into Halperin's four paradigms, which he enumerates as follows:

> The four pre-homosexual categories of male sex and gender deviance that I have identified so far can be described, very provisionally, as categories of (1) effeminacy, (2) paederasty or 'active' sodomy, (3) friendship or male love, and (4) passivity or inversion.[6]

Halperin stresses that the name of each of these categories is 'heuristic, tentative, and ad hoc' (p. 110). Nonetheless, they strike me as eminently useful, so I adopt them without alteration.

Effeminacy: Halperin clarifies that ancient concepts of effeminacy tend to associate it with excesses in what we would now call heterosexual rather than homosexual practice. Men who want to attract women are more likely, according to this construction, to make themselves smooth by shaving, use cosmetics, cultivate social virtues and, as a result, make themselves less martial, athletic, and virile. John Addington Symonds' rejection of effeminacy in his account of the ancient Dorian valorization of same-sex desire, cited above, is a clear illustration of this concept. Wilde's male procreative ideal, however, is predicated on effeminacy as a kind of virtue, at least when joined to the individualistic athleticism of a Cyril Graham or the overwhelming personality of a Dorian Gray. Rather than the association of same-sex desire with the hyper-masculinity of warfare (perhaps in the eyes of Cyril Graham the least acceptable of all team sports), Wilde's version of effeminacy stresses a productive internal combination of masculinity and femininity, in which the effeminate body is shaped by the indwelling masculine spirit. This results in a softened male body, much along the lines of classical effeminacy, but it divorces such soft masculinity from the attraction of women.[7] Wilde's is a celebratory effeminacy that excludes the female body.

One of Wilde's distinguishing physical features, beside his large and rather soft body, was his choice to be clean-shaven in an age in which almost all men wore copious facial hair. George Ives recalled in his diary that when he first met Wilde in 1892, he asked the 25-year old Ives what he was doing at the Authors' Club 'among the bald and the bearded'.[8] John Gray, Bosie Douglas, Robert Sherard, and Robbie Ross were likewise clean-faced while part of the Wilde circle. This does not make a naked face the precise equivalent of the green carnation, but it does connect bodily smoothness with classical effeminacy, as well as the valorization of youth, which is closely connected to the second category.[9]

Paederasty or 'active sodomy': Halperin differentiates paederasty from orientation-era homosexuality by stressing how the former focuses exclusively on the desiring subject. Paederasty is above all an uneven relationship: it is characterized by a desiring man and a male object of that desire. Almost invariably, a difference in age and/or social class reinforces this erotic difference; in either case the difference is most often articulated by referring to the object of desire as a boy. Sexual desire thus belongs to the man, and the boy's desire or enjoyment is not part of the equation. Sexual negotiations take the form of monetary payment, social advancement, or threats. This type of relationship is basically a reinforcement of social hierarchy: the privileged man gives something to the subordinate boy and takes sexual pleasure from him. Additionally, paederasty need not be a matter of erotic exclusivity in object choice: participating in it as the active, insertive partner need not associate the man with effeminacy nor imply that he is uninterested or incapable of sexual relations with women. Halperin cites a body of classical literature in which debates between privileged male characters center on the question of whether boys or women are the more enjoyable sexual objects, and such conversations are carried on very much in the spirit of connoisseurs discussing matters of taste (p. 116).[10] Sexual pleasure remains a matter of phallic supremacy under this regime.

Like effeminacy, paederasty has deep classical roots. Of course, as a student of Greats in Benjamin Jowett's Oxford, Wilde was thoroughly immersed in many of the texts that record and express this tradition, Plato's *Symposium* chief among them. Male procreation is very much based on this paradigm, with male sexual desire being aroused by the fair young ephebe and the sexual creation of ideas resulting from this attraction, much as the procreation of human bodies results from male attraction to receptive female beauty under a phallocentric understanding of physical reproduction. All of the same-sex pairings in Wilde's fiction feature a differential in age: even if, as in the case of Erskine and Cyril Graham it is only a matter of a year or two, it still makes all the difference. Wilde's own sexual relations were focused almost exclusively on younger men. Even if, as Wilde claimed, it was Robbie Ross who first seduced him in 1886 rather than the other way around, Ross was still seventeen while Wilde was thirty-two. There was a sixteen-year difference between Wilde and Bosie and twelve years between Wilde and John Gray. The renters who testified at Wilde's trials were all teenagers. And with the renters most obviously, a gap in social class accompanied the gap in age. To what extent any of these relationships with younger men excluded mutual desire is something that remains outside the ability of literary-historical research to discover, yet with the renters especially, irrespective of Wilde's good treatment of them, money rather than erotic desire was certainly the primary motivation.

Male friendship and love: where paederasty thrives on asymmetrical relationships, the ideal for friendship is social equality, a situation in which neither friend has anything material to gain from the other. In its classical exemplars, friendship excludes sexual desire. Though readers in the era of orientation tend to read latent or repressed sexual desire into the passionate language of friendship (in addition to Halperin's examples of Montaigne and Dryden we might add the friendship of Hamlet and Horatio, as well as Tennyson's 'In Memoriam'), male friendship maintains a separate existence, *philia* as opposed to *eros*. As Halperin succinctly puts it, 'sexual love, in the light of the male friendship

tradition, actually sounds like a contradiction in terms: sexual penetration is not the sort of thing you would do to someone you really
love' (p. 121). Friendship is nonetheless a central part of the genealogy
of homosexuality because it provides a language of fervent same-sex
attachment between equals, which then becomes the ideal for many
gay relationships in the orientation era.[11]

Only a thoroughly cynical reader could, I think, take all of Wilde's
relationships with younger men to be paederastic to the exclusion of
friendship. Though male procreation does require a certain amount of
asymmetry in that one party must play the begetter and the other the
vessel for the begotten idea, as the previous chapters have tried to demonstrate, specific roles can be quite flexible within the paradigm. A considerable amount of mutual respect is necessary for male procreation to
work as it is designed to do, as both the lover and beloved are assumed
to operate on something other than a purely material level. Wilde's
relationships with younger men who were more or less his social equals
(such as Robbie Ross) or who had artistic aspirations to add to their
working class origins (such as John Gray) tended to be paederastic relationships initially and then become friendships when the sexual ardor
had cooled or, what may or may not amount to the same thing, when
the boy matured sufficiently to be treated as a peer. The prison letter, in
addition to being one of the great literary love letters, also participates
in the discourse of male friendship from a negative perspective; Wilde's
disappointment lies in, among other things, Bosie's complete inability
even to approximate a selfless friend.

Passivity or inversion: inversion functions as a kind of necessary
counterpart to paederasty insofar as a receptive or, to speak in the
stereotypically phallic language in which the great majority of sexual
constructs have participated, passive partner is required for paederasty to work. As detailed above, paederasty does not oblige the object
of affection to desire or enjoy penetration. Especially in its classical
iterations (including the *Symposium*), it seems to prefer that the object
specifically not desire penetration, or at least not to appear to do so.[12] In
fact, pre-orientation cultures tend to assign a very pejorative valence to
a man who enjoys a passive role in intercourse: he becomes the *kinaidos*
or *cinaedus* of classical Mediterranean culture, the medieval catamite,
the eighteenth-century English molly.[13] Unlike the active paederast, the
passive (or pathic) male is effeminate: he sexually identifies with a feminine, receptive role and thus participates in many of the assigned traits
that characterize the first category above. Halperin locates the difference
between effeminacy and passivity in the former's universalizing and the

latter's minoritizing ideas of gender deviance (p. 123). Effeminacy is the kind of softness into which all men may fall if they eschew military discipline for luxury and comfort. The pathic, on the other hand, is a faulty man, someone who is incapable of achieving masculine desire. Femininity is thus implicitly defined as failed masculinity.

Two more aspects of the pathic require comment: first, he is a morphology. The pathic can be and often is 'detected', which of course assumes that there are more or less obvious traits that non-pathics can identify and make the basis of accusations. Generally speaking, the detectable traits center on either literal or symbolic cross-dressing: the pathic man either literally wears women's clothing, make-up, simulated body parts (artificial breasts, most commonly), or he presents himself as symbolically female through a lisping voice, a mincing gait, and other manifestations of a stereotype of femininity. Secondly, the pathic is not defined by object-choice. Passive behavior may be combined with cross-sex desire; even if it is, however, the pathic will continue to be persecuted for failure to perform masculinity correctly.

'Sexual inversion' became a dominant part of nineteenth-century sexology's cataloging of sexual identities; the extent to which such an identity was categorized as pathological depended largely on the sexologist. Karl Heinrich Ulrich's confession that he felt himself to be a woman's soul trapped in a man's body became a paradigmatic case for later third sex or intermediate sex theories such as those espoused by Magnus Hirschfeld and Edward Carpenter. Such discourses retain the minoritizing trend of the classical pathic while attempting to remove the social and legal stigma pertaining to it.[14]

An account of Wilde's relationship to inversion would initially seem to consist entirely in restating his relationship to effeminacy. However, inversion, especially the inversion of the late nineteenth century, does allow for some finer differentiations to be made. Most illustrative, perhaps, is inversion's relationship to cross-dressing. Although Wilde was at least once caricatured in a dress,[15] there is no evidence that he was in actuality attracted to wearing women's clothing or participated in cross-dressing. Nonetheless, Richard Ellmann's biography reproduces a photograph purporting to be 'Wilde in costume as Salome'.[16] As is fairly well known, Ellmann was dying during the completion of the Wilde biography, and this tragic circumstance has been blamed for numerous inaccuracies (perhaps most importantly, Ellmann's thesis that Wilde died of syphilis contracted while an undergraduate at Oxford).[17] I have no interest in recovering old arguments about Ellmann's understandable errors of fact, but this misidentification of Wilde as theatrical cross-dresser is, I think, more than just an error. The picture is not accounted for in the text at all; it is, in fact, a photograph of the Hungarian singer Alice Guszalewicz appearing in a 1906 production of Strauss's opera version of *Salome*.[18] The fact that Wilde's cross-dressing seemed to fit so seamlessly (as it were) into the biography and required no explanation indicates both that inversion remains operative in later, mostly unarticulated understandings of homosexuality, and that the distinction between effeminacy and inversion is potentially quite important to Wilde's sexuality. Effeminacy is central to Wildean sexuality; passivity, especially as manifested through what might be called a kind of symbolic cross-dressing, played a much more nuanced role.

Halperin's work has not gone uncontested; most noticeably, Thomas K. Hubbard's writings on classical sexuality set themselves against what has come to be known as the Kenneth Dover–Michel Foucault–David Halperin tradition, which tends to stress the power differential between the adult *erastes* and the youthful and relatively disadvantaged *eromenos*. Hubbard, on the other hand, produces several classical artifacts, both texts and picture vases, that depict both male and female same-sex erotic interactions in which such an age and power imbalance does not seem to be at issue, and he thus contends that Halperin over-reads one type of pederasty as standing in the place of all same-sex practices.[19] Both Halperin and Hubbard are adept classicists, and it remains well outside of my intention and abilities to weigh in on one side or the other in a debate among specialists on the realties of the sexual institutions and practices of the distant past. For this project, however, the perception of classical reality during the late nineteenth and early twentieth centuries is ultimately of more importance than classical reality in and of itself, and Halperin's description of classical same-sex male eroticism fits, for the reasons I have enumerated above, very well with Wilde's theory and practice. It may well be the case that they fit so well because Halperin reads classical culture from a subject position influenced by the four pre-orientation discourses that he describes; indeed, if he is right about their lingering effects, he must inevitably do so. His position is thus not radically different from that of Wilde, who was searching previous culture for a precedent and a justification for desires that were at least partially products of this previous culture. The circularity of the process is less an indictment of Wilde's (or Halperin's) intellectual honesty than a realization of how culture and subjectivity interact. In any case, though I am perfectly content with Hubbard's idea that classical sexual discourse is more complex than Halperin allows, it nonetheless seems to me that Halperin's articulation of it, even if simplified, provides us with a supremely useful set of angles from which to view Wilde's negotiations with classical precedents for same-sex desire. In other words, Halperin's schema may well provide a better way to address Wilde's understanding of classical sexual culture than it reflects the complexities and varieties of actual classical practices.

In order fully to understand Halperin's schema, it is necessary to include the modern concept of homosexuality, which Halperin insists is not synonymous with any of the four pre-orientation conceptualizations. Rather, homosexuality is 'an unstable conjunction' of orientation, object-choice, and behavior (p. 131). It functions as a nexus that incorporates earlier formulations, such as the four he enumerates, without being reducible to any one of them. Moreover, since the object-choice aspect of homosexuality stems from Freud and his students, it is clear that, historically speaking, Wilde lived and died on the other side of the full formation of modern homosexuality. Freud began writing what would become *The Interpretation of Dreams* a few months after Wilde's incarceration. Wilde lived at a time when modern orientation models were inchoate; if the line of development between nineteenth-century sexology and orientation theory seems clear now, this is doubtless the benefit of hindsight. Moreover, especially in England, sexology did not operate in the clear. Havelock Ellis' struggle with the English language version of *Sexual Inversion* can serve as an example of English resistance to a stereotypically continental (and especially German) scientific approach to sexuality.[20] To see Wilde as unproblematically homosexual or gay is thus anachronistic, though not entirely wide of the mark. Wilde lived at a time when the elements that would eventually form our concept of modern sexuality were beginning to coalesce, which makes Wilde and his writings a fascinating case study for a cultural moment that both is and is not our own. Moreover, as Halperin points out (following Sedgwick), earlier forms continue to operate under the surface of orientation; one of the reasons that our understanding of sexuality is fraught with contradiction is that homosexuality both contains ideas from its genealogy and is separate from them. Effeminacy, paederasty, friendship, and inversion are all part of homosexuality, yet homosexuality is not the same as any one of them. Wilde lived on the cusp of the homosexual. He may, whether he wanted to or not, have helped to form it. But he was not, strictly speaking, homosexual.

This historical situation is also why I have chosen to use the word 'queer' in regard to Wilde's sexuality, both in his life and his writing. It is, in fact, less anachronistic than either 'homosexual' or 'gay'. 'Homosexual' had been introduced as a term in 1869, but it did not have the full meaning that it would generate by the first few decades of the twentieth century, while 'gay' seems to be a product of the mid-twentieth century after the dominance of the orientation understanding had been established. 'Queer', on the other hand, seems to have been taking on its modern meaning during Wilde's lifetime if we can judge by Queensberry's use of the term 'Snob Queer' in an accusation of Lord Rosebery, who was rumored to have been engaged in an affair with Queensberry's eldest son, Francis.[21] 'Queer', moreover, allows us to subsume a number of different pre-orientation concepts of sexuality that stand in distinction to male–female, potentially physically procreative relationships. 'Queer', in other words, does not force us to understand Wilde as homosexual or even proto-homosexual, yet it helps to acknowledge the reality that Wilde's life and writings engaged in non-normative constructions of sexuality that courted moral disapproval and legal condemnation.

One other aspect of Halperin's writing needs to be accounted for prior to a deeper investigation of Wilde as a queer theorist. Halperin's chapter 'Forgetting Foucault', originally an article in *Representations*, has for years now stood as a useful corrective to oversimplifications of the first volume of Foucault's *History of Sexuality*. Most importantly for this project, Halperin seeks to counter what he sees as a common misreading of Foucault, which is that he is often read to claim that prior to the codification of nineteenth-century sexology, there were only actions, not types. Once the nineteenth century invents the homosexual as a noun, in this view, sexuality becomes internalized and scientifically identifiable. Before this invention, then, there were only sexual acts, not sexual identities. People may have (and did) engage in sodomy, for instance, but doing so did not reveal their essential identity as sodomites. Halperin argues that Foucault does not in fact foreclose the possibility of a sexual subjectivity or morphology prior to the invention of nineteenth-century sexuality. The *kinaidos*, for instance, is a sexual type in classical Greece: he is an identifiable type of person who can be spotted by behavioral cues that are not directly linked to his defining enjoyment of being sexually penetrated. The point for Halperin is not that Foucault insists that there are no sexual subjectivities prior to 1869, just that homosexuality in the modern sense is not one of these earlier subjectivities.

Nothing Foucault says about differences between those two historically distant, and operationally distinct, discursive strategies for regulating and deligitimating forms of male same-sex sexual contacts prohibits us from inquiring into the connections that pre-modern people may have made between specific sexual acts and the particular ethos, or sexual style, or sexual subjectivity, of those who performed them. (p. 32)

Understanding Foucault in this way allows us to see how Wilde, whether in his own person or in such writings as 'Mr W. H.' and *Dorian Gray*, might well be identified as queer without assuming that queer is merely a different way to spell homosexual.[22]

Wildean queerness

'I then said to him, "Lord Queensberry, do you seriously accuse your son and me of sodomy?" He said "I don't say that you are it, but you look it" (*laughter*).'[23] This report of a conversation between Wilde and Queensberry illustrates the point of pre-orientation sexual identity nicely, from the grammatical level on up. Wilde asks Queensberry whether he is serious in accusing Bosie and Wilde of a sexual action, while Queensberry replies in terms of a sexual identity. Wilde asks about what he and Bosie do or have done, and Queensberry replies in terms of what Wilde (and perhaps Bosie, but perhaps not) is. Or what he appears to be without, in fact, being. Queensberry accuses Wilde, not of engaging in same-sex actions, but in appearing to be the sort of person who would do so. This is the same kind of accusation that enabled the trial in the first place: the card Queensberry left at the Albemarle Club did not accuse Wilde of being a sodomite (or a somdomite), but as 'posing as' a sodomite.[24] In order for a person to pose as something, there must be a shared cultural understanding of the role that is being posed. A pose that pretends to a role that the people being posed for do not recognize is not going to be a very successful pose. In order for Wilde to 'look' a sodomite or to 'pose as' one, the stereotype of the sodomite must be an established and recognized role to which he could pretend.

Either that or Queensberry could simply have been paranoid and delusional; given his actions and reputation, this is not a conclusion to write off too easily. Nonetheless, the most telling part of the above quotation may be the last word: laughter from the audience in the courtroom. Though the records do not attempt to codify the kind of laughter displayed, nor who laughed, it was sufficient to cause the judge to threaten to clear the court.[25] Queensberry's comment was either so incongruous as to elicit laughter at its confusion and outrageousness, or the laughter was that of recognition. If the latter, it would seem to imply that the audience in the courtroom knew what Queensberry had in mind when he accused Wilde of acting the sodomite. They recognized the idea that someone might display the signifiers of a sexual identity and that these signifiers might be so removed from the actions that they supposedly signify as to open up the possibility that the person might not in fact be guilty of the sexual identity that he or she performed. In other words, they understood that a person could act like one without really being one.

This does not mean, however, that the 'one' in the previous sentence meant then what it means now. Where now the tacit meaning would be homosexual, it may then have meant something more akin to what Halperin names inversion. If so, the audience at Wilde's first trial joined a tradition thousands of years in the making of ridiculing the catamite, the willing passive partner in same-sex penetrative intercourse, and of identifying him via his patent effeminacy.[26] But this also does not mean that the audience had a coherent vision of the invert in its collective imagination. The unspoken identity of which Wilde is accused of imitating need be no more coherent than the definition of 'fag' that operates in modern homophobic accusations; the fact that an identity is not well understood does little to control its deployment and may help to explain the laughter of Wilde's courtroom audience. Perhaps they laughed because Queensberry was trying to express something that they too felt existed but for which they had no commonly accepted name.[27]

In any case, Queensberry's ability to accuse Wilde of posing demonstrates Halperin's point that concepts of sexual identity can and did exist prior to the era of orientation. Queensberry did not accuse Wilde of posing as a homosexual, while his chosen, though misspelled, word of somdomite needs to be read in light of the above contentions about the genealogy of pre-orientation sexuality. Queensberry was accusing Wilde of acting an established, if ill-understood and all but literally unspeakable, deviant sexual identity, and this sexual identity was not that of the modern homosexual. But it was certainly queer.

The use of pre-orientation constructions of sexually deviant identities brings up the question of the relationship between what I am outlining here and some very interesting work done in the 1990s concerning Wilde's influence on subsequent models of male sexuality. Ed Cohen's 1993 *Talk on the Wilde Side* and Alan Sinfield's 1994 *The Wilde Century* both make Wilde into a, if not the, crucial figure in the development of the modern homosexual or, to put it in my terms, the foundation of the orientation system. Cohen argues that the Wilde trials, or more properly, the representation of the Wilde trials in the popular British press, 'crystallized a new constellation of sexual meanings predicated upon "personality" and not practices'.[28] Because the newspapers of 1895 could not directly describe the acts of which Wilde was accused and condemned, they had instead to concentrate on representing his aesthetic style and opinions, thus creating a conflation between deviant sexual practice and Wilde's public personality—and the use of this word may be telling in light of my previous chapter, as this conflation involved not only Wilde's written and spoken words, but his often illustrated body as well. Cohen does not claim that the press by itself was thus able to assign the symbol of Oscar Wilde to the identity of the male homosexual: the entire first half of Cohen's book is dedicated to the various social and sexual discourses that enabled the assignment at the end of the nineteenth century. Nonetheless, the press's use of Wilde's artistic stance as the speakable characteristic that stands in for his unspeakable sexual acts creates a new sexual identity: the artistic, hyperliterate, elitist, effete gay man *avant le lettre*.

Similarly, Sinfield in *The Wilde Century* makes Wilde into a model for twentieth-century homosexual identity, but Wilde's combination of performative effeminacy, artistic accomplishment, and leisure-class insouciance is only seen as a gay paradigm after the trials. Before his guilt became apparent, Wilde could indulge in all kinds of behavior that later generations would identify as camp, yet he remained largely unimpugned by any suspicions on the part of his contemporaries. Like Cohen, Sinfield provides a genealogy of sexual discourses; like Halperin, he stresses that effeminacy prior to the Wilde moment was not necessarily linked to same-sex desire (rather the opposite, in fact). Although I find a tendency in Sinfield's conception occasionally to write as though homosexuality is a fully-formed object waiting to be found in the late nineteenth and early twentieth centuries (for example: 'they were at the point of stumbling on our framework'),[29] he nonetheless helps to clear away a lot of the mythology of a single, transhistorical ideology of sexuality. In its place he gives us the moment at which previous ideas of sexual deviance coalesced around the figure of Wilde: 'the image of the queer cohered at the moment when the leisured, effeminate, aesthetic dandy was discovered in same-sex practices, underwritten by money, with lower-class boys'.[30] This combination of gendered, sexualized, and class-based qualities provides an icon of queerness that more or less exemplifies, if not defines, the male homosexual for the next seventy or eighty years.

Putting Cohen and Sinfield together gives us a Wilde who is created, either by the popular press or by a conflation of social discourses, into the towering colossus, or the ravening monster, of male homosexuality. For good or ill—and Sinfield especially makes clear that the identification of male homosexuality with effeminacy participates in misogyny and gay self-hatred—Wilde becomes the founding figure of gay male identity. From the trials to the era of the Sexual Offenses Act in England and Wales and the Stonewall riots in the US, Wilde presides as the queen of the orientation era. Yet it is important to differentiate this Wilde as the icon of an emergent, incoherent sexual system based on orientation from the Wilde who wrote 'Mr W. H.', *Dorian Gray*, and the 'madness of kisses' letter. It is my contention that the iconic Wilde became a symbol for a system that Wilde the writer would not have recognized nor, perhaps, endorsed had he ever been given the chance. Moreover, as I have attempted to show in the previous chapter, Wilde felt himself forced at his first trial to employ an aesthetic defense of his literary work that distanced it from any kind of sexual politics and/or intervention into discourses of sexuality. Therefore, Wilde's putative intent in writing such texts was taken to be adequately represented by his testimony. In other words, the iconic Wilde that emerges from the trials and into prison, whether seen as a martyr or a miscreant, is a Wilde who denies the connection between his texts and sexual discourse.

My interest at this point, however, lies with what Wilde thought himself to be rather than either how he was forced to represent himself while on trial or what subsequent generations have made of him. And what Wilde thought of himself is not a choice over which he exercised complete control. It is formed through the discourses available at the time; moreover, Wilde is not the only person who gets to speak about them. The voice of public opinion can for this moment be assigned to Queensberry, which brings us back to the question of how an accusation of posing as a sodomite is possible if Sinfield is correct that Wilde's contemporaries did not see him as queer because 'they didn't see queerness in the way we have come to see it. Our interpretation is retroactive; in fact, Wilde and his writing look queer because our stereotypical notion of male homosexuality derives from Wilde, and our ideas about him.'[31] But Queensberry did see Wilde as queer, and it is at least possible that the laughter in the courtroom following Wilde's report of Queensberry's accusation demonstrates Queensberry was not the only one who thought he knew sodomitical behavior well enough to know what Wilde was trying to fake.

Halperin's scheme can be helpful here. Recall that of the four pre-orientation modes described above, inversion/passivity is the one that has tended to be the most socially despised and most closely associated with a detectable pattern of behavior. It is thus plausible to think that what Queensberry reacted to was not so much a glimpse of an incipient queerness to come as a vestige of an ancient and despised male sexual passivity. Moreover, if we grant Halperin's point that Foucault did not claim that there were no such things as sexual identities prior to the sexological invention of the homosexual as a noun, and that in fact the pre-orientation era was quite capable of producing typologies and stereotypes of sexual characters, then it is not necessary to contend that Wilde was seen as utterly normal up to the moment that he was convicted. Wilde may well be a central figure for the formation of the typology of the gay man in the twentieth-century Western world, but such a typology needs to be kept separate from both the typologies that surrounded him in the late nineteenth century and from the understandings of sexuality that he sought to explore, however obliquely, in his writings. Wilde's understanding of male same-sex desire is not that of the modern orientation system, and it defines itself against the contemporary visceral disgust surrounding passivity/inversion. Queensberry accused Wilde of unmanly, if not unnatural, appearance. Carson reiterated this point when he claimed that 'anyone who would allow himself to be connected with that article ['The Priest and the Acolyte'] or who publicly approved of that article would be, at least, posing as a sodomite', and when he accused *Dorian Gray* of being intended as sodomitical.[32] My task at this intersection, then, is to flesh out the theories of male same-sex desire suggested by Wilde's texts and distinguish them from the contemporary surrounding discourse of the pathic and the widespread, incoherent aversion for that position.

As I have suggested in my introduction to Halperin's scheme, Wilde's ideal of male procreation participates in all four of the pre-orientation categories. It requires effeminacy in that the beloved must participate in an essential feminine to the extent that he can incubate and birth ideas that have been implanted by the begetter. It requires paederasty insofar as male procreation is based on an unequal relationship of, if not strictly superior and inferior, then at least active and passive. The inequality is always expressed through age and tends to replicate a standard patriarchal privileging of the man/masculine/begetter over the boy/feminine/impregnated. It requires friendship to counterbalance the inequality of classical paederasty. Procreative male couples are not marriages of equals, but they are marriages of true, though distinct and complementary, minds. Without a mutual respect and love they are infertile.

Lastly, and perhaps most controversially, male procreation needs inversion. However, as I have demonstrated in the first chapter, this is a special kind of inversion, an inverted inversion in that it upends traditional understandings and prejudices about a minoritizing organization of sexual passivity. Where classical understandings of the pathic see him as a pathological (or pathetic) monster whose body both encapsulates and betrays its imprisonment of a spirit of the 'wrong' sex, Wilde wants to turn things around. Much (though not all) of nineteenth-century sexology focused on a kind of recuperation of inversion: Ulrichs, for instance, made '*anima muliebris in corpore virili inclusa*' into a political campaign for German legal reform.[33] If the male Urning was the soul of a woman trapped in the body of a man, he was not to be despised, either socially or legally, for a condition over which he had no control. For Edward Carpenter and other apologists for the intermediate sex idea, the Urning of either sex should be allowed to become a bridge between men and women whose souls and bodies aligned in the more traditional fashion. But for Wilde the male queer is neither an essential woman nor a compromise between the two sexes. It is not the body that is masculine (*corpore virili*); rather, the flesh is strongly associated with the feminine. The connection with a masculine soul in such a way as to produce what in *Dorian Gray* is termed personality gives us the Wildean ideal of the invert. In the only kind of transsexuality in which Wilde was interested, the masculine molds the feminine flesh, thereby producing a figure who is effeminate without participating in the stereotypical weakness and timidity of the pathic. In Wilde's implied mythology, Psyche is a boy.

Likewise, Wilde's acceptance of effeminacy distances him from the ultra-masculine school of inversion as articulated by Symonds, among others. As remarked in the previous chapters, effeminacy was anathema to Symonds, who based his ideal of same-sex love on the Dorian Spartans. In Symonds' construction, these Dorians brought male same-sex practice into ancient Greek culture as a military virtue: a combination of paederasty and friendship would ensure that soldiers would never abandon their comrades in battle, and training for combat jibes seamlessly with gymnastic culture. Symonds' version of the 'problem' of Greek love corresponds quite well with Sedgwick's observation that ancient Greece illustrates the ability of homosocial and homosexual (in the broad, ahistorical sense) discourses to go hand in hand.[34] For Wilde, however, there is nothing particularly redolent of either the barracks or the gymnasium in same-sex love. Though the Wildean ephebe can excel at aristocratic games, as with Cyril Graham's riding and fencing, the definition is too platonic to be seen in such an exclusively corporeal way. Dorian Gray, for instance, is not merely a body, but a personality, which is to say a combination of body and spirit in which an anatomically male body is animated by a spirit that participates in the feminine, thus allowing the possibility for an idea-based fertility. Through worship, the ephebe produces ideas, innovation, and art. Wilde and Symonds may well have agreed on the definition and importance of the idea of personality to the Greeks, but they disagreed on the ideal embodiment of the concept.

Wilde, then, sought subtly to promote an understanding of male same-sex desire that worked against the stereotype of the pathic and of the exploitative, radically unequal and nonreciprocal aspects of classical paederasty. He wanted to demonstrate that Shakespeare did not use Willie Hughes (perhaps yet another pun on Mr W. H.'s surname appears here) as a mere sexual object, but that their relationship was a mutual one in which each inspired the other to new heights of artistic expression. This paradigmatic relationship in turn inspires more modern imitators such as Erskine with Cyril Graham, 'Mr W. H.''s narrator with both Erskine and Cyril, and Basil Hallward with Dorian Gray. Not only Wilde's fiction but his life also feature such relationships with Robbie Ross, John Gray, and, most spectacularly, Bosie Douglas. In all of them, Wilde is not denying that there is a sexual typology outside the constructs of the procreative heterosexual couple; in other words, that there is such a thing as a detectable queer. But rather than either the stereotype of the effeminate pathic or that of the hyper-masculine Lacedaemonian soldier, Wilde wants to offer a type of the effeminized male body as a container for the creative soul, a container, moreover, that participates in what it contains. The Wildean vision of the queer man is that of a literally creative and symbolically procreative figure who is separated from the bulk of humanity not by pathology, but through talent. Whether the Wildean queer was seen as an eternal sexual minority needs to remain, I think, an open question. It is possible that Wilde's vision of classical culture allowed room for all male citizens to be potentially procreative, in which case the stigma of queerness would be removed. But outside the utopian confines of the world envisioned in 'The Soul of Man under Socialism' the Wildean queer was a noble minority whose cultural labor went largely unacknowledged. He embodies the hidden processes that drive culture forward, yet the processes if not always their products remain obscure to almost everyone not directly involved.

So Wilde's idea of male procreation gives us a version of queerness that participates in all four of Halperin's pre-orientation forms. Most strikingly it seeks to redeem inversion from its centuries-long pejorative valence, and it does so by removing inversion from the realm of literal or symbolic cross-dressing and instead making it a matter of the physical feminization, or softening, of an anatomically male body that remains essentially masculine in its animating creativity and power. It thus retains creativity for the masculine, relegating women to the arena of purely physical reproduction. It makes true procreation a process entered into by two men who are differentiated by age and their roles as begetter or impregnated host of the idea. The sexual type of the invert thereby moves from his status as despised catamite and pseudo-female to become the unacknowledged creative cultural force of the world.

And yet perhaps the most distinctive facet of this Wildean queer theory of male procreation is that it does not work. Not only did real life, especially in the form of Bosie Douglas, refuse to play its proper role, but even in the fiction, over which Wilde would seem to have a bit more control, the theory never comes to its full fruition. In 'Mr W. H.', the posthumous version of which constitutes its fullest articulation, the characters' inability to sustain their faith in the theory of Shakespeare's sonnets and the process of their birth gives the lie to their full belief in the procreative theory. In *Dorian Gray* Henry Wotton's unsympathetic manipulation of Dorian undercuts any real procreative potential in the Basil–Dorian relationship. Basil's worship, from this angle an aspect of paederasty as only the lover sees the true worth of the beloved, is knocked aside by Lord Henry's need to influence Dorian without feedback and without any true knowledge of the boy's inner being. Lord Henry fails at paederasty and friendship and Basil, who might have succeeded in both, is left to be destroyed at the hands of his inspiration: a further inversion of the inversion that Wilde inverted in order to produce the potential of male procreation in the first place.

Failing queerly

In order to address Wilde's writing the failure of his theory into its articulation, it will be helpful to look at more recent work in queer theory. Perhaps the most influential and controversial work in queer theory following Halperin's *How to Do the History of Homosexuality* is Lee Edelman's 2005 study, *No Future*. In Edelman's Lacanian reading of the role of the queer in contemporary society and politics, its function is to interrupt heteronormative society's faith in the final signifier by '*embodying* the remainder of the Real internal to the Symbolic order'.[35] It does so by refusing what Edelman calls 'reproductive futurism', which is society's simultaneous investment in and infinite deferral of the arrival of a future that is figured by the abstract symbol of the Child. As an abstraction, the Child lacks the particularity of a human who will grow to be an actual adult; the Child is rather the symbol of a future that never arrives but in whose name all manner of material benefits and symbolic legitimacy may be denied to those who appear to lack faith in the Child, which is to say, those who do not reproduce and for whom sexuality is not the means of maintaining faith in the future, but a *jouissance* of the here and now. The queer thus figures the death drive (p. 9) without actually becoming it (p. 17). The result is a 'queer negativity' whose 'value [. . .] resides in its challenge to value as defined by the social, and thus in its radical challenge to the very value of the social itself' (p. 6).

Such queer negativity and radical undercutting of sociality has, of course, not gone unquestioned within queer studies.[36] In a moment, I will describe several responses to Edelman by recent queer theorists, none of whom wish to substitute for his queer negativity a naively positive insistence on facile progress and assimilation. But first, I want briefly to consider Edelman's theory in and of itself in the context of Wilde's male procreation. Most obviously, Edelman's complete rejection of the Child and the faith in reproductive futurism that the Child embodies seems an almost perfect inversion of Wilde's ideas. The faith in the future that male procreation requires would seem to be no less counter to Edelman's idea than the necessity that same-sex love justify itself in terms of symbolic reproduction and childbearing; in fact, given Edelman's psychoanalytic logic, the two objections would be the two sides of the same coin. The fact that male procreation sees itself as the truly creative process while constructing cross-sex love as merely reproductive would, no doubt, appear a feeble justification in Edelman's terms. Making a mirror image of heterosexuality and thus seeking to justify same-sex love as the platonic original of reproductive futurism would seem to testify to an inability to escape the entrancing power of the Child.

One of the most direct responses to Edelman comes from José Esteban Muñoz's 2009 book *Cruising Utopia*. As the title indicates, Muñoz is concerned with the place of utopian visions of futurity in queer studies and queer culture. Appropriately enough for a queer theorist who looks more to Marxian traditions than to psychoanalysis, he begins his book with Wilde's quip in 'The Soul of Man under Socialism' that 'a map of the world that does not include utopia is not worth glancing at' (p. 1).[37] Partly in response to Edelman's writing off of the future as 'kid stuff' (p. 1), Muñoz writes instead that 'the future is queerness's domain' (p. 1) and laments 'the erosion of the gay and lesbian political imagination' (p. 21) as queer politics has increasingly taken the form of assimilation to mainstream culture rather than any attempt radically to alter it.[38] Where Edelman has heteronormative culture insisting on the future's rights over the present by enshrining the image of the Child, for Muñoz it is 'straight time' that 'tells us that there is no future but the here and now of our everyday life' (p. 22). The characterization of the present is one of the cruxes of difference between the two thought styles represented here. Edelman's present is an orgasmic *jouissance* in which sexuality has and needs no investment in the future to justify its present pleasure, whereas Muñoz's 'here and now' is merely the time in which mundane culture replicates itself without reference to new ways of doing and being. For Muñoz 'the present must be known in relation to the alternative spatial and temporal maps provided by a perception of past and future affective worlds' (p. 27). The past is something that needs to be animated, and that requires an 'understanding that the past has a performative nature, which is to say that rather than being static and fixed, the past does things' (pp. 27–8).

Muñoz's vision of a queer futurity seems much more hospitable to Wilde's male procreation than Edelman's rejection of the cult of the Child. In Wildean theory the future itself, in Muñoz's sense as a utopian possibility rather than a simple extension of the present, is brought about through male procreation, and Wilde's vision includes the image of the offspring of male–male love as children of the mind. Moreover, Wilde's combination of male friendship and paederasty involves a kind of filiation in which the boy is at once lover, friend, and son. Wildean male procreation is based on a utopian future—or at least it is when it is successful.

Queer failure, however, has been another trend in recent queer studies, one that is clearly related to queer negativity. Heather Love's 2007 *Feeling Backward* and Judith Halberstam's 2011 *The Queer Art of Failure* stand as exemplary texts. Love's concern is queer history, and she calls for an increased attention to literary texts written during the formation of the orientation ideology. She characterizes these texts as ones that 'turn their backs on the future'.[39] When queer history is exclusively conceptualized as a progressive march from isolated shame into public pride and acceptance, Love contends, it becomes all too easy to forget that history's overwhelming content of abjection and degradation. Queer history, then, is largely the history of failure, and a gay-affirmative triumphalism in which all evidence must meet the criteria of a progressive narrative thus tends to obscure the majority of what has been queer in queer history. Attempts to heal queer history of its wounded attachments are self-defeating in that 'queer history is, in a sense, nothing but wounded attachments.'[40]

Halberstam's project, on the other hand, involves a cultivation of what she calls 'low theory'; her primary texts are children's animated movies and art photography. In the spirit of Love's engagement with the less triumphant moments in queer history, she includes a fascinating chapter on the historical connection between homosexuality and fascism. But primarily she is interested in recuperating failure. In a culture in which success is defined as mastery, maturity, and the accumulation of wealth under the capitalist regime, failure can become a form of critique. Additionally, by reading pop culture texts whose target audience consists of mostly children, Halberstam introduces a different vision of childhood from the conservative image of the Child rejected by Edelman. It is not too much of an exaggeration to say that for Halberstam, there is something always already queer about the child.[41] For Halberstam, 'children are not coupled, they are not romantic, they do not have a religious morality, they are not afraid of death or failure, they are collective creatures, they are in a constant state of rebellion against their parents, and they are not the masters of their domain'.[42] Far from the guarantor of the Symbolic that Edelman makes the Child, Halberstam's children are proto-queers, only some of whom will eventually be corralled into heteronormativity.[43]

Love and Halberstam's queer failure is relevant to Wilde in two ways. First, Love especially counters the critical tendency to construct Wilde into, not only a gay man, but a gay success story. 'By including queer figures from the past in a positive genealogy of gay identity, we make good on their suffering, transforming their shame into pride after the fact.'[44] Neil McKenna's biography of Wilde is a textbook case of precisely this process. McKenna not only makes Wilde into an orientation-era gay man, virtually ignoring any possibility of historical difference in understandings of sexuality, but McKenna then maps Wilde's life onto a trajectory of progress and sexual liberation. Nowhere is this clearer than in McKenna's account of Wilde's post-incarceration life. McKenna does not deny that Wilde's exile in France and Italy consisted largely of begging various sources for small amounts of money and that with the exception of 'The Ballad of Reading Gaol', written soon after his release from prison, he was incapable of literary production. But all of this is evidence for his 'joy-song' (the title of McKenna's penultimate chapter) because Oscar did not need money or writing, yet alone adequate food or medical care. He could merely contemplate life and be rather than do. Above all he could explore his sexuality:

> To be at one with himself was to be at one with his Uranian self. In Paris he embraced his sexual urges and was in turn embraced and enveloped by them, achieving an erotic state of grace where desire was balanced by satisfaction, and where the contradictory imperatives of love and sex were resolved, merging into a perfect whole. [. . .] No longer encumbered by a wife or by his position in society, Oscar had no need to conceal his sexual self. He was liberated, emancipated from all internal and external constraints.[45]

To use McKenna's theological language, suffering is transubstantiated here into homosexual sainthood. Wilde achieved a mystical *jouissance* in the cheap cafés of Paris, and the loss of his talent, family, home, social status, money (the list could go on indefinitely) is as nothing compared to the opportunity to pursue same-sex liaisons without fear of legal prosecution. An insistence on the metanarrative of homosexual progress transforms an early death in a hotel room Wilde could not afford into a triumphant step toward full liberation. I certainly do not want to deny any legitimacy to understanding Wilde's life as a key part of the changes in understandings and acceptances of deviant sexualities in the last century or so. But I do think that McKenna more than adequately illustrates Love's point that an insistence on a trajectory of progress involves ignoring queer shame and suffering as such, and that doing so gives us a warped vision of queer history. Insofar as queerness always involves an opposition to deeply entrenched mainstream sexual ideologies and practices, it is going to involve no small amount of suffering and failure. Love's emphasis on queer shame as an integral part of queer history helps to explain why Wilde might have built failure into every literary articulation of queer love that he produced.

Interestingly, however, Love's *Feeling Backward* does not take on Wilde directly. Chronologically, she moves from Walter Pater to Willa Cather and Radclyffe Hall, leaving the reader to wonder whether Wilde might not be too successful in the eyes of the straight world truly to fit in her consideration. Halberstam likewise does not dwell on Wilde, including him, for instance, in a list of 'antisocial queer aesthetes and camp icons and texts' that constitutes 'the excessively small archive that represents queer negativity'.[46] Yet Halberstam's version of queer failure is also pertinent to Wilde's male procreation. Most intriguingly, her reevaluation of the child fits well with Wilde's literary career. As Ellmann points out, Wilde hid his prodigious literary output with a mask of indolence. In other words, he did a lot of work while pretending only to play. He nurtured a persona, not only of detachment, but of an ability to maintain what he called in the prison letter 'the Oxford temper': 'the ability to play gracefully with ideas' (*WCL*, p. 686). It is the verb in this sentence to which I want to call attention. Wilde valued play, a cultivated immaturity, a dogged refusal to appear to take things as seriously as the straight/adult world seemed to demand. It is worth remembering as well that Wilde's first real literary success, following the failures of his volume of poems and his first plays, was as a children's author. *The Happy Prince and Other Tales* (1888) was the first volume Wilde published that had anything like the cultural impact he wanted.[47] He returned to the genre in 1891, although in a darker tone, with *A House of Pomegranates*. The ability to play, which Wilde opposed to Bosie's 'violence of opinion' in the prison letter, also informs his lack of fidelity to the ideals of male procreation. The model fails from this perspective because it is far too serious of an idea. The very children it is designed to produce would be too childishly and playfully ironic to maintain their faith in it.

Halberstam's version of the child as proto-queer is also useful in conceiving of areas in which the implications of Wildean male procreation go beyond Halperin's four pre-orientation categories. As mentioned above, male procreation is based on an idea of filiation in which the boy plays a role that is symbolically and simultaneously that of the beloved in classical paederasty and that of the son of the lover. The ephebe in this scenario, distinguished from his beloved by difference in age as well as incarnation of a masculine soul in an effeminate body, both incubates the idea with which the begetter impregnates him and in a sense is that idea himself. Willie Hughes as the actor who embodies, inspires, and enables Shakespeare's major female roles illustrates the ideal perfectly. Without Mr W. H., Shakespeare would not have conceived of the roles: he needed a brilliant boy actor into whose hands he could place Lady Macbeth, Ophelia, etc., before he could write the parts. Willie Hughes, in turn, literally embodies the roles by playing them on stage. The plays then go on to a practically eternal cultural afterlife in which they inspire later acts of male procreation. Willie Hughes is thus at once Shakespeare's paederastic beloved, inspiration, artistic partner, mask, musical instrument, friend, and child. He is a child inasmuch as Willie Hughes as we know him in Wilde's story is a creation of Shakespeare. He is Shakespeare's begotten son in whom he is well pleased and who initiates an orgy of male procreation that lasts throughout the ages. He is also both the subject and object of play in all the word's mundane, juvenile, theatrical, and poststructural valences.

Part of this play, however, is failure. Willie Hughes' failure is simply a failure to exist. Dorian Gray's failure lies in his failed embodiment of the ideal of male procreation: his body is a lie, his productive connection with Basil Hallward is incomplete, and his relationship with Lord Henry Wotton is sterile. *The Picture of Dorian Gray* from this angle looks suspiciously like a study in queer failure. The child does not always grow up to embody an ideal, even an ideal of queerness. In fact, in Wilde's fictive track record, the child never grows up to embody the ideal. True to Halberstam's model of the anarchic queer child, Wilde's ephebic children go their own ways. They follow or make paths that fail to illustrate the points for which they were putatively meant. They illustrate that sometimes queerness queers itself.

Such paradoxes bring us back, I think, to the question of the adequacy of the childbirth model for queer sexuality. As mentioned above, Wilde's idea of male procreation is open both to accusations of rampant misogyny and of a failure to escape from the heteronormative paradigm. The charge of misogyny is accurate. One of the effects of the theory is to assign women entirely to the realm of the physical. Sexually, they are merely reproductive as opposed to creative and metaphysically they are limited to the body, unelevated into true personality by the warming touch of a masculine soul. Despite Wilde's established record as a feminist in his early career (his 1887–89 editorship of the renamed *The Woman's World*, for instance), his platonic sexual theory seems in many ways to grow out of the late nineteenth-century institutions of homosociality. If the vast majority of women are excluded from cultural production from the public schools on up, if they are by and large incapable of creativity, whether naturally or by cultivation through education, then why would a man interested in the production of ideas turn to them for inspiration? Though homosociality is not immune to critique in Wilde's work, in the social comedies especially, there is also a sense in which male procreation remains an extension of the cultural logic of homosociality and the construction of a method that not only creates an all-male version of parturition, but then privileges that version above its female counterpart. Men get true creativity in this scheme, while women must be satisfied with physical motherhood.

There is truth as well to the indictment that male procreation is simply an attempt to justify same-sex love by making it productive. If it can be made an integral part of cultural reproduction, if it can be put to work rather than just left to play, it can be justified as a necessary if currently misunderstood aspect of human social relations. Objections to male procreation are thus not only a matter of critiquing the need to articulate same-sex desire as a version of cross-sex desire, but also of the tendency to justify sexuality in general only to the extent that it is productive, whether physically or culturally. In either case, sexuality is acceptable only as an investment in the future—either in the future of the human race as bodies or in the continued development of ideas that will echo down the ages in ways that are impossible to foresee. Male procreation thus seems to be an answer to an objection that was barely articulate during Wilde's lifetime but has become much louder since then: the contention that same-sex practice is unnatural because it is sterile. By making same-sex love into the primary force of cultural development, Wilde tacitly forestalls such objections. Attacks on the love that dare not speak its name are ultimately suicidal in that society is cutting itself off from the source of its own development.

In short, Wilde's queer theory does buy into what Edelman critiques. Wilde justifies queer desire in terms of futurity and symbolic children, if not, strictly speaking, the Child. In its defense, however, we can also see his ideas as investing in a futurity that might be different from a mere continuation of the stasis of a prolonged now. Like Muñoz's queer utopias and Halberstam's queer child, Wilde's male procreation rests on the possibility of progress as well as the belief that progress might come through unrecognized and formerly despised avenues. Wilde's theory uses the reviled pathic, albeit in a newly inverted way, as the secret engine of social and cultural progress. In male procreation, the children are the future,[48] but this future is not a simple continuation: it retains the possibility of surprise.

And the children are even more surprising than they should be because, as children will, they refuse to stick to the script. All of Wilde's texts fail to illustrate his theory—or, they illustrate more than the theory by also exemplifying its failure. Wilde's children demand to been heard as well as seen. They refuse to stop playing and do as they are told. They fail to illustrate the all-too-perfect theory they were meant to embody. They fail to justify the productivity of the same-sex love that theoretically begat them. As Wilde's true children, it would be disappointing if they behaved in any other way.

4
Oscar and Sons: The Afterlife of Male Procreation

'I don't care to live if I am so degraded that I am unfit to be with my own child.'

Wilde (*WCL*, p. 821)

My previous chapter ended with the image of certain of Wilde's texts as his misbehaving children: rambunctious little brats who refuse to demonstrate the theories that they are supposed to uphold. In this scenario, of course, Wilde is the jolly papa who delights in his children's playful refusals. In turning from Wilde's texts as hints about his implicit theories of sexuality to the afterlife of his texts and how they influenced the development of such understandings in the years following Wilde's death, which is to say the years in which the regime of orientation began to cement its hold on conceptions of sexuality, I want to turn from the figurative to the literal sons of Wilde. I want to look at both Wilde's construction of his role as a father and how, after his death, he was in turn constructed as a father by his literal son Vyvyan and by the younger men of his circle who survived him. For the former question, I will turn to the letter Wilde himself called 'Epistola: In Carcere et Vinculis' (*WCL*, p. 782) but which became better known under Robbie Ross's title of *De Profundis*.[1]

Incest and male procreation in the prison letter

In the previous chapter I briefly mentioned Wilde's prison letter as a document chronicling the failure of the male procreation principle. This point is worth development in the context, not only of queer failure, but also of the role of the child in Wilde's queer theory, for Wilde's letter indicts Bosie Douglas for failing to function as an inspiration, a friend, or a paederastic boy, while it also constructs Bosie as both a child and as a son. In doing so it tests the limits of male procreation and explores the differences between the symbolic offspring, personified in Bosie, and the literal offspring, personified by Wilde's biological son Cyril.

One of Wilde's initial accusations is that his relationship with Bosie was artistically infertile: 'my life, as long as you were by my side, was entirely sterile and uncreative' (*WCL*, p. 685). Wilde characterizes the friendship as 'unintellectual', and 'a friendship whose primary aim was not the creation and contemplation of beautiful things' (WCL, p. 685) and compares it unfavorably to the inspirational relationships he had developed with young men such as Robbie Ross, John Gray, and Pierre Louÿs. Viewed in the light of male procreative theory, the reason for Wilde's disappointment in Bosie is clear: he is inadequate as either begetter or begotten. In fact, he is worse than inadequate in that he has proven himself positively destructive of artistic creation. By the end of the letter, Wilde comes around to another version of this theme. Where Bosie should have been one half of the asymmetric paederastic relationship, playing the role of the passive beloved who is acted upon and influenced, the actual relationship was, again, an inversion of its ideal form. Wilde confesses his complete inability to influence Bosie: 'The "influence of an elder over a younger man" is an excellent theory till it comes to my ears. Then it becomes grotesque' (*WCL*, p. 767). Rather than a passive recipient and incubator of Wilde's ideas, Bosie has proven himself to be an impotent would-be father, incapable of imaginative procreation.

It is at this point that the relationship between Wilde's symbolic and literal children becomes important. Insofar as Wilde's theory involves filiation and builds upon the implicit and symbolic paternity of classical paederastia, Bosie should be Wilde's son.[2] And the one aspect of Bosie that Wilde still sees as tolerable in memory after a year and a half of prison is Bosie's childlike quality. Wilde describes his and Bosie's reconciliation after one of their numerous breaks; in this case, the occasion was the death of Bosie's elder brother. Wilde recalls how Bosie came to him 'very sweetly and very simply', seeking consolation 'as a child might seek it' (*WCL*, p. 701). On the few occasions in which Bosie was able to play the role of ephebe, the young ingénu in need of both guidance and erotic devotion from his older lover, Wilde rediscovers his love. But by far the majority of the time the two were together, according to Wilde's imprisoned recollections in any case, not only was Wilde unable to influence him, it seems that the child was father to the man in that Bosie pulled Wilde along into Bosie's sexual interests. In terms of sexual behavior, at least, Bosie seems to have been the one doing the influencing. Wilde does not want to admit this; rather, he retains power by claiming that, if Bosie ruined him, it was only because Wilde allowed him to do so. Nonetheless, Bosie is made to bear responsibility for Wilde's wholesale betrayal of the male procreation theory; he influenced Wilde to abandon the practice of procreation by seeming to embody it so perfectly. Bosie was young, physically small, beautiful, and literally noble; the nickname 'Bosie' by which he was almost universally known among friends stemmed from his mother's use of 'boysie', which she assigned to him before he was ten years old.[3] He was practically labeled as the perfect ephebe.

Ellmann asserts that it was Bosie who introduced Wilde to the London demimonde of male prostitution.[4] The prison letter contains both Wilde's confessions of fascination with and enjoyment of this world, along with his condemnation of Bosie for his indulgences. A certain amount of hypocrisy may be inevitable, but Wilde works hard to explain himself. For Wilde, this new world is a complement to the rarefied heights of art to which he had become accustomed: 'I surrounded myself with the smaller natures and meaner minds. . . . Tired of being on the heights, I deliberately went to the depths in search for new sensations' (*WCL*, p. 730). The renters themselves 'from the point of view through which I, an artist in life, approached them, were delightfully suggestive and stimulating. It was like feasting with panthers' (*WCL*, p. 758). Bosie's renters, however, are not given the same benefit of the aesthetic doubt: 'Your defect was not that you knew so little about life, but that you knew so much. . . . The gutter and the things that live in it had begun to fascinate you' (*WCL*, p. 684). 'When you could not find me to be with, the companions whom you chose as substitutes were not flattering' (*WCL*, p. 704). Again, what Wilde portrays here is an inversion of classical paederastia: the ephebe is initiating the lover into the mysteries of adulthood rather than the other way round. Wilde attempts to retain his adult superiority by claiming that his experiments in sensuality are a conscious aesthetic choice. Having had his fill of Society, as well as, presumably, sex with others in Society, he contrasts the light with dark in a kind of sexual chiaroscuro. Bosie, on the other hand, simply has bad taste. And rather than play the proper paederastic role of allowing his older lover to guide and form his taste, he instead turns his back on aesthetic contrast and embraces only the dark.

For even when the prison letter is at its unapologetic peak as a document in hedonism ('I don't regret for a single moment having lived for pleasure' [*WCL*, p. 739]), it never leaves platonism behind. Wilde is at pains to point out that his interest in Bosie, though it may be erotic, is not physical, and he maintains the body/soul dichotomy so dear to the metaphysics of male procreation. Wilde characterizes Queensberry's interest in his son as being only in his body, while Wilde's lies in his soul, going so far as to claim that Bosie's body 'did not interest me' (*WCL*, p. 708). In defending his decision not to expose the perjury of the Crown's witnesses in his criminal trials, Wilde claims that he could never have purchased freedom at the price of incriminating others, even if those others (presumably Bosie himself) were guilty. 'Sins of the flesh are nothing', he says of his decision. 'They are maladies for physicians to cure, if they should be cured. Sins of the soul alone are shameful' (*WCL*, p. 714).

There is an economic aspect to Wilde's accusations as well. Of course, Wilde overtly places the blame for much of his financial woes onto the shoulders of the Douglas family, who had promised to cover the cost of the Queensberry trial and then failed to come through with adequate funds. There is also the fact that Douglas' movement of his and Wilde's sexual relations into the marketplace of male prostitution made them now a matter of economic negotiations no matter how well Wilde treated the renters and no matter what aesthetic justification he gave to their relationships. But in addition, late in the letter Wilde briefly explores the economics of paederasty. He insightfully claims that Douglas saw his monetary dependence on Wilde as part of his ephebic appeal. 'To make yourself dependent upon me for the smallest as well as the largest sums lent you in your own eyes all the charm of childhood, and in the insisting on my paying for every one of your pleasures you thought that you had found the secret of eternal youth' (*WCL*, p. 768). Douglas' ephebic appeal may have been magnified in Wilde's eyes as well as those of Douglas during the happier days of their relationship, but Wilde in Reading Prison at least sees a stark contrast between the idealized paederastic relationship between the lover and his beloved and the economic reliance of a child on his or her parents. On a strictly material level, the Wilde–Douglas romance was paederastic, while on the spiritual level Wilde came to see it as a grotesque inversion of true paederastia. Bosie was an ephebe of the pocketbook only.

Here is the point where the symbolic filial relationship of paederasty butts heads with literal paternity. One of the cruelest parts of queer failure under which Wilde was forced to suffer was permanent separation from his two sons. In the prison letter, for reasons about which I cannot even hazard a guess, Wilde's older son, Cyril, is used as a synecdoche for the combination of himself and the younger son, Vyvyan.[5] Wilde several times compares Douglas to Cyril at Douglas' expense. Cyril is 'that beautiful, loving, loveable child of mine, my friend of all friends, my companion beyond all companions, one single hair of whose little golden head should have been dearer and of more value to me than, I will not merely say you from top to toe, but the entire chrysolite of the whole world' (*WCL*, p. 715). Certainly it is possible to interpret Wilde's turn to his literal children as an essentially conservative return to heterosexual family values after it was too late (Wilde was never to see Cyril and Vyvyan again). But I think that there is more to this contest of filiation. Douglas is the inadequate ephebe and thus the bad son. Moreover, not only do Douglas' failures as a junior partner in male procreation affect his and Wilde's relationship, they prevent the germination of Wilde's ideas. Bosie Douglas is thus not only himself the bad son, but he prevents further intellectual offspring. He is the death of Wilde's children of the mind. The children of the body, then, are idealized into a kind of pure potential, an embodiment of the male procreative principle. Cyril becomes the new model of the friend and companion. If he is not exactly an ephebe, he nonetheless participates in the veneration of young manhood that enables male procreation. He is the literal child that symbolizes the child of the imagination. In this instance, Wilde is able to combine the imaginative nature of male procreation with his physical offspring. By playing simultaneous roles as both literal son and partner in potential imaginative creation, Cyril makes the perfect emblem for Wilde's vision of his legacy.[6]

In contrast to this image of Cyril as the perfect child, the proper companion for Wilde and his intellectual development where Douglas had provided only intellectual stultification, one of Wilde's final denigrations in the prison letter portrays Douglas again as a child. This time, however, rather than the clinging dependence of previous accusations, the child comparison denotes a petulant, destructive immaturity. Wilde compares Douglas to a child who has found 'a toy too wonderful for its little mind' (*WCL*, p. 773); since he cannot properly understand what he has come upon, he promptly breaks the toy. 'Having got hold of my life, you did not know what to do with it. You couldn't have known. It was too wonderful a thing to be in your grasp. You should have let it slip from your hands and gone back to your own companions at their play. But unfortunately you were wilful, and so you broke it' (*WCL*, p. 773). Douglas is thus the bad child, the repository for all the negative qualities associated with childhood, while Cyril is allowed to assume the positive image of pure potential. Cyril is at once the literal child of

biological procreation and the figurative child of its male–male counterpart. He supplants Bosie as the perfect ephebe, though a thoroughly
platonized one. Wilde describes the loss of his legal rights as a parent
as a devastating blow, one from which he could partially recover only
through a religious submission: 'I flung myself on my knees, and bowed
my head, and wept and said "The body of a child is as the body of the
Lord: I am not worthy of either." That moment seemed to save me'
(*WCL*, p. 744). From a disavowal of interest in Douglas' body, Wilde has
moved into a substitution, or perhaps a transubstantiation, of Cyril's
body for the soul of the child. In alluding to the moment in the Roman
Catholic Mass just prior to the breaking of the Host,[7] Wilde once again
testifies to the communication between soul and body that informs the
concept of personality. He is denied the body of the boy, and he turns
the denial into an act of faith: his betrayal of male procreation under
the influence of Douglas has left him unworthy of his own offspring,
both physical and cultural. Yet in the Mass, this moment of confession
of unworthiness is immediately followed by the reception of the body.
In denying his worthiness to touch the body of Cyril, Wilde is perhaps
holding out a hope that his confession also prefaces the reception of
what he is unworthy to have. The body of the boy, the son, becomes
Wilde's new object of worship, and one that would remain forever
unattained.

The relation between soul and body is up for constant negotiation.
Where the relationship with Bosie had been based on a supposed disinterest in his body, Wilde communicates his desire for Cyril in fleshy
terms, but the flesh is the eucharistic flesh of the incarnated soul. The
turn from Bosie to Cyril might thus provide a kind of solution to the sexual paradox into which Wilde has worked himself in his relations with
Douglas. I see little reason to doubt Ellmann's description of Wilde's
sexual practice once he had been initiated into the world of renters
by Douglas—other aspects of Ellmann's biography are certainly and
understandably suspect, but no evidence has surfaced that seriously
questions the idea that Wilde and Douglas only rarely had sex with
each other, and then only in the earliest stages of their relationship.
Rather, their practice was to go out together to brothels and pick up
young men in their late teens whom they brought back to hotel rooms
paid for by Wilde. As Ellmann points out, these arrangements might
have allowed Wilde to 'think of their [Wilde and Douglas'] attachment
as an approximation of the Greek ideal'.[8] Douglas was allowed to be
the beautiful, inspirational soul because the renters were there to take
on the merely physical parts of sex. Wilde could thus, at times at least,

construct Douglas into the ideal junior partner in male procreation: effeminate, beautiful, talented, and appreciative of the lover's talents and devotion. He could be Mr W. H., Cyril Graham, and Dorian Gray. In a sense, the arrangement did replay a Greek ideal: two of them in fact. Douglas and Wilde formed a paederastic couple potentially capable of male procreation. At the time, Wilde might well have believed in Bosie as inspiration, even if he would change his mind in prison.[9] Yet they also formed a couple along the lines of one of Halperin's other pre-orientation categories: they were friends. As Halperin explicates it, classical friendship more or less excludes sexual activity. The paederastic relationship demands a denigration, however softened, of the junior partner, while friendship is a condition between equals. The renters, by taking the denigration upon themselves, allowed Wilde and Douglas to achieve a friendly paederastia.

On the other hand, a different way of seeing the same situation might put it far more bluntly. Wilde loved the English aristocrat; he fucked the working class teenagers. The price of his attempt to combine paederastia and friendship into a new queer ideal was the replication of some of the most banal facets of class prejudice, as well as a demonstration that the virgin/whore dichotomy need not be endemic only to cross-sex relations. He also foundered on the logic that formed what Foucault called one of the 'great disjunctions' of ancient boy-love; summarizing Plutarch's *Dialogue on Love*, Foucault states 'if the *eromenos* is virtuous, one cannot obtain this pleasure except by subjecting him to violence; and if he consents, one has to recognize that one is consorting with an effeminate'.[10] Wilde could hardly be unaware of this betrayal of the acceptance of effeminacy he wanted from his ideal self. His attempt in the prison letter to reclaim his relationship with Cyril, while reinforcing the platonic presuppositions on which male procreation is based, might also represent Wilde's attempt to extricate himself from an erotic overinvestment in the metaphysical division between Bosie and the renters, the pure ephebe and the dirty panthers. At the very least, it is an investment in the future, whether conceived in terms of Edelman's conservative reproductive futurity of the Child or Muñoz's potentially radical future of a queer utopia. If we wish to read at all sympathetically with Wilde's vision, we will tend to emphasize the latter possibility.

But I think it is also necessary to acknowledge that Wilde's division of his sexual relations between the personality of Bosie Douglas and the mere physicality of the renters tacitly replays many of the prejudices built into pre-orientation male–male sexuality. In attempting to save the nobility of paederasty, Wilde replicates its prejudices, in that he saves his friend from the disgrace of playing the passive role in same-sex intercourse. This begs the question, of course, that the role must be disgraceful. Friendship, on the other hand, likewise is purified of sexuality, which further invests in the classical prejudice against an erotic element in friendship. Same-sex relations, rather than being an aspect of friendship, become an interest that two friends can share so long as their sexual interests are not focused on each other. Sex, to recall Halperin's phrasing, remains something that you would not do to your friend, although you might do it with him and to someone else.

Simultaneously purging Douglas of the taint of being an object of sexual interest and constructing him as a son, whether an incarnated Word or a prodigal, also allows Wilde to avoid a specter that haunts the discourse of paedersaty as filiation: that of incest. Later in this chapter, I will want to look at the hint of incest that runs throughout Wilde's *Salome*, but first I want to turn back to Wilde's literal sons.

Sons and lovers

Vyvyan Holland, Wilde's younger son, published the memoirs of his childhood in 1954 under the title *Son of Oscar Wilde*. The book chronicles Vyvyan and Cyril's early life of exile from England, the change of their last name from Wilde to Holland, the death of their mother (Constance Wilde died in 1898, just less than a year after Wilde's release from prison), and their education at various boarding schools on the Continent and, eventually, back in England, with Vyvyan attending Stonyhurst and Cyril attending Radley. Throughout the narrative Vyvyan gives an impression of a sense of separation between himself and the rest of society, especially Constance's family, whom he portrays as wanting to push the boys out of sight and thus repress the memory of their father. 'We were told to forget that we had ever borne the name of Wilde and never to mention it to anyone.'[11] Vyvyan, unlike Cyril, spends his youth in ignorance of the nature of the legal charges of which his father was convicted, and with the vague impression that he was dead well before Wilde's actual demise.

Vyvyan also represents Cyril as finding the legacy of their father to be an even heavier burden than in Vyvyan's own experience. Cyril is the one with more knowledge of the family's situation, a knowledge from which 'he wanted to shield me to keep me in ignorance of the truth, so that I should not suffer as he did' (p. 63). Moreover, Cyril from an early age gives himself the task of redeeming the family from ignominy. By the age of eleven, Vyvyan claims, Cyril 'had already started on his determined mission in life to rehabilitate the family name by sheer force of character and by overcoming all weaknesses and obstacles' (p. 107). Much later, when Cyril was an Army officer serving in India a few months prior to the outbreak of the Great War, he wrote an explanation to his brother of how he saw his own life in relation to that of his father. After praising the efforts of Robbie Ross to repair Wilde's damaged reputation, Cyril writes:

> All these years my great incentive has been to wipe that stain away; to retrieve, if may be, by some action of mine, a name no longer honoured in the land. The more I thought of this, the more convinced I became that, first and foremost, I must be a *man*. There was to be no cry of decadent artist, of effeminate aesthete, of weak-kneed degenerate. (Holland's emphasis, p. 140)

The letter, or at least the excerpt from it that Vyvyan provides, concludes with 'I ask nothing better than to end in honourable battle for my King and Country.' Less than a year later, Cyril realized one of his father's quips, that one of the tragedies of life is getting what one wants.

As a personal document, Cyril's letter illustrates part of the queer failure that Wilde's downfall entailed. Cyril felt pressed upon him the need to live in reaction against the stereotype of the Wildean queer: the decadent, effeminate aesthete who, whether because he is really either a woman or a boy, cannot be a man. Cyril felt himself compelled to construct himself instead as a laconic, unplayful adult male without the slightest hint of a feminine personality about him. Joining the military played a large role in this project, despite Vyvyan's contention that Cyril did not get along well with his brother officers: Cyril's refusal of gossip and small talk, as well as his disdain for the aristocratic trappings of hunting, shooting, and athletics, made him an outcast even among those with whom he chose to exile himself (p. 142).[12] Cyril's insistence on masculine maturity, a life lived as much in reaction against childhood as against effeminacy, needs also to be understood as something other than a simple rejection of his father's life and of his symbolic children. Both Cyril and Vyvyan were appreciative of Robbie Ross's efforts to rehabilitate the Wilde name, as different as they were from Cyril's efforts to a similar end. Vyvyan's memoir consistently places both himself and his brother in the Ross camp during the period of time during which litigation made it impossible to remain neutral in the feud between Ross and Douglas. Moreover, Douglas was by this time presenting himself as a public crusader for sexual normality. Cyril's masculinity, in other words, is a conscious inversion of his father's celebration of the playful queer child, but it need not be read as a wholesale rejection of queerness itself. That was to be Bosie's road.

In the context of queer failure, Vyvyan's representation of his and his brother's childhoods, at least after the exile of the family in 1895, contains a bitter irony. Where in the prison letter Wilde used his literal children as a queer ideal, these children saw their own lives as suffering from a foreshortened childhood. The public outrage and the subsequent disbanding of the Wilde family destroyed Vyvyan's childhood as such: from that moment on, as he tells the tale, he lived in a kind of enforced maturity, kept in darkness by Constance's family, yet sufficiently aware of the shadow over him that he could never relax and be playful. When he finally does learn the truth about his father's life, Vyvyan becomes a kind of adopted son to Robbie Ross, thus completing a version of an extended family structure: Ross as Wilde's symbolic child becomes symbolic father to Wilde's literal child.[13] Ross becomes the closest that the adult Vyvyan can get to his father as he was before the trials, and his trust in Ross as expressed in his memoirs is instant and complete: 'from the moment that I met Robert Ross, I knew that I had found a true friend of my own, one who would be loyal and true and never betray me' (p. 186).

Befriending Ross, however, meant making an instant enemy out of that other symbolic child of Wilde, Lord Alfred Douglas. Making sense of the fraught relationship between Ross and Douglas after Wilde's death is a difficult endeavor; even now, both sides have their apologists.[14] The prison letter manuscript plays a central role in much of the conflict. Upon release from prison, Wilde gave the manuscript to Ross with the instructions that he should have two typed copies made and send the original to Douglas. Instead, Ross kept the original and claimed to have sent Douglas a typescript; Douglas, for his part, claimed either to have never received the letter or to have burned it after reading only the first few lines (Douglas' biographer claims that Douglas did burn a letter from Wilde, but it was too short to have been the prison letter).[15] Then, acting in his role as Wilde's literary executor, Ross published a shortened version under the title *De Profundis* in 1905; he removed all the autobiographical elements of the text, including any mention of Bosie. It thus came to be widely if erroneously understood that Wilde's prison letter had been written to Ross. In 1909 Ross made arrangements to deposit the original manuscript in the British Museum where it was to lie unexamined for fifty years, by which point all the principals named in it would be safely dead.

Instead, the prison letter again became a controversy in 1912; in that year, Arthur Ransome published *Oscar Wilde: A Critical Study*, the first book about Wilde that was not a personal reminiscence. And although Ross had refused to edit the final draft of the book, he had nonetheless provided Ransome with considerable insights and documents, including the complete version of the prison letter. Douglas is not mentioned by name in Ransome's book, but he is alluded to in such a way that no one familiar with the Wilde coterie could mistake that Bosie is the person indicated, that he was the intended recipient of the prison letter, or that the letter functions as a personal indictment of him. Douglas himself claimed that reading Ransome's book was the way he discovered that *De Profundis* had begun its convoluted literary life as a personal letter addressed to him.

Douglas was so incensed that he sued Ransome's publishers for libel. Part of the trial involved the complete text of the prison letter being used as evidence for the defense. Douglas lost the case and blamed Ross as the supposed ghostwriter of Ransome's book. Thus when a publisher offered him an advance of £500 to write his own version of events, Douglas jumped at the chance and then had his editorial associate, T. W. H. Crosland, do the writing for him. Douglas had wanted *Oscar Wilde and Myself* to include the complete version of the prison letter, along with his own practically line-by-line rebuttal of it, but Ross held the copyright and prevented this from happening. Legal disputes further delayed the book's appearance until 1914, well after the popular furor cased by the Ransome trial of 1912 had died down, and thus considerably diminishing the book's sales. Ross earned even more of Douglas's enmity.

The Alfred Douglas who thus squared off against Ross was a very changed man from the ephebic Bosie, the constant companion of Wilde. His boyish good looks had not entirely deserted him, but Douglas had married and fathered a son in 1902 and had joined the Roman Catholic Church in 1911. Unlike so many *fin-de-siècle* aesthetes who turned to Catholicism, including Ross,[16] Douglas' new found religion was part of his persona as a moral crusader ridding England of vice and sexual deviance. Rather than hide his previous relationship with Wilde, he now publicly repudiated it at every opportunity. He had even gone so far as to attack Ross physically at a reception in 1912, calling him 'nothing but a bugger and a blackmailer'.[17] He was assisted in his moral campaign by his ghostwriter, Crosland, whose distaste for same-sex love bordered on the obsessive. The unrepentantly queer Ross became their primary target, and they employed private detectives to spy on Ross; his lover, Freddie Smith; and his secretary, Christopher Millard.

In 1914 Crosland was arrested for libeling Ross; Douglas was also under indictment, but he remained in France. Crosland's trial, however, ended in his acquittal. A few months later, the outbreak of war caused Douglas to return to England. Subsequently, he also was put on trial for libeling Ross. He in turn pleaded justification, just as his father had done in Wilde's first trial. H. G. Wells, Edmund Gosse, and Vyvyan Holland testified on Ross's behalf, the last claiming that Ross had been 'a second father' to him.[18] The presiding judge's summation, however, expressed a disparaging surprise that Ross had never condemned same-sex love: 'I don't recall that there is any copy or extract which has been produced indicating that he disapproved or that he viewed this kind of vice with disgust.'[19] The jury was unable to reach a verdict, and Ross ultimately decided not to pursue the case further.

Douglas spent most of the remainder of the war years fuming at Ross and waiting for an opportunity for revenge. Ross's apparent success annoyed Douglas immensely. Ross had been publicly feted by many of the London literary establishment following the unsuccessful trial, and Douglas's response had been a denunciatory poem entitled 'The Rossiad', which blamed Ross and his circle for losing the war. Politics played a role in this resentment in that Douglas was a lifelong Tory while Ross was cultivating friendship with the Liberal Prime Minister H. H. Asquith and his wife, the former Margot Tennant. During this time Douglas also wrote another book on Wilde, this time without Crosland's assistance. The project was designed specifically to destroy Wilde's reputation as a person and as a writer, and thus to undo Ross's labors of the past twenty years. The resulting manuscript, *The Wilde Myth*, was so inflammatory that it was immediately refused by its publisher and, in fact, has never been published. Additionally, in an added irony given the question of filiation with which this chapter contends, Douglas in 1915 finally lost legal custody of his son to his father-in-law, his marriage having crumbled some years previously.

The frustrated, bereft, and nearly bankrupt Douglas got his chance at revenge on Ross with the rise of a right-wing independent Member of Parliament named Noel Pemberton Billing. The events of the Pemberton Billing affair, as it came to be known, are well documented and have been productively analyzed from a variety of popular and scholarly perspectives, and I will merely outline them in order to provide context for the reinsertion of *Salome* into Wilde's posthumous story, as well as its relation to the ongoing Great War.[20] In January 1918, Billing's newspaper, the *Imperialist*, published an unsubstantiated accusation under the heading of 'The Forty-Seven Thousand'. The article claims that 'a certain German prince' retains a book containing the names of 47,000 British citizens who are subject to blackmail due to their twisted sexual tastes. These compromised Britons, subject to vices 'all decent men thought had perished in Sodom and Lesbia', were responsible for the failure of Britain to win the war. Moreover, the article claims that this systematic sexual undermining by secret German agents actually pre-dates the war, having begun twenty years previously, in the late 1890s. The implied chronology, then, has massive German infiltration begin-ning soon after the Wilde trials, resulting in the eventual 'demoralizing' of British sailors and the betrayal 'in Lesbian ecstasy' of 'the most sacred secrets of State'.[21]

The initial article had little impact. The situation changed, however, when the novelist Marie Corelli alerted Billing to the announcement in the 10 February *Sunday Times* of a private performance of Oscar Wilde's *Salome* and suggested that its subscribers would likely form a solid representation of the morally compromised 47,000. As a result, Billing published an even more inflammatory if much briefer article in his newspaper, now renamed *The Vigilante*. It basically restated Corelli's accusation that a significant portion of the 47,000 would be found among the audience for Wilde's play, but it went further in that it spe-cifically named Maud Allan, the dancer/actress who would play the title role, and it published its suggestion that Scotland Yard should seize the list of subscribers under the headline 'The Cult of the Clitoris'.

In an uncanny parallel of the events of 1895, Maud Allan and her producer, J. T. Grein, sued Billing for libel. Billing pleaded justification, and the subsequent trial allowed Billing, as well as Douglas, to subject *Salome* to a hostile analysis that saw it as consciously incorporating sexological (and thus German) ideas such as 'open representation of degenerated sexual lust, sexual crime, and unnatural passions' (p. 109). The supposed discoverer of the black book, Harold Spencer, character-ized the titular character of Wilde's play as 'a child suffering from an enlarged and diseased clitoris' (p. 132); this necessitated an explanation in the court, as no one other than Spencer seemed to know what a clito-ris was.[22] Billing's expert witness, a medical doctor named Serell Cooke, claimed that the play presented in dramatic form a kind of guided tour of the sexual perversions presented in Krafft-Ebing's *Psychopathia Sexualis*, a point that Douglas reiterated when he claimed that Wilde had read Krafft-Ebing prior to writing *Salome* (pp. 145–7). Throughout the trial Billing, acting as his own lawyer, attempted to link Wilde's lin-gering influence toward sexual perversity to Germany's sinister efforts to undercut the British war effort.

He was evidently successful, for Billing was acquitted of all charges. Maud Allan's career never recovered from her association with the trial, and Douglas could feel that he had finally triumphed over Robbie Ross. Ross had opposed going to trial from the beginning and advised J. T. Grein not to sue, but to no avail. After the verdict, which was greeted in the courtroom by raucous applause, Ross wrote to Charles Ricketts 'The English, intoxicated into failure, enjoyed tearing poor Maud Allan to pieces, simply because she had given them pleasure, and kicking Oscar's corpse to make up for the failure of the 5th Army.'[23] Within five months of the verdict, Ross died of a heart attack at the age of forty-nine.

The Billing affair is important for investigating Wilde's posthumous legacy for at least three reasons. First, it demonstrates that Wilde's name was still a major cultural force, both for the progressive and artistic set who rallied around Maud Allan (and included former Prime Minister Asquith and his wife) and for the conservative guardians of public morals, among whom Bosie Douglas now wished to be counted. Secondly, it demonstrates how the sexual, ethical, and legal challenges to Wilde's work continued well after his trials and included the application of the emergent discourse of sexology onto the text of *Salome*. The application was intended to be hostile to both Wilde and sexology, but the strategy of Billing's successful defense hinged on linking Wilde with the almost exclusively continental and stereotypically German medicalization of sexual 'perversion', despite Wilde's own attempts during his lifetime not to allow the meanings of his texts and his ruminations on same-sex love to be tied to such theories. Lastly, Billing and Douglas' opportunistic suture of *Salome*'s perversions as viewed through the sexological microscope to the perceived failures of the British war effort displays the extent to which Wilde was politicized during the Great War. In 1895 *Dorian Gray* was put on trial as evidence of its author's personal foibles. In 1918 *Salome* was put on trial as evidence, however ridiculous, of the use of Wilde as weaponized perversity, part of the German arsenal to defeat Britain at home and thus negate the brave efforts of the troops in Flanders fields.

Billing constantly reinforced the idea that his moral crusade against the ghost of Wilde was part of the greater war effort. As Douglas had put it in his 1916 poetic diatribe 'The Rossiad', 'two enemies thou hast / The German and the sodomite'. Billing packed the Old Bailey with wounded soldiers and referred constantly to the war in his conduct of his own defense, while Douglas for his part ratcheted up the rhetoric from politics to metaphysics, calling Wilde 'a diabolical influence on everyone he met. I think he is the greatest force for evil that has appeared in

Europe during the last 350 years' (p. 152). The timing of the trial was also of great significance. The 'Cult of the Clitoris' article appeared on 16 February of 1918 while the libel trial began in May. Intervening in March and April of 1918 was the last major German offensive of the war, during which the new *sturmtruppen* tactics temporarily broke the stalemate of trench warfare in an effort to knockout the Western allies following the withdrawal of Russia from the war and before the large-scale deployment of US forces. British panic about the offensive had peaked around 11 April with Douglas Haig's 'backs to the wall' general order; in many ways, Billing and Douglas were attempting to ride that wave of panic for as long as they could. But whether as posthumous secret agent or sexual Mephistopheles, the Billing affair constructed Wilde as corrupting much more than a few young Londoners. The lingering influence of Wilde was portrayed as a venereal disease sapping the strength of the nation.

In the reading of *Salome* that follows, I want to bring this paranoid hermeneutic of disease to bear on the related question of incest as described in the first part of this chapter. In short, I will read *Salome* in the context of Wilde's idea of masculine procreation through symbolic filiation which, as I have indicated, always exists in the neighborhood of incest. The beloved ephebe is the symbolic son, potentially both inspiration for and product of same-sex love. Moreover, as I pointed out above, during his prison term Wilde had begun to substitute his biological son for his symbolic one, warding off the specter of incest through the iconography of the Eucharist. Although hinted at in *A Woman of No Importance*, it is in *Salome* that this incestuous logic comes closest to the fore, and the *symboliste* aesthetics of *Salome* are much more amenable to the exploration of non-literal incest than are the realist confines of the social comedy.

In a similar manner to my insistence that we take seriously Edward Carson's accusations of *Dorian Gray* as a coded text, this interpretation of *Salome* will likewise attempt to give the Billing–Douglas account of the play as a taxonomy of satanic perversion, if not quite serious attention, then at least an acquiescent nod. *Salome* is not *Psychopathia Sexualis* translated into drama, and Alfred Douglas' 1918 insistence that Wilde had written the play as a kind of crib of Krafft-Ebing is, I think, about as worthy of factual consideration as are most of Bosie's statements under oath. Nonetheless, the play is deeply concerned with articulations of non-normative desire to the extent that a thoughtful audience is forced to consider whether such a thing as normative desire even exists in the play—and perhaps out of it as well.

Seeing and hearing Salome

That a play that had never been publicly performed in Britain could prove so controversial is itself remarkable. Famously, *Salome* had been refused a license by the office of the Lord Chancellor in 1892, ostensibly because plays depicting biblical characters had been strictly forbidden since the reign of Henry VIII. The first production thus never got out of rehearsal.[24] Wilde wrote the play in French, and an English version with illustrations by Aubrey Beardsley was published in early 1894; Alfred Douglas played some role in the translation process, though how much was a question Wilde and Douglas never agreed upon.[25] The play's first actual production took place in Paris while Wilde was in prison. It became popular on the Continent while remaining ignored in Britain, prompting Robbie Ross to comment in his 1908 edition of the *Collected Works* that *Salome* was 'a household word wherever the English language is not spoken'.[26] A German production inspired Richard Strauss to write his opera, which premiered in 1905, and the success of which inspired Maud Allan to develop her dance 'A Vision of Salome', which she debuted in Vienna in 1906. Her appearance in Grein's 1918 private production of Wilde's play was an effort at once to move from pure dance into acting and to rekindle the 'salomania' that had energized her career before the war. Thanks to Billing, her efforts were unsuccessful. *Salome* was not publically produced in England until 1931.[27]

As I mention above, *Salome* is the Wildean text most directly concerned with incest, yet is a strange kind, or kinds, of incest. Primarily, of course, the plot centers on Herod's desire to see Salome dance; Herod seems to spend the majority of his time on stage staring lustfully at Salome. Yet, as the text is careful to point out, Salome is not Herod's biological daughter. She is the child of Herodias and Herod's brother, the latter of whom Herod had killed prior to marrying the former, and thus she is Herod's niece. Were Herod's blood relationship to Salome the only reason for accusations of incest, Herodias would have to be considered immune to such charges and the prophet's curses should be aimed only at the Tetrarch. But one of Jokanaan's many rejections of Salome is an accusation of her mother: 'Daughter of an incestuous mother, be thou accursed!' (p. 591). Though Herod is related by blood to Salome, he is not so related to Herodias. Where the grounds for an accusation of incest against Herod are obvious, against Herodias they are not nearly so clear. Yet when Herod recalls Jokanaan's accusations, the wording he uses is that the marriage itself is 'incestuous' (p. 598).

Most probably, Wilde had *Hamlet* in mind.[28] Just as Hamlet is the only character in Shakespeare's play to object to Gertrude and Claudius' marriage in terms of incest, Jokanaan is the only one to classify Herod and Herodias' marriage in the same category. Other characters in *Hamlet* respond to accusations of murder; unlike Claudius, however, Herod freely admits that he killed his brother before marrying his wife. Only Jokanaan uses the accusation of incest in the play, and he seems to do so from the same basis that Hamlet does: he interprets Herod and Herodias' marriage as spiritually consanguineous, to use medieval terminology. Because Herodias was married to Herod's brother, she was (and remains) Herod's sister-in-law or, more pertinently, sister-in-the-sight-of-God. Marriage with her is thus tantamount to marriage to a biological sister, or at least it appears this way to Jokanaan just as it does to Hamlet in the case of Gertrude and Claudius. In both *Salome* and *Hamlet*, it is the character with the strongest investment in metaphysical reality that maintains the strictest definitions of incest. Hamlet condemns his mother on evidence provided by his ghostly father, while Jokanaan's status as a prophet of the monotheistic God provides him with the moral backing to get away with insults to the ruling family. Jokanaan's prophetic voice calling from the wilderness of the echoing cistern is able to lay a claim on both Herod and Salome, even while it condemns them.

This voice of Jokanaan, or Jokanaan as a voice, is a dominant aspect of the schematic I want to present for *Salome*.[29] Much scholarship of *Salome* has concentrated on its specularity, its obsession with looking and being-looked-at-ness (in Laura Mulvey's deservedly well known phrase).[30] The visual elements of *Salome* are indeed unmistakable, and Wilde was acutely aware of the status of his play as a visual icon. Even in its published format, the only one it was given in Britain during his lifetime, Wilde wanted a text that was much more fully illustrated than any of his other publications. Yet in balance with this emphasis on *Salome* as a text to be seen, I want to accentuate it also as a text to be heard. Moreover, I want to suggest that the specularity of the text is linked to the Hellenistic elements within it, which is to say its systematic representation of the multicultural Hellenistic world in the microcosm of the Herodian court. The auditory element, on the other hand, I link to the Judeo-Christian characters: the enumerated Jews and Nazarenes, and above all, Jokanaan. Like all schematics of Wilde texts, this one will be subject to revision and rearrangement, but it provides a useful place to begin.[31]

I am suggesting here that one of the main attractions of this biblical story to Wilde, in addition to the extremely well documented history of French literary and artistic fascination with the figure of Salome throughout the nineteenth century,[32] is the opportunity it provided him to present a contrast between two conflicting cultures: the Hellenistic world of Greek culture as exported by Alexander the Great and his disunited heirs, and the Judaic world of concentrated monotheism and constant debate over the minutiae of religious interpretation.[33] Furthermore, this contrast is explored at the exact moment at which a crisis forces these worlds together in a way that will have literally world-altering implications. The rise of Christianity will send waves of Hebraic thought throughout the Greek-speaking world, exporting a version of Jewish monotheism into the Roman empire that echoes the spread of Greek culture throughout the Near East in the aftermath of Alexander's conquests. Wilde represents Herod's court as a meeting place for, on the one hand, worldly pagans such as Tigellinus and, on the other, Jews and proto-Christians (as the Nazarenes seem to be). This meeting place, however, turns out to be less of forum for the exchange of cultural ideas than a common area where the groups are able mutually to ignore each other with convenience and where attempts to cross cultural and ideological boundaries are met with prejudice and lethal violence.[34]

One of the prime contrasts between the Hellenistic and Judeo-Christian cultures lies in the aforementioned emphasis on either specularity or audition. The opening of *Salome* illustrates this sensory dichotomy nicely. We open with the Page and the Young Syrian discussing the appearance of the moon and trading similes that reveal each character's obsessions: death in the case of the Page and the beauty of the Princess Salome in the case of the Young Syrian. Interrupting this discussion of what the moon looks like, we hear but do not see a group of Jews 'disputing about their religion' (p. 583). This offstage hubbub expands the onstage discussion to include more representatives of the Hellenistic near east, including soldiers from Herod's household, a Cappadocian (from central eastern Asia Minor), and a Nubian (from the upper Nile valley). These representatives of the remnants of Alexander's broken empire, currently being reorganized by the Romans, turn their discussion to religion in response to the Jewish debate. The Cappadocian and the Nubian compare their polytheistic backgrounds, with the Cappadocian lamenting the demise of his gods with the coming of the Romans while the Nubian describes the unappeasable gods of his homeland. When confronted with the idea that 'The Jews worship a God that you cannot see' (p. 584), the Cappadocian is flustered and offended, claiming that it is 'altogether ridiculous' to 'believe in things that you cannot see' (p. 584).

The exchange about an invisible God is immediately followed by the introduction of Jokanaan as an invisible voice. He speaks from the depths of his cistern prison and interjects the language of Judeo-Christian scripture into the ongoing Hellenistic discourse. Thus at the beginning of the play Hellenistic paganism is something visible that speaks about the visible, while Judeo-Christianity is represented by the divinely inspired Word emanating from an invisible source. Neither Jokanaan nor his monotheistic God can be seen, and one has to take on faith the idea that Jokanaan's voice speaks words that accurately represent this unseen God. Yet Herod has just enough of this faith, or at least the negative fear that Jokanaan might not be just a madman speaking of his own volition, to keep Jokanaan alive and to maintain a suspension of disbelief about his status as the prophet of the invisible God.

Read from this perspective, *Salome* becomes a struggle between a desire that is caused by what is seen and one that is caused by what is heard. The former we can basically ascribe to Greek classicism: as Socrates claims in the *Symposium*, love enters through the eyes.[35] The Hellenistic characters all look at the moon and develop similes that reveal their own desire. Judeo-Christian desire, however, is aural: like the Holy Spirit at the Annunciation, it enters through the ear. It centers on the divine *logos*.

Moreover, the rhetoric of the two civilizations is likewise bifurcated. The Hellenistic characters deal obsessively in similes. As already mentioned, they spend so much of their time looking at the moon and saying what it is like that Herodias' literal-minded insistence that 'the moon is like the moon, that is all' (p. 592) can be read as a kind of comic relief that interrupts a potentially endless exchange of similes. The Judeo-Christian people of the Book, on the other hand, prefer metaphor.[36] Jokanaan's language especially, which consists of an amalgam of The Song of Songs, several of the latter prophets, and John of Patmos' Revelation, also implies that one thing is like another, but does so by speaking in a code of direct identification, not the explicit comparison of the Hellenistic simile. Each of Jokanaan's hearers can then decide whether any of his utterances are directly relevant to him or her.

Jokanaan's objectless oracular rhetoric can be illustrated by his first speech as he emerges from the cistern and thus becomes an object of sight while still maintaining his status as the source of heard language. Jokanaan fills his first breaths in the open air after an indeterminate imprisonment not with relief, but with invective:

JOKANAAN: Where is he whose cup of abominations is now full?
            Where is he, who in a robe of silver shall one day die in

the face of all the people? Bid him come forth, that he may hear the voice of him who had cried in the waste places and in the houses of kings. (p. 588)

Jokanaan never speaks in similes: 'x is like y' is not part of his vocabulary or his thought process. Rather, he offers images that are at once concrete ('a robe of silver') and vague ('shall one day die'). And he commands this unnamed person to come forth, not to see the prophet of the Lord, but specifically to hear his voice. Yet the vagueness of his commands results in no action, as the Hellenistic characters throw up their hands in frustration at the impenetrability of Jokanaan's rhetorical style.

SALOME: Of whom is he speaking?
THE YOUNG SYRIAN: You never can tell, Princess.

Put simply, the Hellenistic characters can see Jokanaan, but they cannot hear him. The Prophet can hear the Hellenistic characters, especially Salome, but he cannot or will not see them.

 Jokanaan's next speech reinforces the difficulties of communication between these two groups while dragging in a specifically sexual accusation:

JOKANAAN: Where is she who, having seen the images of men painted on the walls, the images of the Chaldeans limned in colours, gave herself up unto the lust of her eyes, and sent ambassadors into Chaldea?

Salome interprets this accusation as a barb aimed at her mother, which the Young Syrian denies. His refusal of the most obvious interpretation provides another important insight into Jokanaan's style that will be repeated often in the play: no matter how contextually unambiguous Jokanaan's accusations become, his insistence on the concrete vagaries of Hebrew oracular rhetoric mean that the Hellenistic characters can always assume, or at least pretend, that his accusations and prophecies are not meant for their most obvious targets. Herodias is, of course, the only possible referent of Jokanaan's accusation of feminine lust within the context of the play. The Young Syrian's denial of the obvious seems to stem from a desire to spare the feelings of the beautiful young princess with whom he is as visually obsessed as Herodias was with her multicolored Chaldeans. He knows as well as anyone that Jokanaan is condemning Herodias, but the Prophet's style always allows an escape. It is thus no less elusive than the Hellenistic similes, the potentially infinite stream of comparisons that can forever tell us what a thing is like, but not what it is. Jokanaan will tell us what a person has done or will do, but the question of who that person is remains indefinitely deferred.

Just as important as the escape hatch that Jokanaan's rhetoric always leaves open, however, is his condemnation of the visual. Just as in the first speech cited above he insists that he must be heard rather than seen, in this speech he portrays visual representation, even the visual sense itself, as sinful. Likewise, when the Princess finally does see Jokanaan, she begins to fit him into the Hellenistic regime of the simile, and she does so initially by making comparisons to describe his eyes: 'They are like black holes, . . . they are like black caverns' (p. 589). Jokanaan unsurprisingly objects to being seen and does so precisely in terms of his wish to remain immune to the visual: 'Who is this woman who is looking at me? I will not have her look at me' (p. 589). Salome's comparison of Jokanaan's eyes to holes and caverns simultaneously calls attention to the fact that Jokanaan has eyes, a fact that he seems to need reminding of, and practically labels them as non-functioning. Part of Jokanaan's visual appeal to Salome is the appearance of his eyes, yet his eyes seem to be a part of himself that Jokanaan rejects. In the remainder of this initial exchange between the princess and the prophet, Salome will move on to Jokanaan's voice ('thy voice is wine to me' [p. 589]),[37] his body, his hair, and lastly his mouth, subjecting each to a series of similes.

Her discourse on Jokanaan's mouth is interrupted by the Young Syrian's suicide, but not before Salome has set up her final speech by promising 'I will kiss thy mouth, Jokanaan. I will kiss thy mouth' (p. 590). By moving from eyes to mouth, Wilde is subtly sliding the princess toward Jokanaan's mode of expression, but not in a way that he can accept. She goes from hearing him as a voice and being intrigued, then having him removed from the cistern, at which point she becomes enamored through the eyes as she sees him as a body. Having gone through two cycles of attraction and disgust based on his body and hair, her fixation on Jokanaan's mouth never turns sour. She desires the source of his oracular rhetoric, the source of his prophetic voice, yet her desire to kiss this source is one that, given Jokanaan's rejection of visual and physical desire, is destined to either frustration or a perverse consummation. She wants his voice, the source of his allurement, but she wants also to shut him up: he will not be able to prophesy when Salome's lips cover his own.

Comparatively, Herod's desire for Salome is straightforward, acceptable, one might even say normal. He is an older man who is delighted by the youth and beauty of a girl, which is a position that, allowing for a change of sex in the beloved object, is indicative of the unequal relationship favored by the tenets of Wildean male procreation. What proves objectionable in this case, however, is not the sex of the ephebe but the symbolic relationship between desirer and desired. As pointed out above, the incestuous relationship to which Jokanaan objects is the marriage between Herod and Herodias; though they are not blood relatives, they are symbolically brother and sister. Herod's desire for Salome, then, though it is no more incestuous than his marriage to Herodias on the literal level, is a potentially devastating case of inter-generational incest between symbolic father and daughter. Salome's simultaneous denial and awareness of her symbolic father's lust is the subject of her first speech:

> Why does the Tetrarch look at me all the while with his mole's eyes under his shaking eyelids? It is strange that the husband of my mother looks at me like that. I know not what it means. In truth, yes I know it. (p. 586)

The almost comically plain contradiction in the speech operates as a kind of guide to the machinations of desire in the play. Characters both know and do not know why they desire and what such desire means. They consciously analyze desire while they simultaneously experience tempestuous and inexplicable shifts in desire that seem to leave them awe-struck spectators at their own contradictory utterances. Salome can thus move effortlessly from a frank admission of her desire ('Jokanaan, I am amorous of thy body' [p. 589]) to an equally frank dismissal ('Thy body is hideous' [p. 590]) in the space of one of Jokanaan's speeches.

The operations of desire can be further illustrated by the fourfold relationship that dominates the play until the entry of Herod. The Page of Herodias looks at the Young Syrian, who looks at Salome, who looks at Jokanaan (who looks at an invisible God). Much like the potentially limitless series of similes that dominate the Hellenistic characters' rhetoric, this series of unrequited relationships based on gazing seems fully capable of maintaining itself indefinitely. Yet from the beginning of the play, the Page is focused on interrupting the gazing. He first warns the Young Syrian that he should not gaze on Salome, claiming that 'it is dangerous to look on people in such fashion' (p. 584). These unsuccessful attempts to distract the Young Syrian from his object continue almost to the moment of the former's suicide. Salome, for her part, needs only to promise to return the Young Syrian's gaze for him to comply with her will to bring Jokanaan out of the cistern: 'I will look at you through the muslin veils. I will look at you' (p. 588). Coquettishly attracting and then withdrawing herself from the Young Syrian's sight, the Princess plays with his gaze. This process begins, in fact, before she even appears to the audience's gaze and is directly juxtaposed to the invisibility of Jokanaan:

THE CAPPADOCIAN:	May one see him?
FIRST SOLDIER:	No. The Tetrarch has forbidden it.
THE YOUNG SYRIAN:	The Princess has hidden her face behind her fan! (p. 585)

Wilde moves unswervingly from the enforced invisibility of the Prophet to the volitional invisibility of Salome, pointing out her tactical use of her withdrawal from the gaze as paralleling Jokanaan's absence from the visual. In both cases, the invisibility just prior to the unveiling into the seen serves to pique the interest of the gazer, whether the Young Syrian or Salome. In both cases, the results of the eruption into the visible are disturbing to the onlookers, and in both cases, the viewers' visual fascination leads to their death.

The Young Syrian's suicide is clearly a reaction to Salome's obvious fascination with Jokanaan, yet his violent rejection of the encounter seems less a refusal of her visual fascination with the Prophet than of her insistence in verbalizing it in utterly naked terms. 'Do not speak such words to him. I cannot suffer them' (p. 590) he exclaims in his final speech. From veiling herself with her fan and offering to gaze at the Young Syrian in her market journey the following day, and then only to look at him through the muslin of a veil, Salome's desire is now stripped of all covering. Her encounter with Jokanaan, in other words, is her first dance of the seven veils; the one she performs for Herod is merely a ritual re-enactment of what her words to Jokanaan have already revealed.

After the Young Syrian kills himself as an act of protest against Salome's symbolic public nudity, the Page reveals his own desire. Though he has been warning the Young Syrian against his visual fascination with Salome with all the suspicion of a jealous lover, the Syrian's death allows the Page to vent the only articulation of same-sex desire that occurs in this deeply queer play. He enumerates the gifts he had given the Young Syrian, much like Wilde's own gifts to the renters that would later be brought as evidence against him. The Page mildly critiques the Syrian's narcissism (though Herod later confirms that he was indeed 'fair to look upon' [p. 592]). Above all, he laments this handsome young victim in terms that combine erotic interest and blood relations: 'He was my brother, and nearer to me than a brother' (p. 591). This confession was sufficiently embarrassing that Strauss wrote the part of the Page for a contralto, thereby changing the sex of the character. Even the premiere of *Salome*, staged in Paris by Aurélien Lugné-Poë while Wilde was in prison, compromised the avant-garde standards of the Théâtre de l'Œuvre by casting the Page as female. For my purposes, however, the incestuous imagery is just as important as its same-sex configuration. By having the Page express his grief in terms of family relations, Wilde subtly introduces the theme of incest that haunts Herod's visual fascination with Salome.

Herod's fascination expresses itself most clearly in his request that Salome dance for him. The request is also the fullest expression of incest in the play, a matter to which I must now return. First, however, it is worth pointing out that a performance of *Salome*, whether as an operatic, a dramatic, or a merely imaginative performance, depends largely on the interpretation of the simple stage direction 'SALOME dances the dance of the seven veils' (p. 600). But whether played as an extended exercise in balletic restraint or as a full-on strip tease, the dance temporarily places Salome outside of language and into the realm of the purely visual. Most basically, it of course has the effect of making the Princess appear to accept the stereotypically feminine role that Herod wants to assign her: she seems to hide any trace of her own desire and perform solely as the object of Herod's masculine gaze and for his scopophilic pleasure. Her performance thus sets up the revelation of her own desire in her demand for the head of Jokanaan. Where Herod had taken pleasure in the spectacle of a young girl dancing at his request without regard to her own will, the nakedness of Salome's desire for Jokanaan's death fills him with horror in place of lust. But to remain with our earlier terms, Salome's dance also places her in the Hellenistic world of the visual and removes her entirely, if momentarily, from the Judeo-Christian regime of the word.

The Hellenistic world of visual experience is also, according to my schematic, the realm of the simile. Herod's incestuous and scopophilic desire for Salome, then, places the princess back into the rhetoric of the endless exchange of comparisons. Moreover, since Herod and Salome are not blood relations, Herod's incest is a simile as well. Salome is like Herod's daughter, but she is not, really. Herod is like her father, but is not, really. Much as Salome both does and does not know what it means when the man who is like her father looks at her, this implied simile simultaneously acknowledges and ignores the incest at the heart of its gaze. At the moment of her dance, Salome appears to be a purely visual phenomenon, a silent object completely removed from the Judeo-Christian arena of the verbal prophecy. And she 'appears' thus, not only in the sense that she will immediately claim her voice in demanding the head of Jokanaan, but also in that her appearance is all that remains of her character at the moment of the dance.

Once Salome returns to the verbal, she claims her will with a vengeance. Her specific demand is a triumph of literalism. This does not mean, of course, that there are no symbolic possibilities for the head of Jokanaan: from the source of his oracular voice to the castration of the patriarchal father, her demand is rife with symbolic possibility. But the moment of her demand constitutes a third in the series of Salome's public disrobings. Again her desire is naked and again the male figure who is visually fascinated with her finds himself appalled by her revelation. Herod takes a much longer time in trying to talk Salome out of her desire, but his results are just as much a failure as the Young Syrian's had been. Salome has definitively moved from the purely visual objectification of the dance into the verbal role of the commander. From moving her body to please her symbolic father, she can now, like Rousseau's child, move the world simply by moving her tongue.

Herod's reaction to Salome's revelation of desire is to try to reason his symbolic daughter back to silence and visibility while accusing her of having removed herself from the reach of human voices. He tries, unsuccessfully, to play the role of Jokanaan in that he uses his voice to coax Salome back into her proper function, telling her that her request 'is not what you desire' (p. 601). He tempts her with a litany of desirable objects represented with typical Wildean flourishes; at times he begins to sound like the narrator of *The Picture of Dorian Gray* as he praises the intricacies of birds, jewels, and gemstones. Doing so inevitably leads him back into similes, as the jewels increasingly become 'like' something else: 'I have a collar of pearls, set in four rows. They are like unto moons chained with rays of silver. They are like fifty moons caught in a golden net' (p. 602). Salome will not be tempted back into the Hellenistic preference for the visual over the verbal, however; she insists on her desire to the point that Herod repeatedly claims 'you are not listening' (p. 601).

Herod's accusation focuses attention on Salome's relation to the verbal as a receiver, a listener. Her captivation by Jokanaan is, as we have seen, a relationship with his voice first and foremost. Salome is swept out of the Hellenistic world of simile and visibility and seduced into the Judeo-Christian discourse of hieratic verbal pronouncement. She hears Jokanaan before she sees him, and her visual relationship to him remains elusive and self-contradictory. She is his listener, and Herod's insistence that she is not listening thus contains a heavy irony, no matter how true the accusation might be. Once seduced by Jokanaan's words, Salome can no longer remain content with strings of similes that endlessly make comparisons but never allow desire itself to be spoken. The oracular voice of Jokanaan seems to offer the possibility of a truer mode of meaning even while Jokanaan uses his biblical language to condemn Salome as 'daughter of Sodom' (p. 589), among several other epithets. Jokanaan's Word of the Lord seems to offer the thing itself rather than endless circles of similes with which Salome has had to content herself until the moment she first hears the voice of one crying in the wilderness. But Jokanaan's language remains something from which Salome is always excluded. She can hear his word, but he cannot, or will not, be seduced into visibility: 'Well, thou hast seen thy God, Jokanaan, but me, me, thou didst never see. If thou hadst seen me thou wouldst have loved me' (p. 604). He remains immune to the lures of the visible until the end, and his end turns his head into a silent, visible icon.

Before moving on to the final scenes of *Salome*, I want to attempt to account for how the various threads I have spun here can be brought together into, if not a seamless garment, then at least a muslin veil. The story of *Salome* from this angle is one of failed conversions. Salome herself is drawn out of the Hellenistic world of the simile and into the Judeo-Christian world of the prophetic metaphor. This turns her from a purely visible but silent object of desire into a speaking subject who is able to articulate her desire without embarrassment. Such lack of decorum, however, is not appreciated by her male Hellenistic compatriots, especially the Young Syrian and the Tetrarch. Moreover, as Salome's desire for Jokanaan moves her toward the Judeo-Christian domain of the Word, she gains access to metaphor and the symbolic. Within the play, however, this represents less a triumph than a deferred moment of failure that will lead to her death.

One of the symbolic meanings that Salome must bear as she moves toward the sound of Jokanaan's prophetic voice is that of the incest that is endemic to Wilde's conception of the male procreative principle. Male filiation is figured primarily in terms of cross-sex desire in the play; the representation of same-sex desire could only be hinted at with the Page and the Young Syrian. Salome must thus bear the burden of queer desire in the play, both in her awkward half-acknowledgement of her stepfather/uncle's incestuous attention and her own erotic obsession with Herod's imprisoned prophet. Her annunciation of that desire breaches all decorum, whether Hellenistic or Judeo-Christian, and leads directly to the deaths of the Young Syrian, Jokanaan, and herself. In other words, the two displays of 'heterosexual' desire on which the play hinges are both seen as non-normative, disgusting, and dangerous, even lethal. They are queer.

Jokanaan's death is thus the result of his refusal to see Salome, while Salome's death is the result of the princess in her full nakedness finally being seen, but more importantly heard, by Herod. Herod gets to play the morally upright father at last when he disavows his incestuous desire, but his rejection spills over from his own desire to the object of it. When Herod hears Salome and is forced to see her as a subject, he finds the scene too revolting to take and has the princess crushed beneath the shields of his soldiers, returning her to silence and invisibility. Thus he kills the thing he loves. His choice is one between incest and necrophilia, and he chooses the latter. There is no possibility of 'normal' desire in this play: all desire is warped into violent death.

At this point, it is important to look carefully at the staging of Salome's final scene. After Salome has given her long speech in celebration of her receiving Jokanaan's head, Herod declares her 'monstrous' (p. 604) while her mother voices her approval of her request. Herod's response is to throw Jokanaan's words back in her face by exclaiming 'there speaks the incestuous wife!' (p. 604), thus linking Salome's monstrosity to her mother's (and his own) sexual sin. Herod then rejects the visual in terms even harsher than those used by the Prophet: 'I will not look at things, I will not suffer things to look at me. Put out the torches! Hide the moon! Hide the stars!' (p. 604). His hyperbolic raving leaves the stage in total darkness from which the voice of Salome delivers her final speech. Salome is thus in the place occupied by Jokanaan at the beginning of the play. She speaks from darkness as an invisible voice. She has completed her movement from silent dancer to invisible speaker, and she speaks until the moon, in disobedience to Herod's directive, casts a ray that immediately sends her back into the visible. Given the juxtaposition between Salome's final speech, the stage directions that indicate the lighting of Salome only after this speech has ended, and Herod's order for her execution, it seems that Herod reacts not so much to what he hears as what he sees. He may find Salome's address to the severed head of Jokanaan monstrous, but he orders the monster slain only when he is forced to confront it visually. Salome's appropriation of Jokanaan's voice is perverse to him, but the visual revelation of the princess holding the mutilated source of that voice crosses the line into the unspeakable and the unseeable.

One way in which to understand these interactions lies in seeing them in religious terms—this is, after all, a biblical play. Much like 'The Portrait of Mr W. H.', the trope of conversion is potentially helpful. The play's setting is divided between, on the one hand, a Hellenistic world characterized by paganism, the rhetoric of simile, and the dominance of the visual, while on the other hand we find the Judeo-Christian world characterized by monotheism, the rhetoric of prophetic metaphor, and a distinct preference for the verbal over the 'sinful' visual. Salome's desire is thus expressed in a failed conversion from Hellenism to Judeo-Christianity. Her attempt fails both because Jokanaan's monotheistic ethical purity refuses any compromise with Hellenistic paganism, and because Hellenistic paganism itself turns out to be much less flexible and tolerant than it seems. Jokanaan's monotheism of course refuses all desire that does not take the invisible God as its object. The various enumerated Jews that form the play's other representation of monotheism are so intolerant that they cannot stop disagreeing about their own religion long enough even to notice how much objectionable material they could find in the Hellenistic culture surrounding them. In contrast, this Hellenistic culture seems to offer plenty of room for all kinds of different desire, however queer or non-normative. But Herod is oddly attracted to Jokanaan's inflexible condemnations of his own marriage as incestuous; in a sense, he is as susceptible to conversion as his symbolic daughter. The Hellenistic culture of the play is thus much less lenient than it appears on two levels: it condemns Salome's desire when she speaks it openly, and it is secretly attracted to the moral clarity and inflexibility of Judeo-Christian discourse.

The Hellenistic, of course, is not the Hellenic. There is a sense in which my reading of the play recycles Matthew Arnold's cultural analysis of Hebraism and Hellenism in *Culture and Anarchy*, yet the play's representation of Greek culture as an export product, a compromised and belated version of classical Hellenic culture, is more than an accident of setting.[38] It is, as stated previously, part of what attracted Wilde to the biblical story. As a cultural expression of classical Greece, Hellenistic culture should revel in desire and reserve a space for male procreation, however disguised it may need to be for enthusiasts of the late nineteenth-century London stage. Compared to Jokanaan's Hebraic rectitude, Hellenistic culture is flexible and lenient, a potential conduit for sweetness and light, as well as more varieties of erotic *jouissance* than Judeo-Christian culture could ever tolerate. Nevertheless, *Salome* provides a Greek culture that has been compromised and weakened as it is further removed from classical Athens in space and time. It is a Greek culture that has had to make concessions as it functioned in cultures more or less unknown to classical Greece. As illustrative of the cosmopolitanism of Hellenistic culture as Herod's court may be, it is significant that one of the few nationalities not represented is Greece itself.

The broadminded acceptance of sexual expression that Salome might reasonably have expected from 'Greek' culture is thus not at all what she gets. She is stuck between an indulgent, apparently lenient Greek world that is in fact much more interested in policing her desire than it seemed to be, and a stark, ascetic culture of Hebraic monotheism. Jokanaan's words have half-converted Salome from visibility to verbalism, and she wants Jokanaan to create with her some kind of cultural middle ground where these characters from different worlds can meet. But Jokanaan will not budge, so she stops his voice and turns him into a silent visual icon. Herod kills Salome when she combines Jokanaan's role of voice emanating from the darkness with her already established visibility. In other words, she tries to create the combination of Hellenistic and Judeo-Christian cultures on her own, and her symbolic father, the man with the incestuous gaze, finds her attempt so appallingly perverse that he must put a stop to it by silencing and hiding Salome.

The final scene of *Salome* is justly famous and, of course, the apotheosis of the objectionable sexuality that set Noel Pemberton Billing and Lord Alfred Douglas afire with excited resentment and patriotic disgust. Salome holds the head of Jokanaan, kisses and even bites it, and declares again her undying love and sadness that Jokanaan will not look at her. One does not need a briefing from Krafft-Ebing to detect perversity here. The most obvious reading to a post-Freudian audience would see Salome as a castrating femme fatale who now holds Jokanaan's severed masculine power in her hands, alternately fondling it and threatening to throw it to the dogs. Moreover, it is such usurpation of the phallus that must be punished by Salome's almost immediate demise, thus making the world once again safe for patriarchal dominance. I do not wish to deny such interpretations, but to supplement them with an iconographic reading that again combines religion and male procreation.

It is helpful to refer back to the quotation from the prison letter that I used earlier: 'The body of a child is as the body of the Lord: I am not worthy of either.' More than a scene of castration, I want to look at this iconography as a perverse eucharist. Salome bites, or threatens to bite, the head 'with my teeth as one bites a ripe fruit' (p. 604). She takes Jokanaan's head as the source of his Judeo-Christian oracular voice. As she taunts, moving back into the rhetoric of simile, 'thy tongue, that was like a red snake darting poison, it moves no more' (p. 604). Yet a few lines later, she adopts the language of biblical metaphor in praising

Jokanaan's physical beauty: 'Thy body was a column of ivory set in a silver socket' (p. 604). In a move that will be complete when she becomes an invisible voice speaking from darkness, Salome has both silenced Jokanaan and become him. In biting the head, she claims the flesh of the chaste prophet in the only way she can. Since he would not look at her, she takes his head and points his eyes toward her body, even if his eyes will not open. Since there was no possibility of an embodied sexual relationship while Jokanaan maintained his separateness and purity, she must now consume his flesh in an action that is both perverse, in that it is not the bodily possession of Jokanaan that she really desires, and spiritual, in that it typologically predicts the most sacred moment of the Christianity that Jokanaan himself also typifies.

When Salome kisses the head of Jokanaan, she tastes something bitter and she hesitates in declaring it the taste of blood or of love (p. 605). The metaphysics of Christianity, of course, suggest that these are the same thing: the blood of Christ is an expression of his self-sacrificing love and the means of salvation for his followers. John the Baptist, already acknowledged as the precursor of Jesus by the gospels, now becomes the predictor of the central Christian ritual. In this sense, Salome's story ends with a kind of deathbed confession and reception into a communion that is only at its most nascent state at the moment of her conversion. She is among the first Christian converts and may be the first Christian martyr. But Wilde, of course, is not interested in unmixed piety. Salome's eucharist is just as much a bringing of Jokanaan down to the level of mortal flesh as it is a sanctification of his flesh into eternal food. It is an inverted as well as a perverted eucharist in that it transubstantiates Jokanaan's spiritual invisibility into flesh and blood. It turns his mouth from the source of his oracular rhetoric to the silent object of Salome's fleshly desire. This silver charger contains, not wafers whose substance is said to be flesh, but literal flesh.

In the prison letter Wilde seeks connection to the bodies of his children through the words of the Eucharistic liturgy. He also tacitly rejects the body of Bosie while doing so. As described in the previous section, this connection reveals the incestuous side of male procreation. Insofar as male procreation centers on the figure of the younger male beloved and is intimately tied to ideas of sexual filiation, the idea of ephebe as son is never entirely absent from its conceptualization.[39] The prison letter marks an attempt on Wilde's part to disown the disappointing symbolic child, Bosie, for the pure potential of the literal child, Cyril. This movement toward the body of the child, however, is disturbing in its incestuous implications and requires religious language to move it into a more clearly non-literal meaning. Nonetheless, I do not think that the incestuous implications of male procreation were lost on Wilde prior to his prison sentence. Filiation is part of the appeal of male procreation. It creates ideas and it recreates the people who inspire or embody those ideas. It turns men into fathers and ephebes into incarnated culture. But it also threatens to expose the paederastic relationship as a case of father–son incest.

Salome as a play to be publicly performed on the London stage in 1892, even in French, could not represent same-sex love even in the relatively coded manner that earlier non-dramatic texts such as 'The Portrait of Mr W. H.' and *The Picture of Dorian Gray* had done. Its exploration of incest would have to occur through cross-sex channels. Even then, *Salome*'s incestuous desire is no more literal than that of the male procreation portrayed in the non-dramatic texts. *Salome* represents all desire as perverse: no one gets what or whom they want, and everyone has to make substitutions so that they can want what they are able to get. In the cases of the Young Syrian and Herod, when they see the nakedness of their desired object, they are appalled and moved to violence, self-directed in the first case and other-directed in the latter. In case of the Princess herself, denial of the object results in the violence of the removal of Jokanaan's head so that Salome may speak to and for it. *Salome* is not the guided tour of specific sexual pathologies that Bosie Douglas would have had the British public believe in 1918, but it is a text that undercuts the very notion of normality that any conception of perversion assumes as a standard of comparison. In other words, it is less an illustration of a Krafft-Ebing type of sexology than it is a complete rejection of the cultural logic on which sexology exists. Its eucharistic typology reinforces the inevitability of perversity no matter which way it is interpreted. If it is read as an unholy communion, then sexuality perverts sacred ritual; if it is read as a sanctification of desire, then it is a perverse desire that is sanctified.

Salome with Jokanaan's head is not only an image that encapsulates the movement of Greek/Hellenistic culture toward Judeo-Christian monotheism. It is also an image of perversity, that which was violently rejected or abjected by both Hellenistic and Judeo-Christian culture, combining and usurping the visual iconography of the former and the oracular rhetoric of the latter. Salome dances with the head and speaks for it. Her dance exposes the façade of Hellenistic culture's sexual tolerance, and her speech perverts the prophetic voice that heretofore had only condemned in the name of God. Salome is Wilde's child, existing for just a moment after she has claimed her queer desire and before she is crushed by the social and political forces who had claimed to love her beauty. In her, as in Willie Hughes, he is well pleased.

Placing the child at center stage as the simultaneous object of desire and subject of perversity, *Salome* puts the most potentially disturbing aspect of male procreation in plain view. By turning both Hellenistic and Judeo-Christian rhetorical styles against themselves, it confronts its audience with the failure, not only of male procreation, a self-indictment we have seen before in 'The Portrait of Mr W. H.' and *The Picture of Dorian Gray*, but the failure of all desire, even heterosexual 'normality'. Its perversity in fact exceeds the accusations against it made by Pemberton Billing and Bosie Douglas; where they saw a celebration of perversity at the expense of the putatively normal, I have argued for the play's perversion of the assumption of normality itself. Finally, this perverse child plays between Bosie as failed son and Wilde's biological children as the true beneficiaries of the brighter future promised by male procreation. She is still as much of a misbehaving brat as 'Mr W. H.' and *Dorian Gray*, but her misbehavior, even more than theirs, is how she promises to fulfill the potential represented in her childhood.

5
Priests of Keats: Wilfred Owen's Pre-War Relationship to Wilde

Sucking the sugar stick: the embarrassment of Wilfred Owen

In 1936, William Butler Yeats famously excluded the Great War combatant poets from his *Oxford Book of Modern Verse*. In the Introduction to that volume, he justified his decision as a matter of thematics and, more subtly, poetic fashion.

> I have rejected these poems for the same reason that made Arnold withdraw his *Empedocles on Etna* from circulation; passive suffering is not a theme for poetry. In all the great tragedies, tragedy is a joy to the man who dies; in Greece the tragic chorus danced. When man has withdrawn into the quicksilver at the back of the mirror no great event becomes luminous in his mind; it is no longer possible to write *The Persians*, *Agincourt*, *Chevy Chase*: some blunderer has driven his car on to the wrong side of the road—that is all.[1]

Ostensibly, the poet needs to remain an active force that cannot be overwhelmed by local conditions, even if these conditions involve industrial slaughter on an unprecedented scale. Additionally, just before the passage excerpted above, Yeats characterizes the war poems as having 'for a time considerable fame';[2] the seemingly throw-away qualifier 'for a time' of course implies that whatever notoriety the war poets had achieved by the mid 1930s was a temporary anomaly. Their passivity was a fad; the Yeatsian active version of the egotistical sublime would soon return to its proper place of dominance.

Yeats does not mention any names in his public repudiation of the war poets, but in his letters to Dorothy Wellesley justifying his editorial decisions, it becomes clear exactly whom he meant to expel:

> When I excluded Wilfred Owen, whom I consider unworthy of the poets' corner of a country newspaper, I did not know I was excluding a revered sandwich-board Man of the revolution & that some body has put his worst & most famous poem in a glass-case in the British Museum—however if I had known it I would have excluded him just the same. He is all blood, dirt & sucked sugar stick (look at the selection in Faber's Anthology—he calls poets 'bards,' a girl a 'maid' & talks about 'Titanic wars'). There is every excuse for him but none for those who like him.[3]

What I find striking about this explanation is how radically it differs from that presented in the Introduction to the anthology itself. There the unnamed poets (presumably including Siegfried Sassoon, Edmund Blunden, and Robert Graves as well as Owen) were wrongheaded in their approach to poetry because they failed to master their conditions.[4] If the conditions were impossible to master, then silence would have been a more appropriate response—and one that Yeats himself took with 1915's 'On Being Asked for a War Poem'. In the Introduction he compares modern war to disease in that it is an experience to be borne and then discarded: 'it is best to forget its suffering as we do the discomfort of fever'.[5] In the letters to Wellesley, however, Yeats' opposition to Owen is personalized, comparatively vehement, and rests on the grounds, not of general thematics, but of the aesthetics of Owen's diction.

Before he takes on Owen's aesthetics, Yeats first feels the need to forestall a political rationale for the rejection. It is helpful here to take some account of the political subtext of both Yeats' Oxford anthology and the letters to Wellesley. The parameters of Yeats' politics at any point of his career have been the subject of voluminous scholarship, and I have no desire to be reductive. Nonetheless, I think it safe to claim that by 1936, though his brief official association with Eoin O'Duffy's far right Blueshirt organization had already ended, Yeats remained anti-democratic and deeply distrustful of writers who advertised any leftward sympathies. Though he included selections from W. H. Auden, Cecil Day Lewis, Louis MacNeice, and Stephen Spender in the *Oxford Book*, he wrote to Wellesley that 'most of the "moderns"—Auden, Spender, etc. seem thin beside the more sensuous work of the "romantics"'.[6] The new guard's celebration of Owen made him modern by association (and despite Owen's obvious affinities for sensuous romantic verse). Throughout Yeats' letters to Wellesley, a now relatively unknown aristocratic poet whom Yeats would publish and champion in the *Oxford Book*, a sense of the factionalism of British poetry in the 1930s runs deep. When Wellesley's book is turned down by Faber and Faber in 1935, Yeats explains that Faber has dedicated itself to 'a certain type of poetry' spearheaded by MacNeice, whom Yeats characterizes as 'an extreme radical' (p. 39). Even sending Wellesley's manuscript to Faber had been 'sending the wooden horse into Troy' (p. 39). Likewise, he sees *The Faber Book of Modern Verse*, in preparation at the same time as his own editing of the Oxford anthology, as political as well as economic competition: 'it will be ultra-radical, its contents having all been approved by Robert Graves and Laura Riding' (p. 40). Thus the fact that editor Michael Roberts included Owen in the Faber anthology (with or without Graves and Riding's approval) places Owen among the leftist Trojans in this particular *Iliad*. Yeats' own anthology by comparison represents a self-consciously conservative voice. All of this is to say that, though Yeats claims that he did not know that Owen was celebrated by the revolutionaries but would have excluded him all the same if he had so known, it is perhaps more accurate to claim that the politics of Owen's banishment was at best a happy accident for Yeats. There is no question of excluding Owen despite his politics or those of his champions; rather, Yeats has reason to forestall the accusation that Owen has been left out merely because of political concerns.

Yet Yeats does claim that Owen's post-war political aura was something unknown to him during his editorial process. The real reason for Owen's exclusion, Yeats would have us believe, lies in his diction: his poetic archaisms, his overwriting, his purple verse (if not prose). This is an odd objection for Yeats to make. Yeats' own poetry is hardly free of self-conscious archaisms: as George Orwell remarked in 1943 'one seldom comes on six consecutive lines of his verse in which there is not an archaism or an affected turn of speech'.[7] Orwell illustrates the point using Yeats' late poetry, thereby establishing that the early Celtic Twilight material was not the only time in Yeats' career when he was self-consciously poetic in his diction. Yeats himself used 'maid' to mean 'girl' in several of his poems, most famously 'Who Goes with Fergus?' 'The Secret Rose' among other Yeats poems uses the word 'bard', and if Yeats did manage to rise above the temptation of 'titanic', he nevertheless anthologized Francis Thompson's 'The Hound of Heaven' without apparently entertaining the possibility that Owen's 'Strange Meeting' could have been alluding to Thompson's journey 'adown Titanic glooms of chasmed fears'.[8] It is difficult not to wonder whether Yeats was blaming Owen for making poetic choices that Yeats himself had made earlier in his career and later come to regret; it is even possible that though he consciously regretted these choices, his style encouraged him to continue unconsciously to make them.

Yeats sums up his distaste for Owen in the objective correlatives of 'blood, dirt & sucked sugar stick'. The first two elements of this triad are relatively simple: blood and dirt are directly represented often enough in Owen's poetry (and combined in 'Inspection' [*CP&F*, p. 95, ll. 8–9), and the iconography of trench warfare is replete with blood and dirt. 'Sucked sugar stick' is something else entirely. The phrase contains an accusation of immaturity insofar as it portrays Owen as writing a form of poetic confection fit for children as opposed to the more savory adult fare that Yeats' anthology purports to offer, and from this angle it seems to reinforce the idea that Yeats is castigating Owen for the aesthetic sins of Yeats' youth. But there is, of course, a sexual element to the denunciation as well. This is not to say that Yeats was aware of the specifics of Owen's sexual life; what I find more interesting is that he almost certainly did not, yet he nonetheless came up with a term of accusation that combines puerility with sexual deviance. If Yeats saw this combination in Owen, he found it in Owen's poetry, not in the life of a dead poet he never met.[9]

Yeats was not alone; Owen's poetry has a rich history of creating aesthetic embarrassment.[10] For every C. Day Lewis who has celebrated Owen's use of post-Swinburnian romanticism as a response to the birth of uniquely twentieth-century warfare, there has been a Yeats who saw the poetry as amateurish and overwritten. A relatively recent example of this phenomenon can be found in Seamus Heaney's introductory essay to the prose collection *The Government of the Tongue*. Entitled 'The Interesting Case of Nero, Chekov's Cognac and a Knocker', the essay makes Owen into the primary example of the twentieth-century poet who has led with his political intention and the validity of whose vision rests more on the extra-poetic content of his biography than on the aesthetic accomplishments of his writings: 'what we might call his sanctity is a field of force which deflects anything as privileged as literary criticism . . . any intrusion of the aesthetic can feel like impropriety'.[11] Nonetheless, at the risk of sounding 'prissy and trivial' (p. xv) Heaney indicts 'Dulce et Decorum Est' for its 'excessively vehement adjectives and nouns' (p. xv); in other words, its 'over-writing' (p. xv).

Though Yeats had chosen 'Strange Meeting' and 'From My Diary' as exemplars of Owen's bad writing, and Heaney's tone is characteristically much more generous, his criticism is remarkably similar to that implied in Yeats' private letter. The reader's sympathy should lie with Owen's combat experiences and his decision to return to combat in order more effectively to represent the attitude of the troops who lacked the access or facility to plead their own case. Owen's motivation to write was impeccable, in other words, but pure motivation does not necessarily make for pure results. 'There is every excuse for him' Yeats had said, 'but none for those who like him.' Heaney, though far more sympathetic, I think, to Owen's politics, nonetheless reserves his praise for Owen's historical condition and withdraws it from his supposedly trans-historical aesthetic trespasses.[12]

The question of whether Yeats' and Heaney's aesthetic ideals are indeed trans-historical need not concern us here; I merely want to use them to make a point about the embarrassment of Wilfred Owen. From the moment when Owen first became identified as one of the most conspicuous poetic voices of the war, he has had his detractors, both political and aesthetic. But what strikes me as interesting about Yeats' objection is that the public denunciation on the basis of theme (poetry should not represent passive suffering) masks a deeper hostility on the basis of aesthetics (his diction is archaic and ridiculous). Heaney, on the other hand, commends the theme but finds the diction similarly overwrought. Whether by the standards of a Pound-influenced inter-war modernism or the post-WWII well made lyric, Owen's war poetry is often construed as missing the aesthetic mark.[13]

The reasons for this, I want to contend, are sexual as well as aesthetic. Or perhaps it would be more accurate to say that the aesthetic to which Yeats and Heaney object has a sexual element to it. Owen's poetry represents in several ways the last stages of a nineteenth-century style; moreover, as I have attempted to demonstrate in Chapter 2, the highly self-conscious and, one might dare to say, overwritten style of Wilde's *The Picture of Dorian Gray* marked that text as one not only about effeminate characters, but one that embodied effeminacy in its own diction. And yet, given the circumstances of Owen's life and his representative status for a generation of young British men who suffered through the ordeal of unprecedented industrial slaughter, accusations of effeminacy by non-combatants were almost unthinkable. Additionally, as Yeats' public objections make clear, Owen's Military Cross was part of his persona; Owen not only participated in that most stereotypically masculine of all activities, he was decorated for doing it extremely well.[14]

In this chapter I want to begin to make a case for seeing Wilfred Owen as the symbolic son of Oscar Wilde. In choosing Owen, I am in many ways simply replicating the common assessment that sees him as the exemplary poet of the Great War. To a certain extent, a number of other war poets could have been as appropriate, or as inappropriate, a choice. Yet, as I will explore shortly, details of Owen's biography and poetic style make him uniquely suited to the role of Wilde's literary heir, chief among these being Owen's relationship with Robbie Ross and his decadent verse style that predates both the war and his introduction to Ross and his circle. Yet the basis of Wilde's and Owen's literary affinity rests largely on a shared but probably independent taste bordering on obsession for Keats.[15]

As James Najarian has shown in his *Victorian Keats*, the reception and use of John Keats' poetry was marked throughout the nineteenth century with a sense of sexual embarrassment. Keats' lush sensuality in what he depicted and, just as tellingly, in the sumptuous diction in which he chose to depict it made him a poet with whom later writers fell in love. Yet these same qualities made the Victorians suspicious of Keats and thus suspicious of their taste for him. Above all, Keats was subject to accusations of effeminacy, of what a reviewer in *Blackwood's* characterized as an 'emasculated pruriency' stemming from 'an imaginative Eunuch's muse'.[16] Such observations were based as much on Keats' sonorous use of language as on any specific events in his biography. In fact, Keats' biography was largely unknown throughout most of the nineteenth century: none of his immediate circle wrote a full-length biography, and his relationship with Fanny Brawne was only revealed with the publication of his letters in 1878 (p. 30). For over sixty years he was thus a blank slate on which later writers could inscribe their suppositions. Najarian traces the negotiation between admiration for and sexual suspicion of Keats through Tennyson, Arnold, Hopkins, Symonds, and Pater, while Wilde is a constant presence and probably the least embarrassed figure on the list. Najarian ends with Wilfred Owen as the final inheritor of this tradition.

Moreover, as Najarian also points out, Wilde was capable of making not only Keats' poetry but Keats himself into a positive instance of effeminacy. On his way back to Oxford from a trip to Greece as an undergraduate in 1877, Wilde had allowed a Roman Catholic friend, Hunter Blair, to persuade him to return by way of Rome. Blair knew of Wilde's interest in Roman Catholicism and hoped that visiting the Holy City might persuade his friend to convert. Wilde and Blair had a brief private audience with Pope Pius IX from which Wilde seemed to emerge suitably impressed, yet later the same day he insisted on stopping at what he claimed was 'the holiest place in Rome', the Protestant Cemetery, where he prostrated himself before the grave of Keats.[17] As he did with many of the adventures of this trip, Wilde turned the event into a sonnet, 'The Grave of Keats', wherein he compares Keats to the young Christian martyr who had long since become a symbol of masculine beauty and was then becoming increasingly associated with the erotic appreciation of such beauty through the masculine gaze:

> Fair as Sebastian, and as early slain.
>   No cypress shades his grave, no funeral yew,
>   But gentle violets weeping with the dew
> Weave on his bones an ever-blossoming chain.
>   (*CWOW1*, p. 36)

The body of Keats is figured here through an iconography that draws on the baroque tradition of representing the saint as a healthy, clean-shaven, nearly nude ephebe. Rather than the saint's flesh being pierced by arrows, however, Wilde gives us flowers that replace Keats' muscles and skin. And in place of the more directly fleshly carnation (if we recall the possible etymology of that flower's name from Chapter 2), Wilde provides Keats' sinews in the form of the small, decorative, and colorful violet, certainly one of the more flamboyant of flowers. For anyone other than dedicated horticulturalists, the terms 'violet' and 'pansy' are often used interchangeably, and 'pansy', of course, places us centrally in the garden of effeminacy.

Wilde quickly published his sonnet in the *Irish Monthly* of July 1877, accompanied by a prose account of his visit. The essay makes clear exactly whose version of Sebastian he is picturing when he imagines the body of Keats:

> As I stood beside the mean grave of this divine boy, I thought of him as of a Priest of Beauty slain before his time; and the vision of Guido's St. Sebastian came before my eyes as I saw him at Genoa, a lovely brown boy, with crisp, clustering hair and red lips, bound by his evil enemies to a tree, and though pierced by arrows, raising his eyes with divine, impassioned gaze towards the Eternal Beauty of the opening heavens. (quoted in *CWOW1*, p. 236)

Here is Wilde's version of religious ecstasy, in which a pilgrimage to a holy site results in a vision of a martyred priest of beauty who takes the form of Guido Reni's painting at the Palazzo Rosso (for there are, in fact, several Sebastians by Guido). This young male figure, naked except for a particularly low-slung loincloth, is tied to a tree with his hands above his head while he gazes seraphically toward the sky despite the two arrows, jarring yet bloodless, that protrude from his torso. In Wilde's mystical ardor, the Sebastian/Keats figure looks upward not so much for the heavenly life to come as toward the platonic realm of ideal beauty for which he seems quite content to die. As the arrows pierce his flesh, his eyes pierce this world and see the ideal world behind it: one is reminded of Symonds' phrase about Michelangelo that Wilde borrowed for 'The Portrait of Mr W. H.', and that I cited in Chapter 1. This bound, pierced, practically crucified 'divine boy' rises up in answer to Wilde's artistic prayer, an effeminate Jesus of neoplatonism that incarnates the spirit of Keats.

Many more examples of Wilde's lifelong idolization of Keats could be provided, but my purpose here is to establish Keats as the common ground on which Wilde and Owen could poetically meet. Owen's fascination with Keats dates back to his teenage years: he made two pilgrimages to Keats' former homes, one at Teignmouth and another at Hampstead.[18] Like Wilde, Owen wrote sonnets to commemorate these quasi-religious journeys. 'Written in a Wood, September 1910' is, like much of Owen's juvenilia, something of a romantic pastiche, but it gives evidence of a young man awestruck with any connection he can make between himself and the object of his poetic ardor. Unlike Wilde, he does not try to embody Keats in this sonnet; rather, he maintains Keats' physical absence for thirteen lines, then provides his faith in the poet's continued presence: 'Yet shall I see fair Keats, and hear his lyre' (*CP&F*, p. 7). Where this first sonnet emphasizes the persona's grief in distinction from a nature that has forgotten Keats, 'Sonnet: Written at Teignmouth, on a Pilgrimage to Keats's House' recruits nature as a mourner for the great poet, ending on images of 'weeping trees / Quivering in anguish to the sobbing breeze' (*CP&F*, p. 10). Finally, an unfinished ode reflects an encounter that probably took place when Owen visited London in 1912. Entitled 'On Seeing a Lock of Keat's [*sic*] Hair', it makes explicit the comparison between Roman Catholic adoration of saints' relics and the persona's fascination with a surviving fragment of a poet's body. Though many lines have been cancelled and only a few replaced, the first stanza clearly evokes 'a scarlet fringe' embraced by 'a pallid nun' who kisses the object 'with lips adorant' (*CP&F*, p. 446). Such material adulation causes the obviously Protestant persona to condescend with 'a pitiful smile' (*CP&F*, p. 446), yet when confronted by a relic of the religion of English poetry, he feels its 'power / voluptuous' (*CP&F*, p. 447) and declares himself a votary of the cult of Keats:

> It is a lock of Adonais' hair!
> I dare not look too long; nor try to tell
> What glories I see glistening, glistening there.
> The unannointed eye can not perceive their spell.
>   (*CP&F*, p. 447)

The entire fragment is riven with signs of literary struggle, evidence perhaps that Owen at the age of nineteen could not yet articulate his ardor to his own satisfaction. The ardor, nonetheless, is all the more palpable for the crossings out and abandoned marginal revisions.

Like Wilde, Owen also expressed his religious adoration for Keats in prose as well as poetry. In a letter to his mother that dates from around the same time as the abandoned ode, he describes his reading of William Michael Rossetti's *Life and Writings of John Keats* in terms redolent at once of poetic hero worship and the ending of the Gospel of John: 'Rossetti guided my groping hand right into the wound, and I touched, for one moment the incandescent Heart of Keats' (*OCL*, p. 161). Such iconography is joined by a kind of self identification with Keats in a slightly earlier letter, written again to his mother. He was in London to sit for a university entrance exam (which he passed, but not sufficiently well to earn a scholarship) and went to the British Museum to view several of Keats' manuscripts. Here he is in love not just with Keats' poetry and biography, nor even a relic of his body, but with the physical trace of his linguistic passing: his handwriting. 'His writing is rather large and slopes like mine. . . . He also has my trick of not joining letters in a word. Otherwise it is unlike anybodies' I know, and yet I seem to be strangely familiar with it' (*OCL*, p. 82). Owen sees Keats as a mystery, but one into which he has special insight. As Wilde said to Max Beerbohm, 'I never read Flaubert's *Tentation de St Antoine* without signing my name at the end of it.'[19] Owen both adored Keats as an unattainable goal and felt that he had written Keats' poems.

Keats, especially the Keats whose mythology was initiated in Shelley's 'Adonais', offered both Wilde and Owen the prime example of the unappreciated poet; largely uncelebrated during his brief lifetime, he was slain on the altar of bourgeois indifference to beauty, yet the two younger poets pledge themselves and nature to his holy memory. From the distance of sixty years (for Wilde) or ninety years (for Owen), the later poet's encounter with Keats leaves him better able to face the embarrassment of writing underappreciated poetry; in fact, the more underappreciated at the time of writing, the better the potential connection with Keats. With Keats himself a martyr to beauty, the priests of Keats will be martyrs to their chosen saint. Like Guido Reni, they will paint their St. Sebastian as looking away from the viewer, gazing abstractly at the revelation of the platonic *eidos*, yet the artist's gaze rests squarely on the body of the saint and implies an understanding that the viewer's (or reader's) path to heaven lies in or through that pierced flesh.

The embarrassment of Wilde's poetic failure has been covered in Chapter 3. Keats was one of many predecessors that Wilde was accused of plagiarizing. But just as the embarrassment over Wilde's *Poems* of 1881 was caused by the sexual deviance of such texts as 'Charmides' as much as by the poetry's obvious borrowings, the embarrassment that Owen's poetry has caused many of his readers lies not just in his use of Keatsian diction but also in the sexual undertones of much of the work. If, as Najarian suggests, 'Owen's literary inheritance and his sexuality are, in fact, the same subject' (p. 163), then the sexual embarrassment is part of Owen's Keatsian legacy. When Yeats objects to Owen's sucked sugar stick, then, it is a candy fashioned by Keats, and both its sweetness and its phallic significance are divine gifts from the Priest of Beauty.

Early criticism of Owen, which tends to address him as the most important and most representative figure of the war poets (meaning in this case, junior officers writing short lyric poems during the war years), tended to shy away from the sexual content of his poetry.[20] Paul Fussell's *The Great War and Modern Memory* (1975) changed this by linking Great War culture to a temporary burgeoning and celebration of homoeroticism and by placing Owen's poetry into this context. Fussell evokes the late Victorian tradition of Uranian verse, which idolized the young, beautiful, and often doomed male figure: what was underground and coded in the 1880s and 90s, in Fussell's construction, experienced a brief moment of widespread cultural acceptance during the war, when large numbers of young doomed men were suddenly the subject of public approbation rather than furtive personal desire. From 1914–18, in other words, imagery that had previously belonged to homoerotic verse with a severely limited circulation suddenly became appropriate for mass public consumption, and such previously obscure works as A. E. Housman's *A Shropshire Lad* were made instantly relevant in an entirely new context. Owen's poetic tastes, formed as they were by Keats and 1890s decadence, made him perfectly suited to the moment: 'the tradition of Victorian homoeroticism teaches him how to notice boys; the war, his talent, and his instinct of honor teach him what to make of them. . . . Before he had seen any of the war he had already made his own the sentimental homoerotic theme which his greatest poems of the war would proceed to glorify.'[21]

Fussell's book marks a watershed of First World War studies. I have previously outlined my objection to its construction of an ideology I termed 'combat gnosticism', which I see as Fussell's uncritical acceptance of an epistemological stance that he inherits from the trench lyricists themselves, Owen among them. In this version of gnosis, only those who have directly experienced combat are able to represent it; at the same time, since combat experience does not have to be related to those who have already experienced it, the audience of the trench lyric consists precisely of those who remain incapable of truly understanding the experience represented. This is, to my mind, one of the primary difficulties with which combatant poetry such as Owen's must struggle, yet Fussell does not so much bring such epistemological difficulties into focus as he replicates the ideology that only the initiated can ever truly understand the combat experience that nonetheless formed the modern world in which we all now live. Moreover, the reduction of the experience of the First World War to the experience of literarily competent infantry soldiers on the Western Front excludes civilian experience entirely, as well as such borderline experiences as those of medical personnel—men and women who witness the physical and psychological effects of combat quite closely, yet who are not combatants in the only way that matters within this gnostic definition. Finally, the equation of war with combat results in the all but complete exclusion of women's voices from representations of the war, a situation that a number of feminist scholars in the decades following the publication of *The Great War and Modern Memory* have sought to rectify.[22]

Nonetheless, Fussell's book is still inescapable some forty years after its publication, and the terms he introduced largely remain those with which we continue to negotiate. The homoeroticism of Owen's poetry is a good example of this phenomenon. Although not the first to remark upon how Owen's sensitivity to male beauty combined with his resentment of the war's destruction of young men, Fussell's analysis of Owen's sexual vision placed it in a larger context of pre-war Uranian poetry as well as a wider cultural movement in which wartime culture generally is seen as more open to homoeroticism at a time when a large number of its young men are simultaneously celebrated for heroism and placed at the mercy of unprecedented technologies specifically designed for their bodily mutilation. Prior to Fussell, Owen's celebrations of the vulnerable male body tended to be seen as his own psychological quirks rather than symptomatic of a wider cultural response. Such recent work in the field as Joanna Bourke's *Dismembering the Male* (1996), Sarah Cole's *Modernism, Male Friendship and the First World War* (2003), and Santanu Das' *Touch and Intimacy in First World War Literature* (2005) have eloquently expanded on Fussell's connection between the war and the male body, whether eroticized or not. Along with the parallel movement of the expansion of the effective definition of war literature beyond the literary production of combatants, the opening up of Great War literature to the questions of homosociality and homoeroticism has been the most significant development in the scholarship of the literature of the First World War.[23]

Interest in homosociality and homoeroticism has not, of course, been limited to its relationship to First World War literature: the increasing visibility of LGBTQ concerns inside and outside of academia has provided a huge palette of ideas and vocabularies to which Fussell did not have access in 1975. His entire analysis of sexuality in the war and of Owen's relationship to it is predicated on a definition of homoeroticism that many will now find problematic: 'I use that term to imply a sublimated (i.e., "chaste") form of temporary homosexuality. Of the active, unsublimated kind there was very little at the front.'[24] First, it would seem that Fussell's definition of homoeroticism is dependent on what since Eve Kosofsky Sedgwick's *Between Men* (1985) we would be likely to call homosociality. Both the armed forces and Western society generally were more rigidly homosocial in the early decades of the twentieth century than they are now, and Fussell's easy slide from homosocial institutions into homoeroticism runs counter to Sedgwick's explanation of how homosociality often goes hand-in-hand with an overt, even violent, rejection of homoeroticism. Moreover, Fussell's explanation of homoeroticism itself as both a sublimation and a temporally limited version of homosexuality begs several questions. First, the term 'sublimation' brings with it a lot of Freudian assumptions, not all of which are likely to be readily accepted by readers open to some of the more recent and less psychoanalytically doctrinaire forms of queer theory. Second, the idea that homoeroticism differs from homosexuality mainly in that the former is a temporary while the latter is a permanent state of affairs ignores not only competing definitions for homoeroticism, but also assumes that homosexuality as an orientation does not require historicization. What counted as homosexuality, in other words, in 1917 is assumed to remain the same thing as in 1975, despite changes in nomenclature, theories, law, and cultural practices.

Homosexuality is assumed to be a thing that has always been there, even though it has only been named as such since the late nineteenth century and then only among sexologists, and even though it was a word apparently unknown to the English poets of the First World War. Both Sassoon and Graves, for instance, were familiar with the work of Edward Carpenter and were much more comfortable with his celebratory concepts of an intermediate or third sex than Krafft-Ebing's foreign and technical (if not pathologizing) idea of homosexuality.

Just to reiterate what I take to be an important point, I do not intend the foregoing to stand as a dismissal, or even an unfriendly critique, of Fussell's work. Fussell's linking of Owen's poetry to pre-war Uranian verse is still one of the most crucial connections ever made in interpreting Owen, and it goes a long way toward explaining why Owen's poetry has been a source of sexual embarrassment ever since its first publication. Whether traced to Uranian homoeroticism or Keatsian sensuousness, Owen's 'overwriting' is an integral part of his poetic style and, consequently, inseparable from his representation of the trench conditions on which his reputation, whether aesthetic or ethical, stands. It is also inextricable from the sexual deviance that is the *raison d'être* of Uranian verse and of which Keatsian poetry was suspected throughout the nineteenth century. The embarrassment of Owen is at once aesthetic and sexual. It is a condition he shares with Wilde.

Fathers and sons: Owen, Wilde, and the Ross circle

The most usual tradition in which to place Owen's work has been the Romantic lyric, and the most influential figure of that tradition has been Keats. Najarian's placement of Owen as the culmination of a book on Keats' nineteenth-century influence, for instance, might seem surprising to Romanticists but immediately apposite to scholars of Owen. More subtly, Swinburne and the Pre-Raphaelites' self-consciously poetic experiments and flirtation with shocking subject matter can be unmistakably traced in Owen. Owen's copy of Swinburne's *Poems and Ballads*, for instance, was sent home along with his officer's pistol after his death, and it may well have been the last book from which he read.[25] The influence of Wilde, however, is a bit of a more difficult matter: ever since his literary career hit its stride in the late 1880s, Wilde has been far better known as a prose writer and dramatist than as a poet. Though ultimately I will want to make the case that the legitimacy of Owen's status as a symbolic son of Wilde lies less on direct influence on the verse than on the ideas and assumptions that it embodies, it will nonetheless be helpful to point out the textual and biographical elements that expose Wilde's fingerprints on Owen's manuscripts.

It is difficult to pinpoint when Owen first became exposed to Wilde's writing. Not only did Owen grow up and become interested in poetry at a time when Wilde's name was a byword for sexual infamy (Owen was barely two years old at the time of Wilde's conviction), he grew up in a world very different from Wilde's. Wilde, the child of a physician and a poet, benefitted from several of the most elite educational institutions available; he was born in a colonial capital and was able to move to the metropole. His parents were Ascendancy Irish nationalists who supported the arts and were fascinated by Irish folklore. Though his father especially objected to his son's interest in Roman Catholicism, Wilde's formative years were not particularly marked by religious strictures. Owen, on the other hand, was raised by a father who worked for the railways and an evangelical, teetotaling mother. Though his mother's family had once been relatively wealthy, the family was never able to recreate the fortune lost by Owen's grandfather, Edward Shaw. Owen's childhood was spent moving between several towns in the west Midlands, including the shipbuilding town of Birkenhead (across the Mersey from Liverpool). He did not attend university; instead, he was apprenticed to a conservative vicar at Dunsden, only a few miles from Reading Gaol where Wilde had been imprisoned some twelve years before. Eventually deciding that his developing political and religious attitudes prevented a career in the church, Owen left England for France, first as a teacher in the Berlitz school in Bordeaux, then as a private tutor. He was in France, and initially remained there, when the war broke out in 1914.

Growing up in an evangelical household presided over by parents acutely concerned with respectability and propriety, Owen was unlikely to have discussed the works of Oscar Wilde during dinner conversation with his family. Keats was certainly covered in Owen's school curriculum, but Wilde's works were no more likely to appear on a state school reading list than in a pastor's sermon. While he was a tutor in France, however, Owen was introduced by his employer to the decadent and anarchist poet Laurent Tailhade. Tailhade was an almost exact contemporary of Wilde and had publicly defended him at the time of his trials and incarceration.[26] Owen and Tailhade met in the late summer of 1914, just as the war began; by October Owen was writing an untitled exercise in decadence beginning 'Long ages past in Egypt thou wert worshipped / And thou wert wrought from ivory and beryl' (*CP&F*, p. 70, ll. 1–2). The poem moves through images of human sacrifice among exotic artifacts, constantly evoking the archaic second-person pronoun but never identifying the addressee. With its often lurid emphasis on blood and sacrifice, it is easy to link the poem to the early stages of the war; Owen's letter to his brother Harold describing a visit to a war hospital and illustrating in detail several of the more grisly wounds is dated 23 September, 1914 (*OCL*, pp. 283–6) and is thus a product of the same general time period. Yet if these sacrifices represent early versions of the war dead he will later elegize in 'Anthem for Doomed Youth' and 'The Kind Ghosts', this 1914 version plays up the ritual and mystery that the later poems will deny. Rather than trench realism, the poem provides reiterations, if not clichés, of *fin-de-siècle* dissipation: 'Thou art the dream beheld by frenzied princes / In smoke of opium' (ll. 17–18) and 'Thou art the face reflected in a mirror / Of wild desire, of pain, of bitter pleasure' (ll. 22–3).

If shades of *Dorian Gray* are possible to detect behind these clouds of incense and opium, those of Wilde's 'The Sphinx' seem unavoidable. The latter is a poem with which Wilde struggled for an uncharacteristically long time. It was begun in his Oxford days and not published until 1894, and it appears in all editions of his collected poems from 1908. In many ways the poem represents a triumph of the effeminate style of writing described in Chapter 2; it combines a variation on Tennyson's *In Memoriam* stanza with a Swinburnian emphasis on trisyllabic feminine rhymes such as 'catafalque' and 'Amenalk' (*CWOW1*, p. 182) or 'purple corridors' and 'moaning mandragores' (*CWOW1*, p. 183). To the extent that is has a narrative element, it concerns the persona's fascination with the Sphinx and its ancient heritage. This fascination becomes increasingly obsessive and increasingly sexual, until the persona finally pleads with the Sphinx to leave him 'to his Crucifix'

> Whose pallid burden, sick with pain, watches the world
>   With wearied eyes,
> And weeps for everything that dies, and weeps for
>   every soul in vain.
>   (*CWOW1*, p. 194)

We know that Tailhade encouraged Owen to read decadent literature in French; he gave Owen an inscribed copy of Flaubert's *Tentation de St Antoine* (a favorite of Wilde, as noted above) as well as Renan's autobiography. It is entirely possible that such reading caused Owen to turn to English decadents, and that he produced a poem that reads as a shortened version of Wilde's 'The Sphinx' because both he and Wilde were copying Swinburne. But the parallels run sufficiently close to cast doubt on such coincidence. Though Owen refuses to name the figure that presides over his poem, Egypt is the first locale identified for its ancient provenance, and the poem ends with images of using the figure 'as a poppy to our mouths, / Finding with thee forgetfulness of God' (ll. 20–1). Like Wilde's poem, Owen's is a fantasy tour of ancient pagan practices as seen through an orientalizing lens. Though its emphasis lies more on violence than on sex, Owen's violence is sufficiently eroticized, and Wilde's eroticism sufficiently violent, to allow Owen's untitled piece to stand as a shortened, blank verse variation on Wilde's theme.

As far as material evidence is concerned, Owen's personal copy of Wilde's *Poems* is the thirteenth edition of 1916[27] and thus postdates this poem; Owen's reading, however, was certainly not limited to the volumes that remained in his parents' home after his death. His library contains no volume of Wordsworth, for instance, yet his early poetry is replete with Wordsworth's influence.[28] Given the thematic and imagistic similarly between Owen's 'Long ages past' and Wilde's 'The Sphinx', we need at least to hold out the possibility that Owen was reading Wilde directly in the last half of 1914 and not merely conjuring a Wildean poem out of Swinburne and Baudelaire.

A more direct connection between Owen and Wilde emerges after Owen's enlistment, which took place in October of 1915. Owen entered the Army via the Artists' Rifles, which offered the possibility of an officer's commission to gentlemen returning to Britain from abroad. It was his status as an officer that would eventually put him in contact with the London literary world, and this process began even before his official commissioning. Owen started his training in London, and he used his post-inoculation leave to visit Harold Monro's Poetry Bookshop in Bloomsbury.[29] Owen had discovered Monro's poetry before going to France; Monro's profoundly non-doctrinaire, Whitmanian version of religious prophecy seems to have been one of the means by which Owen survived the stultifying atmosphere of the Dunsden vicarage, and such early Owen poems as 'O World of many worlds' and 'The Time was aeon' are products of Monro's style as much as 'Long ages past in Egypt' is a product of Wilde's. 'The time was aeon' (*CP&F*, p. 73) is especially interesting in this context. It seeks to invert the Pauline dichotomy of flesh over spirit, and its symbol for the flesh is 'the naked likeness of a boy / Flawlessly moulded, fine exceedingly, / Beautiful unsurpassingly' (ll. 15–17). Whether Owen was ever directly exposed to the late Victorian Uranian poetry that Fussell cites as his inspiration remains unproven; if he did read such material, he certainly did not discuss it in his letters. But Monro's verse offered a poetry that did not merely give voice to aberrant sexualities largely because they were aberrant, which is certainly one way to read Baudelaire, Swinburne, and Wilde's 'The Sphinx'. Rather, Monro gave Owen a model for a poetry that was unembarrassed about constructing beauty as a boy and treated doing so, as had Whitman, as a natural possibility. 'The time was aeon' is not merely homoerotic, however; it also serves as a polemic against Paul's directive in Galatians 5.24 to 'crucify the flesh'. By characterizing Paul as 'a small Jew' (l. 33), the poem turns him into one of the 'Jews' on whom Matthew and John pin responsibility for the crucifixion. In this case, the crucified body is that of a fleshly boy, which brings this poem closer to Wilde's image of the pierced masculine flesh of St. Sebastian.

Whether Wilde's decadence or Monro's Georgian mysticism, by the beginning of the war Owen had several models for poetry in which specifically masculine beauty was fair game, not merely for representation, but for celebration. In another untitled poem from late 1915 Owen narrates an encounter with a 'navy boy, so prim so trim' (*CP&F*, p. 79, l. 1), whom the persona meets on a railway journey. The poem balances its portrayal of the boy as a moral exemplar with a reiteration of his physical attractiveness. The boy has just returned from ten months at sea shipping nitre for the war effort, and he is rushing home to offer all of his pay to his mother. The poem thus implicitly compares two stereotypes of the sailor: rather than the dissolute seadog who immediately spends all his pay on drink and women, this navy boy selflessly spends nothing and devotes all his money to one woman, his mother, 'because she needs it most' (l. 36). Yet interspersed within these acclamations of the boy's moral decency, the poem returns over and over to his physical beauty. 'His head was golden like the oranges / That catch their brightness from Las Palmas suns' (ll. 5–6); 'His face was fresh like dawn' (l. 10); 'His look was noble' (l. 13); 'Strong were his silken muscles hiddenly' (l. 17); 'His words were shapely, even as his lips' (l. 21). The young male body is presented as both an aesthetic and an ethical ideal, admirable on all levels. Just as the persona somehow intuits the boy's body despite his uniform (how does the persona know the boy's hidden muscles are silken?), he also knows through the boy's language and manners that 'all of him was clean as a pure east wind' (l. 14). Moreover, the boy's attraction has a salutary effect on the persona: 'And as we talked, some things he said to me / Not knowing, cleansed me of a cowardice' (ll. 29–30). It is possible to interpret this line, as Dominic Hibberd does, as referring tacitly to Owen's final decision to enlist,[30] yet more generally it also has the effect of making an erotic undertone into a moral overtone. The boy does not know that he is giving the persona a moral lesson, anymore than he knows that the persona is imagining his musculature beneath his uniform, but both effects are all the more profound for being unintended.

Several other of Owen's pre-combat poems also give voice to an eroticized appreciation of masculine beauty, including 'Impromptu' ('Now, let me feel the feeling of thy hand— / For it is softer than the breasts of girls' [*CP&F*, p. 76, l. 1–2]) and 'Storm' ('His face was charged with beauty as a cloud' [*CP&F*, p. 83, l. 1]). Yet probably the best example of a developing Wildean sensibility can be found in a poem that was initially drafted in 1915 and revised in 1917–18; it was thus begun and finished on either side of Owen's initial experience of the trenches in the first four months of 1917. 'Maundy Thursday' (*CP&F*, p. 109) is drawn from Owen's experience as an Englishman raised in an evangelical Anglican tradition encountering the rituals of Catholicism in southern France. Its title is misleading in that the veneration of the cross that it represents is a Lenten practice for Good Friday rather than Maundy Thursday, but Owen's confusion on this point only serves to reinforce his sense of removal both from French culture and from Catholic practice.[31] The octave of the sonnet divides the worshippers into three categories, each with a distinct attitude toward the act of kissing a silver crucifix. For men, the ritual enacts their respect for a belief system, while women kiss 'the Body of Christ indeed' (l. 7). Children, on the other hand, kiss a doll. When the persona reaches the cross, he expresses his veneration for the flesh in his own version of the ritual:

> Then I, too, knelt before the acolyte.
> Above the crucifix I bent my head:
> The Christ was thin, and cold, and very dead:
> And yet I bowed, yea, kissed—my lips did cling.
> (I kissed the warm live hand that held the thing.)
> (ll. 10–14)

This preference for the 'brown hands of a server-lad' (l. 1) at the expense of the object to which the worshipper's lips are supposed to be drawn foregrounds Owen's inverted hierarchy of mundane but living flesh over the sacred variety. Or, perhaps more accurately, what is really sacred is the 'warm live hand', not the 'pallid burden' (to use Wilde's words) of the liturgical property. Use of the word 'lad' is significant as well, since it places the acolyte between the two male categories delineated in the poem: he is neither a man, who worships only in the abstract, nor a child, who recognizes only a toy and cannot truly worship. In other words, Owen is developing not only a veneration for masculine bodily beauty, but constructs it as native to males of a certain age, somewhere between boys and men.

The poem's use of a distanced Roman Catholicism, of course, also places it within a *fin-de-siècle* tradition. As much as Wilde's 'The Sphinx' or his conjuration of St. Sebastian, or even J. F. Bloxam's use of the trappings of Catholicism in 'The Priest and the Acolyte', Owen uses the sensuous appeal of Catholic ritual to bring a sense of the sacred to fleshly sexuality. In this case, he has found his Sebastian literally inside the church. Especially to native Protestants such as Wilde and Owen, Catholicism's use of sensuous appeal in its vestments, liturgy, music, and incense can be simultaneously off-putting and seductive. The cultivation of aesthetic beauty, as opposed to the relative austerity of Protestantism, seemed to invite a further movement from the repressive, crucified flesh of Christianity toward the positive acceptance of the flesh in paganism. Writing to his mother after attending Christmas midnight Mass in 1914, Owen's words might well have been Wilde's a generation earlier: 'How scandalized would certain of my acquaintances and kin have been to see me. But it would take a power of candlegrease and embroidery to romanize me. The question is to un-Greekize me' (*OCL*, p. 311). His sonnet demonstrates how deeply his Greek proclivities, both aesthetic and sexual, could run.

Owen wrote almost none of the war poetry for which he is now famous while physically in the trenches. In this as in many other material conditions, he had the advantage of an 'other ranks' poet such as Isaac Rosenberg, who seems literally to have written an early draft of 'Break of Day in the Trenches' *in situ*. Owen, on the other hand, was still avoiding direct poetic representation of trench experiences at the end of his four-month initial exposure to combat; while being treated for shell shock at the 13th Casualty Clearing Station in May of 1917, he was writing self-consciously literary exercises on set themes in partnership with his cousin Leslie Gunston. Owen's mature voice required not only a period of recollection in tranquility, but also the intervention of Siegfried Sassoon, and both occurred during the months he spent in Craiglockhart Hospital in Edinburgh.[32] Arguably the first direct impact of combat experience in his writing, at least as a matter of representational style rather than pure subject matter, was a letter to his youngest brother, Colin, written at the same time as the entirely non-war-related poems with his cousin. After claiming that on Easter of 1917 'we' had shot down a German plane (it is not clear from the letter whether the plural pronoun means that Owen was involved or is merely citing the 'we' of British troops, but probably the latter), Owen goes on to enquire about the farm at which Colin is now working. His mind perhaps jogged by the juxtaposition of Easter, a farm, the death of the German pilot, and writing to his brother, Owen moves into a kind of biblical riffing on the prodigal son parable from Luke, then goes on for what must have been several manuscript pages in an Authorized Version stream-of-consciousness. For example:

> And he, when he came to himself, saw the stars falling in heaven, like a fig-tree when she casteth her untimely fruits.
>
> But in process of time the devil departed from him, and he arose, and girt up his loins, and sneezed three times, so that the fool said in his heart: It is the coming of a great rain.
>
> But he, stooping down, began to tie the latchet of his shoe. Now because of the new wine and the old leather, it came to pass that the same was rent in twain. And he stood up and cursed them.
>
> And hell followed after. (*OCL*, p. 459)

There is a sense, of course, in which this outbreak of playfulness is simply a bit of fun with the texts that had filled Owen's head since his childhood. There is another sense in which he is indirectly reflecting on the recent events that put him in the hospital: among several other traumatic occurrences, he had fallen into a cellar or hole of some kind and received a concussion. The opening of the excerpt above may narrate in an irreverent New Testament apocalyptic style the experience of being knocked unconscious.

However, when a line such as 'and there was silence for the space of half an hour' (*OCL*, p. 459) occurs, it is difficult to discern whether Owen is merely incorporating Revelation 8.1 into his biblical pastiche or whether his diction also echoes the final sentence of Wilde's prose poem 'The House of Judgment': 'And there was silence in the House of Judgment' (*CWOW1*, p. 172). All six of Wilde's 'Poems in Prose', though darker and more somber in tone, nonetheless operate on a very similar principle as Owen's letter. They play with King James phraseology and aim toward an aesthetic that combines the blasphemous and the beautiful.[33]

Owen was certainly aware of the blasphemous possibility; he initially marked the letter as 'CUM PRIVILEGIO' (*OCL*, p. 460) and forbid that it be shown to his parents. In a subsequent letter to his mother, however, he changes his mind and claims that the exercise was done 'without any reference to the Book, of course; and without any more detraction from reverence than, say, is the case when a bishop uses modern slang to relate a biblical story' (*OCL*, p. 461). Owen is proud of the store of biblical texts that he has retained in his memory and of his ability to manipulate them; as is often the case in his letters, he wants to show off for his mother, yet he fears at the same time as he hopes that her sensibilities will be offended by his performance. In this case, the biblical fantasia serves as an introduction to Owen's defense of his Christianity, albeit a Christianity he finds all but completely absent from the world of English civilian culture. After changing his mind about his mother seeing what he had previously reserved for his brothers and making a prophylactic defense against accusations of blasphemy, Owen then moves into his famous redefinition of Christianity: 'I am more and more Christian as I walk the unchristian ways of Christendom' (*OCL*, p. 461). This paragraph culminates in the claim that one of the essential tenets of Christ was 'passivity at any price! Suffer dishonour and disgrace; but never resort to arms. Be bullied, be outraged, be killed; but do not kill. It may be a chimerical and an ignominious principle, but there it is' (*OCL*, p. 461).

This latter part of Owen's letter has sometimes been taken as the key to his true credo, while others have seen him as far more skeptical of any form of Christianity, however 'primitive' (Owen identifies his religious beliefs as 'Primitive Christian' in a letter from June 1917 [*OCL*, p. 467]).[34] In the same letter he provides a prose statement that will later blossom into his war poem 'Greater Love': 'Christ is literally in no man's land. There men often her His voice: Greater love hath no man than this, that a man lay down his life—for a friend' (*OCL*, p. 461). The opening of his King James pastiche letter also contains the germ of a war poem in Owen's description of his participation in an attack. 'When I looked back and saw the ground all crawling and wormy with wounded bodies, I felt no horror at all but only an immense exaltation at having got through the Barrage' (*OCL*, p. 458) would eventually find expression in 'The Show'.

I want to suggest that the King James passage thus presents a link between Owen's combat experience, which he describes at the opening of his letter to Colin, and his religious thoughts as modified by this experience, which he outlines in the subsequent letter to his mother. First, despite his explanation to his mother that in the biblical passage 'I simply employed seventeenth century English, and was carried away with it' (*OCL*, p. 461), the passage reflects his accumulated war experience, including the fall into the cellar, the attack described in the opening of the letter, being blown into the air by artillery fire, and having to take shelter among the physical remains of a dead comrade whose hastily buried corpse was repeatedly disinterred and dismembered by continued shelling. Understandably shaken by such experiences, Owen took refuge in the shelter of a language he had known since childhood, yet that language, as I have indicated, betrayed his concerns even as it offered him protection from them. Yet this interlude where Owen allowed himself to play with the language that his childhood had taught him to regard as sacred also allowed him to reconfront the doctrines he had also been taught to hold as inviolable. The King James pastiche, far from being an 'innocent' way in which to pass an afternoon while in a hospital with shell shock, proved a necessary passage from a 'whole-some bit of realism' (*OCL*, p. 460), as Owen described his representation of combat experience for the benefit of his non-combatant brother, to the reconsideration of traditional Christian *doxa* that was integral to the development of his voice as a war poet. Conversely, the content of the gospels, as opposed to traditional Christian *doxa*, gave Owen a different way to process his war experiences from that offered by either church or state. Doing so, of course, was contingent on Owen's ability to separate the language of the Bible from its officially sanctioned usage. It was, in other words, a product of his ability to construe the Bible poetically, not just theologically.

Thus, to the extent to which Wilde might be traced in Owen's apparently playful but secretly serious approach to biblical texts, Wilde plays a role in Owen's transition into his maturity as a war poet. Much as Wilde had done with a consciously post-Renan Christianity in 'The Soul of Man under Socialism' and *De Profundis*, Owen is able to divorce the figure of Jesus he finds in the gospels both from Paul's version of Christ and from later Christian interpretations, whether Catholic or evangelical. This is not to say that Owen was incapable of making such a distinction without using Wilde as a model; rather, at the very least it should establish that Owen would be sympathetic to Wildean ideas when he was eventually introduced to them.

This introduction would take place via Robert Ross. While in Craiglockhart, Owen met and befriended Siegfried Sassoon, who was by mid-1917 an officer, a protester against the war, and a published poet. His second book of verse, *The Old Huntsman and Other Poems*, had been published in May of 1917, and he was sent to Craiglockhart in August largely to hush up an anti-war statement he had made after coming in contact with the pacifists Bertrand Russell and Ottoline Morrell. Owen was captivated by the realistic trench poems in *The Old Huntsman*, writing to his mother that 'nothing like his trench life sketches has ever been written' (*OCL*, p. 484). Sassoon began reading and helping to revise Owen's poetry, and when Owen left Craiglockhart at the end of October, Sassoon provided him with an introduction to Robert Ross. Owen first met Ross at the Reform Club on November 9. Owen was invited to lunch with Arnold Bennett and H. G. Wells; through Sassoon and Ross, Owen had been bidden directly into the London literary world. He returned with Ross to the latter's rooms at 40 Half Moon Street and stayed until one in the morning discussing his poetry. In January 1918 he attended Robert Graves' wedding to Nancy Nicholson, where he lunched again with Ross, then after the ceremony spent the evening with Ross and 'two Critics' (*OCL*, p. 528), one of whom Hibberd identifies as More Adey, another member of Wilde's inner circle.[35] The other was Charles Kenneth Scott Moncrieff, now best known as the translator of Proust; at the time, Scott Moncrieff was working at the War Office after having been badly wounded in April. According to his memoirs, he had spent the morning of Graves' wedding day in a Police Court testifying as a character witness for Christopher Sclater Millard, who had been arrested for gross indecency. Scott Moncrieff knew Millard from his public school days at Winchester. As Millard had already served a term of three months with hard labor after pleading guilty to a count of gross indecency in 1906, Scott Moncrieff's efforts were unsuccessful: Millard was convicted and sentenced to twelve months at Wormwood Scrubs. Prior to the war, Millard had for several years been employed as Ross's private secretary, in which capacity he was instrumental in Ross's work as Wilde's literary executor; Millard's personal life also constituted a chink in Ross's armor against Bosie Douglas' litigious campaigns, including the Maud Allan affair outlined in Chapter 4. Most significantly, Millard had, under the penname of Stuart Mason, published a *Bibliography of Oscar Wilde*, the product of years of research and a hugely important element in Ross's work to establish the copyright to Wilde's complete oeuvre.

Thus by the beginning of 1918 at the very latest, Owen had been brought into a world in which he was connected to people with much more privileged social backgrounds and with access to the publishing industry. This group centered around Ross and his rooms at 40 Half Moon Street, which served as an informal salon where poets and writers could discuss work and ideas openly and without the necessity of self-censorship, whether political or sexual. Although not confined to men who actively engaged only in same-sex relations, Ross's world was one in which such proclivities certainly did not need to be disavowed. More importantly, for many of its constituents, the link between poetry and sexual inversion was assumed. Although not a part of this

London-based circle himself, Edward Carpenter was a great inspiration to many of its members; even Graves, prior to his rather hasty marriage, had subscribed to Carpenter's ideal of an intermediate sex with a predilection for poetry and the arts. Ross's circle, in short, functioned as an extension of Wilde's influence well beyond his death. Oscar was a constant trace at Half Moon Street. As Owen's introduction corresponded to the gradual build-up to the Pemberton Billing trial, which itself centered on the performance and meaning of one's of Wilde's plays, Owen could not have avoided exposure to Wildean texts and ideas.

Fortunately, Owen's initiation into the Wildean trace coincided with a period of relative leisure for him. Upon leaving Craiglockhart, he was classified as fit for light duty, but not for a return to the front lines. Instead, he was transferred to an Army camp at Scarborough, where he became an administrator. Though kept quite busy during the day, his evenings were relatively free to spend in a private room with his manuscripts, his books, and his purple slippers. In March of 1918 he was transferred to the Northern Command Depot at Ripon for training duties; he was soon able to rent an attic room outside of camp where he wrote new war poems and revised much of what he had previously written. Thus practically all of the poetry for which he is now remembered was either produced or revised after his entry into the Ross circle.

As a case in point, in a letter to his mother dated February 22, 1918 (and thus written at Scarborough) Owen cites, slightly inaccurately, *De Profundis*. After a Wildean reflection on the importance of flowers ('their odour is disinfectant of souls' [*OCL*, p. 535]) and a decidedly non-Wildean comparison of flowers to military first aid stations ('the Field Daffodils and the Field Dressing Station: these are the best ideas of Heaven and Hell for the senses'), Owen writes 'for as one says "There were many Christians before Christ; The astonishing thing is: there have been none since"' (*OCL*, p. 536).[36] He does not, of course, explain to his mother who this 'one' was; Susan Owen was by this time used to her son's occasionally heterodox religious views, but she clearly would not find them more acceptable because they were linked to Oscar Wilde's name. Yet this reference makes clear that Owen was familiarizing himself with Wilde's writing at this time, and not only with his poetry. *De Profundis* is not a volume within Owen's surviving library, so he must have had another source of books. Robert Sherard's 1909 biography of Wilde, however, is in Owen's library,[37] and may well be evidence of his developing interest in this absent center of the Ross circle.[38]

Owen's poetry of this period also shows an increasing Wildean influence. Simultaneously with his trench lyrics, he was producing a series of short, enigmatic, and sexually charged poems that, on their surface at least, have nothing to do with the war and everything to do with forbidden sexuality. The most clearly Wildean is untitled but generally known as 'Shadwell Stair' (*CP&F*, p. 183), and its stanza pattern, length, and scansion all replicate Wilde's 'Impression du Matin' precisely. Owen's poem also shares with Wilde's an explicitly London dockyards setting: Wilde describes dawn along the foggy Thames, while Owen's titular Shadwell dock stairs lead to the Thames waterfront. Hibberd traces Owen's familiarity with the scene to his pre-enlistment return to London from France, when he spent several evenings haunting the East End.[39] The verb is pertinent in that the persona of Owen's poem identifies himself as a ghost, though one with 'flesh both firm and cool' (l. 5). This ghost passes the night on the industrial banks of the Thames watching the tide turn until 'dawn creeps up the Shadwell Stair. / But when the crowing sirens blare, / I with another ghost am lain' (ll. 14–16). Perhaps because of the poem's relationship to 'Impression du Matin', with its final image of a female prostitute 'with lips of flame and heart of stone' (*CWOW1*, p. 153), Hibberd suggests that the second ghost is a renter;[40] no exchange of money is mentioned or alluded to, however, and the *double entendre* of 'lain' may as easily represent furtive consensual sex as prostitution. What makes haunting an apt image, after all, is not the illicitness of prostitution, but the illegality of same-sex relations. Like a ghost, same-sex desire is both present and not present: its illegal status and its violation of the tastes of polite society relegate it to rough and less accessible districts of city life where it only occasionally becomes visible. Most of these sightings, as in the mythology of ghosts, happen at night. The ghost of Shadwell Stair is Owen's symbol for Douglas' love that dare not speak its name.[41] In Bosie's poem, the sweet youth who personifies same-sex love is labeled as Shame by his rival, and Shame seems partially to acquiesce to 'true Love's' demand that he remain ashamed of himself. Owen's ghost, on the other hand, seems characterized less by shame in the face of socially sanctioned love than patiently waiting for it to go to bed so that he may have that part of the night that both parties have tacitly agreed belongs to him. Normative society is haunted by same-sex desire, but not in a particularly spooky or threatening way. The poem provides a scene designed to be recognizable to those who know how metropolitan cruising works, and so it functions to place its author as someone who has likewise been initiated into the knowledge of these mysteries, if not into the rites themselves.[42]

Haunting is also a useful image for the relationship between this group of poems and Wilde: his ghost is detectable in all of them, though none so plainly as the structural modeling going on between 'Impression du Matin' and 'Shadwell Stair'. 'Page Eglantine', for instance, is a brief exercise in light archaisms with a sly sexual undertone; unless, as has been done with Herodias' page in *Salome*, we choose to make this page female, it reads as a proposition to a younger male lover. 'The Rime of the Youthful Mariner' (*CP&F*, p. 131) is an odd little piece about the title character's repaying of various acts of abuse with violent revenge. It ends with a stanza that sets up the expected mistreatment but not the resulting hint of retaliation:

> One bound my thighs with his muscled arms,
> Whose weight was good to bear.
> O may he come to no worse harm
> Than what he wrought me there.
>
> (ll. 17–20)

Lastly, another untitled piece, this one beginning 'Who is the god of Canongate?' (*CP&F*, p. 132), is constructed around an interrogative, catechistic pattern. One voice asks a question, and another voice answers; the second voice, identified as 'little god' (l. 7) and 'barefoot god' (l. 5), is on a literal level a rent boy, a 'lily-lad' (l. 15) who leads men to his 'secret shrine' (l. 7) where they 'lift their lusts and let them spill' (l. 10). Though Canongate is in Edinburgh, which traces the poem back to Craiglockhart, London and Covent Garden are mentioned as well; the latter area has been associated with prostitution since the eighteenth century. But in addition to representing a prostitute, this evocation of Eros also works with some of the same concepts as does 'Shadwell Stair': it testifies to the existence of a metropolitan same-sex underworld that is actively ignored by mainstream culture, and to which Owen charges himself to bring sympathetic attention. The god of Canongate may not be worshipped publicly, but private veneration is happening all the time in London and Edinburgh. People simply choose to make themselves blind to it.

That these exercises in Wildean homoeroticism are being produced at the same time as 'Apologia pro Poemate Meo', 'Dulce et Decorum Est', and 'Strange Meeting' suggests a connection between the combat gnosticism of the war poetry and the sexual gnosticism of the Wildean poems.[43] The war poems rely on a secret knowledge that is shared only by combatants, as well as an angry resentment of those who are excluded from this knowledge: civilians who willfully avoid the imaginative effort to attempt to understand trench conditions and their effects on those who are forced to endure them. This bitter exclusion is especially marked in the war poems that employ the second-person pronoun to emphasize the persona's separation from the presumably non-combatant reader, poems such as 'Greater Love', 'Dulce et Decorum Est,', and 'Apologia pro Poemate Meo', though other poems, including 'S. I. W.', 'Insensibility', and the under-read 'The Kind Ghosts', accomplish the same goal through different grammar. The Wildean poems are certainly not meant for the same audience; rather than exclusion, they rely on a sense of shared meaning, an assumption that the reader is part of a group that already understands and is sympathetic to the subtle meanings being produced. On a biographical level they were probably written for the exclusive consumption of the Half Moon Street coterie and were designed to be passed around in manuscript by Ross and his friends. None of the Wildean titles appears in the provisional table of contents for *Disabled and Other Poems* (*CP&F*, pp. 537–40) that Owen drafted in the summer of 1918 despite the fact that all of them had been written by then. Yet they are just as reliant on a sense of special knowledge, of a definite line between the initiated and the ignorant, as the war poems; they merely posit a reader who remains on the same side of this line as the writer. Rather than accuse the reader of remaining stubbornly, willfully ignorant, they congratulate the reader on having the sexual perspicacity to understand and to accept their meaning. There is no green carnation in Owen. Instead of openly wearing a symbol that he verbally disavows, Owen writes one kind of poem for a general audience and another for a select one. These audiences are, generally speaking, not supposed to intersect, though it is probably not coincidental that the Ross circle was in general highly critical of the conduct of the war.

Perhaps the most salient exception to this division is the brief untitled lyric beginning 'I saw his round mouth's crimson' (*CP&F*, p. 123). On the most basic level, this is a poem (or fragment, as its status as a completed work remains unclear) of fascinated description of a male face. Although it is never overtly amatory, its extremely close attention to its subject makes it difficult to read as completely innocent of sexual interest in the face represented. Owen lavishes loving Keatsian detail on the mouth, cheek, and eyes of his subject, obsessively noting the reactions as he undergoes a significant change. In a renaissance lyric, or even in Keats, this would be a love poem, and if death was involved, it would be as *le petit mort* of sexual bliss. Here, despite no direct evocation of trench imagery, the timing and the reputation of the poet force us to read the poem as describing a young man's death in combat. Moreover, there is none of the explicit objection to the pointlessness of this death that readers expect from the most famous of the Great War protest poets. Instead, we get death as 'the magnificent recession of farewell' (l. 3) as 'a last splendour burn[s] the heavens of his cheek' (l. 5). The face of the dying lad is compared to a sunset, and the shape and color of 'his round mouth's crimson' (l. 1) lead to a 'clouding' (l.4), followed by the reflection of a night sky in his eyes. The only note of discontent is sounded in the pun of the closing lines:

> And in his eyes
> The cold stars lighting, very old and bleak,
> In different skies.
>
> (ll. 6–8)

As physical description, what makes the skies different when reflected in his eyes is his death: the reflection of the heavens in the skies (as opposed to 'the heavens of his cheek') is affected by the soldier's demise. Or we could also read the change as internal to the speaker: in this case, the skies reflected in the soldier's eyes are different because his death has changed the meaning of these skies for the persona. In this case, the poem would function as a war version of Wordsworth's second Lucy poem ('She dwelt among the untrodden ways'): 'For she is in her grave and oh! / The difference to me.'[44] But if we take 'in different' as incorporating 'indifferent', it places this poem in the same thematic territory as Owen's 'Futility' (*CP&F*, p. 158), with its careful placement of the death of a single soldier in the context of cosmic history and eons of evolution ('was it for this the clay grew tall?' [l. 12]). The soldier's death, though subject to an attention far from indifferent on the part of the persona, also points out the indifference of the physical universe to the annihilation of the subjective universe behind the dead soldier's eyes.

'I saw his round mouth's crimson' thus provides a kind of bridge between the Wildean poems and the very different work for which Owen is well known. It is at once an unembarrassed homoerotic portrait with its roots in the sexually gnostic verse Owen was writing for private circulation within the Half Moon circle, and a war poem in which the death of a single soldier is isolated and placed in a universal context in order to realize the horrors of mechanized mass death without invoking the concrete imagery thereof. It is probably the best example of a poem that bestrides the line between the personal-sexual and the public-protest sides of Owen's work. In the next chapter I want to locate more subtle ways in which the prominent war poetry responds to a reading that brings to bear ideas of male procreation that were developed by Wilde and that lived on in Ross's rooms in Half Moon Street.

6
OW/WH/WO: Wilfred Owen as Symbolic Son of Oscar Wilde

Strange meaning

To retrace our steps momentarily to Chapter 4, Oscar Wilde had two literal sons. The youngest, Vyvyan, was only nine years old at the time of his father's criminal conviction. Vyvyan's autobiography describes the estrangement and repression that dominated his later childhood: his mother changed the family name to Holland and abandoned England to live on the continent. After her death in 1898, two years prior to that of her husband, Vyvyan represents his mother's relatives as actively hiding his true identity, telling him to forget his former name, and even intimating that his father was dead well before his actual demise in 1900. Only after his eventual friendship with Robert Ross was Vyvyan able to come to terms with the legacy of his family. Both he and his own son, Merlin Holland, became instrumental in the gradual rehabilitation of Wilde's literary reputation over the course of the twentieth century.

The other literal son, Cyril, was killed in the First World War. Cyril had chosen a military career in 1905 in a self-conscious attempt to disassociate his family from art and effeminacy. Though he constructed a persona that functioned as a reaction to his father's public character of aesthete and epicure, Cyril's ongoing friendship with Robert Ross demonstrated that Cyril was not attempting to repudiate his father's literary status or sexuality; siding with Ross meant risking the litigious enmity of Lord Alfred Douglas, who by 1912 had dedicated himself to the defense of traditional morality, which meant publicly defaming Wilde and his former associates at any opportunity. Cyril Holland fashioned himself as a resolutely serious and unrepentantly masculine Army officer, but not as an opponent of same-sex love.

In suggesting Owen as the symbolic son of Wilde, I certainly do not wish to erase the innumerable differences between Cyril Holland and Wilfred Owen. Though Cyril's upbringing was troubled to say the least, he nonetheless was able to attend prestigious institutions such as Radley and Woolwich, while Owen came from a much more modest background: he did not attend university and was able to gain a commission in the British Army in 1916 only by virtue of having spent time abroad and by training for an entire year before being sent to the front as a second lieutenant. Cyril Holland was eight years older than Owen; Cyril was killed in 1915, some five months before Owen enlisted. Yet the military service of both of Wilde's literal sons at least demonstrates the point that the war enveloped and damaged the generation to which Wilde's children belonged.[1] Less literally, given the ideas of filiation involved in the concept of male procreation, considering Owen to stand in the place of Wilde's sons is a useful exercise in both the possibilities and the limitations of male procreation. If male procreation aims to produce new ideas through the intellectual and erotic interaction between men, and if an age difference plays an important role in this arrangement, it would make sense that Wilde's ideas would reach fruition in a younger man he never met. The role of Robert Ross as a generational go-between, a man younger than Wilde and older than Owen who had himself played a part in the production of 'The Portrait of Mr W. H.', the closest thing Wilde wrote to an explanatory text on his ideas of same-sex love, is critical. If Owen absorbed any of Wilde's ideas from a source other than his books, it would have taken place through either Ross or members of his circle.

One important point must be clarified before moving on to the war poetry. My approach to Owen's work and my situating him as the symbolic son of Wilde does not hinge on his sexual activity. I say this because since Dominic Hibberd's 2002 biography identified Owen as gay (the slightly anachronistic term Hibberd himself uses), Owen's other biographers have insisted that his actual sexuality remains unknowable. Jon Stallworthy's 2013 revision of his 1974 biography objects to Hibberd's use of the word 'gay', claiming that 'gay' is anachronistic while 'homosexual' is not.[2] Nonetheless, Stallworthy does accept that Owen's 'sexual orientation was "homosexual"'[3] while arguing against Hibberd's contention of an affair between Owen and Charles Kenneth Scott Moncrieff (which I briefly address below). Stallworthy declares himself 'agnostic' on the issue, but what constitutes the issue seems to be Owen's sexual activity rather than his object choice. Similarly, Guy Cuthbertson's 2014 biography wants to substitute 'perhaps bisexuality' for homosexuality while maintaining that gender of object choice is the single determinative criterion; because Owen was 'attracted to girls too', he cannot be consigned to homosexuality, and bisexuality is the only remaining option within the regime of orientation.[4] All three biographies, in fact, assume that orientation is the only possible scheme through which to negotiate Owen's sexuality and beg the question that same-sex attraction means during Owen's lifetime the same thing that it means in the late twentieth and early twenty-first centuries.

Although for reasons that I hope to have made clear above I believe that Owen's sexual identity is about as well defined as it can be for anyone not criminally convicted for actions that were illegal at the time, it is much more important that Owen lived and worked during the most productive and final year of his life with an audience for whom an openness to sex-same desire was axiomatic. It is worth establishing that by far the majority of Owen's extant letters were written to his mother. He was very honest with her about his religious doubts, but he certainly did not tell her everything. As Hibberd demonstrates several times, Harold Owen's editing of his brother's letters was relentless, and he had a record of objecting to what he perceived as accusations concerning both Wilfred's courage and his sexuality. His 'accusers' included Robert Graves, who claimed on more than one occasion that Owen had told him that he had picked up young men in Bordeaux; Graves, however, had considered himself a sexual invert prior to and during most of the war, and part of the purpose of *Good-Bye to All That* was to cover over this history.[5] Whether Owen had sex with any of the Ross coterie or with young French men is not integral to my main point. Owen may well have died a virgin in November of 1918; if so, that fact becomes yet another element of his tragedy. But the relevant point for my reading of Owen's poetry, whether the well-known war poems or the obscure sexual material, remains his familiarity with the Wildean circle gathered around Ross and, secondarily, More Adey. This was a world that was London-based, self-consciously literary, educated in the public school and ancient university tradition, and comfortable with the private expressions of same-sex love. Not only was Owen a member of this group for a brief but extremely fruitful period of his writing career, but even people whom Owen knew who were Ross's acquaintances rather than intimates, such as Harold Monro, the owner of the Poetry Bookshop, and Edward Marsh, the editor of the Georgian poetry anthologies, were also amenable to the discreet use of same-sex love as a poetic topic (at the very least).[6] Lastly, Philip Bainbrigge, an officer also stationed at Scarborough with whom both Owen and Scott Moncrieff had a friendly relationship, wrote only one war poem that has become public: it is a retort to Rupert Brooke's final '1914' sonnet, and it is entitled 'If I should die, be not concerned to know.' It ends with a plea to be remembered for his love of 'Beethoven, Botticelli, beer, and boys'.[7] Like Owen, Bainbrigge was killed in the final weeks of the war.[8]

So, if Owen's sexual behavior is not important to this project, why is his sexuality of significance to it at all? His war poems were written by someone who, irrespective of his personal relationships, was part of a community that defined itself largely through an acceptance of male same-sex love. Owen's reaction to the war is a product of this attitude. The strength of his war poetry lies in its expression of this love. Its reaction to unprecedented mass death is not merely humanist. It is also an anger that the world so hated its own desire for young men that it allowed its celebration of its love for them to take the form of a celebration of their violent death. Owen expresses this anger in a letter from the spring of 1918, remarking bitterly of Johnny de la Touche, one of the beloved boys he tutored in France and had responsibility for bringing back to England in 1915, 'he must be a creature of killable age by now' (*OCL*, p. 544).

Owen's reaction is distinct from what he perceives as the dominant civilian attitude toward the death of young men. It is not that the usual civilian reaction is free of either aesthetic or erotic concern; it is more that it remains willfully blind to its own aesthetic or erotic concern. Owen's love may never speak its name in his war poetry, but it refuses the utter silence insisted upon by Douglas's poem. It realizes that civilian culture is praising a love, but doing so dishonestly. The difference between Owen's war poetry and a public poem such as Laurence Binyon's 'For the Fallen' is not merely that Owen saw combat while Binyon did not. It may not even be that Owen's emotion has a link to sexual desire while Binyon's does not. Rather, I think the difference lies more in Owen's refusal to be ashamed of the sexual aspect of his emotional reaction. The Owen who wrote 'Disabled' is the same Owen who wrote 'Shadwell Stair'. In both cases he insists on calling attention to what dominant culture knows but is too ashamed to admit. Whether it is the existence of the culture of cruising or the eroticized celebration of the bodies of athletic young men before they are physically maimed, Owen's poetry asserts what he believes civilian culture should know, and largely does know, but refuses to acknowledge.

CKSM

Charles Kenneth Scott Moncrieff, who introduced Owen to Bainbrigge and whom I mentioned above as the unsuccessful legal defender of

Christopher Millard, plays a special role in Owen's symbolic relationship to Wilde.[9] Scott Moncrieff's position within the Ross circle was
always a bit tenuous, largely because he had a reputation for being
much more reckless in his sexual relationships than either the more
cautious Ross or the scrupulously chaste Sassoon and pre-marriage
Graves. Scott Moncrieff's willingness to testify on behalf of Millard
seems indicative of his occasionally quixotic refusal of circumspection
in sexual matters. Relations with the Ross circle became further strained
after Scott Moncrieff published a review that was less than enthusiastic about Sassoon's approach to war poetry in *The Old Huntsman*.
Scott Moncrieff worked at the War Office after being badly wounded
in 1917; he tried and failed to get Owen a position either in the War
Office itself or as a training officer in a home unit (a service he was able
to provide for Graves). Whether the reason for this failure lay more in
the pressures on the British Army exerted by the German spring offensive beginning in March 1918 or on a lingering question of cowardice
attached to Owen's shell shock during his 1917 stretch in the trenches
remains an open question. In any case, Owen and Scott Moncrieff
became close; Robert Graves claimed that Scott Moncrieff got Owen
drunk and seduced him.[10] Whether this short affair is the reason or
not, Scott Moncrieff wrote a series of sonnets to Owen. Unfortunately,
only one letter from Scott Moncrieff to Owen has survived, while the
rest most probably were contained in a sack of papers that Susan Owen
burned, on her son's instructions, after his death. Also surviving was
a sonnet written on Half Moon Street letterhead and dated by Owen
May 19, 1918:

> Remembering rather all my waste of days
>   Ere I had learned the wonders thou hast shewn
> Blame not my tongue that did not speak thy praise
>   Having no language equal to thine own
> Blame not my eyes that, from their high aim lowered
>   Yet saw there more than other eyes may see:
> Nor blame head heart hands feet that, overpowered
>   Fell at thy feet to draw thy heart to me.
> Blame not me all that all was found unworthy
>   But let me guard some fragment of thy merit.
> That, though myself in th' earth dissolve, being earthy,
>   In thy long fame some part I may inherit.
> So through the ages, while the bright stars dwindle
>   At thy fresh sun my moon's cold face I'll kindle.[11]

This sonnet and two that followed are addressed to 'Mr W. O.', and Scott Moncrieff explicitly constructs them as illustrations of Wilde's idea concerning the authorship of Shakespeare's sonnets.[12] In making this comparison, of course, Scott Moncrieff was extending the plot line of 'The Portrait of Mr W. H.' He cast himself as Erskine, the slightly older man in possession of the theory who grants it to the younger man. At the same time, calling Owen 'Mr W.O.' casts him as Willie Hughes, the 'onlie begetter' of a new series of sonnets by a new Shakespeare.

Whether the sonnets in question are biographical and discuss a brief or aborted sexual affair is of much less importance than the way they place both Scott Moncrieff and Owen directly into the scheme of male procreation. The poem cited above, for instance, constructs the persona as half of an uneven couple. The speaker is both the lesser talent, 'having no language equal to thine', and the active seducer who 'fell at thy feet to draw thy heart to me'. Despite the failure of a physical relationship or, given the platonic logic of male procreation, perhaps because of it, the persona envisions a cultural afterlife in which he will reflect the solar light of his superior partner. This literary immortality, though also a renaissance trope (as in Shakespeare's Sonnet 18), is a product of worship in the sense laid out in Chapter 2. The persona wants to reflect his partner's fame and to inherit it, as a child inherits the estate of his father. As we have seen, roles in male procreation can become quite fluid; Scott Moncrieff plays with the trope as he uses it, both inside of the poem and in his addressing it to Owen. Scott Moncrieff was older and more socially established than Owen, yet the poem at least partially appeals to Owen as the senior participant. In initiating him into the mysteries, Scott Moncrieff paints Owen not as the acolyte, but as the priest.

We know from the surviving letter that Scott Moncrieff wrote several sonnets to Owen, while only the one cited above survives in manuscript. In 1918–19, however, on either side of Owen's death, Scott Moncrieff published two of them in G. K. Chesterton's *The New Witness*. The first, published June 7, 1918, is thematically similar to the one just cited:

> Thinking Love's Empire lay along that way
>   Where the new-duggen grave of Friendship gaped,
> We fell therein and, weary, slept till day.
>   But with the dawn you rose and clean escaped,
> Strode, honourably, homeward. Slowly I
>   Crept out upon the crumbling otherside,
> And thither held my course where Love should lie

But thorn-set hedges rent my Cloke of Pride,
And stones my feet, that yet no nearer came.
I gazed for you; but you were gone from sight
To Honour in an honest House of Shame.
Should I press on—hills, hide the road, and night.
But if I turn—the bitter pathway lies,
Across that hole were, smothered, Friendship dies.[13]

Scott Moncrieff again constructs a persona that is the ethical inferior of his object: where the object is able to walk away from the grave (or shell hole) of former friendship, the speaker arises from it dishonored and unclean. Though the poem does not explicitly state that the death of friendship is the fault of the speaker, it nonetheless seems heavily implied. Again, it is possible to fit the poem into the personal relationship: a less than successful sexual liaison kills the friendship, and Owen escapes into the 'honest House of Shame' of active military service, where the wounded Scott Moncrieff cannot follow. But again, the meaning exceeds biography. The poem replicates the platonic hierarchy of pre-orientation sexuality in which the ideal of friendship is betrayed by sexual expression. 'House of Shame', of course, is drawn from Wilde's 'Reading Gaol', and thus serves as a hint, a kind of green carnation for the audience of *The New Witness*.

Also during the summer of 1918 Scott Moncrieff began his first sustained project in French translation, rendering the *Chanson de Roland* into a self-consciously antique English. He sent the initial pages of the translation to Owen along with a dedication: 'To Mr W. O. To you, my master in assonance, I dedicate my part in this assonate poem: that you may cover the faults in my handiwork with your name.'[14] By the time that Scott Moncrieff's complete translation was published the war was over and Owen was dead, leaving Scott Moncrieff to offer work that he continued to ascribe to the inspiration of Mr W. O.: 'Any success I may have had in translating the *Chanson de Roland* was due entirely to Owen's criticism, example, and encouragement.'[15] Thus, in addition to writing his most well known work with the support of an audience organized around the absent center of Oscar Wilde, Owen's relationship with Scott Moncrieff had introduced him to the ideal of male procreation, and it had done so not only through the theory of Shakespeare's sonnets contained in 'Mr W. H.', but through Scott Moncrieff's attempt to extend that theory into the reality of at least his own literary production, if not Owen's.

Scott Moncrieff published a third sonnet in *The New Witness* on January 10, 1919; by this time, the grave of friendship had become Owen's literal grave.

> When in the centuries of time to come
>   Men shall be happy and rehearse thy fame,
> Shall I be spoken of then, or they grow dumb—
>   Recall thy glory and forget thy shame?
> Part of thy praise, shall these my dull rhymes live
>   In thee, themselves as life without thee vain?
> So should I halt, oblivion's fugitive,
>   Turn, smile, and know myself a man again.
> I care not: not the glorious boasts of men
>   Could wake my pride, were I in heaven with thee,
> Nor any breath of scandal shake me then
>   Swept from the embrace of immortal memory,
> Beyond the sun's light, in the eternal sky,
> Where two contented ghosts together lie.[16]

Again, there are hints of a personal, biographical meaning: a 'shame' and a 'scandal' that could concern either the sexual relationship or Owen's besmirched war record. But again the primary concern rests more in the literary afterlife caused by a successful act of male procreation or, perhaps more accurately, the disavowal of any desire for a personal artistic afterlife in the face of the possibility of resting as a 'contented ghost' with the beloved. Another green carnation is worn in the last line as Scott Moncrieff refers back to Owen's 'Shadwell Stair' with its final image of coupled ghosts being 'lain'.[17]

Scott Moncrieff thus moved Owen thoroughly and explicitly into a Wildean paradigm of male procreation. That a shared conception of artistic creation based on such ideas greatly affected, if not actuated, Owen's private poetry, the materials meant only or primarily for the Ross circle, is not, I think, a difficult case to make. A more pressing question is to what extent the idea of male procreation affected Owen's war poetry, the material that, after all, forms the basis for any literary afterlife to which Owen might lay claim.

Three war poems as male procreation

In tracing the idea of male procreation into Owen's war poetry, I will confine myself to three of his most well known war poems, namely

'Disabled', 'Dulce et Decorum Est', and 'Strange Meeting'. While all of the poetry of his *annus mirabilis* participates in the idea of male pro-creation to the extent that it is a product of a creative relationship with Wilde through such intermediaries as Ross and Scott Moncrieff, these three poems particularly feature a procreative relationship between the persona and his young male subject. In the first two poems, the persona sets himself up as the only one truly able to appreciate the beauty of the subject, while 'Strange Meeting' reverses the paradigm: it is the subject who holds the answer and who articulates for the persona.

'Disabled' (*CP&F*, pp. 175–7), the title poem of Owen's planned collection *Disabled and Other Poems*, is the most obvious case for a male procreative reading insofar as it is the poem that most thoroughly integrates an erotic appreciation of the subject. 'Disabled' paints its subject as a 'god in kilts' (l. 25), a kind of St. Sebastian in the uniform of a highland regiment. The lad's debilitating injuries are expressed largely in terms of age. Before combat the boy had been even more youthful appearing than his chronological age and had been selected by a potential Guido Reni (or Basil Hallward) for this reason: 'There was an artist silly for his face, / For it was younger than his youth, last year' (ll. 14–15). Since his professed age of nineteen at his time of enlistment was, we are told, 'his lie' (l. 29), his face must have been quite youthful indeed. Now, after his injury, 'he is old' (l. 16), and no longer of interest to the women who 'touch him like some queer disease' (l. 13) or whose 'eyes / Passed from him to the strong men that were whole' (ll. 44–5). The opening of the poem introduces this emphasis on war as age by setting up the subject as listening to the sounds of boys playing in a park. In terms of absolute age, a small number of years separate this lad from the carefree boys; in terms of the artificial age induced by combat, they are separated by a lifetime.

At odds with the comparison to St. Sebastian and its attendant association with a Wildean appreciation of effeminacy, the lad in 'Disabled' is marked both by a more traditionally masculine athleticism and by his appeal to women. Football plays a large role in the lad's decision, both in providing him a positive example of masculine *esprit de corps* and in teaching him to value injury to his body as proof of his commitment and abilities: 'one time he liked a blood-smear down his leg' (l. 21). Moreover, his current rejection by women is significant primarily because he was attractive to them before his injury and the poem works hard to pin responsibility for the lad's ill-advised decision to volunteer on 'the giddy jilts' (l. 27), who are separated from combat experience by the gulf of gender.[18]

Though the pre-combat lad is an unambiguously masculine stereo-type, an athlete and a magnet for female attraction, the injured veteran is not only emasculated, but effeminized. His loss of 'colour' (l. 17) in his war injury is represented in language that is at once orgasmic and castrating: 'Poured it down shell-holes till the veins ran dry, / And half his lifetime lapsed in the hot race / And leap of purple spurted from his thigh' (ll. 18–20).[19] The lad's catastrophe leaves a body that women can-not love and men would as soon ignore: even the 'solemn man' (l. 38) who brings him fruit enquires 'about his soul' (l. 39), not his body. The only one who can appreciate the maimed body of the disabled soldier is the persona, the trench poet who has himself undergone similar experi-ences and is thus able to paint the sympathetic portrait that constitutes the poem. Where civilians turn away from an emasculated shell, the trench poet looks more carefully and more lovingly and sees a figure worthy of close attention. The fact that he is no longer a paragon of traditional masculinity makes him all the more estimable to the poet, and only to him. The lad thus operates as an interesting variation on male procreation: while the athletic, pre-combat lad might inspire the cross-sex attraction that would ultimately result in physical procreation, such possibilities are destroyed now; whether or not we read the poem as implying physical castration, the women's distaste for the disabled body means no physical begetting will be taking place in any event. Instead, the lad's body inspires, not merely the creation of the poem, but the attitude toward the war causalities that it embodies. Rather than the 'pity' that the 'institutes' and their 'rules' (ll. 40–2) may offer, the poem encourages a more fully sympathetic appreciation for the sacrifice of the solider and an indictment of the civilian culture that supports the instantaneous obliteration of his youth. In this sense, the poem creates a procreative couple from the persona and the lad, so long as we acknowledge the lad's representational status as not just a figure in a poem, but a symbol of the millions of dead and maimed young men that the war produced on an unprecedented scale.

In 'Disabled' the persona's aesthetic and erotic appreciation for his subject is almost tangible; in 'Dulce et Decorum Est', at least in its finished form, Owen sets himself the task of producing sympathy for a similarly mutilated young soldier while denying himself the represen-tation of the soldier's former physical beauty. 'Dulce et Decorum Est' (*CP&F*, pp. 140–1) is a double sonnet of sorts, and I will try to account for Owen's use of this unusual form in due time. The first thing to notice, however, is that the poem refuses to single out its final subject for almost the entirety of the first sonnet. Until the eleventh line, the voice is collective, using the first-person plural and insisting on a communal suffering and fatigue: 'All went lame; all blind' (l. 6). The military unit (forty-eight to fifty-two men at full strength if we take the poem as more or less autobiographical of Owen's experience as an infantry platoon leader in 1917), not the individual solider, is the element that registers experience in the early parts of the poem. Only when disaster strikes does the subject, who remains undifferentiated except for his injury throughout the poem, distinguish himself, and then only by failure.

The setting of the early part of the poem seems designed to frustrate civilian expectations of war poetry. Although a piece such as Tennyson's 'The Charge of the Light Brigade' revels in collective action and identity, it does so in the service of a violent attack on the enemy. Owen's war scene features exhausted soldiers moving slowly away from battle; its setting, based on the 'haunting flares' of line three, is nighttime and its soldiers are 'beggars' and 'hags' (ll. 1–2), a far cry from the colorful splendor of nineteenth-century cavalry. Rather than the well-lit, direct and bloody confrontation between sabre and flesh, it gives us combat in the guise of gas shells landing near the troops. Moreover, since the shells are fired by 'tired, outstripped Five-Nines' (l. 8), it is fairly clear that the shells were not aimed at the slowly withdrawing group of passively suffering British troops. The German guns, as exhausted as their victims, are too worn to be accurate, and 'aiming' is a term that would apply only in a qualified sense to nighttime, long-distance, indirect artillery fire in any case. The guns are firing on positions, not people, and they are not hitting the positions at which they are aimed. Any resulting casualties will thus be a case of random bad luck. Additionally, once the subject of the poem is defined and set apart from the rest of his unit, it is not due to his skill at arms or lack thereof so much as his inability to maneuver his gas helmet quickly enough. It is on such almost sartorial actions, Owen subtly indicates, that life and death in modern war depend.

Then, once the victim had been identified, he is separated from the rest of his unit at first by surreal images, then by the poem's understated shift from realist reportage to dream vision.[20] The gas casualty is seen physically only through the 'misty panes' (l. 13) of the persona's gas mask which gives the persona the impression that he is watching a man drown in the sea rather than choke on poison gas directly in front of him. The estranging material conditions of mechanized warfare, in other words, distance the persona from the subject; there is nothing he can do for the victim in any case but fling him in a wagon and watch him die slowly and horribly.

The poem shifts in its approach as the first sonnet ends, yet the transition is smoothed by Owen's extension of the rhyme scheme of the second stanza into the shortened third. Line 15 makes explicit what had been suggested by the surreal underwater imagery of the closing of the first sonnet: the second half of the poem is not the direct, realist representation of a horrendous death in the ugly mud of the trenches that it seems at first glance. Rather it is the persona's attempt to drag the reader into the world of his dreams. This does not mean that the harrowing, visceral descriptions of the final stanza are not based on actual events, nor that their representation is not meant to offer an accurate version of plausible details. It is an admission that the event itself, experienced under surreal conditions and remembered through the involuntary medium of dreams, can only be fully communicated if the reader can be made, not just to see and hear the violent death, but to have it haunt the dreams of the reader and become an unavoidably repeated experience, just as it is for the persona. The dominant grammatical mode of the last stanza is the conditional, signaled by the dependent clauses beginning with 'if': '*If* in some smothering dreams you too could pace' (l. 17) and '*If* you could hear, at every jolt, the blood / Come gargling from the froth-corrupted lungs' (ll. 21–2, emphases added), *then* 'you would not tell with such high zest . . . The old Lie' (ll. 25, 27). It is reminiscent of a romantic chestnut, not by Keats or Wordsworth this time, but by Coleridge:

> Could I revive within me
> Her symphony and song
> To such a deep delight 'twould win me . . .
> (514)[21]

The great romantic vision of Kubla Khan's dome, as well as the even greater romantic vision of the poet who has 'drunk the milk of Paradise' and can thus produce this vision for the reader, are conditions for which the poet wishes, not conditions into which he claims to have entered. But rather than Coleridge doubting his ability to conjure Kubla Khan's garden, Owen doubts his ability to conjure a vision sufficiently appalling that it will inhabit the reader's dreams in the same way as it inhabits the persona's. Whether this self-doubt and removal from a strictly realist aesthetic ameliorates the embarrassment at the 'overwriting' that has haunted many of Owen's readers (even if his dream vision itself has failed to haunt them) is, I think, still largely a matter of a reader's tolerance for a language that so thoroughly calls attention to its own signification. In any case, the grotesqueness of the final stanza has its sights on the reader's dreams, not merely his or her sense of decorum.

As indicated earlier, one of the most noticeable differences between 'Disabled' and 'Dulce et Decorum Est' is that, where the former evokes sympathy for its subject largely by calling attention to his physical beauty prior to his injuries, the latter refuses to give any sense of individuality to its subject until he is set apart by his misfortune. Until the subject is gassed, he exists only as a member of a platoon, and once he is gassed, he exists only as a casualty without a life before or after the war. That this was a conscious decision on Owen's part is borne out by the three surviving early drafts of the poem reproduced in Stallworthy's edition. Each of these drafts has a very different version of lines 23 and 24. With minor variations the early versions read, following the evocation of 'froth-corrupted lungs' (l. 22), 'And think how, once, his head was like a bud, / Fresh as a country rose, and keen, and young' (*CP&F*, p. 293). Other versions have 'face' for 'head' (*CP&F*, p. 295) and 'clean' or 'pure' for 'keen' (*CP&F*, p. 297), but in all cases the soldier's current state of agony is compared to his former pastoral beauty as a rose. This is not the highly charged eroticism of Wilde's description of Bosie's 'red rose-leaf lips', and it certainly flirts both with cliché and with vagueness: compared to the brutal specificities of the lines preceding, 'keen and young' does not provide much of a picture. Nonetheless, it does provide a positive if stereotypical image of the subject's physical beauty before war inflicted its artificial aging on him and insofar as it does, it aligns the subject of 'Dulce et Decorum Est' with that of 'Disabled'. Eventually, Owen cut these lines and substituted for them lines that replace the embarrassment of the appreciation of young male beauty with the related embarrassment of visceral 'overwriting':

> Obscene as cancer, bitter as the cud
> Of vile, incurable sores on innocent tongues,—
>
> (ll. 23–4)

lines that exchange a standard evocation of beauty with a shockingly novel representation of ugliness. The final lines offer a distasteful image based on ruminant digestion, of all things: the effects of poison gas, which destroys the soldier's lungs and causes them to fill his mouth with blood and froth, is compared to a ruminant regurgitating the contents of its stomach into its mouth as part of its inhuman digestive process. Even the scansion of the lines is far less regular and predictable than in the earlier version; line 24 especially practically abandons iambic rhythm and becomes something much closer to a military drummer's triplet-based cadence. Owen's cancellation of the earlier version of the lines could hardly be more emphatic. With the loss of the country rose any hint of the soldier's pre-war individual existence is rejected and Owen requires that the reader's attention be fixed exclusively on the event itself and on its traumatic aftershocks in the form of recurrent nightmares.

This status of the poem as a dream vision disguised as reportage is another way in which it acts as a transition between 'Disabled' and 'Strange Meeting'. 'Disabled' produces its complexity largely through its negotiation with time: the current, tragic state of the subject is alternately compared to his past as a paragon of male beauty and his predictable future as a social and sexual pariah who can only be worshipped by the combatant poet. 'Dulce et Decorum Est' lacks a past and future for its subject; instead, it makes its future statements about the reader, and they are not so much predictions as wishes. The second sonnet includes the reader through the use of the second-person pronoun, making the poem one of Owen's most directly accusatory texts. In doing so Owen violates one of the central rules of the romantic lyric, a form he esteemed quite highly. John Stuart Mill's formulation of it was that while 'eloquence is *heard*, poetry is *over*heard'. 'Poetry is feeling confessing itself to itself',[22] which makes all poetry, or all lyric poetry anyway, into soliloquy. 'Disabled' may be soliloquy, but 'Dulce' is not. By directly addressing the reader, Owen may provide additional embarrassment by writing poetry that is heard rather than overheard, but he does so in order to incorporate a more complete picture of the rhetorical exchange on which the trench lyric is based. The speaker relates an experience that he has witnessed in which something violent and tragic has happened to the subject, and the speaker attempts to relate the effects of that experience to the reader who has not witnessed it. The inclusion of the reader in 'Dulce' makes the goal of the trench lyric clearer while also bringing into focus the poet's doubts about his ability to achieve the goal. Owen wants to create the psychological effects of combat in those who have not experienced it. He wants to initiate the reader into the gnosis of combat, yet he also knows that only the experience itself will suffice. Combat gnosticism thus leads him into a paradox in which the lesson he wants to teach is the one that he knows cannot be learned without the direct experience that a poem cannot provide.

I do not believe, however, that combat gnosticism remains an utterly insoluble problem for Owen. The desired or imagined effect of 'Dulce' on the reader is not to achieve the impossible task of placing the reader into a combat experience that he or she has not lived. Instead, it is to produce the psychological effect of that experience without the experience itself. Owen does not underestimate the difficulty of this undertaking, but he also does not confuse it with asking the poem to erase the difference between combat experience and the literary representation of combat experience. His final refusal to paint a portrait, however small, of the pre-war beauty of 'Dulce's' subject changes the trajectory of the poem's desired effect on the reader. 'Disabled' is, in its own small way, an act of male procreation, but one that uses the inspiration of the beautiful soldier to engender a sympathy for actual wounded veterans without explicitly calling on a reader who is incorporated into the poem. By refusing the representation of the past beauty of its victim, 'Dulce' extends male procreation into the future. Sympathy is no longer contingent on seeing the former bodily beauty underneath the present war-induced suffering. Moreover, by giving an explicit future result for the reader, a haunted conscience whose dream life will show that the poem has taken root in the reader's mind, Owen opens up a space for the poem to register its desired effect. As conditional as it may be, if the poet can do his job well, then the non-combatant reader will live in a different future, one in which civilian recycling of the old Lie will have no place. And if such a future can be brought about, it will have been achieved through the procreative activities of the male couple, victim and articulator, that enact the poem.

This optimistic undertone in a relentlessly bleak poem is not a complete anomaly in Owen's war verse. In 'The Next War' (*CP&F*, p. 165), for instance, he writes in the first-person plural of how soldiers are friendly with Death, but they feel this way because they know that 'better men would come, / And greater wars: when every fighter brags / He fights on Death, for lives, not men, for flags' (ll. 12–14). The final line bears the influence of H. G. Wells' thoughts on the desired outcome of the war as a new age of internationalism with nonviolent ways of solving political problems, and it may reflect some of the content of Owen and Wells' lunch together under the auspices of Ross. Another sonnet, 'On Seeing a Piece of Our Heavy Artillery Brought into Action' (*CP&F*, p. 151), begins with seemingly unironic praise of the 'Great Gun' (l. 2) whose violence is deployed to 'reach at that Arrogance which needs thy harm' (l. 5), though whether that arrogance is specifically German militarism or bellicosity on the part of any nation remains unclear. The poem ends, however, with an appeal that 'when thy spell be cast complete and whole / May God curse thee, and cut thee from our soul!' (ll. 13–14). At least at times during his short career as a war poet, Owen was able to express a belief that the horror of combat experience would produce a sadder and a wiser post-war culture as well as a politics that would eliminate any further need for the kind of mass warfare that made his poems necessary. War itself would become the enemy, and the fruits of combat experience would enable a world that had learned too much from the trenches ever to allow itself to return to them.

'Strange Meeting' (*CP&F*, pp. 148–50) bears the trace of these Wellsian optimisms, yet it comes to bury rather than praise them. In this context it needs to be read not only as a more thorough-going dream vision and thus a less realist war poem than 'Dulce', but also as an expression of the frustration of the irrevocable damage that the war has done to male procreation and to the continuing *fin-de-siècle* style of thought and literature that produced and articulated it. It is also helpful to trace the final poem's origins in two of Owen's fragments. The first (Fragment 120 [*CP&F*, pp. 492–3]), drafted in London in late 1917 when Owen was first becoming acquainted with the Ross circle, represents an encounter between the persona and a strange, 'madmanlike' figure who accosts him. Like Coleridge's ancient mariner, this figure waylays the persona, but he apparently lacks the mariner's poetic gift of knowing precisely whom to stop; the figure admits that 'You are not he but I must find that man.' The next lines begin 'He was my Master / Him I wounded unto slow death', but a variety of cancelled options hover above the ending of these lines, including 'whom I worshipped' and 'revered'. The fragment then moves into a variation on the most distinctive line from Wilde's 'Ballad of Reading Gaol': 'For each man slays the one he loves.' It ends almost immediately thereafter.

The second fragment (Fragment 131 [*CP&F*, pp. 514–17]) comes from late 1917 to early 1918 and was sent to Siegfried Sassoon as an attempt to dissuade him from seeking martyrdom at the front.[23] Formally, it is much closer to 'Strange Meeting', as the underlining structure of para-rhymed couplets is detectable if not fully realized. Some of the characteristic dialog between the published poem's persona and dead Other is present in the fragment:

> Beauty is yours and you have mastery
> Wisdom is mine and I have mystery

and

> Then when their blood has clogged the chariot wheels
> We will go up and wash them from deep wells
> Even the wells we dug too deep for war.
>
> (*CP&F*, p. 514)

What differs, of course, is the verb tense. In the fragment, Owen contrasts Sassoon's poetic gifts with his own in the present tense, then offers the future-tense eventuality that, having survived the war, the two of them will repair the damage done. In 'Strange Meeting' these lines are given to the dead soldier, and they are recast as past tense in the first case ('Courage was mine, and I had mastery' [l. 30]) and past perfect tense in the second ('I would go up and wash them from sweet wells' [l. 35]).

Looking at 'Strange Meeting' as a combination of these two fragments places the finished poem as a combination of two pieces about male couples. The first fragment gives us the guilt-ridden madman who has destroyed his partner in an uneven relationship that bears the requisite hallmarks of male procreation. The second fragment, read in the biographical context in which Hibberd places it, puts Owen himself as the junior partner in a potentially procreative male couple, in this case with Siegfried Sassoon: the junior partner pleads with the senior to stay alive and help to undo the damage caused by the war. 'Strange Meeting' recasts these relationships slightly by turning the speaker's encounter with the enemy he has killed into an apparent encounter between peers. Nonetheless, the Other seems placed in the senior position insofar as he has the answers: the 'courage', the 'wisdom', and the 'mastery' are, or were, his, as well as the ability to communicate these gifts to a world that might have been finally able to accept them due to years of unprecedented warfare. The speaker, of course, was aware of none of this when, 'yesterday', he 'jabbed and killed' (l. 42). His dream vision is among other things his coming to terms with his own role in destroying the relationship that could have, if not exactly redeemed the war, at least allowed its veterans to use their war experience to enlighten civilian culture and permit the participant nations to benefit from the horror of the trenches.[24] As Mark Rawlinson points out, the poem's dream vision ends without the expected reawakening, and 'crucially, the "truth untold" remains unsaid, the oracular vision cannot be brought back'.[25]

Moreover, if we allow the trace of Wilde to reenter 'Strange Meeting' through the quotation of 'Reading Gaol', even though it is missing in the final version of Owen's poem, it does allow the poem some additional meaning. Even though Owen ultimately cut the line 'for each man slays the one he loves', nonetheless allowing it to inform a reading of the poem makes more explicit the intensity of the relationship between the persona and the Other. It makes 'Strange Meeting' a love poem, albeit of the same kind of vexed and problematic love as 'Reading

Gaol' depicts. Moreover, though the poem itself begins as an iteration of male procreation insofar as part of its genesis lay in Owen's unsuccessful attempt to convince Sassoon to remain out of battle, the poem nonetheless represents a betrayal of the love that produced it. The persona kills the one he should have loved; though the poem is produced through his encounter with this other who begets the wisdom of the poem, this wisdom will never have the chance to affect the larger civilian world because the war that positioned these men as a couple has also ordained the collapse of the relationship in the most direct and tragic way imaginable: the culturally sanctioned murder of the one the persona loved effected by the persona himself. The persona only learns what has happened after the fact. He enters the 'profound dull tunnel' in a state of ignorance, unaware of whom or what he has killed. Only by escaping the real world of the trenches and invading an imaginative space outside of combat is the persona able to hear the voice of the other as his friend as well as his enemy. He is thus moved from a state of naïveté to one of increased knowledge, yet that knowledge is impotent. Had the persona not killed his enemy, friend, and the one he loved, the world could have emerged from the war scarred but with the wisdom of experience. Now that the other is dead, it is too late.

Reading the poem in light of Wilde gives us the encounter as an inversion of male procreation. We are presented with an encounter in which the callow persona should have been educated by his relationship with the enemy other. The relationship is potentially fertile: it could have been a case of Willie Hughes and William Shakespeare begetting a new idea for the world to profit by. Instead, the persona learns about male procreation at the same moment in which he also learns about his role in having destroyed it. From the optimism of the fragment to Sassoon, the finished poem moves toward resignation and defeat. In this version of 'The Portrait of Mr W. H.' Erskine does not forge his own suicide; he is killed by the narrator and the narrator is decorated for his act of valor.

Reading this way also marks out 'Strange Meeting' as working against the assumptions of combat gnosticism. Rather than an Owen whose primary task is to castigate a civilian audience for its willing complacency in sending soldiers to suffer under conditions that the civilians refuse to confront honestly, 'Strange Meeting' implicates soldiers as well. In making his persona a figure of ignorance who is initiated into mysteries too late to do anyone any good, Owen inverts his usual persona of a knowing conduit between an ill-informed audience and a combatant subject who is too protective to expose this audience to an accurate representation of trench conditions. By assigning the 'Strange Meeting' persona the central role in destroying the possibility of male procreation, Owen undercuts his usual accusatory stance and accepts at least partial combatant responsibility for the destruction wrought by the war.[26]

This destruction cannot be limited to the literal casualties, though it of course includes them. Owen is also marking an important stage in the war: by the spring of 1918, when Owen composed 'Strange Meeting' in more or less the form in which we have it today, he no longer considered it possible for the war to produce wisdom that would be easily communicated and accepted by a post-war civilian populace. He could, in other words, no longer sustain a Wellsian optimism. There are, of course, historical and military reasons for this change: the German offensive that began in March of 1918, after the Russian withdrawal from the war, destroyed any remaining hopes he had retained that the war could be ended through any means other than continued attrition.[27] Owen had been cleared for active duty just prior to the offensive, and he wrote 'Strange Meeting' while confronting not only the military situation at the front, but also his own increasingly likely return to the trenches and his interim role training enlisted men for their consignment to combat. Scott Moncrieff's efforts to place him at the War Office or in a permanent training position were failing at about this time.

Yet there is more here than simply an elegy for doomed youth, yet alone Owen's fears for his own continued safety and career. 'Strange Meeting' is also a threnody for the *fin de siècle*, and specifically for Wilde's beautiful if always fictive dream of male procreation as the hidden driver of cultural progress. In its eccentric reduction of the tragedy of the war to a male friendship that never existed because one man was forced to kill the thing he loved, the poem encapsulates the cost of the war in terms of the lethal damage it inflicted on the dream of male procreation. As the layers of fictive irony in which Wilde encased the dream in 'The Portrait of Mr W. H.' demonstrate, the dream was always a rather tenuous thing. After the war, it became impossible.

Fifty years after the beginning of the war, Philip Larkin attempted to register the cultural change it had wrought with his all but literally monumental poem 'MCMXIV'. After offering a sepia-tinged representation of an England that had maintained a continuity with Norman times ('fields / Shadowing Domesday lines'), Larkin sums up the pre-war cultural moment with 'Never such innocence again.'[28] Relying on the reader's familiarity with the tropes of the trench lyric, Larkin has no need to evoke barbed wire and gas attacks. Instead, he chooses as a final image the domesticity that the war would interrupt—'The thousands of marriages / Lasting a little while longer'—and suggests that even the

Armistice could not put them together again. Less Wilfred Owen than Edward Thomas, Larkin's evocation of the war stresses its interruption of quotidian life and submits that the war now represents a break from a past to which we can never return, irrespective of whether or not we might see such a return as an unmitigated good.

Perhaps another half-century later we can readdress the war less in terms of a lost innocence than as a loss of faith in innocence's apparent opposite, decadence. Larkin's version of the idyllic summer of 1914 has no place for the queer. Its rampant normality would be compromised by any hint of a lingering 1890s influence, any intimation of a persistent decadence or a haunting by a Wildean spirit. Shadwell Stair is just another way down to the dockside in this vision of pre-war England. Yet Larkin cannot help but evoke Rupert Brooke's similarly titled '1914' sonnet sequence, and its lead poem, 'Peace', which gives a significantly different representation of pre-war culture. It welcomes the war in ways that even by 1917, yet alone 1964, seemed to many hopelessly naïve: 'Now, God be thanked Who has matched us with His hour, / And caught our youth, and wakened us from sleeping.'[29] Though not as well known as 'The Solider', 'Peace' allows Brooke to speak in the first-person plural and thus more nearly become what he was commonly taken to be: the spokesman of his voluntarily self-immolating generation. Yet, rather than fiery images of destruction, the poem centers on the striking image of the war as offering a mass baptism, a chance for the generation 'to turn, as swimmers into cleanness leaping'. Of course, if they are in need of bathing, they must be dirty, and the poem does not shirk this implication:

> Glad from a world grown old and cold and weary,
>   Leave the sick hearts that honour could not move,
> And half-men, and their dirty songs and dreary,
>   And all the little emptiness of love!

As Vincent Sherry has noted, the early Georgians, Brooke included, saw decadence as 'a residual susceptibility' that it was their responsibility to purge from English poetry (37).[30] In addition to a very complicated emotional life from which Brooke may have well felt a desire to escape, his commitment to use the war to turn his generation away from 'half-men' and 'dirty songs' would certainly include Wilde among the decadents to be rejected. Owen who, as explored above, was discovering decadence generally and probably Wilde specifically during the opening months of the war, would not have agreed.

Brooke's 'half-men' points also to the fate of effeminacy during the war and in its poetic representation. Part of the meaning of combat gnosticism is its gender exclusivity; the causalities of the First World War, unlike most of the twentieth-century wars that were to follow it, were confined mainly to men on active service. As Cyril Holland's choice of career demonstrates, military service prior to the war could be read as a public statement against effeminacy, though we need not to conflate such anti-effeminacy with wholesale rejections of same-sex love. Brooke's welcoming of the war as a divine cure for decadence can similarly be seen as a retreat from effeminacy and an embracing of a putatively unmixed form of clean masculinity. Owen functions as Wilde's symbolic son in this context also. His version of male procreation is not a clone of Wilde's; as much as Cyril Holland, Owen (and Sassoon as well) rejected any version of effeminacy that would compromise his status as an officer and thus as an effective leader of men in the military structure. Many of Owen's war poems use women and cross-sex love as negative comparisons to the true love that binds men together in violent self-sacrifice ('Apologia pro Poemate Meo', 'Greater Love', and 'The Kind Ghosts' for example). Yet as we have seen several times with male procreation, its purpose is to produce children that will grow up to disobey their parents, and it should be no surprise that Owen's ideal of male procreation, though owing much to Wilde, should also differ in its rejection of the effeminacy that Wilde celebrated. Cyril Graham may have been a capital fencer and rider, but an ideal junior infantry officer he certainly was not.

I have attempted to show elsewhere the trench poets' tendency to appropriate elements of traditional femininity from women and thus expand masculinity to include caring for other men as well as benefitting from an ethics that privileges passivity and suffering.[31] Owen's version of male procreation relies on an imaginative relationship between two soldiers, and their status as soldiers means that they exclude the kind of effeminacy that Wilde valued, yet they incorporate an ability to love and care for their fellow soldiers that those who have not been initiated into the mysteries of combat would never suspect to be a central part of the masculinity that allows the potential for imaginative procreation. Thus Owen's vision of how male procreation should work may not entirely exclude Brooke's rejection of 'half-men' and their decadent 'emptiness of love'. Owen's immersion into the aesthetics of decadence, precisely the kind of late Victorian writing that the Georgians defined themselves against, certainly puts him at odds with Brooke's apparent welcoming of the war as a solution to all things decadent. Yet

Owen's acceptance of the war's simultaneous expansion of masculinity to include 'feminine' care as a virtue with the concomitant rejection of any hint of effeminacy as a compromise of martial competence demonstrates his sympathy with Brooke's position. In the same way that Owen's grisly trench lyrics were admired in Robbie Ross's sumptuously appointed rooms in Half Moon Street, the war produced strange combinations of masculinities: new and old, aberrant and mainstream combined in heretofore unknown ways. Owen's particular combination resulted in a masculinity that was at once battle scarred and gently appreciative of the unarticulated suffering of men.

Nonetheless, the war put extraordinarily destructive pressures on male procreation, no matter how Owen may have nuanced it to exclude overt effeminacy. These pressures can be accessed through Sarah Cole's important distinction between friendship and comradeship, terms that she contends have too often been used as synonyms both during and after the war.[32] Friendship for Cole is a voluntary personal intimacy where comradeship is impersonal and dependent on military structure, 'the endless substitution of one man for another'.[33] These meanings are not only distinct, but often mutually exclusive. The war relies on comradeship but destroys friendship.

In Chapter 3 I indicated that Wilde's ideal of male procreation includes friendship as one of its indispensable elements, and that it does so in distinction to classical articulations of friendship, which tend to construct same-sex friendship as mutually exclusive of same-sex sexual relations. The First World War's sacrifice of friendship in favor of the more militarily useful comradeship is thus a potentially devastating blow to Wildean male procreation; insofar as friendship becomes increasingly unsustainable during the war, the Wildean model of the production of new ideas through an unequal but complementary cooperation between male intellects necessarily becomes increasingly precarious.

Similarly, Santanu Das has called attention to the problematics of queering First World War literature by pointing out that, although many of the major writers that emerged from the conflict are rightly construed as homosexual under the orientation regime, the war affected sexuality by changing the way in which the body was experienced: 'In the trenches, the male body became an instrument of pain rather than of desire.'[34] What later generations see as homoeroticism is for Das often an attempt by soldiers to reclaim the body from its consignment to a mere means of suffering: 'the threat of homoeroticism was arrested by the absence of the desired object and the conception of the body as a seat of pain' (131).[35] If the war affected bodily experience at the most basic epistemological level for those who participated in it, which Das makes very difficult to doubt, then male procreation faced pressure not only in what constituted friendship, but what constituted sexual desire.[36]

These twin pressures help to explain my final contention, that male procreation, like Wilde's biological and symbolic sons, did not survive the trenches. Yet it is worthwhile to consider how the war made male procreation a more beautiful if unattainable vision for Owen. 'Strange Meeting' expresses a desire for a male relationship that will benefit the post-war world. No matter how much pressure we may or may not choose to place on its erotic elements, it is (or was) a potential friendship: 'I am the enemy you killed, my friend' (l. 40). The tragic end of this friendship stands in the place of all of the friendships that the war destroyed, and it testifies as well to Das' point about the war turning the body into a seat of pain rather than desire. In this case, however, the body is as much a means of inflicting pain as it is of bearing it ('so you frowned / Yesterday through me as you jabbed and killed' [ll. 41–2]), which turns the poem into a reflection on how the war became the means of destroying its most positive creation: the friendship and intimacy on which male procreation depends. The mass destruction of men included the mass destruction of male friendship along the entire continuum from chaste pals to ardent lovers.

The search for the exact cultural moment when the orientation regime gained its pervasive hold is a chimerical one.[37] The First World War is not the single event that dictated the termination of male procreation and the triumph of object choice and internalized psychological identity. Nonetheless, the war is an event in that history, and it is not long after its end that orientation can be seen increasingly to take its place as the dominant cultural logic of sexuality. The idiosyncratic idea that culture progresses through a love that that same culture had come to despise becomes displaced by psychoanalytic categories of libido and object choice, as well as an increasing insistence on a fixed or fixable sexual identity rather than Wilde's ideal of the 'complex, multi-form creature'. Something so fragile and tenuous as male procreation could not withstand the trenches.

Male procreation as history

Owen thus represents not only a product of male procreation and an attempt to continue it, but also its end point. And yet there remains an irony in this death of an idea, and it is this note on which I wish to end. In the last two decades, self-consciously revisionist military historians have sought to correct what they see as the mainstream British and US cultural interpretation of the Great War. Brian Bond, whose *The Unquiet Western Front* will serve as my base text for this controversy, is probably the best-known apologist for this school, though he cites several predecessors and allies, especially Corelli Barnett.[38] The version of the war they see as both dominant and erroneous has several aspects. Politically it constructs the war as avoidable (for the UK, at least) and in hindsight as best avoided. Once engaged in, however, it became an exercise in meaningless mass death that featured an incompetent general staff, personified most often in Field Marshall Douglas Haig, who bore the responsibility for the high casualty rate because of their unimaginative leadership style, ignorance of true frontline conditions, and unwillingness to adopt new tactics. These donkeys, so the myth goes, led an army of lions, brave and stoic men and junior officers who shouldered the burden of the war. Finally, the Allies' final victory was pyrrhic in nature, a product of the Germans having run out of soldiers prior to the Allies reaching the same inevitable end. No credit goes to the military leadership for bringing the war to a victorious close.

Bond's version of the war is the opposite in almost all respects. The First World War was 'a necessary and successful war'[39] that the UK was justified in joining in both political and idealistic terms. Politically, Germany was a threat to the continued dominance of the British Empire, and philosophically the UK was more democratic than Imperial Germany; additionally, the violated neutrality of Belgium was not merely an excuse for Britain to join the war, but a legitimate issue that Britain could not afford to ignore. Once hostilities were engaged, the British general staff faced an initially steep learning curve, but by mid-1918 they had essentially adapted to the material conditions of the Western front and the victory in the last hundred days represented a triumph of such adaptation rather than a bleeding stumble to the finish line. And, though the morale of British troops had its ups and downs, there were no large-scale mutinies, and most soldiers were justifiably proud of their military accomplishments.

Why, if all this is true, has the mythological account of the war been dominant for the last century? Part of Bond's answer is that in fact it has not: the mythic version of the war is largely a product of the war book boom of the late 1920s, the most famous example of which remains Remarque's *Im Westen nichts Neues*. The mythic war thus reflects the disappointment of the late twenties and early thirties more than anything in the war years themselves. This historical distortion was exacerbated by the 1960s, when the fiftieth anniversary of the war coincided with student unrest, the growth of the British nuclear disarmament movement, and US military intervention into Vietnam. The specifics of the war have thus been lost in successive waves of appropriation by movements that were 'anti-war' generally and thus not truly focused on the actual events and conditions of 1914–1918.[40]

In 'The Legacy of the Somme' Jon Stallworthy sums up the conflict in the icon of a British coin: 'On one side, the realistic profile of a real Queen, and on the other, an imaginative representation of Britannia ruling the waves. . . . Here are two ways of looking at history: the one realistic, the other symbolic.'[41] For Bond (though Stallworthy is more directly writing back to Barnett), history is a matter of the realistic side of the coin. He wants to study the First World War 'simply as history without polemic';[42] his primary criterion throughout the book is objectivity. Scholars who see the war primarily as symbol, Fussell chief among them, are thus obscurantists. Yet the question of what scholars such as Fussell mean by 'myth' are underplayed. Bond cites Samuel Hynes' *A War Imagined* several times. Hynes' book is largely dedicated to exploring the myth of the war, but by 'myth' Hynes does not mean anything as simple as historical inaccuracy; rather, he is concerned with what the war has come to mean in subsequent culture. Likewise with Modris Eksteins' *The Rites of Spring*, which Bond characterizes as reaching 'a similarly dismal conclusion form a historian's standpoint'[43] that the war can best be understood subjectively and symbolically. Perhaps the prime concept at stake in such discussions is whether the concept of objectivity itself became a casualty of the Great War; certainly the idea that 'history' is synonymous with 'political relations between nations as viewed by the highest echelon of leaders' became increasingly suspect.[44] There are, of course, severe epistemological problems with an approach that equates 'history' with 'objectivity': 'objectivity' too often means a top-down view in which a tacit sympathy is offered to the powerful, such as the British general staff in this case. Very few people will argue that an individual solider in the trenches, whether an enlisted man or a platoon commander, can gain an objective sense of the immense historical violence that threatens to swallow him up at any moment. The question is whether any person, whether one of Sassoon's scarlet majors or a military historian, can obtain the kind of objectivity that leaves him or her entirely unimplicated in the events being observed. The begged question that it is both possible and desirable to do so is enough to make Walter Benjamin's angel of history weep.

Epistemological questions aside, however, Bond's prime culprits for this misinterpretation of the war are the poets. A literary rather than a historical frame has come to dominate the meaning of the war, and this literary frame is in fact based on a very small and unrepresentative sampling of the poetic output generated by the war: 'a narrow selection of poems, especially those of Owen and Sassoon'[45] continues to be the basis on which most people interpret the war. These poets, moreover, are characterized as much by their personal 'hang-ups' as their reaction to the material realities of combat: 'a large element of their mental turmoil, frustration, and anger was due to sexual problems deriving from their education and repressive home environment'.[46] 'Sexual problems' clearly do not qualify as 'history', so subsequent readers have been saddled with an ahistorical version of the war in which their view of its meaning is almost entirely dependent on personal, subjective, and sexually idiosyncratic angles of observation, Wilfred Owen's being, by the 1930s at least, the most prominent.

In other words, though I disagree that it constitutes a tragedy, I think that Bond is correct in his view that the First World War is still seen as, to use Fussell's term, 'a literary war'.[47] Anglophone people especially are likely to understand the war in terms of suffering, futility, and interrupted trajectories of progress, and this remains largely true whether or not they are able to cite from memory two consecutive lines of Owen's verse. Yet it is to Owen and a few other statistically insignificant poets that we owe the interpretation of an event that killed over eight million people and altered the course of world history.[48] Owen's poetry did not save one of those lives, nor did it shorten the war by a single day. It has, however, affected the way that countless people understand the First World War, and war in general, for most of the last one hundred years.

For this reason, though it may well represent the death of male procreation as a pre-orientation ideal, it may also represent the ideal's greatest and most lasting triumph. Wilfred Owen is probably better known now in Britain and the US than is Douglas Haig. More importantly, Wilfred Owen's interpretation of the war has become more pervasive than that of Douglas Haig or one that is sympathetic to him. And perhaps more importantly than that, Wilfred Owen's subject position, the trench-eye view, the experience of being in front of the front while waiting for death by shellfire (see *OCL* pp. 427–8), has become more indicative of the war than is the objectivity of a senior officer staring down at a map. Whether we celebrate or lament this condition, it is the case and has been so for most of the last century.

This symbolic interpretation of the war is a product of male procreation. Wilfred Owen gave birth to it after being inspired, not just by the events themselves, but by a series of male begetters: most immediately Siegfried Sassoon, but also Robbie Ross, More Adey, C. K. Scott Moncrieff and, of course, Oscar Wilde himself. Owen received from these genealogical figures both the intellectual idea of male procreation, but more importantly the example of how it worked. He learned how a small group of people, operating as a community out of the sight of mainstream culture, is able to generate ideas that profoundly affect that culture, even to the extent of producing a new version of it, despite the culture's utter failure to recognize how these new ideas were produced. Whether an interpretation of Shakespeare's sonnets or of a worldwide cataclysm, the new idea had the potential to affect how people would experience culture for generations. The ongoing controversy over whether the symbolic interpretation of the First World War is a correct or responsible one rests on its success as a cultural phenomenon, and that success is a product of male procreation. The way we see the First World War is a product of Mr WO, but it was begotten by Mr OW.

Afterword

Between July and November of 2014 volunteers gradually covered the moat around the Tower of London in 888,246 ceramic red poppies, one for every British and British colonial life lost in the First World War. For five months, the Tower looked as though surrounded by a lake of blood fed from a torrent that gushed from one of the windows, a sanguinary image reinforced by the installation's official title, 'Blood Swept Lands and Seas of Red', which was taken from an anonymous combatant poet's unsigned will. Striking by day and positively eerie by night, the commemoration was popularly judged a great success; the Royals, as well as over five million others, visited the site, and after 11 November 2014 the ceramic poppies were sold with the proceeds going to military charities. There were some dissenting views as to the effectiveness of the event, most notably from the *Guardian*, but they were largely dismissed as too highbrow and unpatriotic.

On 30 November 2011, the 111th anniversary of his death, a glass barrier was erected around Oscar Wilde's grave in Père Lachaise. Sometime in the late 1990s, a tradition developed among Wilde's fans of kissing his sepulcher while wearing bright red lipstick. As the trend grew, even parts of the monument that would be extremely difficult for the tallest of Wilde's enthusiasts to reach with their lips bore the red badge of devotion; the resulting palimpsest of fading lip prints eventually began to eat into the stone of the crypt. Though a considerable fine was threatened for anyone caught defacing the tomb, it had little effect. In the past few years, the lipstick marks and graffiti, an overwhelming amount of it in shocking red, have begun to appear on the glass barrier.

Here, then, are two distinct forms of cultural commemoration. With the Tower installation we have an event that is state-sponsored, temporary, extremely public, and vaguely patriotic without demanding a specific political meaning. With the practice of tomb kissing, we have a practice that is spontaneous, of lasting (if unintended) effect, furtive, and vaguely queer without demanding a specific sexual meaning. The Tower poppies ask their audience merely to gaze and consider in a place of great national significance, while kissing Wilde's tomb requires them to participate actively, and to do so while the authorities are not looking.

In both cases the color red is the dominant compositional element. More than that, the red stands in contrast to the white stone of either the medieval military architecture of the Tower or Jacob Epstein's modernist, neo-primitive sculpture. Yet the color would seem to be asking for different interpretations in these different settings. The red of the Tower display clearly wants to evoke blood, and quite a lot of it. Viewed from a distance, the installation looks like a still frame from a horror film, with blood pouring out of the window to inundate the fields below. Once one is close enough to see that the corpuscles consist of small, imitation poppies, the reference to the flower as an emblem of Remembrance Day becomes clear. Perhaps if the observer knows something about First World War poetry, he or she will think of John McCrae's 'In Flanders Fields', though its imagery of poppies blooming in a military cemetery is not always now associated with the jingoist tone of the conclusion of the poem. Perhaps, if he or she is more deeply read in First World War poetry, Isaac Rosenberg's 'Break of Day in the Trenches' will come to mind, though the observer will look in vain for Rosenberg's 'queer sardonic rat',[1] the complement to his single, earth-dusted poppy. But Rosenberg also claims that the color of poppies, poetically at least, comes from their roots in the veins of the dead. There is no choice about the ceramic poppies, in other words: the red of the poppies is still the red of blood.

The layers of lipstick on Wilde's tomb, or on the glass that now surrounds it, offer a different study in red. The externality of spilled blood seems less the referent than the rushing internal blood of sexual desire. There remains an irony, of course, in the fact that it seems to have been mostly women kissing the tomb for the last two decades. Certainly more than one pair of male or transgendered lips must have donned lipstick in order to leave its trace, but every photograph I have been able to locate of someone kissing, about to kiss, or smiling proudly next to their fresh imprint, has been that of a woman. And yet there is something queer in this mostly cross-sex practice: insofar as the kissing tradition has grown up at the same time as the broadening acceptance of public same-sex relations, women kissing the final home of a male figure (actually two of them, since Robbie Ross's ashes rest in the tomb as well) so closely associated with the definition and gradual liberation of a specifically gay male sexuality can easily be read as itself an act of polyvalent queerness rather than a simple attempt to drag Wilde back into the arms of heterosexual normality.

But the redness fading into pink of Wilde's tomb offers another possibility, that of a trickle of passion in the House of Death. Much as the swallow kisses the statue in 'The Happy Prince', privately and out of sight of the city authorities who do not value such things, the lipstick traces on a single tomb in the crowded confines of Père Lachaise provide an apt image of the place of the queer: a love that remains illicit, sly, and quite possibly destructive of what it seeks to adore. The swallow and the prince both die in Wilde's fairy tale, after all, and the lipstick on Wilde's tomb does actively damage the stone in addition to being unsightly in the eyes of officialdom. Yet the love, at its best, remains love and though it does not conquer all, it refuses to have its trace entirely removed.

Thus it may be that what I have tried to do in this book can be summarized visually by inserting the trace of the red on Wilde's tomb into the lake of red surrounding the Tower of London in the last half of 2014. Seeing Wilfred Owen as the symbolic son of Oscar Wilde means, among other things, seeing the cultural dominance of Owen's vision of the war as gaining its unique mode of expression, as well as Owen's ability to express it, from his indirect relationship with Wilde. Rather than merely inserting the relatively private discourse of the queer into the public discourse represented by the Tower installation, however, I want to contend instead for the necessary trace of the queer within the public and normative. At first glance, the ceramic poppies flooding the Tower of London seem to have nothing to do with the lipstick on Wilde's tomb, yet alone the green carnation in his buttonhole. But if my arguments have been at all successful, we have to see Owen not as just one of the poppies in the Tower's moat, but as part of the meaning of the display itself. And a large part of this meaning of the War is a product of Owen's status as Wilde's queer child.

This has some implications for ideas about queerness and its cultural role. As I have been at pains to point out, Wilde's conception of male procreation was already falling out of favor in Owen's brief lifetime. By the mid-twentieth century it was all but a relic, a vestige of 'the belief in the absolute value of Greek' that Auden uses to indicate that which had become outmoded in his 1937 poem 'Spain'.[2] Yet as cultural orthodoxy about sexuality has changed over the last century, the queer has changed with it. Male procreation seems even stranger to us now than it did in the late nineteenth century; 'The Portrait of Mr W. H.' was published, after all, in a serious and conservative magazine. In the century since, discussions of same-sex attraction generally do not take place in such public forums. Acceptance of homosexuality as an identity category is widespread and in many ways constitutes a triumph, yet it comes at the cost of becoming unable to see outside of the paradigm of orientation and its identity assumptions. Insofar as acceptance of the homosexual as an identity category, the recognition of which is fundamentally a matter of civil rights, has become normative, that which is queer is that which refuses to fit this paradigm.

More generally, finding the lipstick trace in the poppy field means remaining open to queer meanings that may well exceed common contemporary forms of the queer. And it certainly means placing grand political gestures in the context of apparently much smaller and more private acts and feelings of desire. Much though kissing Wilde's tomb may by now be a practice that finds itself in danger of becoming a mere tradition in the sense of something done only because that is what people do (like kissing the Blarney Stone), its history as an act of queer desire, a claiming of alliance with and love for a man who died exiled and outcast, marks it as a custom worth preserving, at least for as long as it retains this trace of queer desire. But more importantly, so long as queer desire retains the power to inflect the mainstream public gesture, whether war commemoration, legal reform, or literary interpretation, it remains dangerous to ignore.

Notes

Introduction

1. Jeffrey Weeks, *Sex, Politics and Society: The Regulation of Sexuality since 1800*, 2nd edn (London: Longman, 1989), p. 10.
2. Michel Foucault, *An Introduction: Volume 1 of The History of Sexuality* (New York: Vintage-Random House, 1978), p. 37.
3. Richard Kaye provides an excellent overview of sexuality-based Wilde scholarship up to 2004, including the controversy over Christopher Craft's 'Alias Bunberry', which represents *The Importance of Being Earnest* as a coded gay text; see Richard Kaye, 'Gay Studies/Queer Theory and Oscar Wilde', *Palgrave Advances in Oscar Wilde Studies*, ed. Frederick S. Roden (Basingstoke: Palgrave Macmillan, 2004), pp. 189–223, and Christopher Craft, *Another Kind of Love: Male Homosocial Desire in English Discourse, 1850–1920* (Berkeley: University of California Press, 1994), pp. 106–39. The identification of Wilde as unproblematically 'gay' or 'homosexual' continues, especially in texts that are not centrally engaged with questions of sexuality. Heather Marcovitch, *The Art of the Pose: Oscar Wilde's Performance Theory* (Bern: Peter Lang, 2010), p. 10, for instance, identifies Wilde as 'a gay man', and Paul L. Fortunato, *Modernist Aesthetics and Consumer Culture in the Writings of Oscar Wilde* (New York: Routledge, 2007) consistently uses 'gay' throughout his book on the consumerist Wilde.
4. Richard Ellmann, *Oscar Wilde* (New York: Vintage-Random House, 1988), p. 277.
5. For intriguing interpretations in the context of Wilde's subversive politics of precisely the texts I push to the background see Sos Eltis, *Revising Wilde: Society and Subversion in the Plays of Oscar Wilde* (Oxford: Clarendon-Oxford University Press, 1996).
6. Ellmann, *Oscar Wilde*, p. 281.
7. Ian Small, *Oscar Wilde: Recent Research* (Greensboro: ELT Press, 2000), pp. 37–8.
8. Jon Stallworthy, *Wilfred Owen* (Oxford: Oxford University Press, 1974), p. 281.
9. Joanna Bourke, *Dismembering the Male: Men's Bodies, Britain, and the Great War* (Chicago: University of Chicago Press, 1996), pp. 127–8.
10. E. M. Forster, *Maurice: A Novel* (New York: W. W. Norton, 1971), p. 159.
11. A landmark case of similar age in the UK is Dudgeon v. United Kingdom, a 1981 case decided by the European Court of Human Rights to the effect that the UK's 1885 Criminal Law Amendment Act (the law under which Wilde was convicted) was in violation of the European Convention on Human Rights. This case was in turn cited by the US Supreme Court in Lawrence v. Texas, which overturned Bowers v. Hardwick in 2003.
12. Eve Kosofsky Sedgwick, *Between Men: English Literature and Male Homosocial Desire* (New York: Columbia University Press, 1985), p. 35.

196

13. Compare to Thomas K. Hubbard, 'Introduction', *Homosexuality in Greece and Rome: A Sourcebook of Basic Documents* (Berkeley: University of California Press, 2003), pp. 7–8: 'There was, in fact, no more consensus about homosexuality in ancient Greece and Rome than there is today.'

1 Sexual Gnosticism: Male Procreation and 'The Portrait of Mr W. H.'

1. Richard Ellmann, *Oscar Wilde* (New York: Vintage-Random House, 1988), p. 297.
2. Morris B. Kaplan, *Sodom on the Thames: Sex, Love, and Scandal in Wilde Times* (Ithaca: Cornell University Press, 2005), p. 154.
3. See Timothy d'Arch Smith, *Love in Earnest: Some Notes on the Lives and Writings of English 'Uranian' Poets from 1889 to 1930* (London: Routledge and Kegan Paul, 1970), pp. 4–11, for background on Johnson Cory's foundational status for the Uranian poetry movement. Brett succeeded his father as Viscount Esher in 1889 and became a confidant of Edward VII and a great influence on British military politics leading up to the First World War.
4. See Alan Sinfield *The Wilde Century: Effeminacy, Oscar Wilde and the Queer Moment* (New York: Columbia University Press, 1994), pp. vii, 156.
5. *The Picture of Dorian Gray* is specifically cited in Queensberry's plea of justification, which formed the basis of Edward Carson's defence during the first trial. Carson cites the 1890 *Lippincott's* version of *Dorian* as well as 'Phrases and Philosophies for the Use of the Young' throughout the first day of the libel trial; see Merlin Holland, *The Real Trial of Oscar Wilde* (New York: HarperCollins, 2003), p. 290 for the plea of justification, pp. 26–151 for the first day's testimony. 'The Portrait of Mr W. H.' is alluded to in the libel trial when Wilde claims that his literary theme of homoerotic adoration was 'borrowed from Shakespeare I regret to say' (p. 92). Carson replied with an accusation that Wilde had written an 'article pointing out that Shakespeare's sonnets were practically sodomitical', to which Wilde countered with 'I wrote an article to prove that they were not so . . . I object to the shameful perversion being put on Shakespeare's sonnets' (p. 93).
6. Joseph Bristow's Oxford edition reprints both versions of the novel, making a comparison between them readily accessible. I refer here to the kinds of changes in the 1891 text that Bristow delineates in his introduction; see *CWOW3*, pp. lii–lv. I take up the textual history of *Dorian Gray* more extensively in Chapter 2.
7. Horst Schroeder, *Oscar Wilde, The Portrait of Mr. W. H.: Its Composition, Publication, and Reception* (Braunschweig: Technische Universität Carolo-Wilhelmina zu Braunschweig Seminar für Anglistik und Amerikanistik, 1984), p. 25.
8. Schroeder, *Oscar Wilde*, pp. 25–6.
9. For more on the dissolution of the Bodley Head partnership see James G. Nelson, *The Early Nineties: A View from the Bodley Head* (Cambridge, MA: Harvard University Press, 1971), pp. 266–79. See Josephine Guy and Ian Small, *Oscar Wilde's Profession: Writing and the Culture Industry in the Late Nineteenth Century* (Oxford: Oxford University Press, 2000), pp. 171–6 for a

description of the Bodley Head's tentative plans for the book version. See Ian Small, 'Wilde's Texts, Contexts, and "The Portrait of Mr W. H."', *Oscar Wilde in Context*, ed. Kerry Powell and Peter Raby (Cambridge: Cambridge University Press, 2013), pp. 374–83, for the importance of seeing 'Mr W. H.' as a text with multiple versions that hail from various stages in Wilde's writing career: to make my position explicit, I see 'Mr W. H.' as the primary repository of many of Wilde's ideas about male–male love as these ideas developed, and I am thus most interested in the posthumous version of the story as the representation of his most fully developed conceptualization.

10. Oscar Wilde, 'The Portrait of Mr W. H.', *The Soul of Man under Socialism and Selected Critical Prose*, ed. Linda Dowling (London: Penguin, 2001), pp. 31–101 (p. 41). Hereafter cited parenthetically in the text. As the Oxford *Complete Works of Oscar Wilde* edition of Wilde's short fiction is not published at the time of this writing, and as Robert Ross's 1908 Edition prints only the earlier, shorter text, there is still no commonly accepted standard edition of the longer 'Mr W. H.' I have thus chosen to use Linda Dowling's 2001 Penguin edition, which I checked against the manuscript of the longer version housed in the Rosenbach Museum and Library in Philadelphia. This manuscript consists of a copy of the shorter version as printed in *Blackwood's* with Wilde's handwritten additions either as marginalia or as interspersed sheets of paper.

11. The tracts were entitled *A Problem in Greek Ethics* (1883) and *A Problem in Modern Ethics* (1891); Thomas Wright, *Built of Books: How Reading Defined the Life of Oscar Wilde* (New York: Henry Holt, 2008), pp. 203–4 contends that Wilde must have read them but offers no material evidence.

12. *Scots Observer*, 5 July 1890, iv, p. 181; cited in Karl Beckson, ed., *Oscar Wilde: The Critical Heritage* (New York: Barnes and Noble, 1970), p. 75.

13. Ellmann, *Oscar Wilde*, p. 324.

14. Douglas Murray, *Bosie: A Biography of Lord Alfred Douglas* (New York: Hyperion, 2000), pp. 14–17.

15. For the significance of Jowett to the Oxford study of classical culture generally and Plato specifically, see Linda Dowling, *Hellenism and Homosexuality in Victorian Oxford* (Ithaca: Cornell University Press, 1994), especially pp. 64–77. Jowett's Clarendon edition of the dialogues was published in four volumes in 1871, just a few years prior to Wilde's arrival at Magdalen College.

16. Lawrence Danson, *Wilde's Intentions: The Artist in His Criticism* (Oxford: Clarendon-Oxford University Press, 1997), pp. 116–17.

17. Danson, *Wilde's Intentions*, p. 125.

18. Dowling, *Hellenism and Homosexuality in Victorian Oxford*, pp. 125–7.

19. Neil Bartlett's *Who Was That Man? A Present for Mr Oscar Wilde* (London: Serpent's Tail, 1988) offers a fascinating relationship with the spectre of Wilde from the perspective of a self-identified gay male Londoner in the mid 1980s. Much of the text involves the negotiations involved in determining whether Wilde is the very basis of an accepted definition of gay or whether his historical and cultural distance disqualifies him from bearing the signifier.

20. William A. Cohen, *Sex Scandal: The Private Parts of Victorian Fiction* (Durham: Duke University Press, 1996), p. 213.

21. Richard Halpern, *Shakespeare's Perfume: Sodomy and Sublimity in the Sonnets, Wilde, Freud, and Lacan* (Philadelphia: University of Pennsylvania Press, 2002), p. 51.

22. 'Perceiving a fallen art world and an unregenerate public, Wilde had two alternatives: he could respond cynically or idealistically. He chose both alternatives and developed two distinct styles to represent them', Regenia Gagnier, *Idylls of the Marketplace: Oscar Wilde and the Victorian Public* (Stanford: Stanford University Press, 1986), p. 19.

23. Wilde used 'Mr W. H.' in precisely this way in his post-prison epistolary flirtation with Louis Wilkinson, a Radley student bound for Oxford. In a letter of 20 March 1899, Wilde asked that Wilkinson look up the story, which he described as expressing his direct thoughts about the meaning of the sonnets: 'I think it was the boy who acted in his plays' (*WCL*, p. 1133).

24. For a fascinating alternative answer to this conundrum, see Rachel Ablow, 'Reading and Re-reading: Wilde, Newman, and the Fiction of Belief', *Wilde Discoveries: Traditions, Histories, Archives*, ed. Joseph Bristow (Toronto: University of Toronto Press, 2013), pp. 190–211, which places 'Mr W. H.' in the context of Wilde's interpretation of John Henry Newman's illative sense and sees Wilde as constructing belief as a form of fiction. Bruce Bashford, *Oscar Wilde: The Critic as Humanist* (Madison: Farleigh Dickinson University Press, 1999), pp. 21–7 presents what is for me a less convincing explanation in which Wilde constructs the story in such a way that the characters only find the evidence for the existence of Willie Hughes to be compelling when they already believe in the theory. Bashford connects this idea of inspiration preceding evidence to Wilde's putative distaste for the damage it does to the humanistic ideal of holistic subjectivity.

25. Ellmann, *Oscar Wilde*, pp. 40–1, 68.

26. The quotation is drawn from John Addington Symonds, *The Fine Arts*, vol. 3 of *The Renaissance in Italy* (New York: Henry Holt, 1888). The complete sentence is 'He alone, in that age of sensuality and animalism, pierced through the form of flesh and sought the divine idea it imprisoned' (p. 518).

27. John Addington Symonds, *Male Love: A Problem in Greek Ethics and Other Writings*, ed. John Lauritsen (New York: Pagan Press, 1983), p. 18.

28. Eve Kosofsky Sedgwick, *Epistemology of the Closet* (Berkeley: University of California Press, 1990), p. 87.

29. Ellmann, *Oscar Wilde*, p. 463.

30. In a sense, though, Bosie eventually became a part of the genealogy when he published in 1933 *The True History of Shakespeare's Sonnets*. He wholeheartedly supports Wilde's theory of the sonnets as a theory but regrets that Wilde couched it within 'a very foolish and unconvincing story'; see Lord Alfred Douglas, *The True History of Shakespeare's Sonnets* (London: Martin Secker, 1933), p. 34. Interestingly, the part of Wilde's theory of which Douglas least approves is the matter of the interpretation of Shakespeare's command to Willie Hughes to beget children: 'it is far-fetched and, I think, unconvincing' (p. 39). After the publication of the book, Douglas completed the cycle of belief by claiming in a 1941 letter to Lady Diana Cooper to have discovered material evidence of a Will Hews's sixteenth-century existence; see Murray, *Bosie*, p. 314.

31. See Joseph Bristow, '"A Complex Multiform Creature": Wilde's Sexual Identities', *The Cambridge Companion to Oscar Wilde*, ed. Peter Raby (Cambridge: Cambridge University Press, 1997), pp. 195–218 which goes into detail on the subject of Wilde's refusal of sexological pathologies.

32. Ellis and Symonds's *Sexual Inversion* was published in German in 1896 and in English the following year. The English version, which had Symonds's name and contributions removed at the insistence of his family, was legally suppressed as obscene. Good recent accounts of this publication history can be found in Heike Bauer, *English Literary Sexology: Translations of Inversion, 1860–1930* (Basingstoke: Palgrave Macmillan, 2009), pp. 54–8 and Sean Brady, *Masculinity and Male Homosexuality in Britain, 1861–1913* (Basingstoke: Palgrave Macmillan, 2005), pp. 140–52; for Symonds' reservations about the term 'inversion', see Brady (p. 191).

33. Joseph Bristow, *Effeminate England: Homoerotic Writing after 1885* (New York: Columbia University Press, 1995), p. 45.

34. Linda Dowling delineates the political implications of effeminacy in her first chapter, 'Aesthete and Effeminatus', though perhaps at the expense of its more directly sexual implications; see Dowling, *Hellenism and Homosexuality in Victorian Oxford*, pp. 1–31. Nonetheless, her observations help to explain why Wilde's writings and persona were perceived as politically threatening to bourgeois English culture. See also Sinfield, *The Wilde Century*, pp. 25–51, which presents a history of British effeminacy that contends that 'effeminacy is founded in misogyny' (p. 26); there is certainly a misogynistic element to Wilde's use of effeminacy, but, unlike the cultural history that Sinfield considers, Wilde uses the term in a nonpejorative sense. As I point out below, Wilde's use of effeminacy promotes a version of femininity but does so by removing it from the female body.

35. Kathy Alexis Psomiades, *Beauty's Body: Femininity and Representation in British Aeshethicism* (Stanford: Stanford University Press, 1997) offers an extremely perceptive tracing of the history of the use of the feminine figure in nineteenth-century British aestheticism in which 'masculinity, feminized, can be loaded with secret depths' (p. 7), which is certainly part of the use of effeminacy in 'Mr W. H.' Psomiades' explicit concern with Wilde, however, is limited to *Dorian Gray* and *Salome*, which she reads as parodic versions of a fallen aestheticism.

36. Wilde's narrator even ascribes the development of feminism to the imitation of female bodies by male actors, speculating that Shakespeare's heroines, inspired by such boy actors as Willie Hughes, laid the foundations for later feminine development: 'lads and young men whose passionate purity, quick mobile fancy, and healthy freedom from sentimentality can hardly fail to have suggested a new and delightful type of girlhood or of womanhood' (p. 73).

2   Shades of Green and Gray: Dual Meanings in Wilde's Novel

1. Robert Smythe Hichens, *The Green Carnation*, 1894 (New York: Mitchell Kennerley, nd), p. 138. Hereafter cited parenthetically in the text.

2. Richard Ellmann, *Oscar Wilde* (New York: Vintage-Random House, 1988), p. 365.

3. Ellmann, *Oscar Wilde*, p. 430. See also Karl Beckson, 'Oscar Wilde and the Green Carnation', *ELT* 43.4 (2000), pp. 387–97. Beckson casts doubt on the facticity of Robertson's account and points out how his story has become an element of the Wilde mythology that has grown in the telling. Nonetheless, Beckson does demonstrate that the green carnation became associated with Wilde and his circle by 1894 at the latest. It may not have been the French secret signifier of same-sex love that later sources would claim, but if it did not signify queer attraction before Wilde began to wear it, it certainly did after he began.

4. Ellmann, *Oscar Wilde*, p. 366.

5. Dennis Denisoff, *Aestheticism and Sexual Parody, 1840–1940* (Cambridge: Cambridge University Press, 2001) reads *The Green Carnation* as a much gentler and campier act of parody than I am allowing for here, although he does admit that it 'threatened the security of those who were in the know by educating others regarding this sympathetic discourse of desire' (p. 111). See also Felicia Ruff, 'Transgressive Props; or Oscar Wilde's E(a)rnest Signifier', *Wilde Discoveries: Traditions, Histories, Archives*, ed. Joseph Bristow (Toronto: University of Toronto Press, 2013), pp. 315–39, which approaches the related question of sexual coding in Wilde's texts through the cigarette case in *The Importance of Being Earnest*.

6. Neil McKenna, *The Secret Life of Oscar Wilde* (New York: Basic Books, 2005), pp. 276–7 offers the most complete account of Hichens' initial meeting with Bosie in Egypt, including identifying Hichens as a Uranian. McKenna's biography is quite willing to draw conclusions on sexual matters on little evidence, so I take Hichens' sexual sympathy with Bosie and the other young men in Cairo as a possibility that would deepen the irony of his writing *The Green Carnation* rather than as a necessary fact. Murray also mentions the meeting, adding that Hichens had a satire of Aestheticism in mind prior to meeting Bosie, though offering no documentation of this; see Douglas Murray, *Bosie: A Biography of Lord Alfred Douglas* (New York: Hyperion, 2000), p. 53. Ellmann also identifies Hichens as a homosexual, perhaps based on an interpretation of one of Wilde's telegrams to Ada Leverson referring to Hichens as 'the doubting disciple who has written the false gospel' (*WCL*, p. 615); see Ellmann, *Oscar Wilde*, p. 425.

7. There are, in fact, now three, since in 2011 Harvard University Press published Nicholas Frankel's edition of Wilde's original typescript that was the basis for the 1890 edition.

8. The aversion in Jeff Nunokawa, *Tame Passions of Wilde: The Styles of Manageable Desire* (Princeton: Princeton University Press, 2003), pp. 71–89 that Dorian Gray is a novel that is not only about boredom but is itself boring rests at least in part, I think, on the dominance of the 1891 version, which Nunokawa cites exclusively. Nicholas Ruddick, '"The Peculiar Quality of My Genius": Degeneration, Decadence, and *Dorian Gray* in 1890–91', *Oscar Wilde: The Man, His Writings, and His World*, ed. Robert N. Keane (New York: AMS, 2003), pp. 125–37 makes the case for preferring the 1890 to the 1891 version. For the past ten years there has been, I believe, an increased sensitivity in Wilde scholarship to the differences in the two versions and a gradual acknowledgement of the earlier version's distinguishing features, including reading the 1890 *Dorian Gray* in the context of the rest of the contents of the July 1890 issue of *Lippincott's*: see Elizabeth Lorang,

        '*The Picture of Dorian Gray* in Context: Intertextuality and *Lippincott's Monthly Magazine*', *Victorian Periodicals Review*, 43.1 (2010), pp. 19–41.

9. This goes back to the first trial, at which Edward Carson cited the 'seduction passage' at length in his opening for the defense; see Merlin Holland, *The Real Trial of Oscar Wilde* (New York: HarperCollins, 2003), pp. 259–60.

10. It is worth noting in this context that the vow in question is part of the conferring of the ring and thus spoken only by the man in the nineteenth century. See the 'Form of the Solemnization of Matrimony' ('WITH this Ring I thee wed, with my Body I thee worship, and with all my worldly Goods I thee endow'). Sexual worship is thus essentialized as an exclusively masculine activity within the ceremony.

11. The 1891 edition revises the first sentence to 'he is absolutely necessary to me' (*CWOW3*, p. 176).

12. The 1891 edition retains Basil's self-quotation in Chapter 9 despite having cut the line he quotes ('as I said to Harry, once, you are made to be worshipped' [*CWOW3*, p. 265]).

13. Frankel's edition demonstrates that Wilde's original version of this sentence was 'It is quite true that I have worshipped you with far more romance of feeling than a man should ever give to a friend'; see Oscar Wilde, *The Picture of Dorian Gray: An Annotated, Uncensored Edition*, ed. Nicholas Frankel (Cambridge: Belknap-Harvard University Press, 2011), p. 172. Moreover, Wilde's editors also removed a complete sentence further in the paragraph: 'There was love in every line, and in every touch there was passion' (p. 172). Frankel contends that the changes made for *Lippincott's* were never approved by Wilde (p. 41); Guy and Small concur but stress that Wilde still used the *Lippincott's* text as the basis for the 1891 volume; see Josephine M. Guy and Ian Small, *Oscar Wilde's Profession: Writing and the Cultural Industry in the Late Nineteenth Century* (Oxford: Oxford University Press, 2000), p. 233.

14. As Wilde put it in an unpublished letter to Sir George Scott-Douglas, *Dorian Gray* 'has beauty for its aim, and ethics for its subject matter' (cited in *CWOW3*, p. li).

15. The extent to which such categories need not be mutually exclusive for Wilde can be illustrated by the relationship between Lord Illingworth and Gerald Arbuthnot in *A Woman of No Importance*.

16. Oscar Wilde, 'The Portrait of Mr W. H.', *The Soul of Man under Socialism and Selected Critical Prose*, ed. Linda Dowling (London: Penguin, 2001), p. 63. The metaphor is also used in 'The Soul of Man under Socialism' to illustrate the passivity of the ideal spectator of art: 'The spectator is to be receptive. He is to be the violin on which the master is to play' (*CWOW4*, p. 258).

17. Wilde also uses the term in a way that fits quite well with our own usage, for example in his exchange with the editor of *The St. James's Gazette* on its review of *Dorian Gray*: 'A critic should be taught to criticize a work of art without making any reference to the personality of the author' (*WCL*, p. 432). The word's use throughout 'The Soul of Man under Socialism' seems to me to retain more or less its common meaning, though it may gain extra valence when read in the light of *Dorian Gray*.

18. John Addington Symonds, *Male Love: A Problem in Greek Ethics and other Writings*, ed. John Lauritsen (New York: Pagan Press, 1983), p. 7.

19. Symonds, *Male Love*, p. 7. 'A Problem in Greek Ethics' also ascribed the character and importance of pederasty in ancient Greek culture to the Dorian people (p. 13), which offers another possibility for homosexual coding in Wilde's novel. The word 'malachia' (μαλακία) is glossed in Henry George Liddell and Robert Scott's *An Intermediate English-Greek Lexicon* (1889) as '1. softness, delicacy, effeminacy' and '2. want of patience, weakness'; see the Tufts University Perseus Digital Library, http://www.perseus.tufts.edu. Symonds is choosing a specifically gendered translation of a term that, as the Perseus site also demonstrates, refers on a literal level to a mollusk without a shell.

20. John Addington Symonds, *Male Love*, p. 53. The word 'personality' also plays an important role in Walter Pater, *The Renaissance: Studies in Art and Poetry*, ed. Adam Phillips (Oxford: Oxford University Press, 1986). In the Preface Pater writes of the 'engaging personality' and the 'fair personality', in both cases 'in life or in a book', as if to bring home the point that the type of aesthetic criticism that he espouses refuses to differentiate between art objects and human beings as 'powers or forces producing pleasurable sensations' (p. xxx). In the Conclusion, however, it is 'that thick wall of personality through which no real voice has ever pierced on its way to us' that keeps each mind 'a solitary prisoner in its own dream of a world' (p. 151). In the first case personality functions as the object of aesthetic fascination while in the second it marks the epistemological limits of subjectivity.

21. Ives seems to have been something of a contradiction in terms: a secret activist. For his friendship with Wilde see John Stokes, *Oscar Wilde: Myths, Miracles, and Imitations* (Cambridge: Cambridge University Press, 1996), pp. 65–88, while for his relationship to the emerging British homophile political movement see Matt Cook, *London and the Culture of Homosexuality, 1885–1914* (Cambridge: Cambridge University Press, 2003), pp. 138–50. McKenna also stresses Wilde and Bosie's involvement in Ives' Order of Chaerona, a kind of Masonic organization for the promotion of same-sex love, though he probably exaggerates the seriousness of their commitment.

22. Oscar Wilde, 'The Portrait of Mr W. H.', p. 66.

23. Oscar Wilde, 'The Portrait of Mr W. H.', p. 65.

24. This caveat leaves room for Jonathan Dollimore's account of the anti-essentialist Wilde, as well as other work that sees Wilde as a forerunner of poststructuralist thought: see Jonathan Dollimore, *Sexual Dissidence: Augustine to Wilde, Freud to Foucault* (Oxford: Oxford University Press, 1991), p. 25 and *passim*.

25. Sterility is an overt concern in another cancelled sentence in Frankel's edition of the *Dorian Gray* typescript, in which the penultimate paragraph of Chapter 7 ends with 'There was something tragic in a friendship so coloured by romance, something infinitely tragic in a romance that was at once so passionate and so sterile'; see Oscar Wilde, *The Picture of Dorian Gray: An Annotated, Uncensored Edition*, p. 175. Dorian is thinking about Basil at this point, though my contention is that sterility comes eventually to encompass all three characters.

26. Oscar Wilde, 'Lord Arthur Savile's Crime', *The Works of Oscar Wilde Volume 4*, 15 vols (Boston: C. T. Brainard, 1909), pp. 3–72; p. 18.

27. Nicholas Frankel, *Oscar Wilde's Decorated Books* (Ann Arbor: University of Michigan Press, 2000), pp. 9–10, 35–8, 79–108 also stresses the importance of signifier over signified in several of Wilde's texts, as well as the emphasis on the signifier implied by the careful material production of these texts as books.

28. See Karl Beckson, ed., *Oscar Wilde: The Critical Heritage* (New York: Barnes and Noble, 1970), pp. 68–9.

29. See Karl Beckson, ed., *Oscar Wilde*, p. 72.

30. See Karl Beckson, ed., *Oscar Wilde*, p. 75.

31. For more on the Cleveland Street affair see Morris B. Kaplan, *Sodom on the Thames: Sex, Love, and Scandal in Wilde Times* (Ithaca: Cornell University Press, 2005), pp. 166–223 and H. G. Cocks, *Nameless Offences: Homosexual Desire in the Nineteenth Century* (London: I. B. Tauris, 2003), pp. 144–53.

32. This coding process can be compared to Richard Dellamora's description of Walter Pater's writing in the 1860s: it 'is discreetly coded so as to "miss" some of Pater's listeners while reaching men sympathetic to expressions of desire between men': see Richard Dellamora, *Masculine Desire: The Sexual Politics of Victorian Aestheticism* (Chapel Hill: University of North Carolina Press, 1990), p. 58.

33. Interestingly, in Wilde's third and final letter to the editor of *The Scots Observer*, Wilde accuses Henley of a similar maneuver of personae in his suggestion that the review, as well as several other letters on the subject, had all been written by Henley under assumed names.

34. These reviews are reprinted in Oscar Wilde, *The Picture of Dorian Gray*, ed. Robert Mighall (London: Penguin, 2003), pp. 219–20.

35. For a slightly different take on how Wilde's apparent rejection of ethics hides a critique of the narrow ethics used to attack his novel, see Joseph Bristow, 'Wilde, *Dorian Gray*, and Gross Indecency', *Sexual Sameness: Textual Differences in Lesbian and Gay Writing*, ed. Joseph Bristow (London: Routledge, 1992), pp. 44–63. Julia Prewitt Brown also stresses the place of ethics in Wilde's philosophy of art, claiming that Wilde offered a synthesis of the ethical and the aesthetic rather than a simple rejection of the ethical: see Julia Prewitt Brown, *Cosmopolitan Criticism: Oscar Wilde's Philosophy of Art* (Charlottesville: University of Virginia Press, 1997), especially pp. 51–67. For Brown, in Wilde 'art's freedom from ethics is the basis of its usefulness to us as ethical beings' (p. 75).

36. For a fascinating interpretation of how the addition of the self-consciously melodramatic James Vane subplot to the 1891 version reflects the controversies caused by the 1890 version, see Neil Hultgren, 'Oscar Wilde's Poetic Injustice in *The Picture of Dorian Gray*', *Wilde Discoveries: Traditions, Histories, Archives*, ed. Joseph Bristow (Toronto: University of Toronto Press, 2013), pp. 212–30.

37. Holland, *The Real Trial of Oscar Wilde*, p. 82. Later in the trial Carson accused Wilde of having 'purged' or 'toned down' the 1890 version for its publication in book form, which charge Wilde denied (p. 219).

38. Holland, *The Real Trial of Oscar Wilde*, p. 51. Hereafter cited parenthetically in the text. I have chosen to use Merlin Holland's recent version of the first trial; for a comparison of the various versions of the trial accounts (primarily H. Montgomery Hyde's *The Trials of Oscar Wilde* and Christopher Millard's

[as Stuart Mason] *Oscar Wilde: Three Times Tried)*, see Leslie J. Moran, 'Transcripts and Truth: Writing the Trials of Oscar Wilde', *Oscar Wilde and Modern Culture: The Making of a Legend*, ed. Joseph Bristow (Athens: Ohio University Press, 2008), pp. 234–58.

39. The complete text of 'The Priest and the Acolyte' is available at http://www. fordham.edu/halsall/pwh/bloxam2.asp

40. My use of the term 'the cause' replicates the language of George Ives, whose foundation of the Order of Chaeronea in 1893 functions as an integral part of McKenna's metanarrative of Oscar and Bosie as homosexual political activists. By use of the term, I do not wish to imply that either person necessarily embraced a vision of homosexuality that replicates a post-Stonewall ideal of gay rights, a matter that I explore further in the next chapter.

41. For the trials as a foundation for modern homosexual identity, see Sinfield, *The Wilde Century* and Ed Cohen, *Talk on the Wilde Side: Toward a Genealogy of a Discourse on Male Sexualities* (New York: Routledge, 1993).

3   Love of the Impossible: Wilde's Failed Queer Theory

1. Richard Ellmann, *Oscar Wilde* (New York: Vintage-Random House, 1988), pp. 143–7.

2. This estimation of Wilde as a derivative poet was continued into the 1970s when Harold Bloom declared him Exhibit A of the 'weak poet' in *The Anxiety of Influence*.

3. Stefano Evangelista, *British Aestheticism and Ancient Greece: Hellenism, Reception, Gods in Exile* (New York: Palgrave Macmillan, 2009), pp. 135–6 points out that Wilde borrowed his sexual coding of 'the love of the impossible/*l'amour de l'impossible*' from Symonds' *Studies of the Greek Poets*.

4. The 1882 edition was actually the fourth through sixth printings of the work: see Fong and Beckson's introduction to *CWOW1* for an explanation of how publisher David Bogue created six 'editions' out of two small print runs (pp. xiv–xvii).

5. Joseph Bristow points out that the sexual excesses of 'Charmides' were directly responsible also for the break between Wilde and Frank Miles, the young artist with whom Wilde lived when he first moved to London. Miles' mother objected to the poem so strongly that she physically excised it from her copy of Wilde's *Poems*: see Joseph Bristow, 'Oscar Wilde's Poetic Traditions: From Aristophanes' *Clouds* to *The Ballad of Reading Gaol*', *Oscar Wilde in Context*, ed. Kerry Powell and Peter Raby (Cambridge: Cambridge University Press, 2013), pp. 73–87, specifically pp. 81–2.

6. David M. Halperin, *How to Do the History of Homosexuality* (Chicago: University of Chicago Press, 2002), p. 109; hereafter cited parenthetically in the text.

7. Perhaps with the exception of one speech by Gwendolen in *The Importance of Being Earnest*: 'The home seems to me to be the proper sphere for the man. And certainly once a man begins to neglect his domestic duties he becomes painfully effeminate, does he not? And I don't like that. It makes men so very attractive'; see Oscar Wilde, *The Importance of Being Earnest*, *The Works of Oscar Wilde Volume 5*, 15 vols (Boston: C. T. Brainard, 1909), pp. 157–329;

p. 267. For the important point that the Wilde trials did not suddenly end effeminacy as a symptom of cross-sex erotic appeal, see Lisa Hamilton, 'Oscar Wilde, New Women, and the Rhetoric of Effeminacy', *Wilde Writings: Contextual Conditions*, ed. Joseph Bristow (Toronto: University of Toronto Press, 2003), pp. 23–53.

8. Quoted in John Stokes, *Oscar Wilde: Myths, Miracles, and Imitations* (Cambridge: Cambridge University Press, 1996), p. 69.

9. Matt Cook points out that the clean-shaven status of the principal figures of the Wilde trials was consistently mentioned in the press; see Matt Cook, *London and the Culture of Homosexuality: 1885–1914* (Cambridge: Cambridge University Press, 2003), p. 61.

10. Compare to Foucault: 'to be sure, the preference for boys or girls was easily recognized as a character trait: men could be distinguished by the pleasure they were most fond of; a matter of taste that could lend itself to humorous treatment, not a matter of topology involving the individual's very nature, the truth of his desire, or the natural legitimacy of his predilection'; see Michel Foucault, *The Use of Pleasure: Volume 2 of The History of Sexuality*, trans. Robert Hurley (New York: Vintage-Random House, 1985), p. 190.

11. Alan Bray's *The Friend* (Chicago: University of Chicago Press, 2003), a painstaking and thorough account of publicly and religiously sanctioned same-sex friendship prior to the rise of civil society in the late seventeenth century, demonstrates the extent to which Halperin may well write off the relationship between friendship and pre-homosexuality too quickly. Bray is careful to indicate that sworn friendships were not merely code for same-sex sexual coupling, but he also stresses the social importance of such 'weddings' in culture prior to the enlightenment and, at significant moments, after it as well.

12. See Foucault, *The Use of Pleasure*, p. 194: 'passivity was always disliked, and for an adult to be suspected of it was especially serious'. As Foucault stresses throughout Volume 2 of *The History of Sexuality*, ancient Greek discourse about male same-sex relations included 'strongly negative judgments concerning some possible aspects of relations between men, as well as a definite aversion to anything that might denote a deliberate renunciation of the signs and privileges of the masculine role' (p. 19). Although the first volume of Foucault's *History* remains by far the best known of the three, both *The Use of Pleasure* and *The Care of the Self* are quite illuminating on the constructions of attitudes toward sex in antiquity, which is a matter of great relevance to Wilde studies.

13. Leo Bersani's foundational 1987 article 'Is the Rectum a Grave?' argues for a version of the pathic to be central to the meaning of the modern homosexual especially in the age of AIDS. The receptive role in intercourse for Bersani should involve a self-shattering and an acknowledgement of the 'strong appeal of powerlessness, of the loss of control', which is precisely what straight culture finds objectionable about homosexuality, and what thus prompts homophobic violence; see Leo Bersani, *Is the Rectum a Grave? and Other Essays* (Chicago: University of Chicago Press, 2010), p. 24.

14. The invert thus most closely resembles Foucault's description of the homosexual under the regime of sexology: 'The nineteenth-century homosexual became a personage, a past, a case history, and a childhood, in addition

to being a type of life, a life form, and a morphology, with an indiscreet anatomy and possibly a mysterious physiology'; see Michel Foucault, *An Introduction: Volume 1 of The History of Sexuality*, trans. Robert Hurley (New York: Vintage-Random House, 1978), p. 43. As Charles Upchurch, *Before Wilde: Sex between Men in Britain's Age of Reform* (Berkeley: University of California Press, 2009), pp. 197–9 points out, Krafft-Ebing reserved his most pathologizing language for effeminate inverts even while trying to remove some of the stigma associated with inversion more generally.

15. Ellmann includes a reproduction of the drawing on the plate prior to the photograph addressed below. Merlin Holland, *The Wilde Album* (New York: Henry Holt, 1997), p. 141 also reproduces the image. It is clear from the context of the fan and cigarette that the illustration is one of Wilde as Lady Windermere and references Wilde's controversial curtain speech addressed at the beginning of Chapter 2 above; in other words, it portrays Wilde as his specific character, not as dressing in just any woman's clothing.

16. Ellmann, *Oscar Wilde*, plate facing p. 429.

17. The most thorough medical debunking of the syphilis theory can be found in Ashley H. Robins, *Oscar Wilde, The Great Drama of His Life: How His Tragedy Reflected His Personality*, (Brighton: Sussex Academic Press, 2011), pp. 98–116.

18. See Merlin Holland, 'Biography and the Art of Lying', *The Cambridge Companion to Oscar Wilde*, ed. Peter Raby (Cambridge: Cambridge University Press, 1997), pp. 3–17, which explains the photograph (pp. 10–12) as well as providing some background on the syphilis theory (pp. 12–14). See Laurence Senelick, 'Master Wood's Profession: Wilde and the Subculture of Homosexual Blackmail in the Victorian Theatre', *Wilde Writings: Contextual Conditions*, ed. Joseph Bristow (Toronto: University of Toronto Press, 2003), pp. 163–82, which adds to the discussion as well as contextualizing the photograph's use by Elaine Showalter and Marjorie Garber prior its authenticity being undermined (pp. 163–6).

19. See Thomas K. Hubbard, *Homosexuality in Greece and Rome: A Sourcebook of Basic Documents* (Berkeley: University of California Press, 2003), pp. 10–16, as well as Thomas K. Hubbard, 'Review of David M. Halperin, *How to Do the History of Homosexuality*, Bryn Mawr Classical Review (2003.09.22)', http://bmcr.brynmawr.edu/2003/2003-09-22.html.

20. For the outlines of the limited reception of sexology in Britain see Upchurch, *Before Wilde*, pp. 186–205 and Heike Bauer, *English Literary Sexology: Translations of Inversion, 1860–1930* (Basingstoke: Palgrave Macmillan, 2009), pp. 52–81.

21. Douglas Murray, *Bosie: A Biography of Lord Alfred Douglas* (New York: Hyperion, 2000), p. 69.

22. In this context, Kerry Powell's rejection of the Wilde trials as the instant codification of homosexual identity that they have often been interpreted as is understandable, though his identification of this interpretation as Foucauldian forgets Foucault in the sense that Halperin laments: see Kerry Powell, *Acting Wilde: Victorian Sexuality, Theatre, and Oscar Wilde* (Cambridge: Cambridge University Press, 2009), pp. 123–30.

23. Merlin Holland, *The Real Trial of Oscar Wilde* (New York: HarperCollins, 2003), p. 58, italics in original.

24. Holland, *The Real Trial of Oscar Wilde*, p. 26.
25. Holland, *The Real Trial of Oscar Wilde*, p. 58.
26. By the cultural logic of pre-orientation sexuality, identifying Wilde as the passive partner would also serve Queensberry by allowing him tacitly thus to identify his son as the active, and thus the masculine and less pathological, partner.
27. Queensberry would thus be engaged in what Cocks, *Nameless Offenses*, calls 'reading the sodomite': 'the Victorian sodomite became modern then, as a figure of equivocation, both reported and unseen, flagrantly visible and at the same time invisible and mysterious' (H. G. Cocks, *Nameless Offences: Homosexual Desire in the Nineteenth Century* (London: I. B.Tauris, 2003), p. 90).
28. Ed Cohen, *Talk on the Wilde Side: Toward a Genealogy of a Discourse on Male Sexualities* (New York: Routledge, 1993), p. 131.
29. Alan Sinfield, *The Wilde Century: Effeminacy, Oscar Wilde and the Queer Moment* (New York: Columbia University Press, 1994), p. 91.
30. Sinfield, *The Wilde Century*, p. 121.
31. Sinfield, *The Wilde Century*, p. vii.
32. Holland, *The Real Trial of Oscar Wilde*, pp. 72, 39.
33. See Gert Hekma, 'A History of Sexology: Social and Historical Aspects of Sexuality', *From Sappho to De Sade: Moments in the History of Sexuality*, ed. Jan Bremmer (London: Routledge, 1989), pp. 173–93 for the political contexts of Ulrichs' attempts at legal reform (pp. 178–9).
34. Eve Kosofsky Sedgwick, *Between Men: English Literature and Male Homosocial Desire* (New York: Columbia University Press, 1985), p. 4.
35. Lee Edelman, *No Future: Queer Theory and the Death Drive* (Durham: Duke University Press, 2005), p. 25, Edelman's italics. Hereafter cited parenthetically in the text. Edelman is using Lacan's triad of the Real, the Symbolic, and the Imaginary, though without the third term in this quotation. The Real in Lacan is that which resists the Symbolic; it may be thought of as the world outside of language (the Symbolic) which language tries to represent. Edelman thus has the queer interrupting the Symbolic with the uncomfortable reminder that the Symbolic is not and cannot contain the Real.
36. Edelman's queer negativity builds on earlier work by Leo Bersani on homosexuality as a refusal of relationality within eros: see especially Leo Bersani, *Homos* (Cambridge: Harvard University Press, 1995).
37. José Esteban Muñoz, *Cruising Utopia: The Then and There of Queer Futurity* (New York: New York University Press, 2009), p. 1. Hereafter cited parenthetically in the text.
38. Objection to the mainstreaming of queer sexuality is a quality shared by all of these queer theorists, though they differ on how to oppose it. For an important earlier articulation of this crisis in queer history, brought about in some ways by the success of the gay liberation movement in bringing homosexual rights into public discussion, see Michael Warner, *The Trouble with Normal: Sex, Politics, and the Ethics of Queer Life* (Cambridge: Harvard University Press, 1999).
39. Heather Love, *Feeling Backward: Loss and the Politics of Queer History* (Cambridge: Harvard University Press, 2007), p. 8.
40. Love, *Feeling Backward*, p. 42.
41. Halberstam's version of the child owes quite a bit, as she points to, to Kathryn Bond Stockton, *The Queer Child: or Growing Sideways in the Twentieth Century*

(Durham: Duke University Press, 2009); for example, Stockton's insistence that 'the child from the standpoint of "normal" adults is always queer' (p. 7), and that the child can and must often 'grow sideways' when confronted with the challenge of 'growing up' into a 'normal' adult. Stockton also is as likely to take a popular film as a literary text as her subject, for instance reading Johnny Depp's performance in the 2005 *Charlie and the Chocolate Factory* as giving Willy Wonka a 'Wildean look' (p. 239).

42. Judith Halberstam, *The Queer Art of Failure* (Durham: Duke University Press, 2011), p. 47.

43. Halberstam engages in a direct critique of Edelman (106–9), especially the politics of his version of queer negativity. I must add that I am happy to discover that I was not the only reader disappointed that a book titled *No Future* fails to engage with the Sex Pistols.

44. Love, *Feeling Backward*, p. 32.

45. Neil McKenna, *The Secret Life of Oscar Wilde* (New York: Basic Books, 2005), p. 454.

46. Halberstam, *The Queer Art of Failure*, p. 109.

47. Guy and Small point out the extent to which *The Happy Prince and Other Tales* was less than a resounding financial success: see Josephine M. Guy and Ian Small, *Oscar Wilde's Profession: Writing and the Culture Industry in the Late Nineteenth Century* (Oxford: Oxford University Press, 2000), pp. 53–6. Nonetheless, it sold out its first edition in less than a year and was certainly successful compared to *Poems*.

48. Unlike the Sex Pistols' 'God Save the Queen', Whitney Houston's wretched 'The Greatest Love of All' is directly referenced and critiqued by Edelman, who characterizes it as the unofficial US national anthem (p. 143).

4 Oscar and Sons: The Afterlife of Male Procreation

1. Ian Small provides an excellent account of the textual history of the letter in his introduction to *CWOW2*. Nonetheless, since my emphasis is on the text's status as a personal letter to Alfred Douglas rather than as a literary text, I have chosen to use Hart-Davis and Holland's version from *WCL*. Put simply, Hart-Davis and Holland use the prison manuscript as their base text, where Small uses a combination of the prison manuscript, typescripts, and Ross's shortened, published version. Since I am using the text of the letter rather than the shortened version that Ross first published in 1905, in deference to Small's preferences I refer to the writing as 'the prison letter' rather than as *De Profundis*; I reserve the latter title for the text Ross excerpted from the letter. See also Ian Small, 'Love-Letter, Spiritual Autobiography, or Prison Writing? Identity and Value in *De Profundis*', *Wilde Writings: Contextual Conditions*, ed. Joseph Bristow (Toronto: University of Toronto Press, 2003), pp. 86–100 and Josephine M. Guy and Ian Small, *Oscar Wilde's Profession: Writing and the Culture Industry in the Late Nineteenth Century* (Oxford: Oxford University Press, 2000), pp. 212–18.

2. André Raffalovich, 'L'Affaire d'Oscar Wilde', *Archives d'anthropologie criminelle, de criminologie et de psychologie normale et pathologique*, 10 (1895), pp. 445–77, claims that Wilde's male admirers were referred to as 'ses fils' and each new favorite was called 'le nouveau *boy* d'Oscar' (p. 490). Raffalovich was

attacking Wilde after his arrest and may well be exaggerating for effect, but his account demonstrates that the language of filiation may have been used by the Wilde circle itself.

3. Douglas Murray, *Bosie: A Biography of Lord Alfred Douglas* (New York: Hyperion, 2000), p. 10.

4. Richard Ellmann, *Oscar Wilde* (New York: Vintage-Random House, 1988), pp. 389–91.

5. Though Vyvyan Holland's claim that Wilde's prison letter does not mention him at all is not strictly true, the frequent invocations of Cyril without his brother are certainly noticeable; see Vyvyan Holland, *Son of Oscar Wilde*, 1954, ed. Merlin Holland (New York: Carroll and Graf, 1999), p. 35. Franny Moyle, *Constance: The Tragic and Scandalous Life of Mrs. Oscar Wilde* (New York: Pegasus, 2011) contends that Cyril was the favorite of both his parents from birth (pp. 108, 115–16), and that Constance Wilde treated the two boys distinctly and with favoritism toward Cyril throughout their upbringing.

6. An early indication of this use of his literal children might be glimpsed in the naming of the participants in 1889's dialog essay 'The Decay of Lying'. In this case, however, the younger child (spelled as 'Vivian' in the text) is privileged as the Socrates figure who has all the answers.

7. The text is based on Matthew 8.8 and has been variously translated. The main idea is that those about to receive Christ's body in the form of the Eucharist put themselves in the place of the centurion and avow their unworthiness to receive Jesus.

8. Ellmann, *Oscar Wilde*, p. 436.

9. Not only does Wilde's prison letter represent a rejection of Douglas, but Wilde's petition to the Home Secretary of 2 July, 1896 claims that he was suffering from 'the most horrible form of erotomania' (*WCL*, p. 657) during his years of association with Douglas. The purpose of the petition, however, was to argue for a shortened sentence on the grounds of 'sexual madness' (*WCL*, p. 656), and Wilde was undoubtedly confessing strategically in an unsuccessful bid for leniency.

10. Michel Foucault, *The Care of the Self: Volume 3 of The History of Sexuality*, trans. Robert Hurley (New York: Vintage-Random House, 1986), p. 201.

11. Vyvyan Holland, *Son of Oscar Wilde*, p. 76. Hereafter cited parenthetically in the text.

12. In this insistent individualism, Cyril Holland recuperates at least some of the characteristics of his fictive namesake Cyril Graham, despite the rejection of effeminacy.

13. Although all these fathers and sons place us dangerously near the Name of the Father, the highly metaphoric, quasi-familial structure at least has some affinities with Eve Sedgwick's avunculate: see 'Tales of the Avunculate: Queer Tutelage in *The Importance of Being Earnest*' in Eve Kosofsky Sedgwick, *Tendencies* (Durham: Duke University Press, 1993), pp. 52–72.

14. The factual material that follows is indebted largely to two of these apologists: Jonathan Fryer, *Robbie Ross: Oscar Wilde's Devoted Friend* (New York: Carroll and Graf, 2000) for Ross and Murray, *Bosie*, for Douglas.

15. Merlin Holland, Vyvyan's son, contends that Wilde probably gave oral instructions to Robbie Ross not to send the original to Bosie once Wilde had named Ross his literary executor: see Merlin Holland, '*De Profundis*: The

Afterlife of a Manuscript', *Oscar Wilde: The Man, His Writings, and His World*, ed. Robert N. Keane (New York: AMS, 2003), pp. 251–67, p. 258. According to Holland, Wilde planned to have the letter published after his death and thus keeping the original manuscript in safe hands was central to maintaining the text's authenticity. Joseph Bristow goes over some of this historical ground, including citing unpublished testimony from Ross to the effect that Wilde told him not to send the original manuscript to Douglas; see Joseph Bristow, 'Introduction', *Oscar Wilde and Modern Culture: The Making of a Legend*, ed. Joseph Bristow (Athens: Ohio University Press, 2008), pp. 1–45, p. 40. For more on the continuing perplexities caused by the *De Profundis* manuscript, see Josephine M. Guy, 'Wilde's *De Profundis* and Book History: Mute Manuscripts', *English Literature in Transition, 1880–1920* 55.4 (2012), pp. 419–40.

16. Ross had converted in 1896, while Wilde was in prison, after more than a decade of becoming steadily more devoted to Catholic practice; see Fryer, p. 123.
17. Fryer, *Robbie Ross*, p. 218.
18. Fryer, *Robbie Ross*, p. 238.
19. Quoted in Maureen Borland, *Wilde's Devoted Friend: A Life of Robert Ross, 1869–1918* (Oxford: Lennard, 1990), p. 237.
20. Philip Hoare, *Oscar Wilde's Last Stand: Decadence, Conspiracy, and the Most Outrageous Trial of the Century* (New York: Arcade, 1997) has, despite its occasional overstatements, become the standard text on the Pemberton Billing affair. Petra Dierkes-Thrun, *Salome's Modernity: Oscar Wilde and the Aesthetics of Transgression* (Ann Arbor: University of Michigan Press, 2011) provides an excellent overview of Maud Allan's career and explains how she became a symbol for women's suffrage despite her own avowed lack of support for the cause (pp. 83–124). Jodie Medd, '"The Cult of the Clitoris": Anatomy of a National Scandal', *Modernism/Modernity* 9 (2002), pp. 21–49 and Deborah Cohler, 'Sapphism and Sedition: Producing Female Homosexuality in Great War Britain', *Journal of the History of Sexuality*, 16 (2007), pp. 68–94 both emphasize the trial's role in the emergence of female homosexuality as a representable cultural and legal discourse, though the latter cautions readers not to take Billing and Douglas' sexually reactionary stance as indicative of British culture generally, despite its momentary popularity. Lois Cucullu, 'Wilde and Wilder Salomés: Modernizing the Nubile Princess from Sarah Bernhardt to Norma Desmond', *Modernism/Modernity* 18 (2011), pp. 495–524 likewise indicates Billing's failure to stem the tide of Salomania as it moved into the new medium of film. William Tydeman and Steven Price, *Wilde: Salome* (Cambridge: Cambridge University Press, 1996) provides an account of Grein's production itself, which tends, both in 1918 and in modern scholarship, to get lost in the political controversy surrounding it (pp. 79–86).
21. Quoted in Hoare, *Oscar Wilde's Last Stand*, pp. 57–8. Hereafter cited parenthetically in the text.
22. The obscurity of the word 'clitoris' in 1918 in fact formed part of Billing's defense against its obscenity.
23. Quoted in Borland, *Wilde's Devoted Friend*, p. 281.
24. Kerry Powell, *Oscar Wilde and the Theatre of the 1890s* (Cambridge: Cambridge University Press, 1990) gives a thorough account of Wilde's miscalculations

with the Lord Chancellor's censor for plays, which included not only *Salome*'s biblical but also its sexual content, as well as Wilde's reliance on the fact that the Victorian London stage had traditionally allowed plays in French to get away with much more than plays in English.

25. The citations from the play below are primarily from the translation in Oscar Wilde, *Salome, Collins Complete Works of Oscar Wilde*, centenary edn (Glasgow: HarperCollins, 1999), pp. 583–605; although this version is identified as 'translated from the French of Oscar Wilde by Lord Alfred Douglas' (p. 583), it is considerably different from the 1894 edition, which is the translation used in *CWOW5*. It will be cited hereafter parenthetically in the text. David Ball, 'Review Essay: Oscar Wilde's French *Salomé* in English', *Translation Review* 84.1 (2012), pp. 43–58 reviews all of the major translations of the play and contends that Robert Ross was responsible for the changes to later editions of the translation though Ross chose not to call attention either to the alterations themselves or to his role in making them (p. 44). I disagree with Ball that 'all Douglas-based translations are essentially the same' (p. 44), as the Ross version (assuming that Ball is correct about Ross being the shadow translator of the later version) seems to me to avoid many of the mistakes and unnecessary archaisms of the Douglas version. Joost Daalder, 'Which is the Most Authoritative Early Translation of Wilde's *Salomé?*' *English Studies* 85.1 (2004), pp. 47–52 agrees that Ross is probably responsible for the translation that supplanted Douglas' version in two editions, in 1906 and in 1912 (p. 47), and greatly prefers the Ross translations, as do I. Joseph Donohue's recent translation is probably the most faithful to Wilde's French, but I have used the Ross translation because, as a revision of the Douglas translation it is much closer to the *Salome* to which Anglophone readers have become accustomed over the past 120 years. Moreover, as William A. Cohen observes in his essay on Wilde's use of the French language, 'the evidence suggests that Wilde took a strong hand in the [1894] translation. Had he not been so committed to publishing an English edition he could approve, one wonders why he would have endured a row with Douglas over it; it is clear that Douglas's name came off the title page as translator because Wilde made changes that Douglas would not countenance'; see William A. Cohen, 'Wilde's French', *Wilde Discoveries: Traditions, Histories, Archives*, ed. Joseph Bristow (Toronto: University of Toronto Press, 2013), pp. 233–59 (p. 243). Both Peter Raby, *Oscar Wilde* (Cambridge: Cambridge University Press, 1988), p. 102 and Guy and Small, *Oscar Wilde's Profession*, pp. 168–9 likewise claim that Wilde controlled the publication of the English version. Additionally, the Authorized Version-style archaisms that dominate the Douglas translation and are toned down without being eliminated in the Ross translation are certainly a part of Wilde's stylistic repertoire in such texts as the fairy stories and the poems in prose, even if they do not accurately reflect Wilde's French text.

26. Robert Ross, 'A Note on "Salome"', *Salome: A Tragedy in One Act: Translated from the French of Oscar Wilde by Lord Alfred Douglas: Pictured by Aubrey Beardsley* (New York: Dover, 1967), pp. xiii–xviii; p. xiii.

27. *Salome* was privately produced in London at the Bijou Theatre by the New Stage Club in 1905 and at King's Hall by the Literary Theatre Society in 1906. Both were small, low-budget productions that were largely ignored by critics

and audiences focused on the West End. See Tydeman and Price, *Wilde: Salome*, pp. 44–57.

28. He was also, of course, using his source texts, the synoptic gospels; this is, in fact, one of the few biblical details Wilde left unchanged. Mark 6.18: 'For John had been telling Herod, "It is not lawful for you to have your brother's wife"' (NRSV). See also Matt. 14.4 and Luke 3.19. Katherine Brown Downey, *Perverse Midrash: Oscar Wilde, André Gide, and Censorship of Biblical Drama* (London: Bloomsbury Academic, 2005) makes clear in her study of Wilde's sources (pp. 96–9) that neither the Gospels nor Josephus' *Antiquities* (which provides Salome's name) make Herod the killer of his wife's former husband. For Josephus, at least, legal controversy centers on the fact that Herodias's husband Philip is still alive, and marriage with Herod thus becomes a travesty of Levirate marriage, which is only required when the husband dies and the wife has no child. In any case, Herod as fratricide seems to be a Wildean innovation and to me, at least, Shakespearian in inspiration.

29. This schematic emphasis on the style of linguistic artifice employed by the separate cultures represented in the play is allied to Chad Bennett's call to move criticism of the play beyond 'plot, character, and other traditional structuring elements of drama', though I will have recourse to these old-fashioned features as well; see Chad Bennett, 'Oscar Wilde's *Salome*: Décor, Des Corps, Desire', *ELH* 77 (2010): pp, 297–324; p. 302.

30. Both Joseph Donohue, 'Distance, Death and Desire in *Salome*', *The Cambridge Companion to Oscar Wilde*, ed. Peter Raby (Cambridge: Cambridge University Press, 1997), pp. 118–42 and J. P. Riquelme, 'Shalom/Solomon/*Salomé*: Modernism and Wilde's Aesthetic Politics', *Centennial Review* 39 (1995), pp. 575–610 provide accounts of the role of visibility and the gaze. This trend actually predates Mulvey, however: the chart in Epifanio San Juan, *The Art of Oscar Wilde* (Princeton: Princeton University Press, 1967) literally maps 'foci of interest' in the play, though it does not foreground the visual nature of such obsession (p. 127). Sharon Marcus, 'Salomé!! Sarah Bernhardt, Oscar Wilde, and the Drama of Celebrity', *PMLA* 126 (2011): pp. 999–1021 puts a new spin on this emphasis through a consideration of the burgeoning celebrity culture of the late nineteenth century: 'not the sheer fact of being seen but control over one's image' (p. 1010).

31. In presenting this schematic I am trying to avoid turning the play into an allegory along the lines of that presented in Jarlath Killeen, *The Faiths of Oscar Wilde* (Basingstoke: Palgrave Macmillan, 2005). Killeen brings to bear several relevant discourses including religion and Wilde's Irish nationality and childhood experiences. Nonetheless, the interpretation of *Salome* as an extended metaphor in which Jokanaan represents evangelical English Protestantism while the princess represents Irish Catholicism is one I find rather limiting (see pp. 62–78). Likewise, my schematic is related to the analysis of *Salome* in Bram Dijkstra, *Idols of Perversity: Fantasies of Feminine Evil in Fin-de-Siècle Culture* (Oxford: Oxford University Press, 1986), though for Dijkstra 'the battle between sight and sound represented the struggle between materialism and idealism, between the feminine and the masculine' (p. 396). Dijkstra reads Wilde's play as of a piece with *fin-de-siècle* misogyny in general, and thus sees it as symptomatic of a fearful withdrawal from women 'into celibacy or active homosexuality' (p. 204). His equation of

these two concepts demonstrates the importance of the rise of sexuality as a critical category in constant relation with gender since the publication of *Idols of Perversity* in 1986. I read Wilde as far more sympathetic to Salome's plight than Djikstra's 'call to gynecide' would allow (p. 396); the interpretation I offer in this chapter is generally more sympathetic to the reading in John Paul Riquelme's 'Shalom/Solomon/*Salomé*', in which 'Wilde stages in the central character's actions and words the patronizing, exploitative tendencies of men gazing possessively at women' (p. 590). Likewise, I read the play as an indictment of homophobic culture that, to use Kevin Kopelson's words, 'successfully interpellated [its audience] as a murderous homophobic subject' to the extent that they sympathize with Herod's execution of Salome; see Kevin Kopelson, *Love's Litany: The Writing of Modern Homoerotics* (Stanford: Stanford University Press, 1994), p. 43. Nonetheless, this is not the only possible interpretation: Kerry Powell's more recent reading of the play, for instance, like Dijkstra sees it as an anti-feminist polemic, this time aimed at New Women purity activists such as Josephine Butler: see Kerry Powell, *Acting Wilde: Victorian Sexuality, Theatre, and Oscar Wilde* (Cambridge: Cambridge University Press, 2009), pp. 61–5.

32. Salome became a recurring icon in French art and literature in the 1870s. Gustave Moreau's several pictures of Salome immediately preceded Flaubert's 'Hérodias' (1877), and Huysmans' *À Rebours* (1884) featured Des Esseintes' fascination with one of Moreau's paintings of the dancer.

33. Iain Ross stresses Wilde's keen awareness of contemporary debates on the role of classical studies in modern culture, including the question of whether Hellenic (5th century BCE) or Hellenistic Greek culture provided a more accurate analog for the late Victorian world: 'The extended appeal to the circumstances of the period "when Alexandria began to take the place of Athens as the centre of culture" suggests Wilde's differing from Arnold over which period of Greek history offered the closest analogy with modern Britain'; see Iain Ross, *Oscar Wilde and Ancient Greece* (Cambridge: Cambridge University Press, 2013), p. 93; the quotation comes from Wilde's early reviews; see also pp. 129–36.

34. S. I. Salamensky sees the Jews in Herod's court as further evidence of Wilde's lingering anti-Semitism: 'Wilde's treatments of the Jew throughout his *oeuvre* are remarkably boorish, clumsy, and coarse'; see S. I. Salamensky, 'Oscar Wilde's "Jewish Problem": Salomé, the Ancient Hebrew and the Modern Jewess', *Modern Drama*, 55 (2012), pp. 197–215, p. 207. This may well be the case with the theatre manager in *Dorian Gray* and Baron Arnheim in *An Ideal Husband* (though the latter is never explicitly identified as Jewish), but my reading of the play does not rely on seeing the treatment of the Jews in *Salome* as any more or less sympathetic than its treatment of the Greeks. Wilde has also been accused of anti-Semitism based on his post-prison association with Major Esterhazy, the actual villain of the Dreyfus affair. Although J. Robert Maguire's *Ceremonies of Bravery* is quite detailed on the involvement of both Wilde and his friend Carlos Blacker in the affair, the book does not address whether Wilde's association with Esterhazy stemmed from racial prejudices. What is clear is that Wilde claimed that he would not have drunk with Esterhazy had he not considered him guilty and thus a fit companion for a broken exile; see J. Robert Maguire, *Ceremonies of Bravery:*

Oscar Wilde, Carlos Blacker, and the Dreyfus Affair (Oxford: Oxford University Press, 2013), p. 112.

35. Foucault reinforces this point: for the ancient Greeks 'the gaze was thought to be the surest vehicle of passion; it was the path by which passion entered the heart and the means by which passion was maintained'; see Foucault, *The Care of the Self*, p. 138.

36. Ian MacDonald, 'Oscar Wilde as a French Writer: Considering Wilde's French in *Salomé*', *Refiguring Oscar Wilde's* Salome, ed. Michael Y. Bennett (Amsterdam: Rodopi, 2011), pp. 1–19, points out that Wilde's frequent use of 'on dirait' is often translated using 'like', although MacDonald's reference for the English text is the Douglas translation (pp. 4–5). This construction is limited to the Hellenistic characters in the original French.

37. The Ross translation of this line seems to break the pattern of Salome consistently preferring simile to metaphor as she does not say 'Thy voice is *like* wine to me.' However, Wilde's French, 'Ta voix m'enivre' (*CWOW5*, p. 522), is more literally translated as 'your/thy voice intoxicates me'. The Ross translation seems to have wanted to keep the concrete images flowing, even to the extent of supplying a few where Wilde's French is more restrained. Douglas' translation of the same line, 'Thy voice is as music to mine ear' (*CWOW5*, p. 713), is even further afield. Joseph Donohue's relatively informal 2011 translation uses the most direct rendering; see Oscar Wilde, *Salomé: A Tragedy in One Act*, trans. Joseph Donohue (Charlottesville: University of Virginia Press, 2011), p. 25.

38. See Matthew Arnold, *Culture and Anarchy*, 1869, ed. J. Dover Wilson (Cambridge: Cambridge University Press, 1932), pp. 129–44. Arnold uses Hebraism and Hellenism as convenient labels for opposing cultural forces, of 'duty, self-control, and work' (p. 129) for the former term, while the latter denotes a critical intelligence that is more flexible and less doctrinaire than Hebraism. Hebraism is, of course, primarily biblical, while Hellenism draws on classical Greek literature. My point in the context of *Salome* is that Arnold's Hellenism is grounded in 6th to 4th century Athens; Wilde's late Hellenistic setting is thus not 'Greek' in the same way that Arnold's identification of critical intelligence with classical 'Greece' (meaning Athens) implies.

39. See Gregory Woods *Articulate Flesh: Male Homo-Eroticism and Modern Poetry* (New Haven: Yale University Press, 1987), pp. 81–212. The 'Childless Fathers' chapter provides an excellent overview of some of the possible relations between male queer sexuality and filiation.

5   Priests of Keats: Wilfred Owen's Pre-War Relationship to Wilde

1. William Butler Yeats, Introduction, *The Oxford Book of Modern Verse, 1892–1935* (New York: Oxford University Press, 1936), pp. v–xlii, pp. xxxiv–v.

2. Yeats, Introduction, p. xxxiv.

3. William Butler Yeats, *Letters on Poetry from W. B. Yeats to Dorothy Wellesley* (London: Oxford University Press, 1940), p. 124.

4. Yeats characterizes the poets as 'invariably officers of exceptional courage and capacity' (p. xxxiv), which excludes the work of enlisted men such

as Ivor Gurney and Isaac Rosenberg; interestingly, Yeats turned down the chance to write an introduction to Rosenberg's first collected volume in 1922; see Nicholas Murray, *The Red Sweet Wine of Youth: British Poets of the First World War* (London: Little, Brown: 2010), p. 204. Another enlisted man, David Jones, had not yet published his monumental *In Parenthesis*. Yeats anthologized none of Graves' poetry and only one each of Rupert Brooke's and Edward Thomas's poems; he also choose Sassoon's 'On Passing the New Menin Gate' (p. 259), which is a war poem but clearly a product of post-war reflection rather than the mid-war anger for which Sassoon is best known.

5. Yeats, Introduction, p. xxxv.
6. Yeats, *Letters on Poetry*, p. 81. Cited hereafter parenthetically in the text.
7. George Orwell, 'W. B. Yeats', *My Country Right or Left: 1940–1943*, vol. 2 of *The Collected Essays, Journalism and Letters*, ed. Sonia Orwell and Ian Angus (Boston: Godine, 2000), pp. 271–6, p. 271.
8. Francis Thompson, *Poetical Works* (London: Oxford University Press, 1969), p. 89.
9. Jay Winter, 'Beyond Glory: First World War Poetry and Cultural Memory', *The Cambridge Companion to the Poetry of the First World War*, ed. Santanu Das (New York: Cambridge University Press, 2013), pp. 242–55 offers the idea that Yeats rejected Owen because Yeats read him from a non-British perspective. As Edna Longley points out, Yeats' omission is not a result of a single reason but of 'complex denials'; see Edna Longley, 'The Great War, History, and the English Lyric', *The Cambridge Companion to The Literature of the First World War*, ed. Vincent Sherry (Cambridge: Cambridge University Press, 2005), pp. 57–84, p. 76.
10. Owen created embarrassment for reasons of social class as well. Siegfried Sassoon told Stephen Spender that Owen 'was embarrassing. He had a Grammar School accent'; see Jean Moorcroft Wilson, *Siegfried Sassoon, The Making of a War Poet: A Biography 1886–1918* (New York: Routledge, 1999), p. 400. This was at a time, however, when Owen had more or less eclipsed Sassoon as the chosen poet of the war, especially among the Auden generation. Sassoon was obviously annoyed that Spender showed no interest in Sassoon's own continued writing and wanted only to use him as a conduit to Owen; also see Max Egremont, *Siegfried Sassoon: A Life* (New York: Farrar, Straus and Giroux, 2005), pp. 350–1.
11. Seamus Heaney, *The Government of the Tongue: Selected Prose 1978–1987* (New York: Farrar, Straus and Giroux, 1988), p. xiv. Cited hereafter parenthetically in the text.
12. Lest this seem like a baseless accusation of Heaney, the essay in question turns from Owen to Osip Mandelstam, whom Heaney constructs as an immaculately aesthetic poet whose 'purely artistic utterance' (p. xx) put him in conflict with Stalinism. In Heaney's Nobel lecture, he places Owen into his poetic genealogy as 'a poetry where a New Testament sensibility suffers and absorbs the shock of the new century's barbarism'; see Seamus Heaney, *Crediting Poetry: The Nobel Lecture* (New York: Farrar, Straus and Giroux, 1995), p. 12. Fran Brearton, '"But That is Not New": Poetic Legacies of the First World War', *The Cambridge Companion to the Poetry of the First World War*, ed. Santanu Das (New York: Cambridge University Press, 2013), pp. 229–41 usefully contrasts Heaney's relationship to Owen with that of

Northern Irish poet Michael Longley, whose imagination, Brearton argues, is much more 'haunted' by the Great War than is Heaney's (pp. 237–8).

13. More recent scholarship has offered defenses of Owen's aesthetics, what Jahan Ramazani calls his 'overwrought rhetoric' and 'verbal excess'; see Jahan Ramazani, *Poetry of Mourning: The Modern Elegy from Hardy to Heaney* (Chicago: University of Chicago Press, 1994), p. 80. Stuart Sillars, *Structure and Disillusion in English Writing, 1910–1920* (New York: St. Martin's, 1999) opens his chapter on Owen ('Wilfred Owen and the Subjugation of the Poetic', pp. 62–92) by considering how 'Dulce et Decorum Est' could have benefitted from a Poundian editor. He also describes Owen's full rhymes (as opposed to pararhymes) as often 'ponderously outlandish and contrived' (p. 77). Sillars always gives credit, however, to Owen's self-consciousness about his style: Sillars sees Owen as using poetry against itself in service to his ethical ideal. Likewise, Peter Howarth, *British Poetry in the Age of Modernism* (Cambridge: Cambridge University Press, 2005) sees Owen as actively indulging in bad taste as a rejection of a Kantian disinterest that had no applicability in the trenches. Owen is 'both sincere and knowingly tasteless' (p. 137) because 'such intense excess insists against neutrality' (p. 199). Howarth also offers an exemplary reading of Owen's concept of pity (contrasted to Wilde's), including but not limited to its sexual dimensions. Tim Kendall, *Modern English War Poetry* (Oxford: Oxford University Press, 2006) opens his chapter on Owen with an overview of other poets' negative estimations of Owen's poetic ability (pp. 46–51). These poets include Craig Raine and Donald Davie. Finally, Santanu Das' virtuosic reading of 'Dulce et Decorum Est' calls attention to its 'excessive music', but also explains how this aesthetics of excess is integral to the poem's meaning; see Santanu Das, *Touch and Intimacy in First World War Literature* (Cambridge: Cambridge University Press, 2005), p. 157.

14. As Dominic Hibberd demonstrates in his first two books on Owen, Owen's younger brother Harold substituted a falsified citation for Owen's Military Cross into the *Collected Letters*; Hibberd reproduces both versions of the citation in Dominic Hibberd, *Wilfred Owen: The Last Year, 1917–1918* (London: Constable, 1992), p. 174. The version in the published letters claims that Owen captured a number of prisoners, while the official citation has him capturing an enemy machine gun and using it to inflict casualties on its former owners. Owen mentions his recommendation for the MC in a letter to Sassoon and tells only of 'having taken a few machine guns (with the help of one seraphic lance corporal)' (*OCL*, p. 582). It is unclear as to whether Harold Owen wished to spare his mother's feelings or support the public image of his brother as a war-scarred pacifist, though both could well be the case.

15. Sandra M. Gilbert, 'Wilfred Owen', *The Cambridge Companion to the Poetry of the First World War*, ed. Santanu Das (New York: Cambridge University Press, 2013), pp. 117–28 also stresses Owen's relation to Keats.

16. Cited in James Najarian, *Victorian Keats: Manliness, Sexuality, and Desire* (New York: Palgrave Macmillan, 2002), p. 1; cited hereafter parenthetically in the text.

17. Richard Ellmann, *Oscar Wilde* (New York: Vintage-Random House, 1988), p. 74.

18. Dominic Hibberd, *Wilfred Owen: A New Biography* (Chicago: Ivan R. Dee, 2003), pp. 55, 60.

19. Ellmann, *Oscar Wilde*, p. 376.
20. Bernard Bergonzi, *Heroes' Twilight: A Study of the Literature of the Great War*, 2nd edn (London: Macmillan, 1980), originally published in 1965, reads 'Greater Love' as a rejection 'both of women and of normal sexuality' (p. 130). Jon Silkin, *Out of Battle: The Poetry of the Great War*, 1972 (New York: Routledge and Kegan Paul, 1987), in many ways the most important pre-Fussell text on First World War combatant poetry, generally reads Owen as a political poet of compassion (in other words, exactly that to which Yeats objected); Silkin sees *fin-de-siècle*, Swinburian eroticism, however, as a 'contagion' that infected Owen's poetry (p. 234).
21. Paul Fussell, *The Great War and Modern Memory* (Oxford: Oxford University Press, 1975), pp. 287–8.
22. See James Campbell, 'Combat Gnosticism: The Ideology of First World War Poetry Criticism', *New Literary History*, 30 (1999), pp. 203–15. Kate McLoughlin, *Authoring War: The Literary Representation of War from the* Iliad *to* Iraq (Cambridge: Cambridge University Press, 2011) situates combat gnosticism in terms of her concept of 'autopsy', or first-hand experience of conditions being represented (pp. 42–3); McLouglin's brief but impressively comprehensive text considers many aspects of war writing in all genres. Probably the most thoroughly oppositional text to Fussell's is Jay Winter, *Sites of Memory, Sites of Mourning: The Great War in European Cultural History* (Cambridge: Cambridge University Press, 1995) which stresses European cultural continuity in dealing with the pressures of the war and de-emphasizes the war's role in the birth of a new and modern worldview.
23. See James Campbell, 'Interpreting the War', *The Cambridge Companion to The Literature of the First World War*, ed. Vincent Sherry (Cambridge: Cambridge University Press, 2005), pp. 261–79 for an account of the development of scholarship until the early 2000s. More recently, the further expansion of focus beyond the combat experience of European men on the Western Front is marked by Santanu Das, ed., *Race, Empire and First World War Writing* (New York: Cambridge University Press, 2011) as well as Simon Featherstone, 'Colonial Poetry of the First World War', *The Cambridge Companion to the Poetry of the First World War*, ed. Santanu Das (New York: Cambridge University Press, 2013), pp. 173–84.
24. Fussell, *The Great War and Modern Memory*, p. 272.
25. Jon Stallworthy, *Wilfred Owen*, 1974, p. 288; *OCL* p. 589.
26. See Richard Hibbit, 'The Artist as Aesthete: The French Creation of Wilde', *The Reception of Oscar Wilde in Europe*, ed. Stefano Evangelista (London: Continuum, 2010), pp. 65–79 for a description of Laurent's defense (p. 77), as well as indication that many of Wilde's French comrades renounced him in 1895. Emily Eells, 'Naturalizing Oscar Wilde as an *homme de lettres*: The French Reception of *Dorian Gray* and *Salomé* (1885–1922)', *The Reception of Oscar Wilde in Europe*, ed. Stefano Evangelista (London: Continuum, 2010), pp. 80–95 points out, however, that though Laurent may have protested Wilde's conviction and the conditions under which he was forced to serve his prison term, he nonetheless thought Wilde a derivative and unoriginal writer (p. 81).
27. Stallworthy, *Wilfred Owen*, p. 322.
28. Elizabeth Vandiver, *Stand in the Trench, Achilles: Classical Receptions in British Poetry of the Great War* (Oxford: Oxford University Press, 2010) also makes

this point in the context of Owen's use of classical texts that are likewise not found in his surviving library; see pp. 119–21.
29. Hibberd, *Wilfred Owen*, p. 104 suggests that this visit was not Owen's first to the Poetry Bookshop: it is the first mentioned in his letters, but he seems to be already familiar with the location.
30. Hibberd, *Wilfred Owen*, p. 157.
31. The actual religious service was probably Good Friday of 1915, which Owen mentions in a letter to his mother. He also describes the following Easter Mass, half ironically, to the evangelical Susan Owen as 'real, genuine Mass, with candle, with book, and with bell, and all like abominations of desolation' (*OCL*, p. 328).
32. Douglas Kerr, *Wilfred Owen's Voices: Language and Community* (Oxford: Oxford University Press, 1993) provides particular insights to how Sassoon opened up Owen to writing about combat in a way that neither war experience itself nor the examples of other poets had been able to do. Sassoon proved both that 'to hate and speak out against the war was not necessarily an act of cowardice' and that it was also not 'an attack on the army' (p. 311), in this case meaning the troops. Kerr's book is an excellent Bakhtinian study of Owen's negotiations with various linguistic discourses, though it does not emphasize queer culture as one of them.
33. Owen was later to write in a similar manner to Osbert Sitwell in response to his poem 'Ill Winds'. The letter described Owen's efforts at training troops in a paragraph-length prose poem that, though less biblical than the earlier letter, is even more redolent of Wilde's poems in prose, e.g. 'with a piece of silver I buy him every day, and with maps I make him familiar with the topography of Golgotha' (*OCL*, p. 562).
34. Kerr, *Wilfred Owen's Voices*, pp. 67–142 makes the important point that, irrespective of his theological beliefs, the linguistic discourses of the New Testament and of evangelicalism remained with Owen always.
35. Hibberd, *Wilfred Owen*, p. 298.
36. Wilde's actual words are 'there were Christians before Christ. For that we should be grateful. The unfortunate thing is that there have been none since' (*WCL*, p. 753). The editors of Owen's *Collected Letters* note of the quotation that 'we have failed to find the source of this' (*OCL*, p. 536), which suggests that Harold Owen did not know it was from Wilde and, if he had, the letter might well have been censored to eliminate the quotation.
37. Stallworthy, *Wilfred Owen*, p. 320.
38. Hibberd, *Wilfred Owen*, p. 405 claims that Owen also read Sherard's *The Real Oscar Wilde* in December 1917, but does not cite evidence.
39. Hibberd, *Wilfred Owen*, p. 301.
40. Hibberd, *Wilfred Owen*, p. 303.
41. Matt Houlbrook, *Queer London: Perils and Pleasures in the Sexual Metropolis, 1918–1957* (Chicago: University of Chicago Press, 2005) identifies 'Shadwell Park Stairs in the Rotherhithe Tunnel' (p. 49) as a site of relative privacy for male–male sexual liaisons in early twentieth-century London. The entire second chapter of Houlbrook's *Queer London* illustrates the role of 'public queer culture' (p. 44) in the metropole in Owen's time. Similarly, chapters 2 and 3 of H. G. Cocks, *Nameless Offences: Homosexual Desire in the Nineteenth Century* (London: I. B. Tauris, 2003), provide an excellent overview of the relationship between metropolitan queer culture, the police, and public discourse

that 'simultaneously referred to homosexual desire, and tried to cover all traces of its existence with circumlocution and evasion' (p. 78).

42. Owen writes to his mother in a similar vein about a slightly more mentionable topic. Describing tea at the Shamrock Tea Rooms, 'perhaps the most eminently respectable exclusive and secluded in Town', he goes on to claim that 'I happen to know that a few stories higher in the same building is an Opium Den. I have not investigated. But I know. That's London' (*OCL*, p. 471).

43. Neil Corcoran, 'Wilfred Owen and the Poetry of War', *The Cambridge Companion to Twentieth-Century English Poetry*, ed. Neil Corcoran (Cambridge: Cambridge University Press, 2007), pp. 87–101 remarks on the simultaneity of the two strands but dismisses what I am calling the Wildean texts as 'callow poems of unalloyed homoeroticism' (p. 90). Harry Ricketts, *Strange Meetings: The Poets of the Great War* (London: Chatto and Windus, 2010) represents the two strands as doing battle 'for Owen's poetic soul' (pp. 144–5), which certainly implies their incompatibility.

44. William Wordsworth, VIII ('She dwelt among the untrodden ways'), *The Poetical Works of William Wordsworth* Vol. 2, ed. E. de Selincourt, 5 vols (London: Clarendon-Oxford University Press, 1952), p. 34.

6   OW/WH/WO: Wilfred Owen as Symbolic Son of Oscar Wilde

1. It is interesting to consider that, had Vyvyan Holland not been on active service during the time that Owen was most directly involved with the Ross circle, the two would almost certainly have met.

2. Jon Stallworthy, *Wilfred Owen*, revised edn (London: Pimlico-Random House, 2013), pp. 301–2.

3. Stallworthy, *Wilfred Owen*, revised edn, p. 301.

4. Guy Cuthbertson, *Wilfred Owen* (New Haven: Yale University Press, 2014), pp. 147, 58. Cuthbertson also seems to me rather dismissive of the Ross circle, writing of 'Robert Ross and other homosexual hangovers from the 1890s' (p. 258) and going on to characterize Ross and Wilde's relationship through an uncontextualized and parodically camp quotation from Augustus John's autobiography (p. 259).

5. See Paul Fussell, *The Great War and Modern Memory* (Oxford: Oxford University Press, 1975), pp. 203–20 for the question of Graves' factual reliability and Adrian Caesar, *Taking It Like a Man: Suffering, Sexuality, and the War Poets: Brooke, Sassoon, Owen, Graves* (Manchester: Manchester University Press, 1993) for Graves' pre-war sexual identity. For Graves' claim that Owen confessed to picking up young men in France see Dominic Hibberd, *Owen the Poet* (Athens: University of Georgia Press, 1986), p. 199 and Dominic Hibberd, *Wilfred Owen: A New Biography*, pp. 145, 277.

6. Monro used appreciation for male beauty as an integral part of his war poetry in his 'Youth in Arms' sequence; see Harold Monro, *Collected Poems*, ed. Alida Monro (London: Duckworth, 1970), pp. 166–70.

7. Philip Bainbrigge, 'If I Should Die, Be Not Concerned to Know', *Lads: Love Poetry of the Trenches*, ed. Martin Taylor (London: Constable, 1989), p. 69.

8. Timothy d'Arch Smith, *Love in Earnest: Some Notes on the Lives and Writings of English 'Uranian' Poets from 1889 to 1930* (London: Routledge and Kegan Paul, 1970), pp. 148–50 cites a representative passage from Bainbrigge's bawdy verse play *Achilles in Scyros*.

9. Jean Findlay, *Chasing Lost Time: The Life of C. K. Scott Moncrieff: Soldier, Spy and Translator* (London: Chatto and Windus, 2014), especially pp. 140–63, provides the most complete account of the relationship between Owen and Scott Moncrieff.

10. Hibberd, *Owen the Poet*, p. 199 cites Martin Seymour-Smith as getting the story from Graves, who in turn claimed to have gotten it from Ross; see also Findlay, *Chasing Lost Time*, p. 319. Graves also claimed to Seymour-Smith in 1943 that 'Owen was a weakling really; I liked him but there was that passive homosexual streak in him which is even more disgusting than the active streak in Auden'; see Martin Seymour-Smith, *Robert Graves: His Life and Work* (New York: Holt, Rinehart and Winston, 1982), p. 63. Graves also referred to Owen as 'an idealistic homosexual with a religious background' in the 1957 revision of *Good-Bye to All That*. As Seymour-Smith points out, both of these dismissive summations come from decades after Owen's death and do not seem to be reflected either in the extant letters between Graves and Owen or in Graves' recorded comments about Owen during the war.

11. Cited in Hibberd, *Wilfred Owen: The Last Year*, pp. 118.

12. Hibberd, *Wilfred Owen*, pp. 315–16.

13. Charles Kenneth Scott Moncrieff, 'Sonnet', *New Witness* (7 June 1918), p. 108. This sonnet is practically identical to that reproduced in Findlay, *Chasing Lost Time*, p. 59; she identifies it as coming from Scott Moncrieff's private poetry book, dated April of 1909 and titled 'My Mistake'. He apparently recycled the sonnet for Owen, but its usefulness in different situations at least makes apparent that the tension between physical desire and platonic idealism affected Scott Moncrieff throughout his life.

14. Cited in Peter France, 'Scott Moncrieff's First Translation', *Translation and Literature*, 21 (2012), pp. 364–82, p. 367.

15. Cited in France, 'Scott Moncrieff's First Translation', p. 367.

16. Charles Kenneth Scott Moncrieff, 'Sonnet', *The New Witness* (10 Jan. 1919).

17. Scott Moncrieff used this poem in the dedication to his translation of *The Chanson de Roland* in a slightly bowdlerized form, changing among other things 'thy shame' to 'this name' and altering the final couplet to 'Beyond the stars' light, in the eternal day / Our two contented ghosts together stay'; see Charles Kenneth Scott Moncrieff, 'To W. E. S. O.', *The Song of Roland: Done into English, in the Original Measure* (London: Chapman and Hall, 1919), p. vii.

18. See James Campbell, ' "For You May Touch Them Not": Misogyny, Homosexuality, and the Ethics of Passivity in First World War Poetry', *ELH*, 64 (1997), pp. 823–42 for more on the misogyny of much of the First World War trench lyric.

19. J. D. Reed, 'Wilfred Owen's Adonis', *Dead Lovers: Erotic Bonds and the Study of Premodern Europe*, ed. Basil Dufallo and Peggy McCracken (Ann Arbor: University of Michigan Press, 2006), pp. 39–56 demonstrates Owen's use of Bion's 'Epitaph on Adonis' in these lines, as well as the implications of Owen's appropriation of them.

20. By 'surreal' here, I do not mean to imply that Owen was directly influenced by Freudian ideas of the unconscious and its role in artistic creation, nor by poets that consciously employed such theories. Instead, I mean to describe a depiction of a reality so estranged that it appears dreamlike even when approached according to the traditions of realism.

21. Samuel Taylor Coleridge, 'Kubla Khan or, A Vision in a Dream', *Poetical Works I*, vol. 16 of *The Collected Works of Samuel Taylor Coleridge*, ed. J. C. C. Mays, 16 vols (Princeton: Princeton University Press, 2001), pp. 509–14, p. 514.

22. John Stuart Mill, *Essays on Poetry*, ed. F. Parvin Sharpless (Columbia: University of South Carolina Press, 1976), p. 12.

23. Hibberd, *Wilfred Owen*, pp. 289–90.

24. Any reading of 'Strange Meeting' rests on assumptions, one of the most important being whether the reader assumes that the dead enemy soldier is a *doppelgänger* figure, and thus a double of the persona, or whether the persona's encounter represents a meeting of the persona and an other and thus a true moment of alterity. The first possibility is exemplified by Daniel Hipp, *The Poetry of Shell Shock: Wartime Trauma and Healing in Wilfred Owen, Ivor Gurney and Siegfried Sassoon* (Jefferson: McFarland, 2005), pp. 94–8, while the latter is articulated using Emmanuel Levinas' language by Kate McLoughlin, *Authoring War: The Literary Representation of War from the Iliad to Iraq* (Cambridge: Cambridge University Press, 2011), pp. 192–4. My own reading is more sympathetic to the second assumption, male procreation being a product of alterity.

25. Mark Rawlinson, 'Wilfred Owen', *The Oxford Handbook of British and Irish War Poetry*, ed. Tim Kendall (Oxford: Oxford University Press, 2007), pp. 114–33, pp. 128–9.

26. In this sense 'Strange Meeting' places its persona in a similar role to that described by Ramazani in his reading of 'Mental Cases', one that places the speaker 'between mourner and mourned, voyeur and victim'; see Jahan Ramazani, *Poetry of Mourning: The Modern Elegy from Hardy to Heaney* (Chicago: University of Chicago Press, 1994), p. 79.

27. In the same letter in which Owen called Johnny de la Touche 'a creature of killable age', he wrote of the German offensive 'the enormity of the present Battle numbs me. Because I perfectly foresaw these days, it was that I said it would have been better to make peace in 1916. Or even last Autumn. It is certainly "impossible" now' (*OCL*, p. 543).

28. Philip Larkin, *Collected Poems*, ed. Anthony Thwaite (New York: Farrar Straus Giroux, 1989), pp. 127–8.

29. Rupert Brooke, *The Collected Poems of Rupert Brooke* (New York: Dodd Mead, 1980), p. 83.

30. Vincent Sherry, 'First World War Poetry: A Cultural Landscape', *The Cambridge Companion to the Poetry of the First World War*, ed. Santanu Das (New York: Cambridge University Press, 2013), pp. 35–50, p. 37. Kathy J. Phillips, *Manipulating Masculinity: War and Gender in Modern British and American Literature* (New York: Palgrave Macmillan, 2006) outlines the use of 'war as a cure for decadence' (p. 26) in twentieth-century warfare generally (pp. 26–33).

31. See Campbell, 'For You May Touch Them Not'.

32. Sarah Cole, *Modernism, Male Friendship and the First World War* (Cambridge: Cambridge University Press, 2003), pp. 144–5.
33. Cole, *Modernism, Male Friendship and the First World War*, p. 145.
34. Santanu Das, *Touch and Intimacy in First World War Literature* (Cambridge: Cambridge University Press, 2005), p. 117.
35. Das, *Touch and Intimacy in First World War Literature*, p. 131.
36. I do not mean to imply that Cole and Das entirely agree in their conceptions: Das' allowance of the military usefulness of tactile contact ('In the military, bodily contact is often the primary means of fostering loyalty, trust and unity within an army unit') would seem to make it as much a sign of Cole's comradeship as friendship; see Das, *Touch and Intimacy in First World War Literature*, p. 118.
37. Attempts to locate the paradigm shift of sexuality have varied widely. To cite just one example, Randolph Trumbach, 'Modern Sodomy: The Origins of Homosexuality, 1700–1800', *A Gay History of Britain: Love and Sex Between Men Since the Middle Ages*, ed. Matt Cook (Oxford: Greenwood, 2007), pp. 77–105 sees the early eighteenth century, when an effeminate minoritized subculture of sodomites in northern Europe began to emerge, as the moment when 'the first European men who might reasonably be called "homosexuals"' (p. 77) became evident in the historical record. Yet in the same volume, Matt Cook claims that it was not until the late 1950s that 'more polarized ideas about sexual identity had taken hold, and . . . who you desired and had sex with defined who you were. Identity politics in relation to homosexuality had been in play since at least the 1890s, but by the late 1950s, it seemed like it was virtually the only way to think about love and sex between men'; see Matt Cook, 'Queer Conflicts: Love, Sex and War, 1914–1967', *A Gay History of Britain: Love and Sex Between Men Since the Middle Ages*, ed. Matt Cook (Oxford: Greenwood, 2007), pp. 145–77, pp. 173–4.
38. Dan Todman, *The Great War: Myth and Memory* (London: Hambledon and London, 2005) offers a slightly more recent version of a historian's objection to the overemphasis of the war poets, Owen especially. Like Bond, Todman is reluctant to engage with Owen's poetry in any detail, but his account of Owen's rise to cultural dominance, especially in British secondary schools in the 1960s and after, is impressive and meticulous; see pp. 153–72.
39. Brian Bond, *The Unquiet Western Front: Britain's Role in Literature and History* (Cambridge: Cambridge University Press, 2002), p. 1.
40. Historians less explicitly committed to undoing the poets' interpretation of the war have nonetheless engaged with their legacy. Hew Strachen, *The First World War* (New York: Viking, 2003), p. xviii, for instance, challenges John Keegan's contention in his similarly named volume that the war 'was a tragic and unnecessary conflict'; see also John Keegan, *The First World War* (New York: Knopf, 1999), p. 1. Strachen emphasizes the desirability of understanding the war as its contemporaries did at the time, uninflected by the war books of the twenties and thirties. Niall Ferguson, *The Pity of War: Explaining World War I* (New York: Basic Books, 1999), p. xxvi predates Bond in identifying the war poets as the source of 'the persistence of the idea that the war was "a bad thing"'; Ferguson's book nonetheless draws both its title and one of its epigrams from Owen.

41. Jon Stallworthy, 'The Legacy of the Somme', *Survivors' Songs: From Maldon to the Somme*, (Cambridge: Cambridge University Press, 2008), pp. 98–108, p. 98.
42. Stallworthy, 'The Legacy of the Somme', p. 75.
43. Bond, *The Unquiet Western Front*, p. 40.
44. Although the discussion is largely a debate between military historians and literary scholars, Allen J. Frantzen, *Bloody Good: Chivalry, Sacrifice, and the Great War* (Chicago: University of Chicago Press, 2004) represents a more literary and mythic reading of the war that nonetheless opposes Owen's dominance of its meaning. Frantzen is interested in reclaiming the chivalry of the war, as well as the positive value of sacrificial violence more generally. He reads Owen's 'Strange Meaning', for instance, along lines compatible with what I offer above, but he rejects Owen's 'dismal hermeneutic circle' (p. 262) as an interpretation of either Owen's war or war more generally.
45. Bond, *The Unquiet Western Front*, p. 88.
46. Bond, *The Unquiet Western Front*, p. 31. Bond cites Adrian Caesar's *Taking It Like a Man* on this point, thus reinforcing the idea that the 'sexual problems' remarked on include same-sex desire, though Bond never makes this explicit.
47. Fussell, *The Great War and Modern Memory*, p. 155.
48. For the extent of the statistical insignificance of the trench lyric in the poetic output of 1914–1918, see Catherine Reilly, *English Poetry of the First World War: A Bibliography*. (London: George Prior, 1978). For its minority status as a representation of combatant experience irrespective of genre, the account of war writing in Jessica Meyer, *Men of War: Masculinity and the First World War in Britain* (Basingstoke: Palgrave Macmillan, 2009) is helpful.

Afterword

1. Isaac Rosenberg, 'Break of Day in the Trenches', *The Poems and Plays of Isaac Rosenberg*, ed. Vivien Noakes (Oxford: Oxford University Press, 2004), p. 128.
2. W. H. Auden, 'Spain', *Selected Poems*, ed. Edward Mendelson (New York: Vintage-Random House, 1989), pp. 51–5, 1. 21.

Bibliography

Ablow, Rachel, 'Reading and Re-reading: Wilde, Newman, and the Fiction of Belief', *Wilde Discoveries: Traditions, Histories, Archives*, ed. Joseph Bristow (Toronto: University of Toronto Press, 2013), pp. 190–211.

Arnold, Matthew, *Culture and Anarchy*, 1869, ed. J. Dover Wilson (Cambridge: Cambridge University Press, 1932).

Auden, W. H., *Selected Poems*, ed. Edward Mendelson (New York: Vintage-Random House, 1989).

Bainbrigge, Philip, 'If I Should Die, Be Not Concerned to Know', *Lads: Love Poetry of the Trenches*, ed. Martin Taylor (London: Constable, 1989), p. 69.

Ball, David, 'Review Essay: Oscar Wilde's French *Salomé* in English', *Translation Review*, 84.1 (2012), pp. 43–58.

Bartlett, Neil, *Who Was That Man? A Present for Mr Oscar Wilde* (London: Serpent's Tail, 1988).

Bashford, Bruce, *Oscar Wilde: The Critic as Humanist* (Madison: Farleigh Dickinson University Press, 1999).

Bauer, Heike, *English Literary Sexology: Translations of Inversion, 1860–1930* (Basingstoke: Palgrave Macmillan, 2009).

Beckson, Karl, ed., *Oscar Wilde: The Critical Heritage* (New York: Barnes and Noble, 1970).

——, 'Oscar Wilde and the Green Carnation', *ELT*, 43.4 (2000).

Bennett, Chad, 'Oscar Wilde's *Salome*: Décor, Des Corps, Desire', *ELH*, 77 (2010): pp. 297–324.

Bergonzi, Bernard, *Heroes' Twilight: A Study of the Literature of the Great War*, 2nd edn (London: Macmillan, 1980).

Bersani, Leo, *Homos* (Cambridge: Harvard University Press, 1995).

——, *Is the Rectum a Grave? and Other Essays* (Chicago: University of Chicago Press, 2010).

Bloom, Harold, *The Anxiety of Influence: A Theory of Poetry* (New York: Oxford University Press, 1973).

Bond, Brian, *The Unquiet Western Front: Britain's Role in Literature and History* (Cambridge: Cambridge University Press, 2002).

Borland, Maureen, *Wilde's Devoted Friend: A Life of Robert Ross, 1869–1918* (Oxford: Lennard, 1990).

Bourke, Joanna, *Dismembering the Male: Men's Bodies, Britain, and the Great War* (Chicago: University of Chicago Press, 1996).

Brady, Sean, *Masculinity and Male Homosexuality in Britain, 1861–1913* (Basingstoke: Palgrave Macmillan, 2005).

Bray, Alan, *The Friend* (Chicago: University of Chicago Press, 2003).

Brearton, Fran, '"But That is Not New": Poetic Legacies of the First World War,' *The Cambridge Companion to the Poetry of the First World War*, ed. Santanu Das (New York: Cambridge University Press, 2013), pp. 229–41.

Bristow, Joseph, '"A Complex Multiform Creature": Wilde's Sexual Identities', *The Cambridge Companion to Oscar Wilde*, ed. Peter Raby (Cambridge: Cambridge University Press, 1997), pp. 195–218.

———, *Effeminate England: Homoerotic Writing after 1885* (New York: Columbia University Press, 1995).

———, 'Introduction', *Oscar Wilde and Modern Culture: The Making of a Legend*, ed. Joseph Bristow (Athens: Ohio University Press, 2008), pp. 1–45.

———, 'Oscar Wilde's Poetic Traditions: From Aristophanes' *Clouds* to *The Ballad of Reading Gaol'*, *Oscar Wilde in Context*, ed. Kerry Powell and Peter Raby (Cambridge: Cambridge University Press, 2013), pp. 73–87.

———, 'Wilde, *Dorian Gray*, and Gross Indecency', *Sexual Sameness: Textual Differences in Lesbian and Gay Writing*, ed. Joseph Bristow (London: Routledge, 1992), pp. 44–63.

Brooke, Rupert, *The Collected Poems of Rupert Brooke* (New York: Dodd Mead, 1980).

Brown, Julia Prewitt, *Cosmopolitan Criticism: Oscar Wilde's Philosophy of Art* (Charlottesville: University of Virginia Press, 1997).

Caesar, Adrian, *Taking It Like a Man: Suffering, Sexuality, and the War Poets: Brooke, Sassoon, Owen, Graves* (Manchester: Manchester University Press, 1993).

Campbell, James, 'Combat Gnosticism: The Ideology of First World War Poetry Criticism', *New Literary History*, 30 (1999): pp. 203–15.

———, '"For You May Touch Them Not": Misogyny, Homosexuality, and the Ethics of Passivity in First World War Poetry', *ELH*, 64 (1997): pp. 823–42.

———, 'Interpreting the War', *The Cambridge Companion to The Literature of the First World War*, ed. Vincent Sherry (Cambridge: Cambridge University Press, 2005), pp. 261–79.

Cocks, H. G., *Nameless Offences: Homosexual Desire in the Nineteenth Century* (London: I. B. Tauris, 2003).

Cohen, Ed, *Talk on the Wilde Side: Toward a Genealogy of a Discourse on Male Sexualities* (New York: Routledge, 1993).

Cohen, William A., *Sex Scandal: The Private Parts of Victorian Fiction* (Durham: Duke University Press, 1996).

———, 'Wilde's French', *Wilde Discoveries: Traditions, Histories, Archives*, ed. Joseph Bristow (Toronto: University of Toronto Press, 2013), pp. 233–59.

Cohler, Deborah, 'Sapphism and Sedition: Producing Female Homosexuality in Great War Britain', *Journal of the History of Sexuality*, 16 (2007), pp. 68–94.

Cole, Sarah, *Modernism, Male Friendship and the First World War* (Cambridge: Cambridge University Press, 2003).

Coleridge, Samuel Taylor, 'Kubla Khan or, A Vision in a Dream', *Poetical Works I*, vol. 16 of *The Collected Works of Samuel Taylor Coleridge*, ed. J. C. C. Mays, 16 vols (Princeton: Princeton University Press, 2001), pp. 509–14.

Cook, Matt, *London and the Culture of Homosexuality, 1885–1914* (Cambridge: Cambridge University Press, 2003).

———, 'Queer Conflicts: Love, Sex and War, 1914–1967', *A Gay History of Britain: Love and Sex Between Men Since the Middle Ages*, ed. Matt Cook (Oxford: Greenwood, 2007), pp. 145–77.

Corcoran, Neil, 'Wilfred Owen and the Poetry of War', *The Cambridge Companion to Twentieth-Century English Poetry*, ed. Neil Corcoran (Cambridge: Cambridge University Press, 2007), pp. 87–101.

Craft, Christopher, *Another Kind of Love: Male Homosocial Desire in English Discourse, 1850–1920* (Berkeley: University of California Press, 1994).

Cucullu, Lois, 'Wilde and Wilder Salomés: Modernizing the Nubile Princess from Sarah Bernhardt to Norma Desmond', *Modernism/Modernity*, 18 (2011), pp. 495–524.

Cuthbertson, Guy, *Wilfred Owen* (New Haven: Yale University Press, 2014).

Daalder, Joost, 'Which is the Most Authoritative Early Translation of Wilde's *Salomé?*', *English Studies*, 85.1 (2004), pp. 47–52.

Danson, Lawrence, *Wilde's Intentions: The Artist in His Criticism* (Oxford: Clarendon-Oxford University Press, 1997).

Das, Santanu, ed., *Race, Empire and First World War Writing* (New York: Cambridge University Press, 2011).

——, *Touch and Intimacy in First World War Literature* (Cambridge: Cambridge University Press, 2005).

Dellamora, Richard, *Masculine Desire: The Sexual Politics of Victorian Aestheticism* (Chapel Hill: University of North Carolina Press, 1990).

Denisoff, Dennis, *Aestheticism and Sexual Parody, 1840–1940* (Cambridge: Cambridge University Press, 2001).

Dierkes-Thrun, Petra, *Salome's Modernity: Oscar Wilde and the Aesthetics of Transgression* (Ann Arbor: University of Michigan Press, 2011).

Dijkstra, Bram, *Idols of Perversity: Fantasies of Feminine Evil in Fin-de-Siècle Culture* (Oxford: Oxford University Press, 1986).

Dollimore, Jonathan, *Sexual Dissidence: Augustine to Wilde, Freud to Foucault* (Oxford: Oxford University Press, 1991).

Donohue, Joseph, 'Distance, Death and Desire in *Salome*', *The Cambridge Companion to Oscar Wilde*, ed. Peter Raby (Cambridge: Cambridge University Press, 1997), pp. 118–42.

Douglas, Lord Alfred, *The True History of Shakespeare's Sonnets* (London: Martin Secker, 1933).

Dowling, Linda, *Hellenism and Homosexuality in Victorian Oxford* (Ithaca: Cornell University Press, 1994).

Downey, Katherine Brown, *Perverse Midrash: Oscar Wilde, André Gide, and Censorship of Biblical Drama* (London: Bloomsbury Academic, 2005).

Edelman, Lee. *No Future: Queer Theory and the Death Drive* (Durham: Duke University Press, 2005).

Eells, Emily, 'Naturalizing Oscar Wilde as an *homme de lettres*: The French Reception of *Dorian Gray* and *Salomé* (1885–1922)', *The Reception of Oscar Wilde in Europe*, ed. Stefano Evangelista (London: Continuum, 2010), pp. 80–95.

Egremont, Max, *Siegfried Sassoon: A Life* (New York: Farrar, Straus and Giroux, 2005).

Ellmann, Richard, *Oscar Wilde* (New York: Vintage-Random House, 1988).

Eltis, Sos, *Revising Wilde: Society and Subversion in the Plays of Oscar Wilde* (Oxford: Clarendon-Oxford University Press, 1996).

Evangelista, Stefano, *British Aestheticism and Ancient Greece: Hellenism, Reception, Gods in Exile* (New York: Palgrave Macmillan, 2009).

Featherstone, Simon, 'Colonial Poetry of the First World War', *The Cambridge Companion to the Poetry of the First World War*, ed. Santanu Das (New York: Cambridge University Press, 2013), pp. 173–84.

Ferguson, Niall, *The Pity of War: Explaining World War I* (New York: Basic Books, 1999).

Findlay, Jean, *Chasing Lost Time: The Life of C. K. Scott Moncrieff: Soldier, Spy and Translator* (London: Chatto and Windus, 2014).

Forster, E. M., *Maurice: A Novel* (New York: W. W. Norton, 1971).

Fortunato, Paul L., *Modernist Aesthetics and Consumer Culture in the Writings of Oscar Wilde* (New York: Routledge, 2007).

Foucault, Michel, *The Care of the Self: Volume 3 of The History of Sexuality*, trans. Robert Hurley (New York: Vintage-Random House, 1986).

——, *An Introduction: Volume 1 of The History of Sexuality*, trans. Robert Hurley (New York: Vintage-Random House, 1978).

——, *The Use of Pleasure: Volume 2 of The History of Sexuality*, trans. Robert Hurley (New York: Vintage-Random House, 1985).

France, Peter, 'Scott Moncrieff's First Translation', *Translation and Literature*, 21 (2012), pp. 364–82.

Frankel, Nicholas, *Oscar Wilde's Decorated Books* (Ann Arbor: University of Michigan Press, 2000).

Frantzen, Allen J., *Bloody Good: Chivalry, Sacrifice, and the Great War* (Chicago: University of Chicago Press, 2004).

Fryer, Jonathan, *Robbie Ross: Oscar Wilde's Devoted Friend* (New York: Carroll and Graf, 2000).

Fussell, Paul, *The Great War and Modern Memory* (Oxford: Oxford University Press, 1975).

Gagnier, Regenia, *Idylls of the Marketplace: Oscar Wilde and the Victorian Public* (Stanford: Stanford University Press, 1986).

Gilbert, Sandra M., 'Wilfred Owen', *The Cambridge Companion to the Poetry of the First World War*, ed. Santanu Das (New York: Cambridge University Press, 2013), pp. 117–28.

Guy, Josephine M., 'Wilde's *De Profundis* and Book History: Mute Manuscripts', *English Literature in Transition, 1880–1920*, 55 (2012), pp. 419–40.

Guy, Josephine M. and Ian Small, *Oscar Wilde's Profession: Writing and the Culture Industry in the Late Nineteenth Century* (Oxford: Oxford University Press, 2000).

Halberstam, Judith, *The Queer Art of Failure* (Durham: Duke University Press, 2011).

Halperin, David M., *How to Do the History of Homosexuality* (Chicago: University of Chicago Press, 2002).

Halpern, Richard, *Shakespeare's Perfume: Sodomy and Sublimity in the Sonnets, Wilde, Freud, and Lacan* (Philadelphia: University of Pennsylvania Press, 2002).

Hamilton, Lisa, 'Oscar Wilde, New Women, and the Rhetoric of Effeminacy', *Wilde Writings: Contextual Conditions*, ed. Joseph Bristow (Toronto: University of Toronto Press, 2003), pp. 230–53.

Heaney, Seamus, *Crediting Poetry: The Nobel Lecture* (New York: Farrar, Straus and Giroux, 1995).

——, *The Government of the Tongue: Selected Prose 1978–1987* (New York: Farrar, Straus and Giroux, 1988).

Hekma, Gert, 'A History of Sexology: Social and Historical Aspects of Sexuality', *From Sappho to De Sade: Moments in the History of Sexuality*, ed. Jan Bremmer (London: Routledge, 1989), pp. 173–93.

Hibberd, Dominic, *Owen the Poet* (Athens: University of Georgia Press, 1986).

——, *Wilfred Owen: A New Biography* (Chicago: Ivan R. Dee, 2003).

——, *Wilfred Owen: The Last Year, 1917–1918* (London: Constable, 1992).

Hibbitt, Richard, 'The Artist as Aesthete: The French Creation of Wilde', *The Reception of Oscar Wilde in Europe*, ed. Stefano Evangelista (London: Continuum, 2010), pp. 65–79.

Hichens, Robert Smythe, *The Green Carnation*, 1894 (New York: Mitchell Kennerley, nd).

Hipp, Daniel, *The Poetry of Shell Shock: Wartime Trauma and Healing in Wilfred Owen, Ivor Gurney and Siegfried Sassoon* (Jefferson: McFarland, 2005).

Hoare, Philip, *Oscar Wilde's Last Stand: Decadence, Conspiracy, and the Most Outrageous Trial of the Century* (New York: Arcade, 1997).

Holland, Merlin, 'Biography and Art of Lying', *The Cambridge Companion to Oscar Wilde*, ed. Peter Raby (Cambridge: Cambridge University Press, 1997), pp. 3–17.

——, '*De Profundis*: The Afterlife of a Manuscript', *Oscar Wilde: The Man, His Writings, and His World*, ed. Robert N. Keane (New York: AMS, 2003), pp. 251–67.

——, *The Real Trial of Oscar Wilde* (New York: HarperCollins, 2003).

——, *The Wilde Album* (New York: Henry Holt, 1997).

Holland, Vyvyan, *Son of Oscar Wilde*, 1954, ed. Merlin Holland (New York: Carroll and Graf, 1999).

Houlbrook, Matt, *Queer London: Perils and Pleasures in the Sexual Metropolis, 1918–1957* (Chicago: University of Chicago Press, 2005).

Howarth, Peter, *British Poetry in the Age of Modernism* (Cambridge: Cambridge University Press, 2005).

Hubbard, Thomas K., 'Introduction', *Homosexuality in Greece and Rome: A Sourcebook of Basic Documents* (Berkeley: University of California Press, 2003), pp. 1–20.

Hultgren, Neil, 'Oscar Wilde's Poetic Injustice in *The Picture of Dorian Gray*', *Wilde Discoveries: Traditions, Histories, Archives*, ed. Joseph Bristow (Toronto: University of Toronto Press, 2013), pp. 212–30.

Kaplan, Morris, *Sodom on the Thames: Sex, Love, and Scandal in Wilde Times*, (Ithaca: Cornell University Press, 2005).

Kaye, Richard, 'Gay Studies/Queer Theory and Oscar Wilde', *Palgrave Advances in Oscar Wilde Studies*, ed. Frederick S. Roden (Basingstoke: Palgrave Macmillan, 2004), pp. 189–223.

Keegan, John, *The First World War* (New York: Knopf, 1999).

Kendall, Tim, *Modern English War Poetry* (Oxford: Oxford University Press, 2006).

Kerr, Douglas, *Wilfred Owen's Voices: Language and Community* (Oxford: Oxford University Press, 1993).

Killeen, Jarlath, *The Faiths of Oscar Wilde: Catholicism, Folklore and Ireland* (Basingstoke: Palgrave Macmillan, 2005).

Kopelson, Kevin, *Love's Litany: The Writing of Modern Homoerotics* (Stanford: Stanford University Press, 1994).

Larkin, Philip, *Collected Poems*, ed. Anthony Thwaite (New York: Farrar Straus Giroux, 1989).

Longley, Edna, 'The Great War, History, and the English Lyric', *The Cambridge Companion to The Literature of the First World War*, ed. Vincent Sherry (Cambridge: Cambridge University Press, 2005), pp. 57–84.

Lorang, Elizabeth, '*The Picture of Dorian Gray* in Context: Intertextuality and *Lippincott's Monthly Magazine*', *Victorian Periodicals Review*, 43 (2010), pp. 19–41.

Love, Heather, *Feeling Backward: Loss and the Politics of Queer History* (Cambridge: Harvard University Press, 2007).

MacDonald, Ian Andrew, 'Oscar Wilde as a French Writer: Considering Wilde's French in *Salomé*', *Refiguring Oscar Wilde's* Salome, ed. Michael Y. Bennett (Amsterdam: Rodopi, 2011), pp. 1–19.

Maguire, J. Robert, *Ceremonies of Bravery: Oscar Wilde, Carlos Blacker, and the Dreyfus Affair* (Oxford: Oxford University Press, 2013).

Marcovitch, Heather, *The Art of the Pose: Oscar Wilde's Performance Theory* (Bern: Peter Lang, 2010).

Marcus, Sharon, 'Salomé!! Sarah Bernhardt, Oscar Wilde, and the Drama of Celebrity', *PMLA*, 126 (2011), pp. 999–1021.

McKenna, Neil, *The Secret Life of Oscar Wilde* (New York: Basic Books, 2005).

McLouglin, Kate, *Authoring War: The Literary Representation of War from the* Iliad *to* Iraq, (Cambridge: Cambridge University Press, 2011).

Medd, Jodie, '"The Cult of the Clitoris": Anatomy of a National Scandal', *Modernism/Modernity*, 9 (2002), pp. 21–49.

Meyer, Jessica, *Men of War: Masculinity and the First World War in Britain* (Basingstoke: Palgrave Macmillan, 2009).

Mill, John Stuart, *Essays on Poetry*, ed. F. Parvin Sharpless (Columbia: University of South Carolina Press, 1976).

Monro, Harold, *Collected Poems*, ed. Alida Monro (London: Duckworth, 1970).

Moran, Leslie J., 'Transcripts and Truth: Writing the Trials of Oscar Wilde', *Oscar Wilde and Modern Culture: The Making of a Legend*, ed. Joseph Bristow (Athens: Ohio University Press, 2008), pp. 234–58.

Moyle, Franny, *Constance: The Tragic and Scandalous Life of Mrs. Oscar Wilde* (New York: Pegasus, 2011).

Muñoz, José Esteban. *Cruising Utopia: The Then and There of Queer Futurity*. New York: New York University Press, 2009.

Murray, Douglas, *Bosie: A Biography of Lord Alfred Douglas* (New York: Hyperion, 2000).

Murray, Nicholas, *The Red Sweet Wine of Youth: British Poets of the First World War* (London: Little, Brown: 2010).

Najarian, James, *Victorian Keats: Manliness, Sexuality, and Desire* (New York: Palgrave Macmillan, 2002).

Nelson, James G., *The Early Nineties: A View from the Bodley Head* (Cambridge, MA: Harvard University Press, 1971).

Nunokawa, Jeff, *Tame Passions of Wilde: The Styles of Manageable Desire* (Princeton: Princeton University Press, 2003).

Orwell, George, 'W. B. Yeats', *My Country Right or Left: 1940–1943*, vol. 2 of *The Collected Essays, Journalism and Letters*, ed. Sonia Orwell and Ian Angus (Boston: Godine, 2000), pp. 271–6.

Owen, Harold, *Journey from Obscurity: Wilfred Owen 1893–1918: Memoirs of the Owen Family*, 3 vols (London: Oxford University Press, 1963).

Owen, Wilfred, *Collected Letters*, eds Harold Owen and John Bell (London: Oxford University Press, 1967).

——, *Complete Poems and Fragments*, ed. Jon Stallworthy (London: Chatto and Windus, Hogarth Press, and Oxford University Press, 1983).

Pater, Walter, *The Renaissance: Studies in Art and Poetry*, 1873, ed. Adam Phillips (Oxford: Oxford University Press, 1986).

Phillips, Kathy J., *Manipulating Masculinity: War and Gender in Modern British and American Literature* (New York: Palgrave Macmillan, 2006).

Powell, Kerry, *Acting Wilde: Victorian Sexuality, Theatre, and Oscar Wilde* (Cambridge: Cambridge University Press, 2009).
——, *Oscar Wilde and the Theatre of the 1890s* (Cambridge: Cambridge University Press, 1990).
Psomiades, Kathy Alexis, *Beauty's Body: Femininity and Representation in British Aestheticism* (Stanford: Stanford University Press, 1997).
Raby, Peter, *Oscar Wilde* (Cambridge: Cambridge University Press, 1988).
Raffalovich, André, 'L'Affaire d'Oscar Wilde', *Archives d'anthropologie criminelle, de criminologie et de psychologie normale et pathologique*, 10 (1895), pp. 445–77.
Ramazani, Jahan, *Poetry of Mourning: The Modern Elegy from Hardy to Heaney* (Chicago: University of Chicago Press, 1994).
Rawlinson, Mark, 'Wilfred Owen', *The Oxford Handbook of British and Irish War Poetry*, ed. Tim Kendall (Oxford: Oxford University Press, 2007), pp. 114–33.
Reed, J. D., 'Wilfred Owen's Adonis,' *Dead Lovers: Erotic Bonds and the Study of Premodern Europe*, eds Basil Dufallo and Peggy McCracken (Ann Arbor: University of Michigan Press, 2006), pp. 39–56.
Reilly, Catherine, *English Poetry of the First World War: A Bibliography* (London: George Prior, 1978).
Ricketts, Harry, *Strange Meetings: The Poets of the Great War* (London: Chatto and Windus, 2010).
Riquelme, J. P., 'Shalom/Solomon/*Salomé*: Modernism and Wilde's Aesthetic Politics,' *Centennial Review*, 39 (1995), pp. 575–610.
Robins, Ashley H., *Oscar Wilde, The Great Drama of His Life: How His Tragedy Reflected His Personality* (Brighton: Sussex Academic Press, 2011).
Rosenberg, Isaac, *The Poems and Plays of Isaac Rosenberg*, ed. Vivien Noakes (Oxford: Oxford University Press, 2004).
Ross, Iain, *Oscar Wilde and Ancient Greece* (Cambridge: Cambridge University Press, 2013).
Ross, Robert, 'A Note on "Salome,"' *Salome: A Tragedy in One Act: Translated from the French of Oscar Wilde by Lord Alfred Douglas: Pictured by Aubrey Beardsley* (New York: Dover, 1967), pp. xiii–xviii.
Ruddick, Nicholas, '"The Peculiar Quality of My Genius": Degeneration, Decadence, and *Dorian Gray* in 1890–91', *Oscar Wilde: The Man, His Writings, and His World*, ed. Robert N. Keane (New York: AMS, 2003), pp. 125–37.
Ruff, Felicia J., 'Transgressive Props; or Oscar Wilde's E(a)rnest Signifier', *Wilde Discoveries: Traditions, Histories, Archives*, ed. Joseph Bristow (Toronto: University of Toronto Press, 2013), pp. 315–39.
Salamensky, S. I., 'Oscar Wilde's "Jewish Problem": Salomé, the Ancient Hebrew and the Modern Jewess', *Modern Drama*, 55 (2012), pp. 197–215.
San Juan, Jr., Epifanio, *The Art of Oscar Wilde* (Princeton: Princeton University Press, 1967).
Scott Moncrieff, C. K. 'Sonnet', *The New Witness* 7 June 1918, p. 108.
——. 'Sonnet', *The New Witness* 10 Jan. 1919.
——. 'To W. E. S. O.', *The Song of Roland: Done into English, in the Original Measure* (London: Chapman and Hall, 1919), p. vii.
Schroeder, Horst, *Oscar Wilde, The Portrait of Mr. W. H.: Its Composition, Publication, and Reception* (Braunschweig: Technische Universität Carolo-Wilhelmina zu Braunschweig Seminar für Anglistik und Amerikanistik, 1984).

Sedgwick, Eve Kosofsky, *Between Men: English Literature and Male Homosocial Desire* (New York: Columbia University Press, 1985).
——, *Epistemology of the Closet* (Berkeley: University of California Press, 1990).
——, *Tendencies* (Durham: Duke University Press, 1993).
Senelick, Laurence, 'Master Wood's Profession: Wilde and the Subculture of Homosexual Blackmail in the Victorian Theatre', *Wilde Writings: Contextual Conditions*, ed. Joseph Bristow (Toronto: University of Toronto Press, 2003), pp. 163–82.
Seymour-Smith, Martin, *Robert Graves: His Life and Work* (New York: Holt, Rinehart and Winston, 1982).
Sherry, Vincent, 'First World War Poetry: A Cultural Landscape', *The Cambridge Companion to the Poetry of the First World War*, ed. Santanu Das (New York: Cambridge University Press, 2013), pp. 35–50.
Silkin, Jon, *Out of Battle: The Poetry of the Great War*, 1972 (New York: Routledge and Kegan Paul, 1987).
Sillars, Stuart, *Structure and Disillusion in English Writing, 1910–1920* (New York: St. Martin's, 1999).
Sinfield, Alan, *The Wilde Century: Effeminacy, Oscar Wilde and the Queer Moment* (New York: Columbia University Press, 1994).
Small, Ian, 'Love-Letter, Spiritual Autobiography, or Prison Writing? Identity and Value in *De Profundis*', *Wilde Writings: Contextual Conditions*, ed. Joseph Bristow (Toronto: University of Toronto Press, 2003), pp. 86–100.
——, *Oscar Wilde: Recent Research* (Greensboro: ELT Press, 2000).
——, 'Wilde's Texts, Contexts, and "The Portrait of Mr W. H.,"' *Oscar Wilde in Context*, ed. Kerry Powell and Peter Raby (Cambridge: Cambridge University Press, 2013), pp. 374–83.
Smith, Timothy d'Arch, *Love in Earnest: Some Notes on the Lives and Writings of English 'Uranian' Poets from 1889 to 1930* (London: Routledge and Kegan Paul, 1970).
Stallworthy, Jon, 'The Legacy of the Somme', *Survivors' Songs: From Maldon to the Somme* (Cambridge: Cambridge University Press, 2008), pp. 98–108.
——, *Wilfred Owen* (Oxford: Oxford University Press, 1974).
——, *Wilfred Owen*, revised edn (London: Pimlico-Random House, 2013).
Stockton, Kathryn Bond, *The Queer Child: or Growing Sideways in the Twentieth Century* (Durham: Duke University Press, 2009).
Stokes, John, *Oscar Wilde: Myths, Miracles, and Imitations* (Cambridge: Cambridge University Press, 1996).
Strachen, Hew, *The First World War* (New York: Viking, 2003).
Symonds, John Addington, *The Fine Arts*, vol. 3 of *The Renaissance in Italy* (3 vols) (New York: Henry Holt, 1888).
——, *Male Love: A Problem in Greek Ethics and Other Writings*, ed. John Lauritsen (New York: Pagan Press, 1983).
Thompson, Francis, *Poetical Works* (London: Oxford University Press, 1969).
Todman, Dan, *The Great War: Myth and Memory* (London: Hambledon and London, 2005).
Trumbach, Randolph, 'Modern Sodomy: The Origins of Homosexuality, 1700–1800', *A Gay History of Britain: Love and Sex Between Men Since the Middle Ages*, ed. Matt Cook (Oxford: Greenwood, 2007), pp. 77–105.
Tydeman, William, and Steven Price, *Wilde: Salome* (Cambridge: Cambridge University Press, 1996).

Upchurch, Charles, *Before Wilde: Sex between Men in Britain's Age of Reform* (Berkeley: University of California Press, 2009).

Vandiver, Elizabeth, *Stand in the Trench, Achilles: Classical Receptions in British Poetry of the Great War* (Oxford: Oxford University Press, 2010).

Warner, Michael, *The Trouble with Normal: Sex, Politics, and Ethics of Queer Life* (Cambridge: Harvard University Press, 1999).

Weeks, Jeffrey, *Sex, Politics and Society: The Regulation of Sexuality since 1800*, 2nd edn (London: Longman, 1989).

Welland, D. S. R., *Wilfred Owen: A Critical Study* (London: Chatto and Windus, 1960).

Wilde, Oscar, *The Complete Letters of Oscar Wilde*, eds Merlin Holland and Rupert Hart-Davis (New York: Henry Holt, 2000).

——, *The Complete Works of Oscar Wilde*, gen. ed. Ian Small, 7 vols. to date (Oxford: Oxford University Press, 2000-).

——, *The Importance of Being Earnest, The Works of Oscar Wilde Volume 5*, 15 vols. (Boston: C. T. Brainard, 1909), pp. 157–329.

——, 'Lord Arthur Savile's Crime', *The Works of Oscar Wilde Volume 4*, 15 vols (Boston: C. T. Brainard, 1909), pp. 3–72.

——, *The Picture of Dorian Gray*, ed. Robert Mighall (London: Penguin, 2003).

——, *The Picture of Dorian Gray: An Annotated, Uncensored Edition*, ed. Nicholas Frankel (Cambridge: Belknap-Harvard University Press, 2011).

——, 'The Portrait of Mr W. H.', *The Soul of Man under Socialism and Selected Critical Prose*, ed. Linda Dowling (London: Penguin, 2001), pp. 31–101.

——, *Salome. Collins Complete Works of Oscar Wilde*, centenary edn (Glasgow: HarperCollins, 1999), pp. 583–605.

——, *Salomé: A Tragedy in One Act*, trans. Joseph Donohue (Charlottesville: University of Virginia Press, 2011).

Wilson, Jean Moorcroft, *Siegfried Sassoon, The Making of a War Poet: A Biography 1886–1918* (New York: Routledge, 1999).

Winter, Jay, 'Beyond Glory: First World War Poetry and Cultural Memory', *The Cambridge Companion to the Poetry of the First World War*, ed. Santanu Das (New York: Cambridge University Press, 2013), pp. 242–55.

——, *Sites of Memory, Sites of Mourning: The Great War in European Cultural History* (Cambridge: Cambridge University Press, 1995).

Woods, Gregory, *Articulate Flesh: Male Homo-Eroticism and Modern Poetry* (New Haven: Yale University Press, 1987).

Wordsworth, William, VIII ('She dwelt among the untrodden ways'), *The Poetical Works of William Wordsworth* vol. 2, ed. E. de Selincourt, 5 vols (London: Clarendon-Oxford University Press, 1952), p. 34.

Wright, Thomas, *Built of Books: How Reading Defined the Life of Oscar Wilde* (New York: Henry Holt, 2008).

Yeats, William Butler, Introduction, *The Oxford Book of Modern Verse, 1892–1935* (New York: Oxford University Press, 1936), pp. v–xlii.

——, *Letters on Poetry from W. B. Yeats to Dorothy Wellesley* (London: Oxford University Press, 1940).

Index

CPSIA information can be obtained at www.ICGtesting.com
Printed in the USA
LVOW04*1320140915

454092LV00008B/30/P